A F

# Return
# of
# The Rose

Theresa Ragan

# DEDICATION

Much love to my husband, Joe, for filling my life with laughter and love.


Thanks to Cathy Katz, my sister and friend, for her never-ending encouragement and support. Cathy read my book too many times to count, killing off characters and brainstorming scenes while busy earning a degree in English Literature.

# BOOKS BY THERESA RAGAN

A Knight in Central Park
Finding Kate Huntley
Taming Mad Max

ABDUCTED (T.R. Ragan)

# PROLOGUE

*England, 1420*

"You have twin daughters, my lord, but the second born is not faring well. There is naught that can be done to save her."

Richard Forrester, Earl of Silverwood, stood in his bedchamber and gazed upon his sleeping wife, the midwife's words still swirling about in his mind. Tenderness for the woman he loved flowed through him, and something besides…a protective instinct so strong his hands curled into fists. What now? What could he do? Gladly, he would fell a thousand knights to preserve his family's safety. But this…he was helpless against this.

Tearing his gaze away, he left his wife's side and headed for the nursery. With a curt wave of his hand, Richard dismissed the attendants and then knelt by his daughters' cradles. The first-born's smooth skin gleamed a healthy color of ivory flushed with coral. The other baby was a pale, bluish shade.

He lifted his sickly daughter in his arms and brought her close, until her small hand brushed against his bearded jaw, and he could smell the sweet newness of her.

"Don't fret, my little one," he murmured. "I will find someone to cure your raspy breathing." But the promise rang empty, for he could see that she struggled hard for each breath. A tear wet his cheek. *God help me, I will not let you die.*

The earl's shoulders jounced in rhythm with the movement of the carriage as he sat alone, cradling his newborn daughter in the crook of one arm. Apprehension gnawed at his insides, along with fear. His daughter was not yet a day old and yet he'd been driven to such a desperate measure.

Briefly, he considered returning to the castle, but one glance at the ailing babe, hastily named Morgeanna after his grandmother, gave him the courage to continue on.

Pushing the window covering aside, Richard glanced outside as the carriage made a sharp left into a forest glade. A decrepit cottage, nearly hidden by the waxy green leaves of ivy and small nameless flowers, came into view. The thatched roof was singed in one corner, as though it had survived a fire, and the wattle and daub walls were crumbling. A well stood just outside the front door, along with a foul-smelling privy.

In the midst of it all stood the Witch of Devonshire, as if she had been expecting him. He'd heard rumors that she used potions and magic to cure the sick. Although he did not believe in witchcraft or wizardry, he did believe in miracles. And now it seemed a divine act of God and an enormous amount of faith were his only hope.

With a tap to the ceiling, Richard signaled the driver to come to a halt. He wrapped the baby tighter in her fur-lined coverlet and stepped out into the cool morning air. His gaze met the old woman's, prompting him to hold Morgeanna closer to his chest.

"So you came after all," she said, her voice hoarse, as though she seldom spoke.

"Aye. How did you know?"

Her laugh erupted as a sharp crow.

"Please—"

"Let me see her," the woman snapped. Her gaze riveted to the bundle in his arms and her thin fingers shook with apparent anticipation.

The earl stopped short of the crone's grasp. "Can you help her?"

"Do you know what you ask of me?"

"Her lungs are weak. She needs your help," Richard pleaded.

"She cannot make it here."

"But—"

The woman's claw-like hands waved him to silence as she hovered closer, her eyes still feasting on the babe. "There is a place. Or rather, a time."

A time? The witch spoke in riddles. Richard nearly turned away but Morgeanna's skin had purpled like a plum. The babe wouldn't survive the ride home. "Speak plainly witch or I shan't leave her."

"You have no choice and we both know it. There is naught anyone can do for the child. Give her to me."

She was right. He'd already visited two physicians before dawn. He had no choice. "What will you do?"

"I will send her to a new tomorrow, another day. And she will live."

With moisture filling his eyes, Richard placed a leather pouch filled with coins on the ground. "Tell no one," he said. "My people have been sworn to secrecy and my wife knows naught of this twin. Why should she suffer?"

"I promise only that the child will live."

Swiftly kissing the dewy-cheeked babe, Richard fastened a strand of leather from which hung a rose-shaped amethyst around her small neck and whispered, "I send you away to give you life, Morgeanna, with all my love."

Then he relinquished his daughter to the old woman's gnarled hands and returned to the carriage, never once looking back, trusting in God...and the Witch of Devonshire.

# CHAPTER ONE

<u>*Lafayette, CA - Present Time*</u>

Morgan Hayes rushed into her mother's antique store and changed the open sign to closed. "Mom, wait until you see this!"

Her mother finished pricing her newest acquisition, a Windsor chair with a spindle back, before making her way across the room. Together they gazed upon a drawing of a fully armored knight sitting straight and tall upon a cloud-white horse.

"It really is him," her mother said, her voice brimming with excitement. "I can tell by the intricate detailing of the brigandine."

"And the gold inlay of his visor," Morgan added, tapping the drawing. "He's definitely our knight. It says here that the armor once belonged to a man known as the Earl of Kensington."

Her mother took the leather bound book from her and began to read while Morgan went to where the armor stood before the front window, the sun radiating off the silver plates like streaks of lightning. Morgan was nine when her mother had acquired the armor, and still, her heart pounded every time she looked at him. She brushed her fingers across the smooth hard steel of his breastplate and closed her eyes, imagining for the millionth time what he might have looked like back when he was alive and breathing. "It's hard to believe he finally has a name."

"And an earl at that," her mother said. "It says here on page twelve that 'the Earl of Kensington was forced to marry and even found himself taken with his new wife. Unfortunately, he was bitterly disappointed in the end.'"

Morgan crossed the room and leaned over her mother's shoulder as she read.

"'The earl believed his wife betrayed him. When his wife left him he did nothing to stop her. Soon after, the earl came to believe he'd been wrong about her. Sadly, in his haste to find his wife he was struck down and killed in an ambush near Swan Lake. He died in 1444.'"

"Swan Lake," Morgan said as she skimmed the text, hoping to learn what became of the woman who had stolen the Earl of Kensington's heart. According to the tale, the woman had simply disappeared, never to be seen again.

Later, as they set about closing shop, Morgan set the book aside and regarded her mother with open fondness. Years ago her mother had lost her husband and daughter in a fatal car accident, and yet she never complained. Neither did she ever talk about the little girl she lost. But Morgan knew her mother ached for her daughter because more than once she'd awoken to her mother's anguished cries as she called out for her little girl named Ashley.

Morgan's thoughts turned to her biological parents and the thought that they hadn't loved her enough to keep her…instead, leaving her on a stranger's doorstep. They didn't deserve a second thought but today was Morgan's twenty-fourth birthday and once again she found herself wondering if she had her mother's smile or her father's eyes. Where were they now and did they ever think about the daughter they gave up so long ago?

Her mother dusted off an old box as she came to stand before her. "Are you going out tonight?"

Morgan shook her head. "I think I'll just hang out here a while longer and get the bookkeeping up to date."

Her mother set the box on a chair, removed the lid, and drew out a blanket. "This is for you."

Morgan stood and scooped the old blanket into her arms. She smoothed her fingers over the crushed red velvet intricately embroidered with gold thread and lined with fur surprised by the odd pang she felt in her chest. "It's beautiful."

"It was wrapped around you when you came to me all those years ago. I was saving it for when you had children of your own," she added thoughtfully, "but I haven't been able to stop thinking about it. You should have it…it's yours. And what better time to give it to you than on your birthday?"

Morgan hugged her mother tight. Then she held the richly woven fabric to her cheek. Closing her eyes, she inhaled the strange musty smell of it, hoping to breathe in some sense of where she came from; maybe get a glimpse of the person who had wrapped her in it long ago.

Instinctively she felt for the necklace she always wore around her neck. Like the blanket it had been left with her when she was a baby. The leather string had been replaced with a chain but the rose-shaped amethyst was still the same.

Tears glistened in her mother's eyes. "I'm sorry I kept it from you for so long."

Oh, Mom." Her throat tightened as she drew her mother close again.

"I'm heading home now," her mother said after Morgan released her.

"Thanks for the gift, Mom. I love you."

"I love you, too."

By the time Morgan finished tallying the receipts for the day a strong wind stirred the trees, making the branches dance. The air, suddenly too cold for a summer night, chilled her as she shut and locked the windows. Morgan turned off the lights except for one small lamplight and picked up the blanket her mother had given her earlier. Then she noticed the Earl of Kensington's armor in the shadows.

She Moved toward him and pressed up close to the hard steel of his armor as she looked up at his closed visor. "Time for me to go home," she said with a sigh, wiping dust from his metal shoulder. "Why do I feel completely alone in the world except when I'm near you? Can you tell me that, Mr. Metal Man?"

Outside, thunder rumbled. Strange, she thought, that a storm might be brewing in the middle of summer. She tried to step away from the armor, but her T-shirt had become snagged in the metal plates. As she struggled for her freedom, the humor of her predicament struck her, making her laugh. "We really must stop meeting like this."

Standing on tiptoe, she tried to peek beneath his visor. The coldness of the steel touched her face. Her chest ached to think that this hollow suit of armor could never be her true, flesh and blood knight.

Ridiculous.

But still, it pained her to know that he would never remove his armor as she'd often imagined him doing in her dreams. She'd never see his smile or feel his warm hands about hers.

Thunder boomed. She clung to the armor. Fingers of lightning struck the front window, rattling the glass. Her heart drummed against her ribs. The armor suddenly became a blinding blur of metal and bright light.

*What was happening?*

As her body became weightless, her panic mounted.

She thought of her mother...smiling, comforting her, and she reached out a hand to fight for normalcy. Desperately struggling to return to the dimly lit room, she tried to focus on the familiar...the antique cash register, the upholstered settee where her mother used to read to her when she was small, the Pembroke table. But all of her mother's treasures grew dim, shrinking in size, until it all disappeared.

And then darkness swallowed her whole.

# CHAPTER TWO

<u>*England, 1444*</u>

A gust of rain-spattered wind spanked the high windows of the king's chambers. Flames upon stout candles danced as drafts seeped through unseen crevices.

Derek Vanguard, Lord of Braddock Hall, looked upon King Henry VI with concern. The English king of the House of Lancaster looked frail as he lay in his bed, clothed only in a thin linen shirt, rambling on with his newest request.

Nobody held the king in higher esteem than Lord Vanguard, and yet at this moment, Derek stood before His Majesty with hands clenched at his sides. He knew he could not deny the king any service…it mattered not how large or small the task. But never had a request of Henry's had the same disturbing effect as this particular assignment.

Derek tried to keep the muscle in his jaw from twitching when he spoke, but it proved difficult considering he wanted to shake some sense into the man. "Your Majesty. I mean no disrespect, but surely you recall how I feel about marriage."

Henry waved his hand as if Derek had not spoken at all. "'Tis nonsense. Not all women are like your mother."

"I understand, but—"

Henry snorted. "It is with great anticipation I await your forthcoming marriage. Peace for our people is all that concerns me. This union between you and the daughter of the Earl of Silverwood gives me great hope. It is an honor I have chosen you to be her husband." The king finished his sentence with a hacking cough.

Derek lifted an aggravated brow. He knew the king used his failing health to manipulate others but this was too much. "As you well know, sire, I vowed long ago never to marry."

"Hogwash," the king spouted with another wave of his pale hand. "You are not getting any younger. It is time you had sons. Who better to serve me when you are too old to watch over my lands?"

As the king babbled on, Derek's thoughts wandered back to his childhood when his prayers went unanswered for too long. He knew not which was worse—a mother abandoning her child or a father who treated his only son with hatred and indifference. Derek trusted no one, had no room in his heart for any child. And he certainly had neither the patience nor the time for a wife.

"I am told that Lady Amanda is praised for her beauty and has not an equal in the entire kingdom. What have you to say to that?" King Henry questioned.

There was no arguing with the king, and that caused the veins at Derek's temple to throb. His voice remained calm, but every muscle he possessed grew stiff with dread. "If the quest, my lord, is a thing that is in my power to undertake, I will undertake it. Unto that, I pledge to you my knighthood."

"Then you will do as I bid?"

"You thought otherwise?"

They exchanged knowing gazes before Derek added with less strain, "I am confident any alliance you feel necessary must be so."

The king sat up a bit, his chest puffing.

"I also find it an honor, my lord, that you have chosen me. Now, if you are done, I should get back to defending Your Majesty and His people."

The coughing spasms resumed and King Henry excused him with a thrust of his hand. "I knew you would see it my way," he croaked. "Now away with you. Give a dying man some peace."

Derek bowed, thankful to be leaving. Although his displeasure had not completely subsided, he found himself amused by King Henry's exaggerations, for they both knew he had but a cold.


Morgan opened her eyes. The smell of damp, dewy leaves drifted up her nostrils. Dirt...leaves.

Where was she?

She sat up and spit leaves from her mouth. A dense growth of trees and underbrush surrounded her. Her heart thumped against her chest. She couldn't remember leaving her mother's store. How did she get outside?

It was eerily quiet. No birds chirping. Nothing except a faint rumbling noise. Cocking her head, she listened closer. The blanket her mother had given her lay a few feet away. The dry scattered leaves moved ever so slightly. The rumbling grew louder until it sounded like dozens of horse hooves crashing against the earth. Her breathing quickened. And then a giant pig-like animal shot through the brush, giving her a start.

Before she could get away, three men on horses charged through the same dense thicket and headed straight for her. She scrambled to her feet but didn't have time to run for cover. Instead, she crossed her arms over her face and stood frozen in place.

The men wrenched their giant horses to a skidding stop, mere inches before colliding into her. Her heart thundered against her chest as she gathered the courage to peek through trembling fingers. The men wore woolen tights and knee-length leather boots. Their shirts were ragged and stained with dirt and blood. They looked vicious in their muddied coats, exhibiting such predatory expressions. A man she assumed to be their leader dug his heels into his mammoth stallion, urging the animal forward until she felt the beast's breath on her head.

This was completely insane!

She squeezed her eyes shut, praying they would all be gone when she opened them and she would be back in her mother's store. Damn. No such luck.

The man before her wore a dagger in his belt and held a short primitive bow in his soiled hand. Handcrafted, deadly looking arrows protruded from a deep leather pocket at his side. She winced at the cruel smile he wore, which served only to make him more repulsive. Clumps of mud matted his long, stringy beard. A jagged scar ran across his bottom lip causing his yellow teeth to show even with his mouth closed. This was no dream. It was a nightmare.

"Look what we caught ourselves," the ugly man said, painfully reminding her that the nightmare was not going to end any time soon.

"Aye, a treasure for certain," another man commented.

As if the sight of her made him hungry, the leader licked his lips. "I fear she let our dinner get away. It seems only fair that we keep her in its stead. What say you to that, wench?"

The smoldering, greedy gazes of his men feasted upon her. Her jeans and T-shirt were on the snug side but other than that...what was the problem? Certainly no reason for them to drool in such a disgusting manner.

She narrowed her eyes. Nobody treated Morgan Hayes like a mere object to be drooled upon. "I beg your pardon, gentlemen, pig-hunting warriors or whatever you are, but I have no idea what this man is talking about. I don't know who sent you here all dressed up but I can tell you one thing—it's not funny. The gag is up, boys."

Plunking hands on hips, she looked at them with set jaw and tight lips, hoping to hide her growing terror beneath an angry glare. Then she turned and walked off, quickening her pace with each step. If she could just reach the denser area of the woods...

The gait of a horse sounded behind her, prompting her to break into a full-blown run, yelping as she was jerked off the ground and into the ugly man's bulky arms. The horrid smell of rotted breath and dried blood saturated her senses, nauseating her. "Let go of me!"

As if that weren't enough, another man on a horse suddenly vaulted through the dense brush. He yanked on the reins, coming to a halt a few feet away. He was an older man and twice as big as the one who held her. Chain mail covered his large frame but he wore no headgear.

"Put her down, Otgar. Now!" the older man barked.

Whiskers hung over Otgar's upper lip as his mouth drew back in a snarl. "Stay out of this, Hugo, she's mine. I found her and I intend to keep her."

Otgar and Hugo. This was too much. Figuring she'd stumbled into the middle of a movie set, she looked around for a cameraman. But there were no cameras to be seen. No director yelling "Cut!"

She struggled to get loose, but Otgar tightened his grip. Hugo's eyes narrowed to dangerous slits of steel. Although she'd never had two men fight over her before, and the idea did have a certain appeal, the Ugly against the Old hardly seemed worth bragging about.

"The king's bidding it is that she's betrothed to another," Hugo warned.

"And why should I believe you?" Otgar asked, spittle hitting her cheek. "What would the king have to do with a harlot found alone in the forest? The feast of a pig she's lost to us and she must pay for her foul deed. Leave us be, Hugo, or you, too, shall pay."

Having no desire to be left with Otgar and his men, Morgan prayed Hugo wouldn't abandon her. Although Hugo was covered with metal links and daunting in size, he appeared old and wise…and his eyes hinted at kindness. But then again, she had a doozer of a headache and she couldn't be sure.

Without warning Otgar tossed her to his closest man as if she were a sack of grain. "Ooomph."

The horse beneath her stamped the ground with one of its massive hooves. Her heart lodged in her throat. "I really need to get off this animal. I won't run away, I promise. Just let me down...nice and slowly." She'd never been fond of horses, scared to death of them, actually. Even on carousels she tended to pick the pig or the boring sled that didn't move.

Otgar merely snorted at her complaints while the man holding her lowered his nose to her neck and sniffed.

She slapped his head. "Stop that!"

Hugo, she noticed, peered toward the denser area of the forest. She followed his gaze, disappointed to see nothing but woodland.

"The woman you hold captive is Lady Amanda, daughter of the Earl of Silverwood," Hugo said to Otgar. "Do you not believe me you have only to look around her neck for proof of what I say. You will see that her pendant bears the Forrester crest."

Morgan frowned. "My necklace has nothing to do with this earl guy." She lifted her hands in exasperation. "Lady Amanda," she said with a snort. "Do I look like a lady?"

Otgar's men mumbled and shook their heads.

"Hand her over now," Hugo added irritably, glaring her way, "and I am sure Lord Vanguard will reimburse you the loss of your dinner. If you refuse, take heed, for King Henry and Lord Vanguard will have your heads within a fortnight."

"And what would Vanguard have to do with any of this?" Otgar questioned.

"'Tis Lord Vanguard who is to marry the lady," Hugo answered.

Marriage to a lord. And just when she'd thought her predicament couldn't get any worse. Why hadn't she awoken yet?

Otgar laughed. "The very blackguard who caused my own brother's death plans to marry?"

"Aye," Hugo answered calmly. "Release her. Let there be no bloodshed today."

For a moment she considered telling Hugo that she wasn't Amanda at all. But what if Hugo believed her and left her with Otgar? What then? The crisp pine-scented air and the pungent body odor of the man who held her confirmed her suspicions. This was no dream. Her mind spun with the absurdity of her situation. Losing her mind would not get her home. For now, she decided, she would let them think she was Amanda.

Rage flickered in Otgar's cold sea-green eyes. He raised his sword, apparently ready to wage war.

A wave of terror swept through her. She gazed toward Hugo, praying the older man might help her, but he was gazing toward the forest again. This time he waved his sword above his head as if signaling to someone.

Looking in the direction he beckoned, she saw a man encased in metal charging straight for her. Her eyes widened in alarm. And then she screamed.

Scooped up like a worm snatched by a bird and tossed to the horse's rump, she clung to cold interlinking metal rings of armor covering the rider. The horse dodged a maze of pine trees and thorn covered shrubs. Her chin bumped against his back with every turn. Behind them, fading in the distance, she saw Hugo take down both of Otgar's men before knocking Otgar to the ground. Hugo then chased the horses off.

Otgar threw his weapon to the ground as he watched her disappear through the regiment of trees.

When they finally cut through the forest's edge into a clearing of grasslands, the horse slowed to an excruciating trot. Morgan struggled for her release. "P-Put me d-down!" She thumped the man in armor, hurting her fist in the process.

"Hold still!" the man ground out as Hugo caught up to them.

The horse's gait made it hard for her to speak. "L-let me go. I'm not who you th-think I am."

"Is that so, my lady? And who might you be?" Hugo asked, clearly exasperated.

She glanced over her shoulder, back toward the forest for any sign of Otgar, deciding she still had no desire to be left alone. "Oh, never mind. Where are you taking me? And could you please tell me where I am?"

The horse stumbled, forcing her to clutch at the man to keep her balance. "You're not that Lord Vanguard guy they were talking about, are you?"

The man slid the helmet from his head, then hooked his visor to the front of his saddle. "Nay, I am Emmon McBray, the very knight who escorted you from Silverwood two days ago before you ran off and left me looking the fool. But go ahead," he said in a clipped tone, "play your ill-advised game. For when you meet your betrothed, you will regret such foolish sport."

"Wonderful," she muttered. He wasn't a man at all, but an adolescent. Much too young to be dressed up in armor and playing with swords.

The man-boy looked over his shoulder and lifted a youthful brow. "I want to know what you put in my drink to make me sleep? And my horse. A finer stallion there is not. What did you do with my horse?"

"I have no idea what you're talking about. Hugo," she called over her shoulder, deciding she liked him better. "I bumped my head before you came to my-uh—rescue. Where exactly are we?"

"I warned you we should not have gone after her," Emmon growled. "She is dimwitted, unfit to marry Lord Vanguard."

Hugo ignored Emmon and focused on her instead. "We are in England, my lady, a short distance west of Braddock Hall."

"And the year is 1444," Emmon added sarcastically.

"That can't be right," she said.

Emmon's fist curled about the leather reins and spasms of irritation crossed his face. "I will tell you what is not right. It is not right that you ran away, making fools of us. Nor is it right

17

that you speak suddenly like a jackanapes and lie about who you are. And lastly it is not right that Lord Vanguard be bound to a wench such as you."

Morgan's stomach clenched. Not because of what Emmon was saying but because things like this just didn't happen. The trees looked the same. The sky was blue, the grass green. But the conviction in Emmon's voice told her he was speaking the truth.

"Too bad you may not live to see The Year of Our Lord 1445," he added almost gleefully.

"What do you mean?"

"Lord Vanguard frowns heavily upon the betrayal of his people. No telling what he might do when he hears of your running away."

"I didn't run away. You've got the wrong woman."

Emmon regarded her with cold speculation.

She sighed. "You're only trying to scare me because you think I stole your horse."

Emmon laughed. "Think what you will. Too bad though that the rumors you've surely heard about Lord Vanguard are all true."

Shivers crawled up her spine. "They are?"

"Aye," he said. "Lord Vanguard has the countenance of a dragon monster. No," he amended, putting a gloved finger to his chin. "I would say he more resembles a humongous, long-haired ogre. But that is not the worst of it."

She rolled her eyes, wondering how it could get much worse than that.

"My lord's poor temper is very nearly as hideous as his misshapen face…and when he learns that his betrothed tried to run off."

"What will he do?"

"Emmon, what are you saying?" Hugo cut in from a distance.

Emmon pulled back on the reins. "I was merely telling her ladyship what to expect when she arrives at Braddock. Are we stopping soon?"

Hugo exhaled. "Nay, we have been delayed too long. If we keep up this pace we should reach Braddock before morning."

The hairs at the back of Morgan's neck stirred. The year was 1444 and not only was she being held against her will, she was mistaken as the bride-to-be of the ugliest man in the world.


Nightfall had come and gone by the time Morgan awoke. The steady beat of the horse's gait told her she had yet to return to her time. Every muscle ached. Her bottom felt as if it had been shot full of Novocain. She rubbed her eyes and when she opened them, she nearly fell off the horse.

Braddock was indeed a castle, a mighty fortress with massive towers surrounded by high stone walls.

The sun's morning light peeked over the horizon and thin curls of smoke appeared above the castle. They rode down a hill and passed by an orchard. The scent of burning iron and manure intermingled with the smell of fruit. People stopped to stare. Most of the men had short-cropped hair above the ears. They wore brown tunics, thick hose, and leather boots. The women wore frowns and gave her sour looks.

Morgan frowned. "What's wrong with them?"

"I told you before," Emmon said. "Nobody betrays his lordship by running away. 'Tis unheard of."

Shivers coursed over her. If these people truly believed her to be the woman who had betrayed their lord, would she be sliced and diced? Hung by a thick scratchy rope from an ancient tree? Maybe his lordship would spare her her life and relieve her of only a finger or two. She eyed her pinky with misgiving.

"My lady! My lady!" a woman shouted, pushing her way through the crowd.

Emmon pulled back on the reins while Hugo rode on toward the stables.

"Young knight. Help her ladyship down," the woman ordered.

Emmon obeyed, dropping Morgan into the plump woman's arms before clicking the reins and heading toward the stables.

Tired of being thrown around like a sack of potatoes, she glared at Emmon's backside as he rode off.

"Lady Amanda, did those blackguards hurt you?"

Gray strands of hair stuck out from beneath the woman's headgear. Her long shirt-like dress was stained and her hands were callused. Both eyes appeared cloudy as if she had cataracts.

"Nobody hurt me," Morgan assured the woman before lowering her voice. "And my name isn't Amanda. It's Morgan Hayes."

The woman wagged a finger in her face. "Your father warned me of your spoiled ways, my lady. Although we've had only a short time to become acquainted, I am not so easily fooled. If you believe, I, Odelia Beaumaris, will fall for this newest ploy of yours, you are gravely mistaken." She clutched onto Morgan's arm and firmly ushered her through the growing number of onlookers.

"You have gone too far," the woman said under her breath, "dragging me across the countryside, letting me dry your tears. And what do you do to thank me? You run away, leaving me with Lord Vanguard's men. And all the while you meant to meet with Robert?"

"Robert?" Morgan asked.

The woman huffed. "So this is the game you wish to play?"

Morgan didn't know what to say to that so she kept quiet while the castle folk gawked and pointed, stealing what little optimism she was trying hard to hang on to. The outer gates were open. She could run, but where to? This was a crazy horrible nightmare that refused to end. Dismayed, she decided once again that it may be in her best interest to play the part of

Amanda for a bit longer. Feigning remorse, she looked to the ground and said, "I'm sorry. I don't know what has gotten into me lately."

A smile crossed Odelia's face, revealing a row of gray-brown teeth. "Oh, my lady, I am glad you are safe. Verily you try my patience but you are here and you are safe. Now tell me, when did you learn to speak in such a curious fashion?"

"Well, you see…when I left you and those men, I-er-I think I fell. Yes, that's it. I fell and hit my head on a rock. More like a boulder," she amended when skepticism crept into Odelia's hazy eyes. "When I awoke, a gang of foul-smelling men surrounded me. And then…Van Gogh's men came."

"Vanguard's men," Odelia cut in, eyeing her suspiciously.

"That's what I said. Vanguard's men came and voila, here I am."

Odelia examined her closely and Morgan was sure the woman was on to her until the lines about Odelia's face softened. "Perhaps you should change your clothes before you meet your betrothed. Where ever did you find such dreadful garb?"

"It's a long story," Morgan said.

Odelia wrinkled her nose before ushering her along again. "Your mother and father would have me on the ducking stool if they saw you now. The Lord of Braddock has not made an appearance in the entire two days I have been at the castle. Perchance Lord Vanguard's rumored disfigurement is worse than we suspected."

Until that moment Morgan had forgotten about Emmon's warning. But now images of Lord Vanguard swirled within her mind. Three heads maybe? Four bloodshot eyeballs? Certainly no man could be uglier than Otgar.

With much trepidation, she followed Odelia into the castle. As they went along, she caught whiffs of rose and mint. No signs of the dirty, musty smells she would have expected. Rows of rough wood benches lined the room and elaborate tapestries hung from limestone walls. Tables were being set, and unlike the villagers outside, the people within appeared too busy to take notice of her.

After Odelia was called away, she continued on, peeking through thick oak doors until she came to a room stocked with a vast array of old books and papers. Unable to resist the seductive pull these ancient works had on her, she forgot all about waiting for Odelia and entered the room.

Using a stool to get a closer look at the collection of books, she touched the leather bindings, surprised by the inner peace that washed through her...the same calmness she felt whenever she stood near her beloved armor in her mother's store.

A shuffling of papers startled her. A man sat at a large desk at the far end of the room.

He stood, and she realized he wasn't a man at all. He was a giant, and he was coming her way. "I'm sorry," she said, shoving the books back into place.

"No need to apologize, I assure you." His deep voice reverberated off the stone walls.

She always tried to look people in the eyes when she spoke to them, but for the first time in her life it was more than difficult; Not only because of his towering stature but because of the power radiating from his mahogany eyes. He was magnificent to look at. And there was something about him. Something oddly familiar, and yet she was sure she'd never seen him before. Never had she gazed upon such raw masculinity—not in the movies, not in any magazine, not ever.

He crossed his arms. "It is a book you are looking for?"

She shook her head.

"Your first day here at Braddock?"

Standing on top of the stool, she wanted to speak, but no words would come.

"Have you no voice?"

"Of course I do," she finally managed. "It's just that you surprised me. I didn't see you lurking over there in the dark."

The corners of his mouth curled upward. He wore a dark green, short-sleeved tunic that clung to his sculpted arms and snug pants that would have looked ridiculous on anyone but him. Massive in proportions, he possessed thick muscular shoulders, raven-black hair that touched his collar, and a very kissable mouth. A few of the men she'd dated had been handsome, but never did the sight of any of them take her breath away.

His chuckle made her realize she was staring at him as if she'd never laid eyes on a man before. She planted her arms across her chest. "What's so funny?"

He was becoming less God-like by the second. And if his dark eyes weren't looking right through her, making her feel tingly and anxious beneath his gaze, she might have thought of something clever to say. But with him staring at her so intensely, it was impossible to think, let alone speak.

Get a grip, she told herself, and as she shifted her weight, the stool toppled. She gasped as she fell, but he caught her in his arms and pulled her close. Close enough for her to feel the rise and fall of his chest and the heat of his body against hers. An eternity passed before she realized he wasn't in any hurry to let go of her. She pushed at his chest. "Put me down!"

Instead, he raised his foot to the fallen stool so she was straddled upon one very substantial thigh...her mouth mere inches from his brawny chest.

"Let me go-or-or I will report you to your boss."

He looked amused by such a threat, but once again he failed to loosen his hold. Leaning forward, he covered her mouth with his as if it was his right to do so, as if he could do whatever he pleased, as if...

His lips grazed over hers in a mere whisper, taking her breath away. Something stirred deep inside of her and heat spread through her like wildfire. His lips melded over hers and all thoughts of pushing him away evaporated. In that instant she knew that for this kiss alone she'd been sent to another century.

He drew away too soon, prompting her to open her eyes. He stared down at her with dark, smoldering eyes...angry eyes, and then released his hold and dropped his foot to the floor.

She staggered backward like a broken wind-up doll. Once she regained her balance, surprise turned to anger as she realized he'd dropped her on purpose.

As his hands came to rest on his hips, his eyelids drooped lazily. "Now," he said, his voice deep and rich with a full measure of conceit. "Perchance you have learned your lesson and will be more careful in the future as to where you wander without permission."

She clenched her teeth.

"Unfortunately, I have important work to attend to," he went on before she could reply. "Had you come at a more convenient time I would have been happy to further assist you in your schooling."

"In my schooling?"

"Aye," he said, examining his cuticles. "All new maidens who come to Braddock seek my instructions eventually. Though it would seem you are more eager than most. Perhaps another time."

"Of all the egotistical—" There he stood with that vainglorious smirk. "You think I came in here looking for you? Hoping to be trained?"

He didn't need to respond. She could see it in his eyes, in the way he stood, in his cocky grin. What an idiot she was to let him kiss her like that. What was wrong with her? "Listen here, Mister conceited, arrogant man. I happen to be engaged to a very important man at Braddock Castle. My name is Lady—"

A thin dirt-stained man came rushing into the room just then, nearly bowling her over. "You must come quickly. There is trouble...in the village," the man said between breaths. "A small band of men without colors or crest—" he inhaled "—was spotted moments before the village went up in flames."

Both men bolted from the room leaving Morgan standing there like a fool, pointing her finger at no one. One minute she was letting the big oaf have a piece of her mind and in the next he was gone. Dispiritedly she glanced around the sparsely decorated room. A draw-leaf table, serving as a desk, sat before the hearth. The walls were ornamented with tapestries depicting men hunting in the woods. The men were dressed exactly like Otgar and his entourage.

Drawn to the writing desk, she headed that way and slid her fingertips over the burled oak. The papers strewn about were scribbled with numbers. Obviously the arrogant man had been having trouble with his math. Assuming he was the castle's accountant, she scanned the document and smiled triumphantly when she easily figured out what the problem was.

As if she'd been living in the fifteenth century all of her life, she took hold of the feathered quill, dabbed its fine point into the inkwell, and made the necessary adjustments. Plunking the quill back into its holder, she left the room with a smile on her face.

Upon returning to the Hall, pandemonium greeted her. She dodged out of the way as frantic people, young and old, grabbed buckets, bowls, pots and kettles, whatever they could find before running out the main entrance of the castle.

Not one to be left behind, she grabbed an iron cauldron from the hearth and followed the crowd. Struggling to keep up, she realized the cauldron had to weigh at least fifty pounds. As she trailed behind an old woman and small children the pain in her wrist slowed her. As the last of the castle folk disappeared around the bend, she stopped to catch her breath.

Within seconds a heavily built man on a horse came barreling around that same curve and skidded to a stop in front of her. "Hugo!"

He gave a small bow. "My lady."

She snorted. "You really don't need to do that."

"What?"

"You know, bow and call me your lady. It's totally unnecessary. In fact, I was just looking for your boss before all hell broke loose."

His eyes widened.

"Excuse my French," she said with another wave of her hand.

He cocked a puzzled brow.

An explosion and screams from the village broke into their exchange. Picking up the cauldron again, she started off, but Hugo leaned over and grasped her shoulder with his large hand. "I've been instructed to see that you stay in the castle, my lady."

"By who?"

"By his lordship."

"Ridiculous," she said. "I might be able to help."

Another man on a horse appeared around the same curve in the road. Morgan cursed her bad luck when she saw it was Emmon, the man-boy who thought she'd stolen his horse.

"Gustaf and his boy are trapped beneath the stables," Emmon said to Hugo, "we need your help."

Morgan gestured toward them both as if she were shooing away a couple of flies. "Go on, I'll be right behind you two."

Hugo smiled broadly as he leaned over and took the heavy cauldron from her. Emmon leaned low, too, a scowl on his face as he plucked her from the ground and grunted as if she weighed two hundred pounds.

"I'd rather walk," she protested, but Emmon ignored her, clicking his heels into the animal's sides. The horse raised its front hooves before taking off, leaving her no choice but to clutch onto the boy for dear life.

As the village came into view and the animal slowed, Morgan jumped from the horse, although she could have sworn she was half pushed. Emmon, she thought sourly, had an attitude problem.

"Stay put, my lady!" Hugo ordered before they rode off, blending into the chaos and taking her cauldron with them.

26

"Will do," she muttered. Then she marched off in the opposite direction.

Dozens of people ran back and forth between the river and the burning homes, throwing water on dwellings still in flames. Horses, oxen, goats and chickens ran loose, adding to the madness. Pitiful cries of children and animals blended together with the sounds of crackling fire.

She approached a group of people huddled in a circle. They all seemed to be talking at once, gesturing and pointing at something on the ground. The horror and panic covering their faces caused Morgan to push her way through the crowd until she saw what the commotion was about. Lying in a woman's arms was a small boy she guessed to be hardly a year old. He had a bluish-gray tinge to his face and he wasn't moving.

A movement to her right caught her attention. She looked up, surprised to see the same obnoxious man who'd kissed her in the castle. He carried a small girl, seemingly from the same fiery cottage the baby had come from. The child was a few years older than the boy. Her cry was piercing.

He quickly placed the little girl in a woman's arms then disappeared into the thick smoke before Morgan could ask him to help with the baby.

Nobody was doing anything. The baby's face had turned purple. He was dying right before their eyes. Morgan's heart lodged in her throat. She bit at her lip, tried to conjure up every 911 episode she'd ever seen.

Knowing she might be the baby's only hope, she seized the baby from the helpless woman's arms and quickly laid the infant on the ground. She tilted his head back then carefully inserted her finger to make sure his tongue wasn't lodged in his throat. Next, she gave him four quick breaths of air before listening for a pulse.

Nothing. The boy didn't stir.

"He's dead!" someone shrieked.

"She killed him!" another wailed.

Ignoring the protests, Morgan proceeded to breathe air into the boy's lungs. She'd only taken two CPR classes in her entire life but she wasn't ready to give up. She blew four short breaths into the baby's nose and mouth. Using two fingers from both hands she gently, yet firmly, pressed two times into his chest beneath his tiny ribs. Another four breaths…massage…four breaths…massage.

It had to work. The baby couldn't die. She listened for a pulse and prayed to God for help. Four more breaths…massage.

The child's face wrinkled as he turned bright red. Then he let out a piercing wail, stinging her ears and filling her heart with joy. Tears fell from her cheeks as relief flooded her insides. Never had she been so relieved to hear a baby cry. As she cradled the small boy in her arms, a firm, gentle hand framed her shoulder. She looked up into the brown eyes of the man she'd kissed earlier, and the elation she felt from having saved the boy caused her to smile at the man. He smiled back and the crowd cried out in approval.


Hours later when the fire was out and the people without homes had found lodging, Lord Vanguard found himself once again face to face with the maid who had saved the small boy from certain death. "Come," he said to the maid. "There is not much more we can do here."

He had no idea why he felt inclined to invite the woman to join him but inclined was putting it mildly. Earlier in his study, he'd been absorbed in his work when she'd entered. But that failed to stop him from becoming mesmerized by the way her eyes lit up at his collection of books. Knowing of no woman who could read or write, he had determined she had come looking for much more than a good read. But it was he who had been taken aback when he kissed her earlier. His chest had grown tight with desire. The fact that this woman gave him even the slightest pause made him uncomfortable. Women were trouble. They had the characteristics of spiders, spinning their webs, waiting for a clumsy fool to fall within their net. He'd seen it happen to too many men; strong warriors transformed over night, lured into a life of deception and turmoil.

The maid stopped short, tugging her arm free as they approached his mount.

"I don't like horses," she said stubbornly. "And I can't believe you'd think I'd come with you after the way you treated me in the castle."

He shrugged. Any fool could see that the maid was playing hard to get. An intriguing game, he mused, considering it had been years since any woman had bothered. As he murmured soothing words to his stallion, he decided he had not the time for games. Without giving her another thought, he untied his horse and walked off, leaving her behind.

"Hey!" the annoying wench shouted after him.

Impatiently, he glanced over his shoulder, promptly drawn to the curve of her hips within the absurdly snug breeches she wore. A ponderous sigh erupted as he wondered when he'd started getting soft in the head. "Are you coming, or not?" he asked.

"I don't even know you." She plunked a hand on her hip.

"Nor I you," he said matter-of-factly.

"But you're a man."

"Aye," he said, his gaze caressing every inch of her. "And you are very much a woman."

Her cheeks blossomed with color, surprising him, for it was usually the inexperienced maidens who blushed, not brazen wenches such as she. He was due to leave shortly to visit the king's holdings and this wench tempted him sorely. But he wasn't about to play the fool simply because her eyes sparkled like rare jewels and her silken hair made his palms itch. Frowning, he gripped the leather reins and yanked his horse onward, reminding himself that he cared not whether she followed. He was tired and he needed a rest.

Morgan hurried to catch up to him. If she were in her own time she might think twice before going into the woods with a stranger, but she'd seen first hand how the people in the village respected him and how he risked his life to save those children. Besides, he was an accountant, and he wasn't exactly begging her to come with him. "Where are we going?"

"There is a lake close by," he said without glancing her way, "and I am hungry. I thought to share my food and drink but if you have training to get to, perhaps you should be on your way."

"My afternoon's pretty clear," she said, struggling to keep up with his long strides. "And if you don't mind my asking, what kind of training are you referring to?"

"Your womanly duties at Braddock, of course. Perhaps Matti will start you off with needle or shuttle, though it would depend on your age and other such things."

She lifted both brows. "Like?"

"For example, how many children do you have...five, ten?"

She snorted. "I'm twenty-four. I don't have any children."

His eyes widened. "Most women, assuming they have survived the dangers of childbirth, have had more than a dozen by the time they reach four and twenty."

"That's ridiculous."

"Are you married? Widowed?"

"Neither."

He stopped in his tracks and looked her over with growing speculation.

"What is it?" she asked.

"Four and twenty and you have not married? Perhaps you are flawed in some way. Let me see your teeth."

She shooed him away. "Nothing's wrong with me. I'm in great shape. I do aerobics twice a week and I eat plenty of fruit and vegetables."

He winced as if her words pained him. "It is a strange French accent you have?"

"More like a new-old sort of English."

"Hmm. I would appreciate your use of intelligible English when in my presence. Now then, do as I say and reveal your teeth to me."

Morgan rolled her eyes before impatiently flashing him a glimpse of her pearly whites.

He merely grunted before starting off again, following a worn path through patches of dogtooth violets and tall broadleaf trees.

"Wait up," she called before she caught up to him and walked briskly at his side. "So? What did you think?"

He gave a noncommittal shrug. "I have seen better."

"Just like a man," she muttered.

"What is that?"

"Stubborn...hard to please," she said.

He huffed and then said over his shoulder, "It is women who cannot be relied upon, who say one thing yet mean another."

"Men don't know how to listen," she shot back.

"Women talk too much—"

"Men talk with their—"

He glanced back at her when she failed to finish her sentence.

"Oh never mind," she said, waving him onward, "you win."

He shook his head, once again fixating his gaze on the beaten path as he kept a steady onward pace.

The man was tough to figure out, Morgan decided. Although he walked and talked with the confidence of a dozen men, he seemed at a loss whenever he looked into her eyes. Maybe he wasn't as harsh as he liked to appear. That had to be it. Her instincts told her he possessed an inner gentleness that made her soften towards him. "You wouldn't happen to know Lord Vanguard, would you?" she asked after a few moments of silence passed between them.

"Why do you ask?"

Because she was curious as to whether her head was going to be cut off by the ugly troll. Instead she said, "Because rumors have it that the man's nasty temper nearly matches his repulsive face."

He laughed, but said no more. Morgan didn't know whether that meant the stories were true, or not, but she decided to leave it at that since she would be meeting the hideously ugly lord soon enough. "Do you believe in miracles?" she asked next, filling gaps of silence with questions, something she did out of habit, especially when she was nervous.

"Nay."

"Why not?"

"Because I believe truth and logic are always involved in occurrences others are quick to call a miracle."

"What about the birth of a baby? Don't you think that's a miracle?"

"Nay. God has created women for such purpose."

Maybe, she thought, that inner gentleness she'd sensed was a fluke. Either he was preoccupied or he wasn't used to revealing any sort of emotion. It was hard to tell. But she wasn't exactly a psychiatrist and she certainly didn't plan on being here long enough to help this man with his inner self.

As she struggled to keep up with him, she said, "I guess it would be safe to bet then that you didn't believe in the Easter Bunny or Santa Claus when you were a boy?"

They arrived at their destination. He turned and looked down at her, making her feel four feet tall. "You speak in riddles," he said. "But I can tell you that I believe in naught that I cannot see with my own two eyes." With that said, he led his horse to the nearest tree and proceeded to tie the leather reins to a low branch.

As she watched him fiddle with his horse, she found herself admiring his iron-muscled physique. She decided to enjoy the moment along with the view; try to think of her time in this new world as an adventure. Until she figured out why she was here and how she was going to get home, it wouldn't do her any good to panic.

While he secured his horse, she took in a long deep breath of pine-scented air. They had walked far enough away from the lingering effects of the fire. She plunked down on the grass next to the lake's edge. Birds chirped and squirrels rustled through the trees. If not for the man's ancient breeches and soft boots with turned down cuffs, she would have thought she was back in her own time.

From the traveling pack, the man withdrew a chunk of crusty bread. Then he untied a leather bag from the saddle and took a drink from it. After giving the animal a pat on the rump, he advanced her way. He handed her a chunk of bread before sitting beside her. The inside of the bread was chewy and had a buttery aroma. Her stomach grumbled.

She took a gulp of the drink he offered and almost gagged as the thick, tangy wine slid down her throat. She was thirsty though and it wasn't long before she acquired a taste for the stuff. For the next twenty minutes, between swigs of wine and nibbles of bread, she stole peeks at the medieval man out of the corner of her eye. Flecks of amber glinted beneath lashes that seemed too long for a man. She took note of the hard outline of his jaw and his thick, dark hair and the way it curled at his neck where a thin scar began, ending inches lower near his collar bone. Apparently he was a man of few words. She wondered what he was thinking and was glad when he spoke and she didn't have to ask.

"What kind of witch are you that can breathe life into the dead?"

She laughed; a nervous, slightly tipsy laughter, stopping only after realizing he wasn't laughing with her. She tried to look serious and that made the corners of his mouth tilt upward the slightest bit.

"Anybody can do it," she said, before taking another mouthful of wine. "Even you." She poked his stone hard chest in a friendly gesture and just that small touch caused a fluttery tingle in the pit of her stomach.

As he leaned back on the grass, using his elbows to keep himself propped upward, he watched her closely, intensely. For some ridiculous reason she reveled in the attention he gave her as he kept his gaze focused on her. "Want me to teach you?" she asked playfully.

His brow arched.

"Lie down and pretend you're dead," she told him.

"The sun will be setting soon," he told her. "Perhaps another time would be just as well."

"Oh, come on. Are you afraid of little ol' me?" She gently pushed at his chest with both hands until his back lay firmly on the grass. She hovered over him. Gazing into those gorgeous eyes, she knew suddenly what it was like to feel complete and utter lust. She laughed at the thought.

"I am amusing?"

"Oh…hush. You're supposed to be dead, remember?"

He groaned but obeyed nonetheless. His dark eyes bore into hers, daring her to finish what she'd started. The sun's last rays reflected off of his face, taking her breath away. Suddenly, as she looked into his eyes, she couldn't remember what she was supposed to be doing. Those eyes, that mouth. Once again, if only for a fleeting moment, she thought she recognized him. Had they met before? No. Ridiculous. The notion had to be the result of too much wine. She shook her head and then smiled devilishly as she recalled what she was about to do.

She was going to kiss this fine warrior and wake him from the dead. Slowly, she brought her mouth to his until she felt the firm fullness of his lips pressed against her mouth. He tasted of herbs and fruity wine. She was supposed to help him breathe, she reminded herself. But instead of giving him breath, he took hers away, deepening their kiss, hungry with passion until she was consumed by the thrilling realness of his fiery kiss. Every part of her tingled and shivered with pleasure, hoping this time the kiss would not end too soon, but he gently pulled away and said softly, "It seems I am needed once again."

Leaves crunched behind her.

She turned about, gasping at the sight of two men hovering over them. One man wore chain mail and a helmet adorned with a bright red plume. The other wore brown tights and a tunic and no headgear at all. Both men wore sheepish grins as they made their apologies.

With hands splayed against his chest, she pushed herself upward, making him grunt from the full weight of her. "Why didn't you tell me they were here?"

"Verily you had me pinned to the ground. How was I to know?"

"I didn't pin you to the ground."

He came to his feet, casually brushing grass from his breeches before he went to his horse. "Call it what you will," he said over his shoulder. "Though it was obvious to all," he added, reminding her that they had witnesses, "that you were in full command."

As he mounted his horse he called out, "Julian! See that the maid returns to Braddock safely." He rode to where she stood and gazed upon her, his expression filled with longing. "I must go. But I fair say I shall be quick to return for another of your lessons."

At her obvious embarrassment, a grin tugged at his lips. Chuckling, he used his legs against his horse to accelerate to a gallop, leaving her frustrated and standing alone once again. Whether her frustration stemmed from his cocky attitude or because she hadn't wished the kiss to end, she wasn't sure. Nor did she care to know.

# CHAPTER THREE

Three days later, Hugo and Matti watched Lord Vanguard stride through Braddock's keep with barely a nod and only a disturbing scowl to greet them.

"Does he think his people are blind to the fury sprouting within him?" Matti asked her husband. "Ever since the king informed Lord Vanguard that he was to marry, he has been more irritable than usual. For days his betrothed has been at Braddock, and yet he has made it clear he has no intention of ever meeting her."

Hugo opened his mouth to speak, then promptly closed it when Matti continued.

"What is Lord Vanguard planning to do? Wait until the wedding day comes upon us, speak his vows, and be done with it? Without benefit of introductions? Not if I have any say in the matter."

Hugo sighed. "My dear, Matti. 'Tis not sound for you to question his lordship when he is in such foul temper."

"Oh, but he has gone too far this time, I fear." Matti paced the floor. "Ignoring Lady Amanda since her arrival…his manners are downright boorish. I am going to see that an introduction is made this very day."

Hugo's shoulders sagged.

Determined strides brought Matti to Lord Vanguard's study. She tapped her knuckles firmly on the sturdy oak door. Without waiting for a reply, she entered his den.

Derek sat in his high-back chair hunched over his paper-cluttered desk. He didn't bother to glance up even after Matti cleared her throat for the second time.

"Good to see you have returned in good health," Matti said. "You will be joining us for the morning meal?"

"Nay."

"My lord, you cannot hide in here forever. Your betrothed has been quite patient in waiting to meet you. Your avoiding her will only make matters more difficult."

"Me avoiding her? If I recall correctly it was Lady Amanda who ran away from my men in hopes of finding her lover."

"So you have heard."

"Bloody right. If not for Hugo and Emmon tracking her down, we would not be having this discussion. It seems Lady Amanda has no more desire than I to go through with this marriage. Verily I am surprised she is still here."

"But she is here and you cannot put off meeting her any longer."

"How can you be certain she has not run off again? Have you checked her bedchamber recently?"

Matti sighed. "Once you meet Lady Amanda you will see what a charming young woman she is. She has made quite an impression on Braddock's people while you've been gone."

He wished to hear no more of Lady Amanda. When Hugo had first told him of Lady Amanda's escape, Derek had thought his problems were solved. No bride, no marriage. A wife would only bring him pain.

*I will not be hurt again.*

All the prayers in the world had failed to bring his mother back. And nothing he did to please his father had helped him gain his father's love. His heart was now impenetrable. He preferred it that way.

Matti's shoulders sagged. "It is not as bad as it appears, my lord. According to her maid, Lady Amanda was injured in a fall and does not remember what happened the day she was found in the woods."

A deep, theatrical guffaw echoed off the dense walls. "And I suppose Lady Amanda has a stream of castle folk thinking she's as pure as unsullied water from a new rain. Hog's turd...all of it." He shook his head and looked back to his papers.

"My lord, I am only asking that you meet your betrothed. If not for me, or for the king, do it for your people. A quick introduction is all I ask."

"I am against marriage, Matti. A wife would bring me naught but strife."

Matti remained silent.

Derek leaned back in his chair and rubbed his temples. "Do not distress yourself for I have every intention of going through with this bloody wedding...providing she is still around. But I must warn you," he added carefully, "cease in your endeavor to convince me of her endless endowments, or I may change my mind and bow out altogether."

After a moment, he glanced up to see Matti still standing there...waiting. Derek sighed. The woman had raised him, after all; he supposed it would not pain him overly much to give into her request...just this once. "Send her to me, but make it quick. I have much business to oversee before nightfall."

Noticing dark shadows beneath Matti's eyes, his voice softened. "Someday, Matti, you will see that I am right. If I know women, and I can well assure you I do, she has other intentions altogether. Perhaps she has not run off because she and her lover hope to get their clutches on Braddock itself. Marriage to the lord of Braddock would be the swiftest way to accomplish that."

Matti stiffened. "Do not speak of such things. King Henry would never have forced a woman such as that upon you."

"The matter will be out of our hands soon enough," he said with a ponderous sigh. "Nothing good can come of this union, Matti. Nothing at all."

Morgan raked her fingers through her tangled hair since there was not a hairbrush in sight. She then brushed her teeth using water and a rag. It had taken her over an hour to figure out all the laces and doohickeys on the medieval dress Odelia had left out for her. The long-sleeved chemise as Odelia referred to it trailed to the ground. The outer kirtle was velvet and about the same length. She tied a belt of cloth at the waistline, bringing the garment high enough from the ground so that she wouldn't trip.

She was ready to head downstairs when the door flew open. Odelia rushed in. "He has returned-and he wants-to see you," she said between ragged breaths.

"Who?"

"His Lordship. And we have little time." Odelia paused suddenly, her brows drawing together as she scrutinized Morgan's dress. "Was it that new lass, Maren, who helped you dress, my lady?" Odelia's eyes twinkled with sudden amusement.

Morgan failed to see the humor. Maybe people back home would laugh at her outfit but Odelia actually lived in this century. She wore this stuff every day. "I dressed myself, thank you very much."

Odelia smiled. "I am sorry, my lady, but you have put your kirtle on backwards. 'Twould seem your garb is going in one direction whilst her ladyship is going in another."

Hastily, as if she'd just that second remembered why she'd come, Odelia began unlacing Morgan's gown. "We must hurry. I've been told that Lord Vanguard does not like to be kept waiting."

Morgan rolled her eyes. "He doesn't like to be disobeyed, he doesn't like to be kept waiting. The man sounds a little controlling and uptight."

Odelia sighed. "It will do no good for you to be showing your true colors so soon. If you behave, I am certain Lord Vanguard will take a liking to you."

39

"Take a liking to me? I could care less if the ugly beast likes me or not. In fact," Morgan said, a sly smile curving her lips, "it would be to my advantage if he wanted nothing to do with me." She swished Odelia away and then used both hands to muss her hair in defiance. "There," she said, "show me the way. We wouldn't want his lord and master to be kept waiting."

Odelia made tsking noises as she followed her out the door, doing her best to retie a few laces as they moved along. "Naught but sympathy I have for this Lord of Braddock Hall, whom I have yet to meet."

"Did you say something?" Morgan asked.

"Nay, my lady."

Moments later, Odelia and Morgan stood outside the very same room Morgan had entered on her first day at Braddock. The room with the wonderful books, journals, and...and that man. "Are you sure this is Lord Vanguard's study?"

"Aye, my lady. I am certain." Odelia knocked on the door.

An impatient voice snapped, "Come in."

Odelia wished Morgan luck before she hurried off.

A chill raced up Morgan's spine. Within the time it had taken her to get to his lordship's den, she'd gone from feeling like a determined, gutsy woman to a cowardly, spineless one. Her stomach turned and her hands trembled as she pushed the door open.

Inside, the heavy curtains were pulled shut. Except for the meager light produced by a fire in the hearth, the room was dark. Flames flickered here and there, casting eerie shadows on the walls. Her eyes took a few minutes to adjust.

Then she spotted him.

Her fiance sat at his desk near the fire. Thankfully his back was to her because suddenly the idea of seeing his hideously repulsive face made her cringe.

Without bothering to turn about, he raised a hand and idly waved her forward. How rude, she thought, that he couldn't bother to acknowledge his betrothed with a nod or a simple "hello."

He was bent over his desk, seemingly absorbed in a pile of disorderly papers. She wondered if he'd thanked his accountant for his help the other day. The high-backed chair he sat in made it impossible for her to see the extent of his disfigurement. He was definitely large because his shoulders stuck out on either side of the wide chair.

As she took a seat on a simple wood bench nearby, burning logs crackled in the fireplace. "I see you are busy, sir—My Lord..." She winced, having no clue as to the proper way to address him. "...so I will try to make this quick."

She wrung her hands in her lap as she searched for the right words. To hell with it. She would tell him the truth and be done with it. "I'm not the woman you think I am," she blurted. "My name is not Amanda Forrester. It's Morgan Hayes and I'm from another time. The year 2011 to be exact. A century you might view as technological chaos with its fast-moving cars and planes, buses and trains. I grew up there...in the future. But last week, the strangest thing happened. I was in my mother's antique store when suddenly I was suddenly swept through time...to this century. I know it sounds crazy, but it's true. When I first arrived I thought it was a dream."

A bit of nervous laughter escaped her before she went on, "A nightmare really. But now I know, as impossible as it sounds, it really happened. Somehow I was transported back in time and I have no idea why or how. The worst part is that I don't know what to do about it. Obviously I have no relatives to go to. I tried closing my eyes and tapping my heels while chanting, there's no place like home, there's no place like home, but that didn't work."

Silence. Her smile faded as she tried to explain herself. "You see there was this movie where a girl named Dorothy ends up in a strange place called Oz, and she—oh, never mind, it's kind of hard to explain. I guess what I'm trying to say is that I know this must be hard for you to believe when I hardly believe it myself. But the simple truth is that I am not who you think I am. And I thought you should know."

A strong urge to see what he looked like swept over her and she stood and took a step closer. Her heart suddenly went out to this "elephant man" who hid himself during the day. And what of night? Did he come out of hiding then? She practiced making a straight face since she did not want to give away the pity she might feel when she finally saw his deformities up close.

"This must be quite a shock to you," she said, only inches between them now. "Once this Amanda woman comes to her senses, I'm sure she'll come to Braddock to seek you out. It's obvious you take good care of your people and your castle. Just because you look the way you do..." Grimacing, she added, "I mean...it's the inside that counts."


Derek stiffened. He did not need to turn around to see that the woman babbling on was the same woman who had shared his wine and kissed him as if there was no tomorrow. The same woman, he thought resentfully, whom he had envisioned in his mind much too often these past days.

Her strange dialect could not be mistaken for anyone but her. The wench could definitely babble on and if she continued for too much longer he would run away himself.

"I do have one favor to ask of you," she said, making him further ponder his unusually bad luck. King Henry, it seemed, had bound him with a madwoman for certain.

"It's about Odelia, Amanda's maid," she went on. "She's innocent in all of this. She hardly knew Amanda before she was asked to accompany the lady to your castle. And I don't think Odelia can see very well either...it looks to me as if she has cataracts. Maybe there's a doctor around here who could take a look at her eyes. Anyhow, Odelia honestly thinks I'm Lady Amanda, so if you wouldn't mind letting her stay on until her boss or master, the Earl of Forrester, can be informed, I'm sure she'd appreciate it."

A maddening tick set within Derek's jaw as he lifted himself to his feet and turned around.

Morgan gawked in disbelief. "You can't be—"

"And why is that?"

"Because Lord Vanguard is so ugly he kills men, women and children with his looks alone."

Derek found her surprise to be amusing, not to mention her hair, which stood out in all directions like a bird's nest after a storm. That, coupled with the fact that her outer garment was in reverse, made him chuckle.

She stuck her chin out defiantly. "What's so funny this time?"

"I find it humorous, my fair wench, that although you compare my countenance to that of an ogre and insult my intelligence by expecting me to believe you are from a world far beyond the horizon," he threw his arms in a wide arc, "I have not yet strangled you with my own two hands. Which I am quite certain is what it would take to silence you since it seems you have not expired from staring at me as you thought you might. Verily judging by the way you have ogled me of late I would guess you were more than pleased by what you saw."

She very nearly growled, her hands curling into fists at her sides as she said, "I did not make up that story. It really happened. And who are you to call me a liar when you knew all along that you were Lord Vanguard and yet you didn't just tell me."

"I do not recall you stating your name the other day," Derek said as he scratched his stubbled jaw. "Ah, but now that I ponder our first meeting further, I do recall you mentioning you were engaged. I can only assume you were about to inform me that you were engaged to me." He pointed at his chest. "But now suddenly you claim to be Morgan Hayes, a time-traveler, no less."

Morgan snorted. "I don't care what you think or if you believe a word I've said. The truth is I wouldn't marry you if you were the last man on earth."

With a few steps he closed the short distance between them. "Is that so?"

He noticed her chest rise and fall with each breath as she nodded, refusing to cower. The thought of holding her again made every muscle in his body grow taut. The notion that he wanted to touch her at all inflamed him all the more. So much so, that with one swift movement of his arm, he pulled her tight against his chest. He felt the brisk beat of her heart as he slid the palm of his hand behind her head and brought her lips to his. Although she took a bit longer than before, she did succumb, melting in his arms like newly churned butter.

With his mouth pressed against hers, he eagerly awaited the overpowering sense of potency he usually felt after conquering a wench such as she, but instead, an unfamiliar ache of intense longing swept over him. Pulling away from her, he gazed into her eyes. "You wouldn't want to be leaving for that other world of yours without a farewell kiss, now would you?"

He put a finger to her lips before she could respond. "You need not say another word, my sweet angel from beyond. For I believe your response to my touch has already answered my question."

She pushed away from him, her eyes narrowing. "Once again I've let you get the best of me, but it won't happen again. I can't believe I thought there might be a hint of warmth hidden beneath that hardened exterior of yours!" She turned to leave.

"It will not work," he called out.

She paused at the door. "What won't work?"

"Your ploys to have me believe you are someone else. Think hard before you continue this game of yours," he said coolly as he made his way back to his desk. "Whichever name you wish to claim, it will not change the situation. And Amanda—"

"My name is Morgan."

"Amanda," he said hotly. "You'll not be leaving Braddock, so abandon any ideas of trying to escape. The banners have been posted. The king along with your father will be arriving at month's end to see us married. Neither of us has a choice in the matter." He shuffled through the papers before him and then looked up. "I am finished. You may leave now."

"I'm not a child awaiting your every order. So you can wipe that pompous, self-important smirk clean off your—"

"Out!" he snapped, making her jump. He pointed a finger at the door.

She stood her ground, peering into his eyes, unblinking.

He watched her closely, seeing nothing but stubborn pride in her stance. Another man might find her mulish behavior infuriating, but he did not. She was like thunder on a clear day, and she aroused his interest like no other.

Without another word spoken, she turned and left. The door slammed shut, sobering him from such wearisome thoughts. Every muscle tensed. King Henry may as well have strapped him before an arrow slit during battle...'twould have been much more considerate. Marriage to the wench would be the end of him.

# CHAPTER FOUR

Morgan returned to her room, plunked herself on the feathered mattress and tried to think. What was she going to do? She needed to find the real Amanda, quickly, preferably before she was forced to marry a medieval man with a medieval attitude. Where was the woman anyhow? Had she really run off to be with her lover? And how, she wondered, could she and this Amanda woman look so much alike? The questions spun inside her head like the rotors on a helicopter.

She couldn't sit around the castle doing nothing. But roaming the forests in search of Amanda lost its appeal as visions of Otgar came to mind. According to Lord Vanguard the marriage was to take place at the end of the month. That gave her a few weeks to come up with a plan. Until then she was stuck. Unfortunately she was stuck with an arrogant, overconfident lord who refused to believe a word she said.

Iron hinges creaked as the door to her room came open. Odelia backed into the room, holding a tray of food that she placed on a high table near the bed.

"Tell me I didn't just meet Lord Vanguard," Morgan said with a groan. "Tell me it was his stable guy or his cook, or the castle's contractor."

"I am afraid 'twas indeed Lord Vanguard."

"How long has he given us to pack?" Morgan asked.

"Don't be a shandy fool. Nobody is leaving Braddock."

"Even after I told him I wasn't Lady Amanda?"

"He believes you are Amanda," Odelia whispered into her ear, "because you are Amanda. And, according to the others—"

"Others?"

"Aye, the castle folk. There is Maren, the new kitchen maid." Odelia used her fingers to keep count. "And Hugo's wife, Matti. Shayna and Ciara the sewing maids, and Maxine, the castle's bloodletter."

"The castle's bloodletter? Oh, never mind, I don't want to know." Morgan collapsed backwards on the bed into the mounds of embroidered pillows. After a moment she propped herself up on an elbow. "Okay, I can't stand it. What did they say?"

Dusting the furniture as she spoke, Odelia said, "They believe Lord Vanguard is quite taken with you and has acted peculiar since you arrived. They spoke of your entering his lordship's study on the day you arrived, unannounced and wearing those ridiculous breeches," Odelia shot her a reproving look, "and they told me of how he mistook you for a serving maid."

"A serving maid?" Morgan felt ridiculously offended.

"A serving maid," Odelia repeated with a good dose of satisfaction.

"If he thought I was a serving maid, then what was he doing kissing me that day?"

"He kissed you?"

"Yes sirree. As far as he knew, his fiancée was right here under the same roof, and yet he kissed me."

"Before you go on, 'tis not jealousy of your own self I am hearing, is it?"

"Me? Jealous?" Morgan laughed a little too heartily. "You're crazy if you think I'd be jealous of that man kissing a serving maid. I couldn't care less if he kissed every Tom, Dick, and Harry in England."

"I do not think 'tis Tom, Dick, or Harry you have to worry about. Especially since it is indeed your own self whom he seems to be infatuated with. Verily, you don't have to convince me though. I just thought perchance, after meeting him, you might have changed your mind about marrying the man."

"That's absurd. I don't ever want to talk to the man again. Except to tell him that I have proof that I'm not Lady Amanda."

"And what proof might that be?" Odelia asked, her shoulders sagging.

"Well, the greatest proof will be when I actually find Amanda. Then you'll all see."

Odelia shook her head in exasperation.

"If I can't find Amanda though, I'll give Lord Vanguard details of the twenty-first century. Things that will happen in the future…history in the making so to speak."

"Since being bumped on the head, my lady, you've become a regular jester. Mayhap you can tell his lordship when the war between France and England will be over?"

Morgan shrugged. "I don't know everything, Odelia. But I do know the French won the war." She frowned. History had always been one of her weaknesses. Brightening she added, "Something called the Black Death will occur, a bubonic plague caused by rats. I wish I could remember the exact date."

Odelia shook her head. "'Tis behind us."

"Oh." Relief swept over her. Rats rated right up there with horses. "I know…I could tell Lord Vanguard about Joan of Arc…how she leads a French army in a siege."

"She became an English prisoner and was burned as a witch," Odelia finished.

Morgan drummed a finger on the bed cover. "Well, I'll think of something."

Odelia wagged a finger at her. "Truly you are not going to continue with these tales of yours, are you? Although your long-time maid was too sick to accompany you to Braddock, she warned me of your constant pranks and went on to say that you were a stubborn, overindulged young lady who would do anything to get her way."

Morgan's shoulders drooped. No wonder Odelia was convinced she was Amanda. Since arriving, she'd definitely not been herself.

"If you want to go on trying to convince me that you are not Amanda, go ahead," Odelia went on. "But I can assure you of one thing. Should you continue to tell Lord Vanguard that you are someone from aloft the horizon he will begin to think you are a mad woman. To make the king happy he will marry you anyhow and then keep you locked in the dungeon. Forever. Indeed, it happens all the time."

Morgan swallowed, picturing herself trapped in a dark musty dungeon with hungry rodents. And there would be bugs, probably stag beetles...the ugly ones with jaws as long as their bodies that branched out like antlers. A prickly unease crept up her spine. "I'll be very diplomatic when I talk to him next time," she promised Odelia. "Besides, you already said he's not going to throw us out. And, if it makes you feel any better, I told him you had nothing to do with any of this."

The maid's plump body wilted. "Whatever you intend to tell his lordship will have to wait. He left for escort duty shortly after you left his study."

"Escort duty?"

"'Tis when a king calls upon his vassals to provide him protection as he visits his holdings."

Odelia straightened a few things, then paused at the doorway and said, "The parents of that little boy you saved wish to thank you. I was told you breathed life into the child. Where did you learn to do such a thing?"

Morgan wanted to tell her about the CPR class she'd taken, but she stopped herself. What good would it do? "I don't know, Odelia. I just knew I had to do something."

"Mayhap we can visit the boy on the morrow."

Morgan nodded. "I would like that." After Odelia left the room, Morgan felt a tightening in her chest at the thought of Lord Vanguard being gone. The last thing she needed was a crush on some arrogant knightly lord whose kisses felt like a moonlight caress on a balmy night with promises of something more.

Suddenly she found herself wishing she'd dated more. Maybe then she'd have something to compare his kiss with. There had to be other men who could make her sizzle like an egg on hot asphalt. A nice, friendly, slightly smaller man, who could make her feel the way Lord Vanguard did. She grimaced at the idea that maybe only conceited, arrogant men like Lord Vanguard could make her dissolve in their arms.

Derek sent his men onward to Braddock, telling his men-at-arms that he would follow shortly for he had personal business to attend. Getting away from Braddock for a few days had served him well, but he still yearned for his old life back; the simple, promising life of an unattached lord.

As he neared Leonie's cottage, a simple wood structure with a chimney, he noted that the windows had been newly covered with fine linen. Dozens of candles flickered from the breeze he let inside when he opened the door, casting a flattering glow upon the woman waiting within. Leonie lay upon a large four-posted bed, her gaze fixed upon him as he set down his sword and removed his tunic.

"Did you miss me?" she asked seductively, eager for his attentions.

"I have been busy. I am afraid I have not had time to think of such pleasures."

"'Tis not what I heard, my lord."

Not used to her meddling, Derek stopped unbuckling his belt. "Exactly what is it you have heard?"

She propped herself on a pillow, making certain he had a clear view of her ample bosom. "'Twas rumored the king plans to force you into marriage. 'Tis not true, is it?"

A frown creased his brow. He had come to Leonie in hopes of relieving the mounting tensions of late. Hoping to erase Lady Amanda from his mind. It was no use.

Panic lined Leonie's voice. "Tell me you do not plan to marry an unseasoned, virginal innocent? Just looking at you would surely put her to her death."

His jaw hardened.

"You are too much of a man for a chaste lass such as Lady Amanda," she said.

He arched a brow. "But what of you? I assume 'tis safe to say I am not too much of a man for you?"

"Never," she burst out. She edged off of the bed, trying hard to regain her composure. Her voice became a whisper. "I have a confession to make." She removed the pins from her hair, letting the thick strands fall past her pale shoulders. Gazing into his eyes, she loosened her belt and let the thin muslin gown she wore slither to the floor around her feet. Slowly, she came toward him, her hips swaying. "I have been burning up with jealousy, my lord, and only you can put out the flames flickering within."

Words and gestures laced with jealousy...this is not what he had in mind. A good mind-numbing romp in the sheets is what he desired. Nothing more, nothing less. Derek turned away, retrieved his tunic from the chair and pulled the soft leather jerkin over his head. He moved to the table and claimed his sword.

'Twas like a dark cloud sweeping toward him as she rushed to his side, clinging to his leg like a woman suddenly possessed by insecurity. "Please, my lord, do not leave. Forgive my presumptuous behavior. Stay and let me satisfy your needs."

"Get up, Leonie. Begging is unbecoming on you."

"I will not let you go," she cried, paying little attention to his words. She clawed at him like a wild animal being denied its supper.

"I always thought you were different." He unclasped her fingers, snatched his mantle from the table, and headed for the door.

51

"You'll regret this day if you leave me, Derek Vanguard. Come back here and satisfy me now. I demand that you do!"

He gazed back at her long enough to shake his head, wondering what he'd seen in her these past months.

"If you marry the noble bitch," Leonie shrieked as he headed for the door, "she will seduce you first with her innocence. Then she will crush your heart in the palm of one flawless hand." Leonie held a fist to the air. "One gentle squeeze. 'Tis all it will take to destroy you as you are destroying me. Aye, you will see."

Holding her gown to her bosom, Leonie followed him outside to where his horse was tied. He threw the reins over his stallion's neck and vaulted to its back.

Still clinging to him, Leonie gazed beseechingly into his eyes, her voice calm as she said, "Unlike myself, my love, you will not survive such destruction of the heart. Your betrothed will see to that."

Derek loosened her hold and rode off. He closed his eyes and let the strengthening wind whip across his face as the steady beat of his stallion helped soothe his weary state. Seeing Leonie had only made matters worse.

The steed quickened its pace as Derek guided the animal to the nearest inn. The scene with Leonie did not bother him nearly as much as the endless visions of his betrothed. Since that first kiss, when he assumed she was no more than a serving maid, Lady Amanda had dared to plague his mind. It was her fine instructions on saving the dead though, that had captured his full attention. He'd been stunned by his unusual reaction to her seemingly inexperienced teachings. And when his men had interrupted their short time together, he should have been grateful. Instead he had found himself aggravated by the interruption.

He took pride in his ability to remain unaffected by those around him...especially women. Women were naught more than a means in which to satisfy a need. Never once had he contemplated turning Leonie away before. The fact that he had, irked him greatly.

He couldn't get to The Boar's Head Inn soon enough. His knuckles turned white as he curled his fingers yet tighter about the reins but nothing stopped the woman from appearing in his mind's eye. Wisps of hair framing a shadowed face along with a petite form told him that the darkly cloaked figure he was seeing was indeed a woman. As a child he had spotted the same hooded figure many times: at fairs and on market day. Once he had seen her outside Braddock's gates, but before he could question the woman she always disappeared. He'd forgotten about the woman until now. *Who was the wench and why did she dare to plague his thoughts?*

Inwardly he cursed his luck when the vision was replaced with Lady Amanda's visage. God's teeth! The wench managed to void all reasoning, pummeling his mind with her enchanting smile and expressive eyes. How was he to counsel the king on important matters when he could not keep a clear head?

As soon as the thatched roof of the inn came into view, Derek flung himself from his horse and tied the animal to a wooden stake. He stalked past two women gathering water from a well then entered the tavern and ordered the strongest drink they had. A plump man with pink skin and a patch of red hair on his head promptly brought him a full horn. A handful of people watched as he guzzled the brew in two swallows.

Bloody hell, he thought after consuming a fair share of the drink. Even the strong ale failed to erase the image of Lady Amanda's velvet lips descending upon his. The notion that his betrothed aroused him even after hearing her tales of being from another world made him question his own sanity. Exactly why he was here. He slammed the empty horn to the scarred table, scowling at the innkeeper as the elfish man hurried to refill it.

There seemed to be no cure for his ailment. Damnation to all women. Particularly Amanda or Morgan...or whatever her name be this day, he thought bitterly. He planned to erase all memories of the noble wench before returning to Braddock, for he was sure she would be gone when he returned. She had runaway before and there was naught to keep her from doing so again. A knot formed in his gut as he realized that the thought of never seeing her again was what troubled him most.

By the time Morgan awoke, shafts of sunlight had broken through the clouds. She dressed quickly in a kirtle of pale yellow. Over that she put something called a surcoat, a light golden brown fabric with gold embroidered trimmings. She was a quick learner. And Odelia, believing she suffered from memory loss due to her head injury, was an admirable teacher.

As she descended the narrow staircase, Morgan realized this was the first time she'd left her room without Odelia at her side. She could've waited for the maid but she was anxious to get outside. It was a beautiful day. And besides, she had no idea how long she'd be staying in this century. The hardest thing about living here, she decided, was having no sense of time. Too bad she hadn't been wearing a watch when her t-shirt had become snagged in the Earl of Kensington's armor. No watch, no makeup, no convenient items to prove her allegations.

She stopped in her tracks and her eyes widened.

*I was not wearing a watch when I was stuck to the earl's armor.*

Her mouth dropped opened. Why hadn't she thought of him before? *The Earl of Kensington. He could very well be the answer to her problem.*

If she recalled correctly, he'd lived during the fifteenth century. Emmon had said the year was 1444. The same year the Earl of Kensington had supposedly been killed in an ambush.

That's why she was here! For the first time since she'd been swept through time, it all sort of made sense. Time travel, of course, was a crazy unthinkable notion, but here she was, in a

strange time with no inkling as to why. Until now. She needed
to find the Earl of Kensington and warn him of the ambush
before it was too late. Her heart soared at the possibility that
she'd been sent to this century to save the earl's life. She took
the stairs two at a time as she envisioned seeing her very own
metal man, a familiar sight in an unfamiliar world. She would
find him!

"Good day, my lady," Matti said, pulling Morgan from her
thoughts as she was greeted by the older woman on the
landing.

They had met once before, Morgan realized. Matti was
Hugo's wife. "Please, call me Mor...I mean Amanda. And that
goes for all of you," Morgan said to the castle folk within
earshot. Her cheeks heated at the thought that all these people
knew what had transpired between her and Lord Vanguard.
Did they think she was crazy? Were they angry with her for
supposedly defying their lord by running off in the forest?

Matti took hold of her forearm and gently pulled her aside.
A note of kindness touched her voice. "You have no need to
fret, my lady. 'Tis only a loyal few who know the extent of
your conversation with Lord Vanguard."

Morgan smiled weakly, surprised by the woman's
perceptiveness.

"Is it true you believe you are not Lady Amanda, or is it as
his lordship says?"

Morgan's palms began to sweat. "What does he say
exactly?"

"That you play childish games and wish only to be with
your lover."

Matti didn't beat around the bush. Morgan chewed on her
bottom lip, wondering what she should say. If she told Matti
the truth, that she was Morgan Hayes from the future, Matti
would think she was either a liar or a nutcase. If, on the other
hand, she told Matti she was Lady Amanda, she would be a
liar, and a contemptible person for dishonoring their lord by
running away in the first place.

Matti raised a hand before she could answer. "I apologize. I should not have asked. Verily I only wished to talk with you for a moment."

Thankful for the reprieve, Morgan followed Matti across the keep, away from curious eyes and ears.

"As you are most likely aware," Matti said softly, "Lord Vanguard is highly respected and greatly loved here at Braddock. To an outsider he might seem a bit gruff, but to the people that know him best, he is…" Matti chuckled lightly. "I must say, now that I think on it, he is extremely gruff, even to those of us who love him most. She placed a hand on Morgan's arm again. "But he is also devoted and unselfish with those he cares about."

Obviously the woman wanted Morgan to like their lord. "I saw him rescue those children in the village," Morgan said. "I'm sure he's a good man, but—"

"You must understand 'tis not an easy life he's had," Matti interrupted.

He has a wonderful castle, Morgan thought, people respected him, and he was gorgeous…what could be the problem?

"Lord Vanguard was once a happy child," Matti continued determinedly. "His laughter used to fill these castle walls, at least until he realized he would never have what he yearned for most…his mother."

"What happened to her?"

"She left when he was but eight years of age, for reasons only God can judge."

"What about his father?"

"Simon Vanguard had never been a doting father, but once Lady Vanguard left, it was Lord Vanguard who received the blunt end of the stick. Simon did unspeakable things to the boy, even went so far as to lock him in an old trunk for more than a day after Lord Vanguard asked about his mother. Never did Simon look the lad in the eye when speaking to him, nor did he ever tell his son he loved him. Verily it gives me gooseflesh to think of it."

Tears welled in Matti's eyes as she shook her head. "By the time Simon passed away, Lord Vanguard had become hardened by life's cruelties. Some say our Lord is void of heart, but Hugo and I know otherwise."

Morgan had never thought of parents in this light before. The mother abandoning her child...she could relate with that aspect of Lord Vanguard's story. But to think Derek grew up with a true biological parent who physically and verbally abused him. No wonder he seemed so cold...so distant. It would have been better to have no parents at all.

Morgan could see that it pained Matti to remember such horrible times. She took Matti's hand in hers. "Thank you for telling me. It must be hard. Caring for someone that way and yet not always being able to help."

Matti nodded and after Lady Amanda excused herself, she watched her ladyship walk off. A tap on her shoulder caused Matti to look behind her.

"How did it go?" Hugo asked.

"She seemed genuinely concerned. I do believe we have our work cut out for us though." She watched Lady Amanda stop to chat with a small child before disappearing through the castle's main entrance.

"Emmon will be watching her," Hugo said.

Matti sighed. "Emmon still holds a grudge and might fail to watch her properly. Our plans to see Lord Vanguard and Lady Amanda married would be for naught."

Hugo rubbed a callused thumb over Matti's cheek. "I had a long talk with Emmon and thus give you my solemn vow that our youthful friend will see Lady Amanda home safely."

Matti turned to her husband and regarded him fondly. "No one in his right mind would fail to honor thy husband's request. Is that not so?"

Hugo's chest puffed. "'Tis so indeed and good to know that my wife has finally seen the moon in its full light."

"Good indeed," Matti said with a smile.

Morgan stepped outside and breathed in the light fragrance of dogwood violets and trilliums. She followed the beaten path, deciding to go to the village and look for the little boy she'd helped save. She would ask the villagers if they'd seen a woman resembling herself or maybe someone could tell her where she might find the Earl of Kensington.

She passed by endless stone walls, massive towers surrounded by lush greenery, and well-manicured gardens. The clanking of iron against rock could be heard in the distance, not to mention the squawks of chickens as they ran underfoot.

As she neared the outer gates, a guard leaned over the tower and shouted, "You there, state your name!"

"Lady Amanda," she called back.

"Lord Vanguard's betrothed?"

Before she could answer another guard shouted, "Who do we have there, Jacob?"

"'Tis the lady who ran off to be with her lover," the first guard answered.

Morgan rolled her eyes. "It's just a rumor. I never ran off and I don't have a lover."

The second guard stepped into the bright daylight, elbowing his partner in the gut. "Of course not, my lady. Many apologies for Jacob's insolence. Go on. You may pass."

As she walked off she could hear them arguing.

"Why did you let her go? I promised Hugo I would not let her through the gates unescorted," Jacob said.

"His lordship ordered that she be allowed to roam free at all times," the other man argued. "Let her go."

"She will not be safe."

"'Tis not our concern."

Lord Vanguard had told her straight out to stay put. Why then, Morgan wondered, had he told the guard to let her pass? When she was far enough away, she gazed back at Braddock. The castle wasn't crumbling and faded like castles she'd seen in the history books. Nor was the castle as colorful and illuminating as depicted in modern films. Braddock was bold and dynamic, bespeaking power, like its master.

As she continued her walk, her thoughts turned to her conversation with Matti. She thought of Derek as a boy, frightened and alone, wanting nothing more than to be held in his mother's arms. Maybe Lord Vanguard was just a lonely soul like herself. He sure wasn't as ferocious as everybody liked to think. His kisses were proof of that. Or maybe she was just making too much out of a few kisses.

Somberly she wondered what her mother was doing now. She missed their morning talks over coffee and even her mother's constant meddling. At the age of eighteen, she had moved to an apartment of her own, but her mother had been lonely and had begged her to move back home and save her money instead. As a dark shadow of a hawk swept across the path overhead, she glanced upward in time to see a man lunging from the higher branches of a tree.

She screamed, but the man clamped a hand over her mouth. She bit down as hard as she could.

"Bloody hell, woman!" He jerked his hand back and peered disbelieving at the teeth marks embedded in his palm. "'Tis me, Robert!"

Her eyes widened at the mention of his name. She took a good look at the young man, noting his scarlet cape and green tights. He must be Amanda's lover, the man Odelia had mentioned on more than one occasion.

"I'm sorry," she said gesturing toward his wounded hand, "but you scared me. I thought you were Robin Hood!"

"'Twould seem my enthusiasm at seeing you has caused me to act foolishly. I should have warned you first of my presence." His apologetic expression turned to a look of perplexity. "Pray tell, who is Robin Hood?"

"A legendary English man in tights who steals from the rich and gives to the poor."

"I have not heard of him."

"It's not important," she said, "but I think he dates back to the 1300s. Does the 'Sheriff of Nottingham' ring any bells?"

"Why is it that you can no longer speak properly?" he asked.

"Because I'm not who you think. I'm not Amanda."

He stepped closer and took her hand in his. "You are lovely even when you are babbling nonsensical rubbish. Being away from you this past year has only served to make my love for you grow stronger. I have missed you." Swiftly and without notice, he drew her snug against his chest and held her tight.

Who did the men in this century think they were? And why couldn't Amanda's lover see that she wasn't Amanda at all? More discouraged than ever, she pushed away from him. The hurt she saw in his eyes almost made her feel sorry for him.

"Amanda, what has happened? What has that depraved man done to you? I need to know."

"You must listen to me, Robert. I'm not who you think I am. I've heard about the love you and Amanda have for each other. That's why you need to find her. She's probably out there somewhere waiting for you."

He hardly flinched at the sincerity of her words. She was beginning to see the hopelessness of convincing him or anyone else of her cataclysmic experience. "My name is Morgan Hayes," she said wearily, "and I'm from another time…the year 2011."

"We both know you are an atrocious liar." A smile tugged at his lips and his hands fell to her shoulders. "You listen to me now. Your father's people are forgiving and their love for you is deep. If you leave with me, they will understand."

She shook her head. "I'm sorry."

"I know why you are doing this," he said. "'Twill only serve to destroy us both, can you not see that? I beseech you to come with me now before it is too late."

"I can't," Morgan said. "But for Amanda's sake and mine, you must find her. She'll have the answers you're looking for."

"You are a stubborn woman, my love. Surely you know I will not give up until you are out of that man's ruddy clutches."

"Whose ruddy clutches?"

"Vanguard's, of course, who else?" He studied her critically. "Could it be that you have not been held prisoner these past days as I feared?" This time when he stepped close he took her firmly about the waist.

She was beginning to feel like a rag doll the way he kept pulling her into his arms as if she had no say in his handling of her. His well-trimmed goatee scratched her cheek. Robin Hood was getting on her nerves.

"Do my eyes dare deceive me?" he went on. "Can it be that you plan to go through with this marriage? Tell me 'tis not so."

She had a headache and her eyelid began to twitch again. Here she was in another time, with yet another good-looking man who thought she was Amanda. "Never a dull moment," she said before digging her heel into his foot.

"Saint Dunstan's Tongs!" he said, wincing in pain and hopping on one foot. "'Tis him, is it not? I will kill him, I will."

Morgan plunked her hands on her hips. "I'm tired of all this talk. Why won't anyone listen to what I'm trying to say? Men. Overbearing control freaks, all of you. Medieval, modern...it doesn't seem to matter."

"You are coming with me," he demanded, ignoring her completely.

"This is the last time I'm going to tell you. I'm not Amanda. I am Morgan Hayes. Read my lips." She stepped closer with each word until he was forced to take a few steps back to avoid a gouged eye or worse. "Nobody's going to tell me what to do or when to do it. Not the men I meet back home, not the conceited, cocky gladiator at Braddock, and certainly not you,

Robin Hood." She gave him her best don't-hassle-me-buster look and then walked off.

"You are not yourself, that much is certain," he called after her. "But my love for you is stronger than all of England's love for their king. My life is nothing without you, Amanda, and I vow unto you this day that I will not give up until you are in my arms where you belong!"

# CHAPTER FIVE

"What do you mean you're not sure where Lady Amanda is?" Hugo asked.

Her ladyship's maid, Odelia, looked from Hugo to Lord Vanguard, her face haggard from worry. "'Twould seem Lady Amanda has taken a walk, my lord. Methinks she will return shortly."

Lord Vanguard sat askew within his chair, his elbow propped precariously upon the table in front of him, expressly confident and cocksure that neither Odelia nor Hugo could bring forth Lady Amanda. "It seems to me," he drawled, his speech the tiniest bit slurred, "that your lady of such lofty virtues has chosen to run away once more…"

"She's here, she's here!" an excited maid said as she entered the room, interrupting Lord Vanguard in her excitement.

Derek studied the messenger. "Who is here?"

"Lady Amanda, my lord. The guards at the outer gate swore 'twas her ladyship who entered just before sunset."

Derek glanced at Hugo in disbelief.

Hugo responded with his own self-satisfied look.

Odelia wiped her perspiring brow and quickly headed for the door, dragging the other maid out with her.

Derek stood and waited for the room to stop spinning, wishing he hadn't spent quite so much time at the Boars Head Inn. He needed proof that the wench had returned. Women never followed orders and for that reason alone he was sure he had seen the last of his betrothed.

"Mayhap it would be preferable," Hugo told him, "if you got some rest and visited your betrothed when you are…shall we say…more yourself?"

Derek strode past the burly man-at-arms without so much as a glance. Not even the strong drink had eased the turmoil Lady Amanda caused him. If indeed the wench had returned, she would surely regret that decision.

Morgan stepped into the round wooden tub filled with warm water, hoping to wash away the frustrations of the day. Maybe she really had hit her head in the forest. Or maybe she was indeed Amanda and her other life in the future was a crazy dream. Why else wouldn't any one else see that she was not Amanda Forrester?

Since the tub wasn't long enough for her to extend her legs fully, she sat with her legs crossed in front of her. She grabbed one of the scented soaps she'd found in Amanda's trunk and used it to bathe.

When she was done washing she let her legs dangle over the edge of the tub and lay her head back on a folded pelt. The room crackled with relaxing warmth. She closed her eyes, but not for long, because suddenly the door swung open. The iron hinges nearly unbuckled beneath the weight of the door. The thick planks hit the stone wall with an ear-piercing bang.

Lord Vanguard stood beneath the heavy-timbered frame, his breathing ragged, and his eyes blazing.

Morgan grabbed the fur pelt and held it in front of her. "Are you insane?"

He appeared to have little regard for her question as he stalked toward her. His intense scrutiny heated her skin as his gaze roamed carelessly, freely, as though the flames of the fire itself coursed over her. He towered over her, his expression hard and unreadable. Then she got a whiff of what smelled like a brewery. "You're drunk!"

He lowered himself on bended knee, placing one of his large hands on her shoulder to keep his balance. He swayed a little to the left, then to the right. She followed his gaze to where his fingers touched her skin.

She gently removed his hand, but he raised that same hand and used it to graze his knuckles over her cheek. For a man of his size, his touch was gentle. He leaned close to her ear as if to tell her a secret, and she leaned forward to listen, absurdly intoxicated by his nearness. The richness of his voice when he spoke was as warm and soothing as the fire that burned within the hearth.

"You came back," he stated more than asked, sending shivers up her spine.

His lips trailed over her ear. She closed her eyes and let her head fall back slightly. The feathered touch of his fingertips upon her arm sent waves of pulsating vibrations through her body. She stifled a groan.


Although her body told him everything he needed to know, Derek had an overwhelming desire to see if her eyes exhibited the same invitation. He pulled back, just enough so that he could see her face. With the ball of his thumb he gently lifted her chin. Who was this woman who dared to bewitch him; this woman who succeeded in intruding upon his every thought since he first laid eyes on her?

He brushed his lips across her cheek, her lips, then moved back to nibble on her ear where he whispered, "What kind of magical hex has befallen me?"

Although she had no answer for him, her face flushed.

The woman drenched his senses with jasmine scented skin and tantalized him with her rosebud lips. He could not torment himself any longer. He kissed her, thoroughly this time.

The useless pelt fell to the ground as he lifted her from the tub. He carried her across the room, pressing her down into the furs that lay before the hearth.

His preferences had always been for the more experienced women, exactly what he assumed her to be, a seasoned wench who could appreciate one of life's pleasures. Although her startled gestures were those of an innocent, he was sure it was a practiced trait of hers that made her even more desirable.

Pulling her lips from his, she said, "We can't do this..." His mouth traveled down her neck. "Too many...unanswered quest—oh, that feels good. Don't stop."

His lips returned to seize the flow of words, words she'd instantly regretted anyhow. Not only were bells ringing, a whole cacophony of trumpets and chimes exploded inside of her. Nothing in her life had ever felt more right than this. Of all the wonderful sights she'd seen in this century so far, things that would turn to faded memories when she returned to the future, she wanted only the memory of Derek Vanguard to linger forever.

His hand curved around her breast, making her quiver as his inspiring mouth easily coerced her lips into parting for him. His tongue scorched her own, teasing, exploring the taste of her. The kiss was demanding and erotic. She reached both of her arms about the thick broadness of his neck and shoulders. When he lifted his head slightly she opened her eyes and saw him staring down at her. She hardly knew the man but she wanted him. Nothing made sense any longer. This place. This man. Regardless, she smiled at him and his reaction was instantaneous. His muscles constricted beneath her fingertips. His scorching look of desire dissolved, leaving in its wake a haunted expression, dark with pain, lined with anger as he loosened her arms from about his neck.

Confused, she kept her eyes locked on his as he raised himself from the floor. "What are you doing?" she asked.

"I refuse to be taken in so easily when we both know 'tis another who floats about in that head of yours."

"What are you talking about?"

An all-knowing smirk covered his lips as he tied the laces on his shirt.

She sat up, covering herself as best she could with her arms. "Oh, I see. The old lover thing. I have no lover."

"Ha!" he spouted.

Disappointed, she watched the surly bull leave without further explanation. He exited the room as quickly as he'd entered, leaving her naked and wet by the fire, feeling like an idiot for being so easily seduced. Rising from the furs, she shivered as she made her way to the bed. Numbly, she slipped one of Amanda's short-sleeved tunics over her head and then crawled under the heaps of woolen blankets and fur pelts. Although the fire still burned, she felt cold as she gingerly touched her fingertips to her lips. She tried to tell herself that she was glad he'd left. It was, after all, the best thing for them both.

Through a small window across the room, stars glittered against a jet-black sky. Her skin burned where Lord Vanguard's unshaven jaw had rasped against her flesh. Overwhelmingly tired, she closed her eyes as she thought of her other life, especially her mother and how much she missed her.

The next morning, Morgan negotiated her way through the great hall where a half dozen maids were in the process of removing dirty hay and grass from the floor. Small children followed behind gleefully tossing fresh straw from a wooden cart as they went along.

After running into Robert yesterday she'd gone to the village. She hadn't been able to find the boy whom she'd performed CPR on, and nobody she'd talked to had ever heard of the Earl of Kensington. Today, she decided, she'd explore the castle, get to know the people. Maybe they could shed some light on her predicament. And, no matter what, she wouldn't give Lord Vanguard and his searing kisses another thought.

Entering the smoke-filled kitchens, she waved to the cook as she passed by. The woman smiled and handed her a warm piece of bread before Morgan exited through the back door that led to the gardens. She ambled up a stone path, enjoying the sweet taste of the bread as she took in the fresh scent of flowers lining the way. She'd never seen such beautiful gardens in her life. Then she spotted Emmon, the man-boy who thought she'd stolen his horse. She was surprised to see him tending to the roses since he didn't seem like the gardener type. "Hi," she said, plunking down on the soft grass behind him. "Mind if I watch you work for a while?"

He turned her way and gave her a frustrated scowl. "Do you have naught better to do?"

"Nope. Not really."

"Surely a noble lady such as yourself would have many interesting hobbies to busy herself with. I, for one," he said, putting a gloved hand to his chest, "have no wish to be the one to begrudge her ladyship of such important doings."

The hostility in his tone was obvious. "I hate to disappoint you," she told him, "but I have nothing I'd rather do right now than watch you tend the roses." She leaned forward, drawing in the sweet aroma of a newly blossomed rose before drawing back and finishing her bread.

Angrily he turned back to his bushes and began snipping away yellow spotted leaves with a vengeance.

His irritability bordered on comical. Done with the bread, she scooted forward and began to remove dead leaves from beneath the bushes. Out of the corner of her eye she caught a glimpse of the beginnings of a fuzzy goatee framing Emmon's chin. He was tall and lanky and with his light hair streaked from the sun he looked like a California surfer boy. "Did you grow up here at Braddock?" she asked.

"Why would you care to know?"

"I just thought since we keep running into each other it would be nice to get to know you."

"Why is it you act as though you have done nothing wrong?" he asked. "As if drugging my water and stealing my horse is naught for me to get upset about. As though we were friends, no less." He stuck his chin out defiantly. "'Twould seem to me you think all men to be fools. Lord Vanguard warned me of women such as the likes of you. And be you a lady or not, I should have listened to him from the start. My horse has never been the same since you stole it from me and rode off in the forest to find your lover, leaving me, Emmon McBray, to look the fool." He stood tall, planted both hands firmly on his hips, and glared down at her.

She stood, too, and brushed dirt from her gown. "As I've said before, I don't have a lover. And I didn't steal your horse. The truth is I wouldn't jump on a horse's back if you paid me." She started to walk off, but then turned back and said, "If I were you, I would not listen to what Lord Vanguard has to say about women. He doesn't know as much as he thinks he does. And by the way," she added, gesturing toward the flowers, "your roses are beautiful."

Morgan walked off, more determined than ever not to let Emmon or Derek Vanguard ruin her mood. Odelia promised to teach her to embroider today. She would find the woman…a friendly face amidst so many strangers. The thought that she had a friend at all lifted her spirits as she walked on.

Rounding the stone path, she saw a dozen children tugging at the skirts of one exhausted looking woman. "Would you like some help?" Morgan asked.

"'Twould be a blessing from God," the maid quickly answered, "but I fear his lordship would be upset with me were I to shed my duties upon his betrothed."

Morgan smiled. "We'll just keep this between me and you."

The woman grinned, her mottled complexion glowing as she made her way to a bench and took a seat. Excited to have someone new to play with, the children instantly battled for Morgan's attention. She laughed as they grabbed her skirts and ran in circles around her.

An hour later, Morgan was still laughing when a mound of dirt hit her square in the chest. She asked the boy nearest her to loan her his slingshot which he gladly handed over. She loaded her borrowed slingshot and fired back.

The other boy ran, dodging for cover behind a thick hedge. After a moment, his little head popped up and with a conspiratorial grin on his face he called truce and at the same time gestured for her to come his way. Then he pointed toward Emmon, and she smiled too. She and the boy crawled on all fours, sneaking up behind their unwitting enemy.

Without making a sound, they attacked, bombarding Emmon's back and side with soft clumps of dirt. Emmon did his best to ignore them, but finally gave in when the smaller boy's ammunition hit him square in the back of his big head.

Emmon quickly retaliated by throwing wilted rose petals and debris their way. It wasn't long before Emmon was showering them with mud balls and had both Morgan and the boy begging for leniency.


Derek watched Lady Amanda through the high window. He was not sure exactly how long he had been watching her entertain the children, but judging by the stiffness of his neck 'twas longer than he'd intended. He chuckled as she determinedly chased a small girl, tickling the child until the poor girl cried with high-pitched laughter.

His eyes widened as Amanda leaned over onto the grass and stood on her head. Her skirts dropped, revealing tight breeches underneath. He looked over his shoulder to see if anyone else was watching. The picture brought to mind all of her ludicrous antics: her ridiculous use of words, how she rambled on when she was nervous, the scrunching of her nose when she was frustrated. Her smile, her soft skin and the way her silky flesh felt beneath his fingertips. Every part of him ached to hold her close and kiss her with the same urgency he felt every time he looked her way. He cursed himself for stopping what he had begun last night. He'd grown used to women whose every movement was rehearsed, in the bedroom as well as out of it. And yet Amanda was different. Every time he expected her to do one thing, she did the opposite. 'Twas imagining her pining for her lover, though, that had caused him to leave so abruptly last night, for he was certain 'twas another man's image filling her every thought. Only days ago she had risked her very life to run off to be with another man, humiliating him before his people. And now suddenly she waltzed about his castle as if she belonged here. She made no sense. Why was she still here? He'd instructed the guards to allow her through the gates and yet she'd returned to his castle on her own free will. *What was the woman up to?*

He was losing control of his emotions, which he vowed had to stop. *How many times must I tell you, boy, that women cannot be trusted. Deceit is behind everything they do...everything!* His father's words resounded in his mind, making his head ache all the more.

Derek gazed upon his betrothed once more. She presented herself as an innocent, and she played the role well. No wonder Hugo and Emmon had been so easily deceived. How could he expect them to do what he could not? She was a woman for God's sake and she had a plan...a plan that would reveal itself soon enough. He was certain of it.

"There you are," a baritone voice came from behind.

Derek jerked about. "God's teeth, man! What are you doing sneaking up on me?"

Hugo chuckled. "I humbly apologize, my lord, but as you might recall, 'tis the only passage leading abovestairs. I am but on my way to bring a bit of cheer to my ailing wife. Of course, that is, if it befits you to let me pass."

Derek's annoyance turned to concern for Matti. "What is it that ails that troublesome wife of yours?"

"She has but a stuffy nose and scratchy throat. Naught that a little Flemish broth cannot cure," he said, nodding toward the steaming cup he carried. "I also thought to cheer her with a bit of spring." He reached for and held up a pewter vase filled with flowers, then stepped forward to peer out over Derek's shoulder. "Hmm, I see 'tis not just the beauty of the day that has you entranced."

A look of disdain crossed Derek's face. "How long before you return to the training of your men?"

Hugo smiled knowingly. "Do I sense an eagerness to be rid of me, my lord?" He placed the flowers to his heart in mock pain. "Aye, but you have chafed me to the quick." Hugo laughed, and then gestured with his chin to Lady Amanda. "'Twould seem King Henry has done well with his choosing of a bride for you, my lord. And I surmise, by the way you ogle her like a besotted schoolboy that you agree. Verily if I did not know you better I would deduct your constant meditations of late to have some sort of veiled meaning...mayhap hinting at feelings of love."

Derek looked Hugo square in the eye. "You have been in the sun overly much, my good man. I am afraid I have been too busy for the likes of such time-consuming sentiments that you speak of. If you must know, 'tis not my heart that yearns for the wench but something else altogether." He forced a grin and slapped Hugo hard on the back, causing the broth to slosh about.

Derek shook his head as he took the last of the steps in a few strides and then strolled down the hall toward his bedchamber. "Love!" he said loud enough for Hugo to hear. "A good-for-nothing endearment if ever there was one."

# CHAPTER SIX

Morgan entered the keep just as the trumpeter blew his horn, announcing the midday meal. Meals at Braddock were usually light, consisting of bread, fruit and wine. If Lord Vanguard's men were home, the meal became an elaborate display of food: stew, salt-cured ham, fatty bacon, fish, an assortment of broth's, egg tarts, fruits, and pastries.

This afternoon was of the latter variety. Today the knights, archers, and squires had yet to begin their training and so the castle was brimming with people as she moved through the castle, making her way to her bedroom so she could quickly change her clothes.

When she reappeared fifteen minutes later, it seemed that even the number of servants had doubled. Before today she'd mostly eaten in her room or in the kitchen with the cooks, but today she decided to sit with everybody else. The people at Braddock seemed to be getting used to her being around, since they didn't stare and point every time she walked into a room.

Odelia spotted her at once and gestured for her to take a seat on the upper dais where a long narrow table had been covered with clean linen.

As Odelia headed toward the kitchen, Morgan glanced around the room glad to know Lord Vanguard wouldn't be joining them for lunch. Odelia had told her that he took most of his meals in his study, which was one of the reasons why there were rumors that he was disfigured. When visitors came to Braddock he seldom made an appearance and his guests went away assuming the worst.

Morgan's eyes widened as a large strapping knight smiled broadly at her before taking a seat beside her. The room quickly filled with a stream of loud knights and squires. Within minutes at least three brawny knights surrounded her. The man to her right had a long mane of reddish-brown hair. His eyes were like those of a lion, his gaze intense as she made eye contact and said good morning. The warrior seated directly in front of her wore a leather tunic that was a size too small, so snug against his swell of hard muscles that she wondered why he bothered with a shirt at all. Like the lion man, his hair, too, hung loosely, so that the ends brushed over the top of his massive shoulders. Next to him, sat a Fabio look alike. She couldn't dismiss the resemblance, and she had to resist the urge to stare.

As mountains of food were served, she tried not to feel insulted when the food instantly took priority over any small-talk she offered these men. She quietly filled her plate, opting for a piece of salt-cured ham and a chunk of dark rye bread.

Hugo entered the room next, and she happily scooted over to make room for him.

"My lady," he said enthusiastically as he took the offered seat. "You are a vision to behold. Verily your beauty inveigles me to close my eyes and sing praise."

Embarrassed, Morgan thanked him; glad she'd had time to change after playing with the kids. She wore a cream-colored gown. The sleeves were decorated with elaborate gold-threaded embroidery and the fabric felt silky against her skin. She felt unusually feminine sitting before this grizzly bear of a man, not to mention, the assemblage of Chippendales surrounding her. "Will Matti be joining us?" Morgan asked Hugo.

"I am afraid she is not feeling well today. But I am certain a visit from you would do her health well."

"I'm sure she would rather rest in peace without any visitors."

Hugo adamantly disagreed, making her promise to visit his wife as soon as she was done eating.

After one bite of her ham, the room grew quiet.

Morgan glanced up and immediately saw the reason. Derek was making an unprecedented appearance. He stalked into the room wearing tight leather breeches and a loose-sleeved shirt. Thank God he couldn't hear the rapid beat of her traitorous heart.

The two hunks seated across from her moved over to make room for him, even after she subtly gestured for them to stay put.

"I see you are being well tended to," Derek said crisply, still standing.

She managed a tight smile. "Unlike some people I know, your men are very attentive and well-mannered. Not one of them has left the table without excusing himself first. Isn't that right, boys?"

A few men mumbled under their breath, but most kept right on eating like a gang of ravenous wolves.

Derek arched a brow. "Ahh, perhaps I should reward them."

"Oh, no. Let me do the honors. I'm sure I can cook up something pleasurable for them."

His jaw hardened. "I am certain you could indeed."

His statement was crammed with innuendo, but before she could tell him she meant that she would bake his men some cookies, Hugo cut in.

"You have not eaten all day," Hugo said to Derek, "have a seat."

"He's probably much too busy," Morgan said.

With a wry smile, Derek took a seat. "I always make time for a meal." He grabbed a roasted chicken leg from the plate set before him and sank his teeth into the tender meat. Swallowing, he then turned his attention back to Hugo.

"'Twould seem I owe you thanks for solving the error in my calculations the other day. If I had known you had a way with numbers I would have sought your help long ago." He shook his head. "For days I worked on those figures. How did you do it?"

Hugo stared blankly at Derek, obviously clueless as to what calculations he was talking about.

"Did you hire someone then?" Derek asked.

"It was me," Morgan informed him.

He nearly choked on his meat. "You are serious?"

"Completely. In fact, I've been wondering when you were going to thank me for fixing such a careless mathematical error."

"I am certain she did not mean careless," Hugo added.

She shrugged.

Derek lifted a skeptical brow. "You expect me to believe you are skilled in the practice of numbers?"

"I'll prove it."

"Indeed. And how will you do that?"

"I'll do your bookkeeping for you." Not only would it give her something to do, she thought, she'd feel as if she were earning her keep while she was here. "I'll start first thing tomorrow morning. And if you don't like the job I do, you can fire me."

"Fire you?"

"You know, send me packing…lay me off." She rolled her eyes at all the blank stares, and then extended her hand toward Derek. "Do we have a deal?"

"'Twill give you more time for hawking," Hugo urged.

Fixing her with a level stare, Derek wiped his hand on a linen cloth, then clasped his fingers firmly about her hand. Goose bumps spread up her arms and heat flowed through her veins.

"One misplaced number," he said gruffly, "one missing shilling and you will surely regret offering your services."

"You can count on me," she said confidently without looking away, her hand still firmly clasped within his.

"Is that so?"

"Absolutely," she said, giving his hand an extra squeeze.

He shook his head as if she'd lost all sense, then he rose from the bench and spouted quick instructions to his men. She thought he was going to say something to her directly when he turned his gaze back on her. Instead, he regarded her curiously and then left without another word.

After visiting Matti and entertaining her with a story about Snow White and the seven dwarfs, Morgan made her way to the sewing room where she found Odelia and two young women, both of whom she guessed were about eighteen.

"Sit here," Odelia said, patting the stool next to her. Then she handed Morgan a linen shirt, a needle, and a spool of wiry thread. The two younger women watched quietly as Odelia told Morgan what to do. Before long they were all chatting and sewing as if they'd met a dozen times before.

To her left, she soon learned, was a young girl named Shayna. Her hair, the color of milk chocolate, fell past her shoulders, and her eyes were a dark forest green. The other woman, Ciara, seemed a bit shy. Her eyes darted about and her hands trembled. Although her teeth were crooked and yellowed from lack of care, she, too, was pretty with curly auburn hair and brown eyes.

"Is it true that Robert DeChaville is wandering nearby villages in search of you?" Shayna asked Morgan. "A more thrilling prospect I cannot imagine; having two men, such as the likes of Lord Vanguard and Robert DeChaville lusting after you."

Morgan looked to Odelia for help. Odelia merely shrugged, her needles clicking away.

"Hogs Turd, I'm sure," Morgan said, quoting one of the kids she'd been playing with, hoping to sound medievalish.

Shayna grinned.

"You know how rumors spread when people have nothing better to do," Morgan added.

"What are you going to wear to the king's banquet?" Shayna asked next, easily flitting from one subject to another.

Morgan chuckled. "I don't think I'll be going to any banquet."

"Aye, you'll be attending," Odelia stated firmly. "'Tis for you after all, in honor of Lord Vanguard and his betrothed, which means you."

Shayna laughed. "I am certain her ladyship does not need reminding of who she is."

Odelia gave Morgan a piercing glare. "You can never be too sure."

Morgan ignored them all as she tried to concentrate on what she was doing. Patiently, she made her stitches the way Odelia had shown her, pleased that an actual design was taking shape on the fabric.

Shayna released a long sigh and said, "You wouldn't want to miss the banquet, my lady. 'Twill be an affair to remember. If you would like, I could design a gown for you."

Morgan shook her head. "Thank you, Shayna, but it won't be necessary." She had no idea when she might suddenly disappear and find herself back in her own time.

"Oh, but it will," Shayna told her. "It is to be held at Windsor Castle and you will be introduced to King Henry himself. There will be feasts every day and tournaments. Dozens of handsome knights will joust for their ladies' pleasure. Is that not romantic?" Shayna leaned closer. "Sometimes a lord will attain special knighthood through the king himself and that knight is honored with a gift of a fine horse, jewels, or land. Oh, and the entertainment," Shayna went on excitedly, "is sure to be spectacular. You must tell us all about it when you return."

"You do make it sound wonderful," Morgan said. Hoping to change the subject since she didn't plan to be around long enough to visit the king, she said, "Have any of you ever heard of a knight known as the Earl of Kensington?"

Ciara shook her head. "The name does not sound familiar."

"If there is an Earl of Kensington, Lord Vanguard would know of him, my lady. 'Twould be a good idea to ask him," Shayna said. "Is he someone you know personally? Is he as handsome as the other men flocking to see you? Is he married?"

Morgan laughed. Shayna was definitely a romantic. "I don't know much about him except that he's well favored by King Henry." She lowered her voice and added, "Truthfully, I need to find him so I can warn him."

Shayna sat up straighter. "Is the Earl in danger?"

Odelia rolled her eyes in disbelief.

"Yes. It's been said that once the Earl of Kensington sets out to find his one true love who has been lost to him, he will be killed in an ambush near Swan Lake."

"Ludicrous," Odelia muttered. "Whoever spouted such rubbish?"

"I don't remember the author's name," Morgan said, "but it's true."

Odelia frowned.

"You are eager to marry Lord Vanguard, are you not?" Shayna asked.

Morgan thought about it before she spoke. "Not all women want to get married."

Shayna scoffed at the notion. "Lord Vanguard is many a young maiden's dream."

"I guess there's no denying he's easy on the eyes," Morgan agreed as she thought of his strong jaw, beautiful eyes and solid physique. "Before I met him though I had been told he resembled a hideous monster and that he was capable of killing a man with a merely a glance."

The room grew deathly silent. Odelia's face had paled to a ghostly white sheen. Apparently the women weren't used to talking so bluntly about Lord Vanguard.

"Well," Ciara added nervously. "He might indeed cause a few people to fall dead if he ever wears that," she said, pointing at the linen shirt in Morgan's hands.

Morgan held the shirt up for closer examination.

Shayna and Ciara tried to hold back their laughter, but as soon as Morgan glanced Odelia's way they all burst out in a wave of hysterics.

When Shayna finally attempted to speak, an unladylike hiccup escaped, causing new peals of laughter. Morgan laughed hard enough to cause her stool to fall over, sending her rolling to the floor with her arms wrapped tightly to her sides.

No one was too sure how long he'd been standing there, but when they did finally notice him. Instantaneously, the room quieted.

Standing beneath the doorframe, Lord Vanguard appeared suddenly to be a foot taller than the last time she'd seen him. So tall, she observed, that he had to bend so he wouldn't hit his head on the wooden beam as he entered the room.

Still on the floor, and getting a worm's eye view of him, Morgan tried to appear nonchalant as she sat up. "Did you want something?"

"You," he said.

Morgan blushed. Her new friends weren't any help at all. They all stitched furiously. Not one of them would look her way.

When Morgan glanced back at Lord Vanguard, he winked, making little effort to hide his strange mood. Maybe, she thought, the overconfident man wanted to make up for leaving her so suddenly last night. Forget it.

As Morgan pushed herself from the floor, she was about to tell him she was having too much fun to stop what she was doing when suddenly he stepped forward, swooped her easily into his arms, and carried her from the room before she could say anything at all.

"Put me down," she said from atop his right shoulder, "you had your chance and you blew it!" She tried to wriggle free, but her attempt to get away was useless.

Derek strode swiftly down the long spiraling staircase. All eyes were on them as they crossed the landing and swept through the great hall. Morgan caught a glimpse of Emmon and Hugo as they passed by. "Do something," she pleaded.

They just stood there...looking extremely pleased instead of horrified by their boss's bad manners. Derek probably carried a different maid over his shoulder every week. The people here at Braddock were most likely accustomed to his barbaric ways.

Morgan clung to the back of his shirt. As they passed through the inner bailey, she heard giggling from a small boy she'd taught to play leapfrog the other day. "See if I teach you any more games," she told the boy, pointing a finger at him.

The boy's big eyes widened in horror before he ran off.

Derek's solid strides didn't slow.

Morgan pounded a fist against his back. "I'm never going to forgive you for this, Vanguard, unless you put me down this minute!"

She kicked her feet and flailed her arms, but it was useless fighting him. The man, without benefit of any armor, was made of steel.

"If you put me down," she said calmly, hoping a different approach might work, "I promise not to run. We'll talk...about everything. I'll listen to every word you have to say without interrupting."

Derek stopped and leaned his head low enough so that he could see her face between the crook of his arm. "When I put you down wench, it won't be to talk." A wry grin spread across his lips.

"What does that mean exactly? That you intend to tease me and tempt me and then run away again?"

A small tic pulsated within his jaw. But instead of spouting his ire, he surprised her by throwing back his head and giving vent to a torrent of laughter before continuing on.

She frowned at his laughing at her, especially in front of the stable boy. Stable boy? What the hell were they doing in the stables?

Derek moved quickly past the horses before he plopped her atop a tall pile of straw, plucked bridle and reins from the wall mount, and then went to his horse, a huge white stallion that snorted and stamped its giant hooves within its stall.

She tried to stand, but her legs sank into the soft hay like quicksand. She crossed her arms over her chest. "If you think I'm riding that beast you're crazy. Besides, I'm allergic to horses," she lied. "I get a terrible rash." She held up her left forearm, revealing a couple of flea bites.


Derek scowled. He had little care for the woman's nonsensical sniveling. If she could manage to take Emmon's horse and run off, then she could handle any steed he had to offer.

After his horse was readied, he mounted the stallion and rode to where she awkwardly stood within the pile of hay, refusing to move an inch.

"Have it your way." He leaned low and with one arm he lifted her, plunking her onto the animal so that she was snug on his lap.

Before she could protest further, he turned the stallion full around in the cramped quarters, leaving the stables far behind as the horse's hooves thundered beneath them.

Derek held his betrothed tightly within his arms. Waves of impatience swept over him at the thought of all the raw emotions the wench had so quickly managed to unleash inside of him. After leaving her at the table earlier, he had found himself in the garden, a place he rarely, if ever, visited. And for what? To find her and listen to more of her ridiculous fabrications? Furious at himself for considering dawdling with a the woman, he had gone to his bedchamber to retrieve his sword. And it was then and there that he had heard enough merriment to fill two castles. Finding his betrothed on the sewing room floor, her eyes sparkling, he had instantly realized what he must do. He would have his fill of her, finish what he began last night, and quickly, before another day was wasted. For he was certain that only after he had taken her would he once again be clear headed and able to finish his growing list of tasks.

His stallion whinnied and relief flooded through his veins as they neared Swan Lake. He knew fair well that he could not take much more of this tortuous ride. With Amanda's buttocks resting full against him he was already as hard as stone.

Bringing his stallion to a halt, he lifted her off of his lap and placed her gently on the ground. Her face had lost all color as if she truly had been afraid for her life.

As he took the stallion toward a group of trees to provide shelter against the sun, he recalled what Emmon had said about Lady Amanda being an experienced rider. If that were true, then what was she afraid of? Surely she was not trying to put on an act for his benefit, pretending to be the fair and chaste maiden. What kind of fool did she take him for? Besides, had she not dared him to finish what he started?

He shook his head as he secured the reins. He wanted her, and thus he would have her. It was as easy as that. Nothing here to stop him now, not even his own foolish thoughts. He needed to get some work done. Until he had her beneath him, once and for all, 'twas useless trying to accomplish anything else. The woman was like a leech on the brain, sucking all reasonable, intelligent thoughts until there was naught but mush. He would not allow this incessant mind-wandering to continue. She was his betrothed, by God, and bedding her would be his right soon enough.

Morgan steadied herself by an oak as she watched him jump from his horse and tie the reins around a branch. Without hesitation, nor modesty, he began to throw off his clothes, one piece at a time, until he was completely naked.

Her eyes nearly popped from their sockets. She quickly directed her gaze toward the ground and tried to catch her breath. When she resumed a fairly reasonable breathing pattern, she felt compelled to take a peek...or two. She hadn't seen him naked in the light of day. Heck, she hadn't seen him naked in the dark either, but she was confident no man would come close to what she was seeing now.

The sunlight struck his profile just so, giving her a striking view of his handsome face. He had a full but firm mouth and a cleft in his chin. His neck was thick, straight and powerful, which by scanning lower she could see was synonymous to the rest of him. Her cheeks grew hot, her palms moist.

He headed for the lake. Standing near the water's edge, he looked like a proud warlord, sun-bronzed and weather-toughened. Even the scars of battle etched across his backside added to his picturesque stance. Dizziness swept over her. Only after he dove into the icy water was she able to regain her composure.

A knot constricted her throat as she tried to decide what to do. She wanted him; that much she knew. Losing her virginity wasn't the problem...she'd been hoping and yearning that the right man would come along for years now. But losing her heart was another matter altogether. She tried to envision making love to him today and then she tried to picture herself back home, in the future, without him.

A cold fist clamped over her heart. She couldn't make love to him. Any intimacy between them would only hurt them both when it came time for her to leave. And she felt unreasonably certain that the time would come sooner rather than later.

She stood, paralyzed, fighting with her emotions, when Derek emerged from the lake. Hadn't she heard somewhere that men took cold showers to cool their sexual appetites?

Well, she'd have to tell all the world when she returned that cold water didn't always work. She had indisputable proof coming right at her. She couldn't move. She had turned into bark and was now a fundamental part of the tree behind her.

Derek didn't just walk toward her; he hypnotized her, his gaze hot and mercurial as he came toward her. He appeared feral as if he were hunting her down without benefit of any weapons. Except perhaps one very large dangerous, yet, unique looking weapon. Her cheeks flared with heat. What was it about this man that made her lose all sense?

Without another single thought, she put her body in motion and ran. She ran as fast as she could, toward the only thing that could get her away fast enough and far enough. She ran toward the horse.


Derek watched with amusement as his betrothed tried hopelessly to mount his steed. His stallion swished its tail and let out a few whinnied snorts as though she were naught but an irritating fly.

Openly frustrated she attempted her fourth jump onto the horse's back. She grasped at its mane and wiggled her legs until she was almost three-quarters of the way up, straining, until finally she reached the top of the animal.

Derek headed that way and reached out a hand to stop her, but it was too late. She dug her heals into the horse's flanks, unaware that this particular stallion needed no goading. The horse reared up and took off in a blinding flash with Lady Amanda clinging dearly to its neck.

Hastily, he grabbed his breeches and yanked them on. In the distance he could see that the reins were about the horse's neck, but the straps were not within her hands. She clearly had no idea what she was doing. Apparently she wished to live, though, since she leaned low against the horse's neck to prevent being clunked in the head by a tree branch.

Every muscle he possessed grew taut. Bloody hell. 'Twas his favorite steed and he had no wish to see the animal hurt. The horse raced into the denser area of the forest, weaving through trees and jumping over small bushes. Derek heard naught but the cracking of branches as he made his way into the forest.

The wench was daft. Clearly Emmon had been wrong about Lady Amanda being an experienced rider. The woman had no clue as to what she was doing.

Derek whistled, and then again as he jumped over a low shrub following the path of broken tree limbs. One signal from his lips was all it usually took to get his steed to return to his side. He used the whistle as a signal for hunting when he needed to leave the animal behind and sneak up on his prey. After which he would signal for the horse's return. But no one had ever been foolish enough to take his horse before. The animal needed only a small jerk of the reins or a click of the tongue. *God's teeth! Not a kick in the ribs.*

He whistled once more, emitting a loud shrill. He kept running, too, grunting with relief when he finally heard the familiar neigh of his horse. His heart stopped when he saw his stallion heading toward him without a rider on its back.

Seconds later he observed the wench hobbling through the last of the thick underbrush. Twigs dangled from her hair and dirt smudged her face. Before reaching him, she crumbled to the ground in one small heap.


Morgan opened her eyes. She was numb. So numb she wasn't even sure if she was alive. Not until she looked up into stormy black eyes as Derek hovered over her. Obviously Mr. Vanguard was not impressed with her riding skills. The tic in his jaw was deeper than ever. But at least he had put on his pants. Now when she looked away from his piercing stare, she had only his naked chest with black curly hair trailing eagerly downward to gaze at. "You're angry, aren't you?"

"Damn it, wench," he ground out, "you could have been killed."

She pushed herself to her feet. "I'm sorry," she offered, rubbing a sore arm, "but you have to admit this was all your fault."

He shook his head, then walked back toward his horse. He pulled the reins from around the animal's neck and led the animal back through the trees to where the remainder of his clothes lay.

She heard him mutter something about an addle-pated monkey. Frowning, she hobbled in pursuit of him, afraid he would leave her in the forest to fend for herself. "I didn't know what to do," she said. "I thought that after the way you treated me last night, you would at least apologize. One minute I'm convinced you care for me in an odd, medieval sort of way, and in the next minute you act as though I don't exist."

A splay of muscles flexed as he donned his tunic, rendering her temporarily speechless. She rolled her eyes at how easily he could distract her. "Don't you have anything to say at all?"

He focused his attention on adjusting the leather sash around his waist.

"Fine then, don't talk to me." She crossed her arms across her chest. "You know what really bothers me, though?"

He finished with the ties on his shirt and looked into her eyes. "Would it stop your prattle were I to tell you I do not care to know?"

"What really gets my goat," she went on, ignoring his remark, "is that you drag me here, expecting me to..." Her stomach fluttered. "You know...act as if I'm going to be thrilled at the prospect of..."

The corner of his mouth turned upward.

At a sudden loss for words, she wondered why she'd started this conversation in the first place.

"Continue, please," he said. "You suddenly have me vastly curious as to what you believe I expected of you."

"Okay," she said, "I'll tell you. You brought me here fully expecting that we would make love to one another."

"Ha!" he said, startling her. "You are wrong."

Her insides tumbled. "I am?"

"Aye. Two people can only make love, you see, if they are in love. I do not love you. Do you love me?"

"Of course not, but—"

He raised a hand. "Let us clear the air, so to speak. You wanted me and I wanted you. No use denying the truth," he added huskily. "'Twas made plain in every ragged breath you took last night and in every candidly scorching gaze you have sent my way since our first meeting."

Her mouth fell open.

He stepped close, smoothing the palm of his hand up the column of her neck. "We both know I brought you here in hopes that you would be a willing participant in some meaningless, yet highly intensive sex." He dropped his hand. "Clear enough?"

She let out a helpless sigh as she realized she was a glutton for punishment. The way he touched her, not to mention listening to him speak so candidly made shivers coarse over every part of her. "Patently clear," she said softly. "But this entire conversation has nothing to do with the point I was first trying to make."

"Pray tell, please make your point, madam, before the sun goes off and leaves us for good."

"That's exactly what I mean," she said. "You make fun of me every chance you get. And when you're not doing that, you're bombarding me with charming advances and hasty exits until my head is left spinning like the vanes of a windmill. Where I come from, the man brings the woman flowers, maybe a note, perhaps a kind word. Anything to make the woman at least feel like kissing…or what you might refer to as two interacting bodies going at it."

"Hmmm," he said, scratching his chin. "I fair say your description is unappealing at best." A smile tugged at his mouth. "But please answer me this: Why is it that the other night you seemed more than willing?" He rubbed again at his stubbled jaw. "I do not recall bringing flowers, nor sending any note before then."

"Oh, forget it," she said exasperated. "I don't know why I bother talking to you at all. Besides, if you ever brought me flowers I would fall over dead from shock."

Derek gave a nonchalant shrug of his shoulders and started off. After a moment he glanced back her way, saw that she'd hardly moved, and then hastily returned to her side. "You can hardly walk. Let me see to your injuries."

"Don't bother," she said.

"You are hurt."

"I'm fine."

"I am going to take a look with or without your permission. The choice is yours."

"Fine." She lifted her torn dress and watched him wince at the sight of red and blue marks against her pale skin.

With a click of his tongue, Derek called his horse to his side once again. He shuffled through the leather pouch attached to the girth and came up with a tin box filled with a greasy concoction. Plunking down on one knee, he began to apply the ointment to her thigh.

She sucked in a breath, feeling no pain, only the gentle touch of his fingers. When he finished, she wasn't sure whether she felt relief or disappointment.

"That was a foolish thing you did," he said.

"I know."

He seemed taken aback by her quick agreement. He put the ointment away, then pivoted back around and leaned forward.

Sure that he was going to kiss her and forgetting all about not wanting anything to do with him, she closed her eyes and waited with tingly anticipation for the feel of his warm lips on hers. His hands gripped both sides of her waist instead. A gasp escaped her as he raised her high in the air and plopped her on his horse.

Taking hold of the reins, he flashed her one of his subtle looks that said "gotcha" before leading them homeward.

"There, you did it again," she said.

"And what is that?" he asked without glancing back at her.

"Oh, never mind." Her thoughts tumbled as she wondered what she was going to do about him.

# CHAPTER SEVEN

Days later, Derek shut his ledger and looked across his writing table at Emmon. "I thought you told me Lady Amanda could ride as well as any man."

"My lord, the woman is trouble," Emmon said, exasperation lining his voice. "She is a two-timing thief who continues to weave a maze of falsehoods day after day..." Emmon paused in mid sentence. "I apologize, my lord, but the wench...I mean the lady sorely raises my ire. Was it not you who taught me that women ply men with ale and strange herbs, then take their moneybag while they are sleeping? Well, you were right about that, except this one took my horse instead."

Derek rubbed his jaw, trying to hide the amusement the young knight provided him.

"When Hugo and I followed Lady Amanda's trail after she escaped 'twas obvious she was a skilled rider. She rode as fast as any storm, she did."

"I do not understand it," Derek said. "That was no act she put on the other day. She has not a clue as to how to ride a horse properly. She could barely sit on the animal without teetering to one side."

"I am telling you she has gotten under your skin, my lord. Like a leech, and even now—"

"You do not trust her," Derek broke in.

"Nay, I do not. I saw her swim like a mermaid, but it would not surprise me if suddenly she could not paddle her way out of a puddle. It is a pity, my lord, that the king has linked you with one such as her."

Derek leaned forward and placed a fatherly hand on the boy's bony shoulder. "I have taught you well…mayhap too well."

After Emmon left his study, Derek wondered if perhaps he had been too hard on the boy in the past. As his squire, the boy had needed toughening. Derek could see he had succeeded in that regard. Like himself, Emmon had no patience for wasting time; and dawdling with a woman was just that.


"I thought I made it clear to you both that Lady Amanda's running off in the forest was to be kept quiet," Matti said to Hugo and Emmon, fixing them both with a disappointed scowl now that she had them alone in the sewing room. "It is difficult enough getting Lord Vanguard's cooperation with his impending marriage without you two adding sticks to the fire."

"More than a dozen men learned of Lady Amanda's folly before Hugo sent them back to Braddock with her maid." Emmon lowered his voice, "'Tis only right I should also tell Lord Vanguard I saw his betrothed in the arms of her lover."

Matti shook her head. "Your eagerness to be rid of Lady Amanda is growing tiresome. You said yourself it was a one-sided kiss. If Robert DeChaville jumped from a tree as you said, then surely she was not expecting to run into him."

"'Twas a kiss nonetheless," Emmon muttered, "and his lordship would surely put her in the dungeon for that. The two of you are playing cupid and unwittingly making a fool of his lordship. I no longer wish to play a part in your ludicrous matchmaking games."

Hugo put a firm yet friendly arm about the boy's shoulder. "Emmon, my boy. You have already been sworn to secrecy on the matter. And although you have made it clear you are not happy with Lady Amanda, have you ever seen Lord Vanguard look happier? Do you not want to see his lordship contentedly settled?"

"'Tis obvious to me," Emmon said, "that she is not of the settling sort. Peculiar is what she is."

"Aye, she is odd at times," Hugo agreed, "but I for one like her courage."

Matti smiled and said, "Indeed. And she is a friendly lass. The castle children adore her already."

"No need to worry about Lord Vanguard squashing her spirit as we first thought," Hugo chimed in as he returned to sit on a stool.

Emmon crossed his arms in exasperation and kept quiet.

"I surmise Lord Vanguard may have found his match," Matti said thoughtfully, "whether he cared to or not."

Hugo gazed fondly at his wife. They both knew if there was one thing Lord Vanguard needed it was a trace of happiness. Something the entire castle could use about now.


Derek's eyes stung as he made his way down the narrow hallway toward his bedchamber. Once again he had worked well into the night without rest. Ever since his steward had run off, he had been burning the candles into the wee hours. He stopped abruptly when he saw Hugo standing like a sentry before Amanda's bedchamber door. "How is she?" Derek asked Hugo.

"I am afraid she is not faring well, my lord."

Derek stiffened. "What do you say? She had but a few scrapes and bruises."

"Matti is with her now but it seems her ladyship could scarcely walk this morning. Her injuries are far worse than you surmised. Naught to fret about, though, my lord, a physician will be here soon to look after her." Hugo gazed about dispiritedly as if he were already mourning the death of her.

"I will see for myself." Derek moved toward the door.

"Take these in for me, will you?" Hugo grabbed a bouquet of flowers from a vase on the hall table and shoved them into Derek's hands before he could protest.

Derek stepped quietly into Lady Amanda's bedchamber. When he saw her happily sharing stories with Matti he felt his hackles rise. Here he stood, he thought, brimming with concern and looking a foolish sop with flowers in hand. And for a wench, no less, whom he had vowed only yesterday to avoid at all times.

Matti smiled and stood, stifling a chuckle as she swept past him, making a quick exit.

He watched Amanda maneuver within the bed to see who had entered. Her chin instantly began a haughty upward climb until she spotted the flowers in his hands. Only then did her icy reserve melt as fast as snow on hot timber. "For me?"

"I am afraid so."

"You are 'afraid so'?"

He sighed as he headed her way and merely thrust the flowers toward her. "I mean naught by it. Here, take them. Now what is this I hear about you not being able to walk?"

She wrinkled her nose. "I can walk. It hardly hurts anymore." She pulled the coverlet aside and raised the thin chemise to her knees. "I mean honestly, the fuss Hugo and Matti have been making these last few days is ridiculous."

A prickly, lusty heat charged through him, and he gritted his teeth to think her bare knees alone could give him pause. Other then a fading bruise and a few well-healed scratches, her creamy skin was very nearly unblemished. He bristled as it suddenly dawned on him that Hugo and Matti were up to something. Even the flowers he would bet were part of their plan. Always scheming those two. "Raise your gown higher so I can see the extent of your injuries."

"Nice try," she said wryly.

He crossed his arms over his chest.

"You're serious?"

He nodded.

She let out a ponderous breath. "You aren't going to leave until I show you, are you?"

"Nay."

A burst of modesty must have consumed her, Derek mused, for she rambled on suddenly as if she hoped to scare him off with her chatter. It was working, too, he thought resentfully. "For two days," she said, "I have been held captive in this room without one visit from you. But now you barge in here, throw me a handful of flowers..." She glanced wistfully at the colorful blooms, "demanding I show you my body. You're truly unbelievable."

He merely cocked a brow and waited.

"Fine, here, take a look." She yanked the silky fabric upward, revealing the upper area of her pale slender thighs.

His throat went dry.

"See? All wounds are healing nicely." She then stretched the gown to her ankles, threw the bedcover over her lap and then looked up at him. "Satisfied?"

"Nay," he answered, taking a seat on the edge of the bed.

She inhaled sharply as he slid the coverlet back down. Slowly he raised the hem of her gown, watching how the silky fabric clung to her shapely legs as he revealed her bare legs once more. Using the ointment Matti had left behind, he felt her body tense slightly when his salve-covered fingers touched her warm skin.

"Nice flowers," she said, her voice quavering. "Are those the roses Emmon grew?"

Much more interested in watching the goose bumps appear as his fingers slid across her smooth thigh, he paid her no heed. Her skin was as soft as goose feathers. Through the silk chemise he could see her body's reaction to his touch.

Morgan closed her eyes at the very first touch. She tried to relax against the mounds of pillows behind her, but it was impossible. There had to be something she could think of other than the thrilling graze of his palms against her skin. Her mouth dried as his thumb trailed over her flesh like a whisper. The masculine scent of him mingled with the roses sent waves of excitement rippling through her body. She leaned her head back, inhaling deeply as his hands worked their magic.

She felt downright feverish, never having dreamt that a man touching her so intimately would or could feel so good. Even with her eyes closed, she knew he was watching her. She should've been blushing with embarrassment. Instead she felt a keen sense of pleasure at the idea of his gaze shadowing the agile movements of his fingers as he massaged and teased. She clutched at the matress as his other hand caressed her jaw before he brought his lips to hers. She lifted a hand and blindly raked her fingers through his thick hair, urging his mouth impossibly closer. He was right, damn it. She wanted him. And damn it, she was going to have him.

A knock sounded at the door. Her eyes shot open, meeting Derek's gaze in shared, frustrated silence. She swallowed dryly.

"God's teeth, man," Derek growled as he swept the covers over her and stood. "Who's there?"

"The doctor has arrived," Hugo answered.

They heard hushed whisperings outside the door before Matti added, "The good doctor has come to see about Lady Amanda's injuries. May we enter?"

"Come in," Derek bellowed, cursing under his breath.

Morgan averted her gaze as Matti led a tall, well-groomed stranger into the room. Judging by Derek's scrutiny of the man, he didn't recognize the physician with the broad shoulders and pretty-boy looks. The doctor gave Derek a courteous nod as he approached her bedside.

"State your name," Derek ordered, blocking the man's way.

"Sir Henry Warcliffe, Doctor of Medicine, my lord."

Derek eyed him skeptically. "As you can see, my betrothed is doing well. She has naught but a few scratches that have already been well tended."

Matti tried to speak. "But—"

"'Tis taken care of Matti. Is that not right, my love?"

Morgan could hardly believe what she was hearing. Was he talking about her? Nonetheless, she nodded in quick agreement and tried not to laugh when Derek took the stunned man by his shoulders, turned him none to gently about and ushered him out the door.

Matti shot Morgan a devilish grin before she followed the two men into the hall. When Derek returned, Morgan was disappointed to see that his look of lusty passion had been replaced with that all too familiar scowl. "'My love?'" Morgan teased.

The fine lines etched across his forehead grew deeper. "'Tis an endearment used by most couples about to be shackled in marriage. I thought it best he knew you were sworn to me."

"I know you don't want to marry, but give me a break. 'Shackled in marriage'? You talk as if the old ball and chain is already heavy about your neck and ankles."

"I do not wish to speak of this."

"Why not?"

"No use whining about life's cruelties when there is naught that can be done to remedy the situation."

"Sometimes talking about life's cruelties helps ease the pain."

"'Twould seem you believe talking to be a cure for all ailments."

"Not for everything," she said coyly, hoping he'd get the hint and take over where he'd left off before they were interrupted.

Unfortunately his frown only deepened.

"I do think it helps people to talk about their problems," she told him. "Otherwise problems tend to fester and grow."

"Hmmm," is all he said, appearing to be deep in thought.

"Matti told me about your mother," she said, hoping to get him to open up.

"I have no mother."

"You did at one time. Tell me about her, Derek. What was she like?"

He grunted and headed for the door. Disappointment swallowed her whole as she watched him walk away. He obviously harbored a deep resentment toward his mother and wasn't ready to open up. "Thanks," she said before he reached the door.

"For what?" His two words shot through the air like bullets.

"You don't have to shout."

"I am not shouting!"

She resisted the urge to roll her eyes at him. "I was going to thank you for the flowers, but never mind." She folded her hands in her lap and stared at the wall, then the ceiling, waiting for him to leave.

Derek grunted, then turned back toward the door to do just that. "I will be in my study should you be in need of me."

"I'm sure I'll be fine."

The door opened and closed. He was gone and yet her body still felt weak from the medical attention he'd given her. The man treated her emotions like a yo-yo: falling and rising, unwinding and rewinding. Resignedly, she reached for the flowers and brought them to her nose, inhaling deeply as she pondered Derek Vanguard, Lord of Braddock Hall. For the life of her she couldn't picture him picking flowers from Emmon's garden. But the thought of him doing so made her smile. He was an exasperating man, she thought wearily. Also pig-headed and full of himself, the worst kind of man. And yet sadly she couldn't wait for their next encounter. She was falling for the man, falling hard and fast.

Derek leaned back in his chair and glanced from Hugo to Matti. "Suppose the two of you tell me what you are up to."

Matti and Hugo looked at each other with feigned innocence and then back at Derek with identical ignorant expressions.

"Do not play the doltish fools with me," Derek said. "I have known you both since I was but a child. So tell me what harebrained scheme the two of you are plotting now."

"Pray tell, my lord, whatever do you mean?" Matti asked with exaggerated innocence.

Derek shook his head. "The two of you have plotted and schemed your way through life. Matti," he added sharply, "I seem to recall a time when you gathered enough spiders to scare away an army, placing them in a certain maid's bedchamber. And why? Because a beautiful fair maiden had batted her thick lashes at your burly warrior over there." He gestured with his chin toward Hugo.

A subtle smile tugged at Matti's lips, obviously recalling that day with great satisfaction. Derek had been nine and most helpful in gathering the ugly eight-legged creatures. After the deed was done the maid had dared not look at Hugo again, and, in fact, went back to her parents not bothering to finish with her training at Braddock.

"And you, Hugo," Derek barked.

Hugo was too busy frowning at his wife to take heed. Apparently his friend had not been aware of the spider incident. But Derek knew full well Hugo could still remember the maid he spoke of.

"'Twas it not you, Hugo, who plotted to rid Braddock of a certain troubadour?"

Hugo's eyes widened.

"What was his name?" Derek asked with feigned interest before answering his own question. "Ah, yes, Philip. I believe even you enjoyed the minstrel's entertainment until the princely Philip managed to attract much of Matti's attentions with his flattering poems and intriguing tales. If I do recall correctly it was you who began the scandalous whispers that the man preferred a masculine touch to that of a soft female."

Matti gasped. The women of Braddock had thought the troubadour resembled a Greek God. When Matti and the other maids heard he preferred a gentleman's attentions, they had all been devastated by the news.

Matti elbowed her husband in the side, and Hugo provided her with a sheepish, lop-sided grin.

"The point of my retelling of these stories," Derek went on, "is that the two of you have been plotting and scheming within these castle walls for many years. Although I had assumed you had absolved yourselves of such childish games, it is clear that is not the case. Those flowers for instance." He frowned at Hugo. "An ingenious feat waiting for me to walk by Lady Amanda's bedchamber so that you could trick me into bringing them to her. A well-laid-out plan I must say, telling me that she could not walk. And the doctor. Strange, I have not seen that young physician around Braddock before."

Matti looked to her feet.

Derek's voice softened a bit. "Anyone can see that the two of you share something most wedded couples do not. I am glad for you. But as I have told you both before…I have no time for such nonsense as love." He shook his head at the mere thought of such absurdity. "Whether there someday be a lady of the castle or not, I expect the everyday administration of this household to remain the same. Do you both understand me?"

"Aye," Hugo said. "We understand, my lord, and I can assure you that we meant no harm."

"But can you not see that Lady Amanda cares for you?" Matti questioned. "Mayhap she is a bit unconventional and has a set mind, but naught that cannot be softened with a bit of coaxing."

"And what do you have in mind?" Regret filled Derek the moment the question flew from his mouth, for he had no intentions of dawdling further with the wench. It was his body that deceived him over and over again when it came to Lady Amanda.

"Hugo and I thought it would be appropriate that you should court Lady Amanda," Matti began. "Bring her flowers and mayhap a small gift every now and then. Possibly bestow her with a compliment here and there."

Derek glowered at Hugo, who raised both brows, cocking his head toward his wife to let Derek know this was all her doing.

"I hate to disappoint you, Matti," Derek said, "but I have no intentions of courting the wench. If the marriage vows are ever spoken, the alliance between Lady Amanda and myself will remain just that: an alliance...an association to further the common interests of the king's holdings. Nothing more, nothing less."

Matti sighed.

A knock sounded at the door before Emmon hurried into the room.

Derek crossed his arms and waited to see what was so damned important. The people of Braddock were making it a habit of disturbing him whenever they pleased.

"I apologize for interrupting, my lord, but I thought I should tell you right away."

"What is it now?" Derek growled.

"Lady Leonie is here to see you. And she has enough trunks with her to last a sennight."

Derek cast a weary sigh. He had thought he'd made it clear to Leonie that he wanted no more to do with her. "Show her in, Emmon. I will see to her momentarily." A thought suddenly struck him. "Before you go, Emmon, you wouldn't happen to be involved with this matchmaking scheme of theirs would you?"

A look of horrified dismay covered Emmon's face. "I am sorely insulted to think you would believe me to have joined in on one of Matti and Hugo's simple-minded schemes. I am as innocent as a newly born babe."

Matti glared at Emmon's back as he hurried out. As soon as the door shut, Matti shot Derek a look of disbelief. "Surely you do not intend to let Leonie enter Braddock when your betrothed lies dying in her bedchamber?"

Derek groaned. "Lady Amanda, I can assure you, is very much alive and kicking."

Twenty-four hours had passed since Derek had brought Morgan flowers. And just like her, the roses were beginning to wilt. Morgan was tired of sitting in bed. It bothered her that Derek hadn't visited, especially after all that had transpired between them. The only thing she knew for certain was that her heart was in trouble. And that realization made her nervous. She'd seen first-hand what her adopted mother had gone through after losing her loved ones. She hated the idea of putting herself through the same life-long torment. Isn't that what would happen if she allowed her feelings for Derek to grow, only to suddenly disappear through time and never see him again? Until she figured out exactly why she was here, she needed to keep her distance from him.

Hearing a commotion outside, Morgan jumped from the bed and went to the window. A long-line of squires and pages carried large trunks across the outer bailey and toward the castle's main entry.

The prospect of having visitors appealed to her. She dressed quickly in a pale blue gown of silk with gold embroidery and matching slippers. She used a ribbon to pull her hair back. Not only did she and Amanda supposedly look alike, they were very nearly the exact same size. *Very strange indeed. Where was this Amanda and when would she make an appearance?*

Downstairs the entire castle bustled with activity. Great puffs of smoke came through the hall as the fires within the kitchen were readied for cooking. Tables once stacked to the side of the hall were being set up front and center and it seemed that all the castle people were chattering at once today.

Seeing Odelia scamper across the keep, Morgan snuck up behind her and tapped her on the shoulder. "Odelia, what is going on?"

Odelia spun around in alarm. "What are you doing out of bed? Verily, I was about to ready your tray and bring it to you."

"Don't bother. I'm bored stiff. I saw all the excitement outside. I couldn't just sit in bed and let you have all the fun." She gave Odelia a teasing jab with her elbow.

"Ow," Odelia muttered. "Nobody important visits Braddock this day, my lady. Go back to your bedchamber and I will keep you company there. You could teach me to play chess as you promised."

"Don't be silly. My legs are healed." She raised her dress to prove it.

"My lady! Put your skirts down before every knight within view comes begging for your attentions."

Morgan dropped the hem of her gown and laughed. "You are wrong, Odelia. Not one knight is coming my way."

Odelia glanced about, then let out an audible sigh. "'Tis only because there are no knights within the hall, my lady."

"You worry too much. And stop looking so serious," Morgan said as she hurried off before Odelia could stop her. Outside by the well-tended gardens, Morgan heard a group of people talking. She edged closer to a tall well-manicured hedge and peered through the leaves. Matti, Ciara, and another woman she'd never seen before talked beneath a willow tree. Dressed to the hilt in a gown made of a rich scarlet cloth, the visitor resembled a voluptuous vogue model. Her dark hair was interwoven with sparkling gemstones, wrapped in perfect swirls about her head. She was a breathtaking sight: tall and graceful with a figure to die for. Even her voice had a pleasant ring to it.

Morgan was about to come out of hiding and introduce herself when the woman pulled out a note and handed it to Matti. "'Twas kind of Lord Vanguard to send for me," she said. "I never would have thought he would be so bold...especially with his betrothed right here under his roof and all."

Frowning, Matti took the parchment, studying it carefully before handing it back to the woman.

*Derek invited her?* The woman tucked the note into a silk sachet tied around her wrist. All gazes turned to Derek as he exited a side door and made his way toward the group. He made an imposing sight with his tight breeches and loose-fitting shirt.

Morgan felt a tap on her shoulder and jerked about. "Shayna! You scared me."

"I apologize, my lady, I did not mean to frighten you whilst you spied on the guest."

Morgan gave Shayna a culpable smile. "Who is that woman?"

"She is a harlot, that one."

"She's beautiful."

"Perhaps on the outside, but inside lurks a hundred snakes preparing to strike."

Morgan feigned a small shiver. "A hundred snakes? Maybe you exaggerate just a bit?"

"Believe what you will. But the woman is here for one reason only."

After a few minutes passed in silence, Morgan said, "Well? What is the reason?"

"Him," Shayna said pointing at Derek. "His lordship is the reason Leonie is here."

Morgan turned back in time to see Leonie rush into Derek's arms and kiss him like a leech sucking blood from its victim. They definitely weren't related, Morgan thought. Having seen enough, she turned to leave.

Shayna followed her. "Don't let Leonie bother you. You are much prettier…and friendlier."

Morgan gave Shayna a well-meaning grunt as she made quick strides toward the kitchen door. "That's kind of you to say, Shayna, but you don't have to worry about me. Seeing that woman in his arms doesn't bother me a bit."

Shayna did her best to keep up with her. "Truly?"

Morgan stopped to look Shayna squarely in the eyes. "Truly. I couldn't care less who that roguish, dog-hearted man kisses. Our engagement is a farce anyhow."

"I do believe she was the one kissing him," Shayna reminded her.

"Maybe," Morgan said with a curt wave, "it just doesn't matter."

The kitchen door opened and both Shayna and Morgan watched Emmon come through the door, stopping short when he spotted them heading his way. Emmon's powder blue eyes met Shayna's emerald green ones and they stared at one another as if Cupid had struck them both smack in the forehead.

Morgan chuckled. "Have you two met before?"

Neither responded, having suddenly lost all touch with the world around them. "Emmon, why don't you show Shayna your roses." Ushering them in the direction of Emmon's well-tended flowers, Morgan watched them walk away. The smile vanished when she caught a glimpse of Derek talking to the woman beneath the willow tree.

# CHAPTER EIGHT

Back in her room, Morgan struggled with the removal of the medieval dress, groaning as she yanked it over her head and tossed it on the bed. She was annoyed with Derek, but mostly she was angry with herself. She knew what kind of man he was, and she knew she had no claim on him. He had made no promises to her. Hell, he'd made it perfectly clear that he hardly even liked her. There was probably a perfectly good explanation for that woman to be wrapped in his arms like that. But the reason didn't matter because she didn't care. She didn't want to know anything more about Derek Vanguard.

Besides, it was time to go in search of Amanda and the Earl of Kensington. She had waited long enough, procrastinating with unreasonable thoughts of lurking danger when the real problem was that she couldn't bear the thought of leaving Braddock, and especially Derek Vanguard. Something about that man made her want to seek him out at every turn. It was time to do something about her situation…time to search for the real Amanda. She would find shelter in the village or at an Inn. She pushed open the heavy lid of Amanda's trunk and rummaged through the neatly piled clothes until she found her jeans, T-shirt, and a small purse filled with coins. She dressed quickly, putting on the tennis shoes she'd had on when she first arrived in this century.

There was leftover bread on the tray from this morning which she shoved into a leather pouch. She needed to get far away; find a way home while her heart was still in tact. Her feelings for Derek were spiraling out of control, causing her to lose direction and focus. Besides, she missed her mother back home. Her mother must be worried sick about her.

She threw on Amanda's woolen cloak, hoping to pass the guards without attracting much attention. With all the excitement over Derek's lady friend, hopefully they'd be too busy to notice her at all.

She made it to the stables without anyone trying to stop her. The blacksmith was busy fitting a horse with new shoes. Further on, two men were digging holes that would be used to empty dirty basins and chamber pots. She heard laughter while passing the gardens, but the stone walls and high shrubs provided cover.

Using the hood of the cloak to hide her face, she kept her gaze straight ahead as she arrived at the outer gates.

"You there. State your name."

Morgan swallowed and said in a low, husky voice. "'Tis Odelia, her ladyship's maid. I have been instructed to go to the village for almonds. It seems our guest likes nuts." She grimaced, praying she hadn't ruined her chance of getting through the gates without Derek's permission.

"You may pass," he said. "Make haste though, for the gates will close at sundown."

Morgan nodded as she hurried past.

It was late afternoon by the time she arrived at the village. Judging by the crowds of people coming and going, she figured it had to be market day which she'd heard Odelia speak of on more than one occasion. Morgan stopped the first woman who passed by. Two children clutched at the woman's stained brown skirts. A basket filled with bruised apples hung from the woman's arm. Beneath the ragged cloth tied to the woman's head was a gray mass of tangled hair.

"Would you mind if I asked you a question?" Morgan pleaded.

"I hath not the time," the woman muttered.

"I need to find a woman who looks a lot like me," Morgan said anyhow, struggling to keep up with the woman as she headed onward. "I'll pay you with coins for your help."

The woman did stop then and watched closely as Morgan slid back her hood. The woman gasped.

"What is it? Have you seen someone who looks like me?"

The woman nodded. "She is prettier than you but she lives at Braddock over yonder. The villagers say she is a witch and breathes life into the dead."

"Thanks," Morgan said half-heartedly as she realized the woman was talking about her. "You've been very helpful." She handed the woman one of two-dozen coins, no longer feeling guilty using Amanda's clothes or spending her money. If Amanda wanted to claim her things, she'd have to come get them.

The woman smiled broadly as her kids clamored to see the shiny coins. Thoroughly disappointed, Morgan set off again. Hours later she was down to her last two coins. As she wondered what to do next, a filthy old man approached her. She couldn't see his face beneath his hooded cloak. She tried not to gag at the sour smell of him as he leaned close to her and said, "I hear you are looking for a woman with golden hair and sparkling eyes," the man said, hacking out the last word.

The man appeared sick and feeble, what harm could he do? Besides, she was desperate for some answers. "I don't know about sparkling eyes," Morgan said, taking a step back so she could breathe easier, "but I'm looking for a woman who looks just like me. Have you seen any such person?"

"Aye," he answered without pause, giving her hope.

"Where?" she asked excitedly. "Where did you see her?"

He was staring at her money pouch.

"Oh, I only have two coins left, but you can have them both if you point me in the right direction."

"For two coins," the man said eagerly, "I will take you there myself."

Night was descending upon Braddock when Odelia burst into Derek's office without waiting for permission. "My lord," Odelia said, glancing nervously at Leonie and then back at Lord Vanguard. "I must speak to you about Lady Amanda."

"What is it?" he asked irritably. His head pounded already as if a battering ram were laying siege to his head. Surely the maid was not going to tell him her ladyship was dying. Paperwork was piling up and he had yet to go over expenses with the cook and the marshal. Never mind the nearby manors needing his attention. And he had yet to reprimand Leonie for coming to Braddock without invitation, exactly why he had asked her to come to his office for a private chat.

Although he'd never seen Leonie looking comelier, he was displeased with her coming to Braddock at all. And he certainly did not like her bringing a small entourage of servants whom he now felt obliged to feed.

Odelia's worried voice brought him back to the matter at hand. "It seems Lady Amanda has gone to the village alone," she said. "I am worried for her safety. The guards at the outer gates told me of a woman dressed in a woolen cloak who left hours ago. She has not come back. Her ladyship should have returned by now, my lord, and I am certain she would have if she was not in danger."

"How can you be so sure? If ever there was a woman who could take care of herself, 'tis your lady Amanda."

The elderly maid's shoulders wilted before his eyes.

Derek raked his hands through his hair, glanced outside at the darkening sky, and found himself suddenly on his feet, surprising even himself at his sudden concern. "Have the stable master ready my horse. I will see what detains your lady."

"Oh, thank you, my lord. God bless you."

After Odelia left, Leonie quickly maneuvered her way around the table until she stood before him. "Surely you do not intend to leave me here to dine alone? I have come a long way to see you, my lord." She slipped her slender arms around his neck, pressing her soft bosom to his chest. "I have missed you," she went on. "I hoped since our last meeting that you have had time to reconsider. Please do not go." She took his hand and placed it firmly on her bosom.

The feel of her breast restrained within its velvety confinement made his loins harden. It had been too long since he'd been with a woman.

He glanced out the window. Night was fast descending upon them. The thought of Amanda out there alone gnawed at some deep hidden conscience he had not been aware existed until this moment. He dropped his hand and headed for the door. "We will talk later."

Morgan walked along with the sickly old man, stopping and waiting for him every few minutes as he coughed and staggered through the brush. As the sky darkened, she became aware of what a foolish thing she'd done, putting her trust in a strange man, following him on a pathless route through the forest. Shivers coursed over her as the small hairs at the back of her neck stirred. "Are you sure this is the way?"

Before he could answer, a heavily bearded man bolted from a thick cluster of tall shrubs and pointed a dagger their way.

Morgan turned toward the old man for help, but there would be no help from him, she realized too late. Obviously this had been their plan all along, and she'd easily fallen into their trap. Without hesitating further, she clutched at the hem of her cloak and ran. If she could get back to the edge of the forest, she might have a chance. She heard the thumping of footfalls and the crushing of leaves behind her. They were gaining on her. She ran faster, jumping over shrubs and dodging low branches. Her pulse raced, branches tore at her clothes. A bolt of pain shot up her side as a man's full weight clung to her and she was yanked to the ground. She kicked at the man on top of her, screaming and scratching at every part of him. It was working, too, until the other man caught up and took hold of both her arms, pinning her to the ground. Rocks and thorns bit into her skin. The horrid smelling man brought forth his dagger. She struggled helplessly as he pressed the sharp tip of his knife to her neck. She screamed for help as he sliced through her cloak and T-shirt, ripping the fabric from her chest. When the knife was at his side, she butted his back with her knee, but he only laughed at her efforts.

The sickly man pulled his hood off, revealing his face.

"Otgar," she said, her eyes wide with disbelief.

"I am flattered by your remembrance of me," Otgar said. "I, too, have not forgotten you. Nor the way you hungered for me the day I found you in the woods. Now we shall both have our due."

"You're a madman," Morgan said through gritted teeth. "I should have known it was you from the horrid smell of you alone, you dirty bastard. Get off me or Lord Vanguard will make you pay."

Otgar laughed like a hyena. "You need not worry about him ruining our fun. It is another comely wench who keeps him busy this night."

Morgan spit in his face.

"You stupid wench! Do that again if you like, for it only makes my loins grow harder to see you squirm and fight. Come now, wriggle your slender body beneath me like an animal in heat."

She did exactly that. It didn't matter what he told her, she wouldn't ever lie still while he groped at her with his stained hands and exhaled his horrid breath on her face and neck. She felt his lips on her throat and she bit down on his ear when he turned his head.

Otgar jerked back with a hiss and jabbed the sharp tip of his knife into her cheek. "Do that again bitch and I will slice your neck clean through as though you were but a deer. Either way I will enjoy your soft mounds of flesh beneath my eager hands. Matters not to me whether you are alive and kicking or stone dead."

Certain that he meant every word, Morgan stopped fighting him. She would live. If only for the sake of seeing Otgar pay for what he was doing to her now. She shut her eyes and waited as he plunged his dagger back into his belt.

Her arms throbbed in pain. They were pulled tight above her head and the other man's full weight was on them. Tears slid down the side of her face as Otgar's repulsive wet lips licked the drop of blood that his dagger had caused on her cheek. One filthy hand fondled her knee and drool seeped out from his crooked mouth as his hand slid up her thigh.

The ground vibrated beneath her, and she was sure it was the devil laughing at her. But then a new awareness registered and the vibrations turned to a heartening drumbeat of thundering hooves. She opened her eyes and saw the white mane of Derek's horse and the steel of his blade flashed through the night. She inhaled, never so relieved to see anyone in her life.

Quicker than his companion, Otgar jumped to his feet and took off running, disappearing into the forest. The other man released her arms and staggered to his feet, standing rigid against a tree. With the tip of Derek's blade already sharp against his belly, the man begged for his life.

She tried to stand, but her legs would not support her. Derek glanced down at her, his gaze taking in the blood and terror on her face. She wasn't sure whether she would have protested or not, but before she could try and move again, Derek's stallion reared up, causing the blade of his sword to finish what it had started.

Blood spurted from the man's body and Morgan threw her hands over her face and cried. She cried for the hideous man's life. She cried for her mother back home, and she cried for the parents she'd never met. And then she cried for the loss of her heart to a man she could never call her own.

Derek came to stand before her. Bending down, he placed his mantle around her shoulders. She didn't stir, not even when he picked her up and carried her home.

Derek watched over Amanda long into the night. He sat near the hearth within her bedchamber, staring blindly into the flickering light. It was well past midnight and the castle was quiet. As he gazed upon her thoughtfully, something inside of him stirred. Tonight she had shed every tear possible. His heart had ached at the sound of her whimpering for they were not the sounds of helpless whining from a feeble woman, but the cry of one who mourned for something lost; something irreplaceable and significant.

She could have been killed. Seeing her trapped beneath those men had made his blood thicken. He had felt no mercy. Never before had he felt such utter wrath. His furor would not rest until Otgar was dead. His jaw hardened and the tic there began to throb. His forbidding expression did not soften as he touched her cheek, soft like the rest of her. He held a loose tendril of hair between his fingers, taking pleasure in its silkiness.

Kicking frantically at the covers, Morgan fought for her freedom and swung her arm outward, knocking a silver goblet from the bedside table.

Odelia rushed to her side and grabbed her shoulders. "My lady, wake up. Amanda, please!"

Morgan opened her eyes. Beads of perspiration gathered on her forehead. "Odelia. Thank God it's you."

"And let us thank the Lord that you are safe."

Morgan's voice cracked. "I don't mean to cause you so much trouble, Odelia. I'm confused and I don't know what's happening to me."

"My lady, if only you would learn to talk to me before you do such things. If you truly do not like it here at Braddock then send message to your father. Tell him you cannot stand the

113

sight of Lord Vanguard. Tell him that you never want to see
him again. Your father will understand. He will listen if only
you tell him the truth."

"I wish it were that easy. It's not that I can't stand the sight
of Lord Vanguard. Actually it's quite the opposite effect he has
on me."

Odelia pointed a finger at her. "Ah-ha, I thought as much.
But why then did you run away?"

"Because he doesn't care for me the way I care for him.
And even if he did…" She might disappear without notice, in
an instant, and he'd think she'd abandoned him. Not wanting to
upset Odelia further, she kept her thoughts to herself.

"'Tis nonsense you speak. If you care for him at all…show
him. Why end something that has not yet begun? Besides, a
broken heart never killed anybody."

Odelia tilted her face upward for a better view of the cut on
her cheek. "Do you have any other wounds?"

Morgan shook her head. "Some bruising is all."

"You will not have Otgar to worry about again. When that
hideous man is found, he will be hung from the highest tree.
Now promise me you will dress yourself and make an
appearance before this day is over."

"Is that woman still here?"

Odelia nodded.

"I don't know if I can stand to see her fondling him again."

"Have it your way," Odelia said, "although you were the
one who his lordship watched over all through the night."

"He was here?"

"Right there," Odelia said, pointing to the chair next to the
bed. All the more reason for you to join his lordship this
evening. No need to hide from that other woman. She is not his
lordship's betrothed. You are, my lady. Besides, you can teach
me how to play chess as you promised."

Derek leaned forward and clasped his hands together on top of his desk, paying no heed to Leonie as she rambled on. The curtains were pulled back. Another day had passed and once again darkness descended as his mind filled with thoughts of last night. When he went in search of Amanda last night, some villagers had sworn they had seen her, but nobody knew of her whereabouts. After heading back toward Braddock and cutting a path through the forest, he had heard a woman's cries for help. Never in his life had he felt such panic as he did in that moment. He was a warrior for God's sake, experienced in warfare and trained to stay calm amidst conflict. But hearing her screams had caused fear to clamp down upon him, twisting his gut without mercy.

"Please, my lord, tell me you are not bothered by my visit," Leonie said again, distracting him from his thoughts. She sat stiffly within the chair before him. Unlike her spine, her voice was soft when she spoke. "I was on my way to visit a friend and thought only to stop by and see how you were faring. That is the only reason I made this untimely visit, I swear."

Derek raised a brow. There had to be more.

"Surely you do not find anything wrong in that?" she asked. Under his stern gaze, Leonie wriggled uncomfortably within the chair. "Tell me I have done nothing wrong, my lord. After all, we have known each other in such an intimate way." She fluttered her lashes and feigned an act of modesty. "I can think of no reason why you would be distraught by my visit. Surely 'tis not because you are afraid of your betrothed's reaction to my coming here?"

Derek saw right through Leonie and still managed to say naught. He knew what she was up to. Womanly games. She was much too predictable. So much so, he was sure she would offer to leave just to please his betrothed. And, of course, expect him to fully decline such an offer so that his pride would remain in tact.

"If my stay would aggravate your betrothed, my lord, I will leave tonight...before sundown."

Derek stood, feeling the weight of these past days on his shoulders. "That would be an unselfish gesture on your part to do so, Leonie." He tried not to smile at her look of sheer disbelief that he would let her leave. "Lady Amanda will surely appreciate the inconvenience you would dare put yourself through for her well being. If you would like, I will have Matti provide you with assistance in your packing. We will have you off and visiting your friend before the morrow." He flashed her his most charming grin.

Leonie's cheeks turned the same reddish hue as the flames in the hearth. With a great huff, she excused herself.


That very night the smell of fresh bread and roasted chicken seeped into the great hall where Morgan and Odelia sat before a small marble table. The twitch in Morgan's eye was worse than ever as she tried to concentrate on teaching Odelia how to play chess. "You cannot move your pawn two spaces, Odelia. You can only do that if it's your pawns first move."

Odelia plunked the pawn back to where it was before. "Seems a foolish rule, if you ask me."

"If you take your hand off the chess piece, like you just did, then your turn is over."

"Well why did you not tell me that rule ere I took my hand off?"

Morgan rolled her eyes. "Go ahead and take your turn. I'm just trying to teach you the rules of the game."

"Nay…I would not want to cheat," Odelia said as if Morgan's offer was an insult.

Morgan tried not to laugh as Odelia eyed her suspiciously, waiting for her to make a slip. The woman had no patience for learning games, Morgan decided as she moved her knight forward. A few more moves and she'd have Odelia's king trapped.

While Odelia pondered her next move, Morgan glanced over her shoulder and saw a large group enter the keep. Derek entered last. He wore dark colors tonight, from his short black cloak to his black leather boots. His mahogany eyes sparkled mischievously as she determined that he'd never looked more handsome than he did at this moment. When he glanced her way, her heart skipped a beat. He had saved her life last night. Knowing him as she did could only serve to make her life richer. For if she returned to her other life tomorrow, she'd know what it felt like to love a man; a flesh and blood man, not an empty suit of armor. She had a strong urge to tell Derek how she felt. She wanted to feel him hard against her and discover all he had to offer. Time was running out. She could feel it. If nothing else, Amanda's father would be coming soon and then their time together would be at an end.

Derek winked, catching her off guard. She looked away, pretending to give her complete attention to the chessboard.

"There, I got you!" Odelia exclaimed as she took Morgan's king with her rook.

"Odelia, you have to say 'check' before you can take my king. And, I hate to break it to you but a rook can only be moved horizontally, not diagonally."

"I surrender," Odelia said, straining to push her full-figured body from her chair. "'Tis an absurd game."

Morgan pinned Odelia with narrowed eyes. Derek had finally entered the keep. They couldn't leave now. "Sit down and finish this game or I will tell that handsome jongleur you keep staring at that you want him here and now."

Odelia's cheeks flushed crimson as she plopped back into her seat. "I am much too old for that fine gentleman, but ahhh, I see what has flared your temper, my lady."

Morgan followed the direction of Odelia's gaze. Derek and Leonie sat near the hearth. Morgan's stomach lurched at the sight of Leonie's hand draped casually over Derek's knee as she chatted with Emmon and Hugo as if they were the best of friends. Matti stood behind Hugo, a possessive hand on her husband's shoulder.

"My temper isn't flared," Morgan said. "For once in my life I just want to finish what I've started…and tonight, my friend, I have started to teach you how to play chess."

Odelia watched her with what looked like amused fascination as Morgan said, "Neither of us will part with our chairs until you can play this game." Morgan moved her queen three spaces to the right.

"Aye, the reason for your sudden ire 'tis clearer than frosted glass, my lady. "Check," Odelia said as she slid her queen across the board.

Morgan opened her mouth, ready to tell Odelia that she couldn't possibly have put her into "check" when she noticed that Odelia had actually won the game.

"I do believe I am growing suddenly fond of this game," Odelia said.

"I'm tired," Morgan said, "I think I'll go to bed now."

"You can do no such thing. That woman will think she has won the game if you do."

"Fine. I'm tired of games. Besides, Derek seems to want the woman. Who wouldn't? Look at her."

They both glanced Leonie's way. The woman was dressed like royalty in an emerald green silk gown with gold brocade. Her thick hair braided loosely, hung down the front of her like black silk against an ivory throat and across breasts that defied gravity by not spilling forth.

"I appreciate your staying with me, Odelia, but I can't do this. I won't leave the castle again though, I promise. I'll be in my room." Morgan stood and turned to leave. Unfortunately there was no way to get to the stairs without passing the happy group.

The striking richness of Derek's voice filled the room as she headed that way. Her heart beat fast against her chest and her palms grew moist. She felt bruised and tired, not to mention, plain and ugly in comparison to Derek's girlfriend, whose gaze burned right through her as she maneuvered around them.

Derek stood as she tried to pass, blocking her path. She could smell his earthy scent as he took her hand and urged her to sit in a padded chair that Hugo pulled forward. She tried to get Odelia to join them, but Odelia pleaded exhaustion and walked off.

"'Tis good to see you up and well," Derek said as he waited for her to take a seat before he took a seat next to her.

"Thanks," she said, feeling completely out of place.

Derek plucked Leonie's hand from his knee and returned it to Leonie's lap. Morgan caught the gesture but didn't think much of it, for Leonie looked just as happy to play with his hair.

"My lord, your hair has grown since I saw you last." Leonie twirled her long, perfect fingers in his wavy locks, adding in a honeyed voice, "Was it less than a sennight when I saw you last, my lord?"

Morgan knew that a sennight was equal to one week. That meant Derek had been with Leonie the same night he'd barged into her room like a drunken sailor and carried her from the tub. No wonder he'd left so abruptly. After being with Leonie, he probably thought he was deranged for seeking her out at all.

"His hair has grown overly long. Do you not agree, my lady?" Leonie asked Morgan.

A mischievous grin curved Derek's mouth. "My betrothed is well aware of how my hair has grown. Is that not so, my love?"

Morgan managed a small, confused nod. He was doing it again

Shayna released a small chuckle.

Leonie wouldn't let it go. She was like the energizer bunny, Morgan decided. She just kept on going...and going and going.

Leonie leaned toward Morgan and said, "Never mind his lordship's fine locks. Such a terrible ordeal you have been through." She gave a *tsk, tsk* before adding, "But only a fool I dare say, would go out unescorted and follow a strange old man through the forest." Leonie put her hands over her lips, feigning a mere slip of the tongue. "Pardon me, I did not mean to imply that you were a fool, I only meant…"

"We know what you meant," Hugo said wearily. "Triston," Hugo called to the jongleur. Sing for us whilst we eat. I believe I heard the horn long ago." Hugo stood, motioning for the visiting minstrel to follow as everyone made their way to the dining tables.

An hour later, Morgan poked at her roasted mutton as she listened half-heartedly to the small talk during dinner. Emmon had situated himself between Leonie and Derek. She knew Emmon didn't like her, but at least he didn't appear to like Leonie any better.

Although preoccupied with catching Emmon's attention, Shayna sat across from Morgan and every once in a while presented her a subtle look of sympathy. More than once, Morgan caught Derek looking at her. A fierce gentleness beamed from his dark eyes, as if he were caressing her without using his hands. A shiver raced up her arms as she wondered what went through the man's head. Why did he keep looking her way? Obviously he enjoyed Leonie's company or he would have already sent her away.

Leonie, Morgan noticed, watched her like a hawk. Whenever Morgan glanced her way, Leonie nearly pushed Emmon off the bench so she could talk to Derek or touch his forearm with her long pale fingers. When the meal was finally over, the men gathered near the fire, while the women listened to the minstrel's songs. When she saw that both Derek and Leonie were missing from the room, she said her goodnights and quickly excused herself. She hurried up the stairs glad to see the halls were empty as she rushed toward her room. Closing the door behind her, she leaned against the cool hard planks and let out a long, weary sigh.

"What took you so long?" a deep voice asked from the shadowy corners of her room.

# CHAPTER NINE

Morgan squinted in an attempt to make out the dark figure across the room. Derek. He appeared only as a large shadowy figure where he sat within a cushioned chair. "Why are you here?" she asked.

"I wanted to be sure you were staying in for the night and not roaming the countryside."

She breathed easier, glad to know he wasn't wrapped in Leonie's arms as she'd envisioned. He was here in her room and she couldn't help but wonder why. "I'm glad you came."

"Is that so?"

She nodded. "I wanted to thank you for saving my life. I would have thanked you earlier but I knew you were busy with your guest."

He stood so fast he startled her, then moved toward her with the smooth grace of a large cat. He took a firm hold of her shoulders and said, "I want to know why you left Braddock yester eve? Who were you looking for?"

Morgan peered into stormy black eyes. "I left because I was confused…confused about my feelings for you."

"I demand the truth."

"I'm telling you the truth." She tried to hide the excited rush of nervous twinges she felt at having him so close. He smelled of fresh linen. His loose shirt gaped open, revealing a soft feathering of black curly hair.

She took in a breath and added, "I left because I can't take anymore of this tension between us. Since the day we met we've been at odds with one another. Fate has thrown us together and I have no idea why."

"I think I do." He played with a lock of her hair, letting it slide between his fingers.

"There is so much for us to understand before we could ever really begin to know each other," she said. "And I want to know you, Derek. About your childhood and the circumstances that have made you who you are."

He tensed. "There is nothing from my childhood worth knowing about."

"A childhood makes people who they are. And I want to know who you are. I find myself yearning to know what's on your mind. I often wonder how you feel about...about me."

His mouth took in her next breath, and the low growl he emitted when his tongue parted her lips made her feel weak in the knees. The wonderful taste of him engulfed her, making her dizzy, until she forgot all her questions and remembered only Leonie. She pulled away. "Why are you kissing me instead of that Leonie woman who has been glued to you for days?"

He gave her an innocent, if not ingenuous look. "For some ludicrous, illogical reason I desire only your lips upon my own."

"The truth," Morgan demanded, as he had earlier.

"Unfortunately, it is the truth I speak. For as hard as I try to expunge you from my mind," he rubbed his thumb across her cheek, "I cannot do so." He put his thumb to her chin and tilted her head upward. "It matters not whether I have before me a flock of kitchen wenches or a lady of great beauty...'tis you who haunts my every thought."

"Are you implying that I'm not a lady of great beauty?"

He smiled softly before he kissed the tip of her nose and then her lips. He lifted his palms from her face and ran his fingers through her hair. "You are by far the most beautiful woman I have ever seen."

A warm tingling surged through her. Although she didn't usually go about asking for compliments, she hung on to his every word.

"As for Leonie," he said, still peering into her eyes, "she is readying to leave as we speak."

"Why would she do that? She didn't look eager to leave."

"I asked her to. It is as simple as that."

His hand slid down the smooth column of her throat and then downward over her shoulders as his mouth nibbled at the sensitive area of her nape. He was doing it again…hypnotizing her with his hands and his lips.

"Amanda," he whispered, "when I kiss you…when we make love…you shan't be thinking of anyone but me."

Making love, she repeated in her mind, trying her best not to get overly nervous.

His warm mouth burned a downward path, stopping to graze upon her ear. Her pulse soared as he whispered a string of endearments. So softly and huskily did he speak that the only words she understood were, "lovely" and "succulent." His hands slid slowly downward over her waist until his fingers entwined with hers. Then he lifted her hands to his chest, her splayed fingers touching the warm skin revealed within the open V of his shirt. She trembled at the feel of his hard pectorals as fine curly hairs crept between her fingers. A rotating display of fireworks shot through her. She'd wanted to touch him for so long and now that she was, she could hardly breathe.

Tremulously, she used her fingertips to make a path across his muscular shoulders. A husky groan escaped him as he removed his shirt and tossed it to the floor.

Slowly, she explored the hard cords of his neck and the steely hardness of his stomach. His breathing became ragged and a shudder rippled through her as she trailed a finger over his chest.

His eyes were dark with passion as he untied the laces of her dress. His mouth grazed over her shoulder and he took the cottony fabric of her gown between his teeth, sliding the dress off as he worked his way downward. She felt the cool air through her thin chemise. His hands smoothed over her calves, then up under the thin fabric, intoxicating her with desire. Her body shuddered.

Straightening to his full height, he took a handful of silk, and with one practiced jerk of his wrist, removed the undergarment completely. She smiled at his sudden impatience as he threw the garment over his shoulder, letting it fall where it may. He caressed her with his eyes instead of his hands, the effect just as rousing. Her cheeks warmed. The corner of his lips tilted upward right before he picked her up and carried her to the bed, leaving her there while he undressed.

She watched as he removed his boots and breeches, trying not to blush at seeing him fully naked and fully aroused. It never occurred to her to look away. His eyes burned into hers as he walked to the bed and lowered himself over her. Gazing into her eyes he said, "No turning back now."

"Never," she whispered, intoxicated by his nearness.

His intense gaze never wavered as his fingers foraged a tortuous path over her collar bone and lower still.

She shut her eyes, overcome with desire.

"Tell me your thoughts. What is it you yearn for?" he asked.

"You," she said between ragged breaths as he brushed kisses across her throat.

"No one else?"

"Only you. Now please stop torturing me!"

"Stop what," he asked, "stop this?"

He kissed her further, slowly as he touched her soft skin until she nearly wept. And only then did he stretch his body over hers until she felt the hardness of him press against her thigh. "Don't stop," she whispered as he teased her with his soft kisses. She felt like a woman possessed as she clutched at his back and shoulders, eager for him to put an end to the agonizing cravings within.

As if struck by lightning, Derek felt a sudden unnatural loss of power over his own body. His blood thickened as he was now driven by a primitive compulsion to have her. He felt a change in her body as her muscles constricted, bracing herself as he entered her and felt the soft wall of resistance.

She was a virgin.

He knew not what to think about that, except to remove any obstruction in his way. He did so, with one swift thrust of his hips.

Morgan drove her nails into his back as her body tightened in pain. She was going to die after all...literally. Not from blissful ecstasy as she had first envisioned, but from dreadful, tortuous pain. Why hadn't any one told her it was like dying? Being stabbed in the gut with a sword and then dying?

He must have sensed her worry or probably knew from experience because his voice was tender when he said, "Try not to move." He held her down with the weight of his body as she wriggled beneath him.

"Please get off me, you're killing me. I've changed my..." Her voice trailed off as he began feathering her neck and shoulders with light kisses.

Although Derek's body screamed for release, he restrained himself, something he never did with any woman, uncaring as to whether they received pleasure or not.

Insanity drove this sudden need to pleasure her as she pleasured him. Every muscle was strained and tense in order to keep from finding his gratification too soon. His jaw clenched tight as he fought against the exquisite feel of being inside of her. If he did not move soon it would be too late.

Her eyes were clamped tight, but he felt her body relax as the pain slowly diminished. She moved her legs as she became more receptive to him, obviously expecting more pain. "Trust me," he whispered. He felt her shiver. She dared to relax one muscle at a time until her hips slowly rotated, her movements instinctive now as he sank deeper.

He had planned to take it slow, but that was impossible. The feel of her wrapped around him, was too much to bear, overwhelming him, taking over his senses as the unleashed fervor between them caused his pace to quicken. She moved her hips in unison with his until the splendid torture was brought to a rapturous end for them both. Her body shuddered before every limb relaxed beneath him.

They stayed close, basking in a moment of tranquility, neither speaking. Derek rolled off of her so that he lay on his back with one knee bent upward. He stretched upon the bed, then brushed her hair from her cheek when she propped her head within the crook of his arm. He'd been caught, he realized. He'd been tangled in the spider's web so superbly weaved. A sad, indistinguishable pain swept over him.

One hand lay beneath his head as he looked to the wooden beams above. By the time he lowered his gaze to the woman next to him, she was asleep. A contented smile across her lips. His eyes coursed over her and a frown wrinkled his brow. It dawned on him that the innocent way she had looked at him all these days had perchance been real. No wonder she had been frightened at the lake. She had been a virgin, and he had made it clear that day that he had no intentions of coddling her.

He brushed the pad of his thumb across her soft cheek. She was more beautiful than King Henry promised. She was also far different from any woman he had ever met. Although she told ridiculous tales of being from another world and had a vocabulary of absurdly strange words, she seemed naught but sincere with her feelings. Somehow she had even managed to bring forth feelings of his own…feelings he had thought dead and buried.

After a few moments, Derek maneuvered himself from the bed, placing her head on a soft pillow. He donned his breeches and wandered to the window where he stared pensively over his lands. After a while he turned back to gaze upon his betrothed, wondering what cruel fate she had planned for him.

Morgan's eyes flittered open the next morning to the sounds of swords clanking together outside. No sweet chirping of the birds today, she thought with a smile as she snuggled closer to Derek, disappointed to find him gone.

She sat up, wincing at the sight of the blood-stained linens. She slid off the bed and rolled the linens into a ball. As she brought the bed sheets across the room, she moaned at the stiffness she felt in her legs and the soreness between them. It felt as if she'd been riding Emmon's horse instead of Lord Vanguard. She chuckled at her own devilish thoughts.

Returning to the bed she picked up the torn chemise. Amanda would not be happy at all when she saw what Morgan had done to her clothes. She chuckled again, surprised by the giddiness consuming her. She walked like a bull-legged cowboy to the basin. How could something so good make her feel so darn sore? She splashed cold water on her face, then dressed in a mauve-colored tunic.

As she returned to the bed, she heard a knock on the door. Before she could say 'come in' Odelia swept into the room with a tray of food. She set the tray down, grabbed the dirty linens and hastily headed for the door.

"Aren't you going to ask me about last night?" Morgan asked her.

"Aye," Odelia said, turning back. "What did you do to the poor man?"

Morgan smiled. "I made the man groan with pleasure. Can you imagine?"

Odelia's cheeks bloomed with color. "Nay, and I have no desire to imagine any such thing."

"Derek Vanguard, Lord of Braddock Hall loves me," Morgan said happily.

"Did he say the words?"

"No, not exactly," Morgan confessed. "But he said we were going to 'make love,' and then we did."

"I have no wish to ruin your mood, my lady, but a man will say anything to get a woman to bed him."

"Maybe," Morgan agreed, "but I saw more than desire in his eyes. He loves me. I felt it every time he touched me."

"The only thing I sensed as his lordship stalked through the keep this morn was fury," Odelia said. "He wore the scowl of a wolf, he did. And without bothering to break his fast he stormed outside before the sun had time to rise."

"Where did he go?"

Odelia shook her head. "I know not."

"That's strange." She began searching for her slippers. "Maybe I should talk to him."

"The chambermaids are heating water for your bath. Perhaps you should wash first."

"Good idea. I'll take a bath first. Thanks for everything, Odelia, especially for being my friend."

Odelia peered into her eyes as if she were searching for something...or someone, as if she wondered who exactly had taken over Amanda's true form. Then she muttered a few nonsensical words and headed for the door again.

"Before you go," Morgan said. "Could you tell me if anyone else in the castle knows that Derek was here in my room last night?"

Odelia smothered a cough with the corner of her apron. "I...methinks they are not..." Odelia dropped defeated arms to her sides. "Of course, they all know. 'Tis the same here as it was at Silverwood. There is naught at Braddock that goes unheeded, my lady."

Morgan cringed. "I guess I'll be considered loose."

"You are his betrothed." Odelia chuckled. "The consummation of a marriage before the actual event is not an uncommon practice. There will be no taunts or jests coming from these friendly people. Now quit your worry."

After Odelia left, Morgan slumped back into the feather mattress. "No big deal," she said aloud, "You lose your virginity to a medieval man, what did you expect? A friendly thank-you note? A good-morning kiss?"

She frowned at the idea of Derek being upset. Men in this century were warriors first, second, and probably third, too. He might as well be a caveman. Did she really think that sleeping with him was going to make a difference in the way he felt about her or the way he treated her? She sighed. She hadn't had time to think about any of that last night. And even if she had, it wouldn't have made any difference. Derek had made her feel things she never could have imagined possible. She had no regrets.

By the time she finished with her bath, Morgan felt her confidence dwindling. Why hadn't he come to say good-morning? Where was he? She hated to think of herself as the jealous insecure type, but images of Derek frolicking outside with a newly trained kitchen wench or bonding with the castle's bloodletter somehow managed to invade her mind.

Without putting much thought into what she was doing she shuffled hurriedly through Amanda's chest, searching for the daring red gown she'd seen more than a dozen times. After she ripped the fur-lined collar off of the dress, she noticed that it had a very revealing neckline, too. She put it on. The silky fabric hugged every curve. The dress was sure to catch Derek's undivided attention.

As she entered the hall, she noticed all eyes were on her, and suddenly she felt sort of stupid. She could hardly walk. Not only because of the soreness between her legs, but because the dress was incredibly tight. She had no choice but to sway, a Mae West kind of stride as she crossed the seemingly never-ending room. She pushed a flimsy strap into place, praying the fabric would keep hold of her very compressed bosom. Her breasts had a rhythm all their own as she made her way outside and down the wide steps.

She followed the sounds of clattering swords. Then stood paralyzed by the spectacular sight before her: Knights, dozens of them, were outfitted in chain mail. Hundreds of tiny links of metal covered each knight from head to foot. Their blades flickered in the sunlight and the clashes of swords reverberated off one another. The heavy shields they held in front of them provided a barrier of defense.

It wasn't hard to spot their lord who stood easily a foot above the others. He wore no helmet and his chain mail covered only his upper body. The man was as big as the jolly green giant. Only he wasn't green and he certainly didn't appear to be too jolly either.

With one quick thrust of his sword, Derek easily knocked his antagonist to the ground before turning quickly to another ready opponent. The man on the dirt yanked off his helmet, revealing the angry red face of Emmon McBray.

Unmistakably peeved at being so easily defeated, Emmon stalked by her without glancing her way. A river of sweat trickled down his pouty face and neck, disappearing beneath his padded armor.

"Did he hurt you?" she asked.

Emmon stopped in his tracks as if she were a rattlesnake ready to attack. He glared at her as he turned back her way. His blue eyes narrowed and his face turned a shade of lavender.

Shoot. She'd embarrassed him. She shifted her weight uncomfortably as he studied her attire with a look of disgust. Then he shook his head and stalked off.

Emmon was beginning to like her, she could tell.

Turning back to watch the men on the field, Morgan suppressed a gasp at the sight of Derek stomping toward her, every stride eating up an incredible length of distance between them. His chiseled jaw appeared hard and his lips looked like a tight line across his face. He was definitely upset about something. As he grew closer, his expression remained stony and unreadable.

"Wench!" he shouted for all to hear.

Every knight on the field looked her way. An incredible wave of heat shot up her neck as she braced herself for what Derek might say or do next.

"Females are not allowed upon these grounds. Has Matti taught you naught? It is a known fact that women of such high-born breeding as yourself are well versed on what is right and what is not. Perchance when we are married I shall have to also rehearse with you your wifely duties?"

Morgan glared at him, refusing to shy away in front of a crowd of lance-toting knights. "Obviously you think I'll wait for you with bated breath every time you waltz into my room and then leave me without a word. I won't. And—"

"Cease your foolish prattle woman or I shall turn you over my knee right here for all to see the castigation of an unruly wench."

"You wouldn't dare!"

He pointed toward the castle and waited for her to leave.

She raised her chin high, refusing to budge.

He cocked a brow and said, "Have it your way." He picked her up and heaved her over his shoulder to the enthusiastic cheers of his men.

Not again! Refusing eye contact with any one of his men-at-arms, she buried her head in the hard metal links of Derek's back as his lengthy strides brought them quickly back to the castle.

Within the keep Shayna waved at her, Matti winked, and three little kids giggled as they followed Derek's quick steps to the bottom of the stairs.

He brought her to his room, dropping her on his humongous four-posted bed as if she were a bolt of cloth. With hands planted on hips, he stared down at her. And he wasn't looking into her eyes.

She pulled at the top of the dress, feeling suddenly cheap and ridiculously modest.

"I would ask that you disrobe," he said in a brusque tone.

"What?"

"Strip for me now," he commanded.

"Me?" She glanced behind her, then back at him. "My clothes?"

"Strip until you are as naked as the day you were born. That is an order—not a prayer."

"You're a madman." She lifted her nose to the air and swished him away. "You'll just have to pursue your shameless, self-enjoyment elsewhere. I'm sure there are other woman waiting in line for your lordly caress." But none that wanted him as much as she did, she thought pathetically. He was visibly firm beneath his tight leather medieval pants. And the fact that she noticed at all made her moan.

"Then I will have no choice but to relieve you of those garbs myself."

"You wouldn't."

"'Twould seem you know me not."

"I can do it myself, but I won't be ordered around by you. Besides," she added haughtily with a small wave of her hand, "I'm not in the mood."

"That meager bit of cloth you wear can only mean you are in the mood for one thing."

She huffed. "It's not my...I mean, I didn't know..." She sighed, frustrated at herself for wearing the ridiculous dress in the first place. "I'll never wear it again, okay? I'd like to leave now."

"Nay. Not until you show me the rest of that which you flaunt about my men."

It dawned on her then, hitting her full force. The man was jealous. Could it be? The idea of it seemed a little bit ludicrous and a whole lot wonderful. "Is that what this is all about?" she asked, unable to stop a wide grin from spreading across her face.

"And what, I am fearful to ask, are you talking about now?"

"You're jealous."

"'Tis not a trait I possess."

She waggled a finger at him. "You are. I can see it scrawled all over your face." She laughed, pleased with the way things were turning out.

His expression remained steadfastly inscrutable.

"Why is it so unbelievably hard for you to open up to me?" she asked. "Did last night mean anything, or was I just another notch on your headboard?"

The puzzled look on his face made her smile.

"Would it make you happy if it were so?" he asked.

"Would what make me happy?"

"If I were to say I was jealous?"

She thought for a moment. "Yes, I guess it would."

"And if I were to confess to being jealous, although 'tis a ridiculous notion, you would then be eager to reveal what little is not already exposed?"

Morgan laughed at that. "Maybc. But only if I choose to and not because of any threats you make. And not, mind you, until you have fully admitted to being jealous."

"Agreed. I, Derek Vanguard confess to having been momentarily envious of every man, boy, and animal whose glance, peep or gander crossed over thy fair maiden's form." He tapped his foot to the floor. "I am waiting."

Morgan swallowed, mortified at the idea of undressing within his sun-drenched room. "One thing," she said, ignoring his impatient scowl. "For every item I remove, you must extract two of your own."

"'Twould seem you drive a hard bargain, my lady." With that said, he hardly struggled at all as he promptly removed the cumbersome chain mail, tossing it to the floor with a clank and a thud. Quickly following was his leather belt along with a clasp of precious stones.

Morgan gulped at the swiftness of his agreement. Smiling halfheartedly, she realized she didn't have many clothes to discard. She eyed her slippers.

Derek cleared his throat impatiently.

"Okay, okay." Slowly, she slipped off her shoes and handed them to him so he could add them to the pile.

"You decry this a fair game, my lady?"

She smiled coyly.

Derek hastily removed two leather boots and his woolen stockings. He stared at her, drumming his fingers against his muscled thigh.

This was not the scene she'd envisioned. First of all she never intended for him to take her seriously. Secondly, she had no desire to stand before him stark naked in the brilliant sunlit room. Sure, he'd seen it all before, she thought, but that was in the midst of passion. She was too embarrassed to reveal her modesty to this cocky warrior though, and she tried his patience to the hilt as she wondered what to take off next.

"It seems you are in need of assistance after all."

"I can handle this myself, thank you very much." She unhooked her necklace, looked at it lovingly, then placed her rose pendant carefully on his bedside table.

He was way ahead of her, throwing his tunic and cotton shirt atop the pile before her necklace was fully removed. He waited another minute as she struggled with what to take off next. "Enough," he said. "I refuse to wait another moment whilst you brood over what to extract next."

Her gaze followed his hand as he reached into the top of her gown. She felt his knuckles against her breasts, and she gave a startled gasp when he ripped her gown clean off with one swift sweep of his hand. Wide-eyed, she watched him throw the dress atop the mounting heap. "You can't go around ripping all my clothes off. I won't have anything left to wear!"

"I will purchase any cloth needed to replenish your wardrobe on the morrow. Now help me out of these," he demanded with a good deal of exasperation in his voice.

Her hands shook as she attempted to loosen the leather laces that held his breeches tight against his thick muscular thighs and narrow waist.

He groaned as her fingers fumbled along and finally he yanked the breeches off impatiently and tossed them to the pile. He towered over her, leaning close so that he could nuzzle her throat as his hands slipped beneath her back.

She eagerly wrapped herself within his arms while his mouth claimed her breast. A small moan escaped as his thumb gently rubbed at her lips.

Her hands explored the lean ripples of his back, wandering lower until she felt the firm contours of his buttocks. She let out a contented sigh of ecstasy as he entered her, slowly, gently. There was a small gentle ache, but no pain this time as he kissed her, moved within her. Her legs quivered and she took pleasure in the sounds of his low, rumbling groans. She tightened around him and sucked in a breath at the quickness of her release as they were both brought to fervid, spiraling satisfaction. A blissful oblivion consumed her as she felt him shudder inside of her.

Still on top of her, using his forearms to hold most of his weight, Derek kissed her chin and then her neck.

"What are you thinking?" she asked after a moment.

Derek considered revealing the truth, letting her know how she unsettled him, wreaking havoc upon his body and mind. He should tell her all that was once stable and rational was now unreliable. And why? Because every wakeful thought was of her emerald eyes and bewitching smile. He no longer had to touch her to imagine fully the velvety smoothness of her skin. He had gone to the training fields this morn in hopes of exuding her from his mind. It had been working, too, until he saw her standing there, fairly naked at that in her crimson gown. Verily his brain was now impotent when it came to concentrating on his duties, and this last thought caused him to say instead, "I was thinking of all the work piling up because of my being here."

Her frown told him that any feelings of pleasure were abruptly eclipsed by irritation.

"Were you always this insensitive?" she asked.

Derek looked to the hearth. Before the fire appeared a ghostly image of his father as the elderly Vanguard poked at the burning logs with a stick. "Go away, boy," his father said, "I have no time for your useless whining."

"But father," Derek tried again, "my horse is dead. The stable master said you ordered it to be so."

"I will not have you coddling a worthless animal before my men. That is a weakness your mother possessed. How many times must I tell you not to get attached to anyone or anything?"

"But he was mine, a gift to me."

His father finally looked into his eyes and said dispassionately, "The blade sliced through the beast's throat so swiftly it hardly suffered. Now be off with you before I am forced to call one of the servants to deal with you instead."

Derek's stomach knotted and his blood surged at the remembrance of his father's hate; a detached, emotionless hate so strong that even the disciplining of his only son was left more often than not for others to handle.

"I'm sorry," Morgan said as she touched his arm. "I didn't mean to upset you."

"It is nothing," he said. The caring in her voice was like hot iron to his skin. He drew away and went about retrieving his clothes from the floor.

"Can't you stay for a while longer?"

He looked at her and sighed. "Is that disappointment I see in your eyes?"

"Me? Disappointed? You've got to be kidding," she said. "Not me. I'm happy as a lark."

He exhaled as she tried to convince him she cared not in the least that he had no time to linger.

"For your information, Lord Vanguard, I happen to be resistant to disappointment." She shook her head and laughed in an exaggerated attempt to show him how unaffected she was by his leaving so abruptly once again. "It so happens that I, too, have better things to do with my time than dawdle in bed with you."

"'Tis good to know," he said as he shuffled through the pile of clothes on the floor.

"Derek?" she said after a few silent moments passed between them.

"Hmmm?" He turned toward her, smiling when he caught her staring. "'Tis something you see to your liking?"

Her face heated and she quickly looked away. He felt himself growing hard again. "Look what you do to me," he said. "'Tis unladylike for you to be ogling me every chance you get."

"That's ridiculous," she said, gazing at a tapestry on the wall. "I wasn't ogling you."

"Call it what you will, but I fair say your eyes stroked me with such heat that I am afraid I will not be able to tie my breeches now."

She sighed, and then quickly changed the subject. "I was going to ask you if you plan to go through with this marriage business? We both know you don't want to marry…so why go through with it?"

"Because it is my duty to do so," he said evenly, tugging his breeches upward.

"What if I were to let you off the hook somehow?"

"It is kind of you to offer but it is too late. You are no longer a young, innocent maiden and no one else would have you."

She crossed her arms over her chest. "I could have anyone I wanted."

He shook his head. "'Tis too difficult for a husband to train a bride of so many years. You are far beyond the usual age. Perchance you are right though and there is a feeble old knight somewhere who would show interest."

Frowning, she said, "I could find someone. And," she added indignantly, "he'd probably pay a king's ransom to have me. It's not important, though, because I don't need a man to make my life complete."

Derek hid the smile that threatened to come forward. The woman had an inner feminine strength about her that made him want her even more. He also knew she was right about the king's ransom.

"Is your life complete?" she asked, apparently unable to let a moment pass without chatter.

He sat on a stool and put on his woolen stockings. "I have not the time to ponder it."

"Are you happy?" she asked.

"Nay. How could I be when no one allows me to get any work done?"

"Now that I'm better, I'll be able to help you with your work."

He came back to her and pinned her to the bed with his body, using his elbows to keep his weight from crushing her. He gazed upon her with admiration, and then brushed a light kiss on her forehead. Unable to stop there he slid his mouth down over her soft cheek until he reached her lips. He pulled away a moment later and went back to finding his clothes, unwilling to accept the fact that she drove him mad with desire even now, so soon after having his fill of her.

Morgan stared at his backside as he rummaged through a wooden chest across the room, wondering why he was so intent on hiding his feelings. Odelia was right. He didn't love her as she loved him. Not yet. But maybe he could if she helped him open up. He was holding back and he was stubborn. Her head ached at the thought of leaving him. She couldn't bear the thought of going through a life of sadness and grief. She could remember the day when she'd found a trunk of memorabilia concerning her mother's accident, the same accident that had caused her mother to lose her husband and child. When Morgan had asked her mother about that day, Cathy had told her everything. How she and her husband, Eric, and their only daughter, Ashley, had left a party early to spend

Christmas Eve at home. What tore at her mother's insides every day since, was that Eric had been leery about driving in the stormy conditions. It was Cathy who'd insisted they go. A sudden deluge of rain had made the roads slippery and without warning, a semi, weaving out of control had blindsided them.

Cathy awoke to the stark whiteness of the hospital. According to police, her husband could have escaped through his side of the vehicle, but instead, he gave up his life saving his wife and then trying to save his daughter. Everything was taken from Cathy Hayes in that one horrible moment. And worse, Cathy felt she was to blame.

Without warning, Morgan had been swept through time to this century. What was to stop it from happening again?

Morgan watched Derek slip a clean shirt over his rumpled head of hair before he gazed back at her with concern. "Did I say something to cause you grief?"

Morgan shook her head, her annoyance with him already receding. "Where are you going?"

"You think I can lay in idleness all day?" he questioned, tucking in his shirt.

"I was beginning to think you enjoyed being with me just a little bit." She squeezed her index finger together with her thumb to show him how much. "I forgot momentarily about your duties, but trust me when I say I won't forget again."

"Good," he said curtly.

She threw a pillow at him.

He ducked and it flew past his head, hitting the wall. As he placed his sword within its ivory sheath, his eyes glimmered with mischief and his voice was thick with lust. "Though you beseech me with your tempting lips of roses and skin of lilies in full bloom," he said, "I decry my fairest maiden, I have training of my men to do. Verily I could only spare the remotest slip of time to punish you for coming to the training fields dressed in a gown befitting a bar wench. Surely my men will be out of commission for most of the day with images of you floating about their unseasoned heads."

Morgan laughed at that. "Under the circumstances, surely the punishment you sentenced me was cruel and unusual," she teased. "Any true knight would have employed a much kinder, gentler act of punishment. Maybe the guillotine...or a good tar and feathering."

Derek chuckled. "Do you dare mock my choice of retribution?" He held a hand to his chest in feigned hurt. "I sorely desire that I could stay and serve out your just penance. Mayhap when I return in a few days, the stretching device within the dungeon could be commissioned for our use."

Her cheeks grew warm at the thought of using his stretching device for that purpose. "When you return?"

He stepped closer, looking handsome in his linen shirt all fine and clean and those wonderful leather breeches. His stubbled jaw gave him a touch of animal magnetism that made her want to drag him back to bed so that he could further discipline her.

Instead he leaned down and gave her a perfunctory kiss on the forehead. "Only a few days must you sorely wait for my embrace, for I must leave before nightfall to do the king's bidding. Until then, I expect you to behave."

"Before you go," she said, "I have one more question for you."

"And perchance I can answer it," he offered.

"I was wondering if you have any knowledge of a man. An infamous knight who goes by the title, the Earl of Kensington?"

Derek gave her a begrudging look. "You sorely tempt my head to throbbing woman."

"What if I told you that this Earl of Kensington was a good friend of mine?"

"I would say, my fairest lady, that methinks you have again imbibed too much wine. 'Tis nonsense you speak," he added, binding his leather boots tightly into place.

"Why is it nonsense?"

His tone made clear his growing agitation. "Because there is not and never will be an Earl of Kensington. The Kensington estates are vast lands still held by King Henry himself. The good king has decried more than once that these holdings are those that he embraces dearly. He would be sorely bereft to ever give them up…whether it be to friend or foe."

"Of course there is an Earl of Kensington," Morgan declared. "He's an honorable knight who fought hard for his people. A warrior who trusted in no one but his sword."

"'Tis nonsense."

She looked panicked as she tried to convince him. "He's a man who loved only one woman, but he didn't comprehend the extent of that love until it was too late. The Earl of Kensington went in search of his true love but sadly he was killed in an ambush…east of Swan Lake. He didn't see it coming until it was too late. I was hoping to find him, warn him of the danger."

All amusement vanished from Derek's face as he towered over her. "There is no Earl of Kensington and will never be. Your fabrications grow wearisome."

"After his death," Morgan said softly, unwilling to believe the earl didn't exist, "the earl's people placed a piece of her jewelry upon his chest before they buried him; a gemstone she'd left behind and that the earl carried with him on the day he died."

The mere thought of the earl's tragic death, made her eyes mist. When she looked back at Derek she saw disappointment in his eyes. "Derek," she called after him, but it was too late. The door slammed shut behind him.

She released a weary sigh. Until he believed her story of coming from the future, he would never understand her. And until he trusted her, nothing would ever be right between them.

# CHAPTER TEN

The night held little comfort for Morgan. She tossed and turned, finding no rest as images of a man beckoned her. An elderly man with dark hair and silvery patches at his temples. The same man she always saw in her dreams. He held a bouquet of flowers, only this time he didn't come toward her with open arms. He seemed unbearably sad as he fell to the ground on bent knees and placed the flowers atop a pile of stones. She thought she saw tears in his eyes. As she moved closer to get a better look she heard the creak of a door.

Morgan bolted upright in bed, fully awake.

"Oh, I apologize, my lady," Ciara said with a hand on her chest. "I fair say I am not nearly as soundless as I try to be."

"That's okay," Morgan said, pushing hair out of her face as she glanced toward the window. "Looks like I slept late again."

"Aye, my lady. I was going to leave this missive for you on the table."

"A note? From who?"

Ciara handed her a tightly rolled paper, tied neatly within a thin strip of black velvet. "The missive was found by one of the scullery maids early this morn."

A note for me? Morgan opened it, slowly, savoring every word as she read.

To my dearest Amanda, whose merest smile makes me dizzy as though I had drunk a good sweet wine. Whose kiss gives my soul a glorious hope and causes my heart to sing like any nightingale.

Keep these words close to your heart until I return to your side once more.

A little corny, but straight from the heart, bringing a knot to her throat. Hadn't she told Derek that women liked to receive flowers and notes? She smiled at the realization that Derek possessed a fanciful inner side after all. And to think she made his heart sing like a nightingale's. She sighed contentedly, satisfied to know he was thinking of her while he was gone.

That same afternoon, dressed and well fed, Morgan followed Odelia around her bedroom, the note firmly clasped in her hands. "Would you like me to read it again?"

"Nay," Odelia blurted. "The note is lovely, my lady. Never a more captivating missive have I heard ere this. But I dare say I have the note well memorized myself."

"A little grouchy, aren't we?"

"If you would let me finish with my chores," Odelia said with a huff, "perhaps we could get to the market before nightfall."

Morgan watched Odelia dust furniture that looked clean enough already. "Come on, Odelia, let's go. It's the dawn of a new day and new beginnings," Morgan said cheerfully. Not only had she received a note from Derek, but a messenger had arrived earlier with a message from Amanda's father. Apparently, problems with nearby manors prevented him from visiting as scheduled. The wedding would be postponed until after the king's banquet at Windsor. She had at least another week before Derek would know the truth.

Odelia and Matti were taking her shopping in the village. According to Matti, Derek had said he hoped to see Lady Amanda dressed appropriately when he returned. She looked back at her note. "Whose image is seen with thy every breath," she said as if she were quoting Shakespeare.

Odelia threw her hands up in defeat, tossing the dirty cloth into the bucket of murky water. She grabbed Morgan's hand and off they went in search of Matti.

It wasn't long before the sun's rays warmed their backs as the three women followed the dusty path into town. Emmon came along too, but he trailed behind, evidently having no desire to listen to their womanly chitchat.

Morgan talked about the bathing suits Ciara and Shayna were going to sew for them and the picnic she was planning for all the castle women. Morgan lectured Matti and Odelia about getting fit with exercise and good eating habits.

As they approached the village, Morgan grew nervous at the possibility of Otgar being near. She glanced back at Emmon, glad to see that he was close by. He sat rigid and alert upon his horse, looking as mean and cruel as any young warrior could. She pressed her fingers to her hip and felt the hardness of the dagger she'd hidden beneath her dress. If Otgar showed up, she'd be ready for him.

The village looked much different today. The structures burnt in the fire were being repaired. The homes they passed were small and unpainted. Some were grouped together, while others stood alone with briars and thorn branches intertwined to make menacing looking fences. Slops were thrown from windows and muck heaps piled up outside doorways. Thanks to a light rain the night before, unpleasant odors arose only occasionally.

Street cries sounded as they drew closer to the vendors. They passed a man with a gray goatee and soiled brown tunic. A pet monkey clambered about the man's shoulders and he held out a battered tin cup. Dogs waited for tossed scraps, wearing the same hopeful look as the mimes and jugglers.

Her eyes widened as they approached a fine selection of fabrics, a kaleidoscope of colored bolts displayed upon long tables, row after row of wool, linen, and silk, and a salesman behind each table, ready to push his wares.

After growing bored with listening to Matti's dickering with the merchants, Morgan made her way down aisle after aisle of tables, admiring rows of hand-carved bowls and cups, iron and brass pots, wonderful elaborate chests, and so much more.

Minutes turned to hours and soon a faint cape of darkness swept through the sky, telling her she'd been gone much longer than she'd intended. She glanced around, panicking slightly when she realized Emmon was nowhere in sight.

Odelia and Matti were probably worried. Emmon wasn't going to be happy with her, she thought, as she hurried back the way she'd come. Weaving through tables that were being packed up for the day, she drew back suddenly when a hand darted out and grabbed her arm. She was about to scream until she saw that it wasn't Otgar, but an old woman instead. The old lady muttered gibberish and took little excited hops, reminding Morgan of one of the patients in the movie *One Flew Over the Cuckoo's Nest*. Her hair stuck out like a porcupine, all silvery-white in disarray. Morgan tried to loosen the woman's grip on her arm. The old lady was stronger than she looked. The few teeth left in her mouth were as yellow as the center of a daisy and her breath smelled of cow dung.

"What do you want?" Morgan asked.

Her answer came in the form of more high-pitched chanting.

With a twist of her arm, she yanked free of the crone's wiry grip and ran off.

"The spell worked! You came back," the witch shouted. "Aye, back from the other world as I knew you would!"

Morgan ran faster. She glanced over her shoulder to see if the woman was following. Bam! She slammed square into Emmon, sending him sprawling to the ground. Emmon jumped to his feet, muttering and cursing as he brushed himself off, not bothering to help her up as he waited impatiently for her to follow him.

"Emmon," she said walking briskly in an attempt to stay at his side. "I'm so glad to see you. I lost track of time and before

I knew it...it was dark." She gave him a look of remorse when he glanced her way, but he was stubborn and he only grunted.

With a sigh, Morgan said, "If you hadn't come, that old woman would have put a hex on me. And if that didn't do the trick, her breath alone could've been the death of me, I swear."

The corner's of Emmon's mouth curved upward.

"Ah-ha!" she said, pointing a finger at him. "I made you smile."

"'Tis useless trying to ignore a ludicrous wench such as yourself," Emmon said. "Aye, you made me smile a wee bit, but so do the foolish jesters that pass through Braddock every so often."

"Well, I'm sorry. I don't try to be so much trouble. I just never seem to be able to do things right. I never really, you know...fit in. Whereever I go it's the same. A curse. I was born with it, I suppose." She let out an exaggerated sigh, and then another after Emmon agreed with her, suggesting she seek help.


Derek squinted in an attempt to see Braddock's towers through the trees. His men were exhausted. It had been a longer journey than expected. The king had called upon his vassals for aid to stop a band of thieves stalking the supply routes to his castle. Derek and his men had been assigned one of the main routes and after three long nights of naught but wolves crossing their paths, a half dozen men were caught trying to sneak out of the king's lands with stolen quarry.

"It will be more than just their heads they will lose for such foolishness," Derek said to Hugo as he spurred his destrier toward Braddock. They had turned the thieves over to King Henry. And now, so close to Braddock, Derek was eager to be home, for no other reason than to find a hearty meal and a warm bed, he told himself, knowing there was a certain wench he yearned to see.

"Did you hear that?" Hugo asked, pivoting in his saddle.

Derek pulled on the reins and brought his horse to a halt. "What?" he asked impatiently. He could view Braddock's towers from here and Hugo's attempt to detain him, if even for a moment, was too much. "Was it not you who wanted to reach Braddock before sundown?" Derek asked sourly. "Eager to be welcomed into Matti's loving arms? My men are hungry and have no desire to stop and listen to every whistling tree and crackling of brush."

Through his thick beard, Hugo gave Derek a sideways grin. "'Tis a good friend," Hugo said with a chuckle, "who abruptly tells the king we must make haste to return home, that we cannot oblige him with his kindly offer of rest, food, and entertainment. Fit for a king, no less. And why? Because his long-time comrade and friend, Hugo," he added mockingly, pointing to his barrel-chest, "is lonely for his wife. A good friend indeed."

Derek shot his gaze heavenward at Hugo's sarcasm. "I possess the patience of a scholar if I dare must remind you once again that no strings tie me here to Braddock. Verily, be glad to have such a friend, for you would not want me as your enemy."

"Aye, you are right on that account, my lord. Your enemy I fair say I would not want to be, for not only have I heard the fearless tales boasted of you, I have—"

Feminine giggles interrupted their bantering.

Hugo gestured for the men close by to be still as he and Derek dismounted. They stalked quietly through the high bushes.

Derek's mouth dropped open at the sight before him. "Pinch me for I am but dreaming."

Hugo, too, stood speechless. Not far from the lake's edge were a dozen maids wearing the tiniest bit of cloth. Lady Amanda twisted and turned, every gesture of hers shadowed by the other women.

A frown creased Derek's brow.

Hugo could barely stop himself from bellowing great gales of laughter, at least until Derek pointed at Matti.

Hugo's wife stood front and center within the group, fairly nude like the rest of them in those tiny bits of fabric.

Hugo paled considerably.

"It appears your dearest Matti is not awaiting your return so eagerly as you first thought," Derek quipped.

"'Tis the woman in charge that causes this outrage, my lord." Hugo nodded to the most meagerly clad of woman with legs spread wide and fingers touching her toes.

Derek's face heated and his blood surged at the sight of his betrothed. He motioned for the other men to take leave and make haste, but it was too late. More than two-dozen knights already surrounded the lake with assorted views. He could not instruct them all without being heard by the women below. "By God and Saint John, the woman is cause for ire! Where in damnation is Emmon?" Muttering obscenities, Derek made a sweeping gesture with his hand for those nearby to follow him back to the castle. He instructed Hugo to stay behind, but well hidden, to see that the women arrived back to Braddock unharmed. He would await his betrothed there and see what she had to say about this when she returned.

Hugo waved Lord Vanguard off, then quickly turned back to watch. He was beginning to enjoy this sampling of his wife he'd never before seen. She was graceful in her gestures as she mimicked Lady Amanda. Her silver hair appeared streaked with golden highlights in the aglow of the sun's last rays. His eyes then feasted on his wife's breasts that appeared round and high, snug within the small pieces of fabric.

The women were gay with laughter as they returned to Braddock. At least until they noticed the great puffs of smoke rising above the castle. Dozens of destriers were being fed and groomed outside the stables.

The men had returned.

The women quickly huddled together, talking quickly and all at once.

Morgan wasn't sure what all the fuss was about until she heard talk of their being punished. One of the cooks was convinced they would be forced to go without food for a week. Another maid began to cry, sure that she was going to be sent packing.

"Do not fret, ladies," Matti said, gesturing with a flick of her hand for all to follow. "Luck is on our side. The tower guards have taken leave for the time being and I know of an underground passage on the eastern side of the keep. We can enter the castle unnoticed," she whispered as they moved past the orchard and through a field of tall weeds.

"Surely his lordship will order us to leave Braddock after he learns of our dallying," another maid whined.

Morgan scoffed at that and said, "Lord Vanguard will never know. And even if he does find out, you don't have to worry. I'll take the blame. If he so much as lectures you, I will…" She rubbed her chin as she pondered what she would do exactly. "I will refuse to marry him. And he will fall to his knees and beg for our forgiveness."

The women all chuckled, except Matti, who looked thoroughly exasperated as she led them to a patch of ground covered with rocks and leaves.

"Anything's possible!" Morgan said teasingly. She liked these women. For the first time in her life she had friends. There was no way she was going to let Derek scare them off because of a harmless picnic.

After they finished removing at least a dozen rocks, Matti pushed aside a couple of wood planks. Morgan peered into the dark hole that disappeared into the ground like a giant gopher hole. Matti plunked down and began to crawl inside. "You don't really expect us to go in there, do you?"

Judging by the scowl on Matti's face, she did.

Reluctantly, Morgan plopped herself onto the ground. She dangled her legs into the dark hole, cringing as she climbed in.

The tunnel immediately widened into an elaborate maze of dark, musty passages. Her heart pounded against her chest, but she was thankful there was room to walk instead of crawl. She cringed at the thought of all the bugs hidden in unseen crevices. Something crunchy crackled under her left slipper. She jerked her foot up and shook it wildly. Reaching forward, she grabbed onto Matti, having no desire to lose her in the dark. It was as black as tar, and she felt her throat tightening. Taking a deep, strangled breath, she told herself this was better than having Derek greet her and a dozen of his employees clothed in string bikinis. Then she remembered his so-called punishment and realized she'd probably been hasty in following Matti after all. A cunning grin curved her lips at the fleeting image of having him scold her as he carried her to the stretching device.

Matti tugged her along. A long wispy spider web slid across her face, making her skin crawl. "Where does that tunnel lead?" Morgan asked, pointing to another route they passed.

"That leads to the dungeons. Many men perished in those cells. Long before Lord Vanguard was ever born."

"Does everyone know about these passages?"

"Truth be known, I am not sure," Matti answered as she carefully maneuvered through the dark passageway. "Hugo used to hide in here when he was a small boy. But he left a trail of clues so that I could find him. That is how I first learned of the tunnels. We kept it our own little secret after that," she said in a mischievous tone. "Braddock no longer has need for such passages though, since it is well protected. No man would dare lay siege to that which belongs to Lord Vanguard."

It warmed her to know she wouldn't have to worry about dodging flaming arrows or gathering buckets of hot tar while she was here.

There were murmurs of relief when they finally reached the end of the dank, musty tunnel. One at a time they followed

Matti up a rickety wooden ladder that was thoroughly encased with the artwork of many spiders.

"This leads to the weaving room," Matti said as she slowly pushed open the trapdoor.

All was clear.

"There is a trunk filled with clothing," Matti said. "If your tunics are wet and you need to change be quick about it. After that, 'tis each for themselves."

Morgan and the rest of the women made it to their rooms unseen. Odelia, bless her heart, had left a bath for her. As she climbed into the warm water, she felt anticipation building at the idea of seeing Derek again after so many days.

After a quick bath, she dressed in a silky rose-colored kirtle and matching slippers. She flayed her head back and forth to help dry her hair, pinched her cheeks for color, and then hurried out the door.

Downstairs, knights and ladies abounded. Despite the noise, half a dozen men already slept on pallets before the fire. More than a few men-at-arms played chess, but the majority of men sat contentedly with their ladies wrapped in their arms.

Thankfully, most of the maids had stayed behind and prepared dinner. The men appeared famished. Gingerly, she tiptoed over meat scraps and chicken bones that had been casually tossed on top of the fresh rushes.

Serving maids with platters of veal and venison, rabbit and duck scurried in and out of the kitchen. She'd never seen so much food in one place before. Already spread on the tables were huge wooden bowls filled with rice, figs and raisins. Ale and wine abounded. The men seated at the tables ate and drank heartily.

The moment she spotted Derek sitting with his back to her at the far end of the table on the dais, her pulse quickened. She felt nervous and excited all at once. She had a strong desire to run her fingers through his hair and kiss him soundly. Instead, she grabbed one of the trays of warm bread from a serving maid and snuck up behind him.

She leaned over his shoulder, her chest pressed against him. "Perhaps some warm bread would help put an end to your ravenous appetite, my lord," she said in a voice dripping with honeyed enthusiasm.

Without glancing around he reached back, turning slightly so he could pull her easily to his lap. Morgan gasped as the tray fell to the floor. He set his mouth full upon hers before she could say another word. A few men guffawed at their lord's actions, but most were intent on finishing their meal and seeking out their own mate.

Derek's eyes glimmered with mischief as he pulled away. "Oh, 'tis only you."

She elbowed him in the ribs. "You think you're funny, do you?"

"Aye, that I do."

"Well, I was going to tell you that I missed you, but never mind now."

Derek shrugged.

Morgan frowned. There was something insufferable about a man being so arrogantly cocksure of himself. "So you don't care whether I missed you or not?"

"'Tis written all over your face. What need do I hath for you to speak of it when it is as clear as rainwater that you pined for me."

"I didn't pine for you, I..."

His warm mouth cut off her words. His lips felt full and inviting and her toes curled as she encircled his neck with her arms, quickly forgetting whatever they'd been discussing. He smelled of leather and herbs, and she closed her eyes, thoroughly enjoying being in his arms again. It had been too long without him. Much too long.

Derek nibbled at her neck and when she opened her eyes, he smiled down at her. "What did you do whilst I was away?"

"Oh, nothing much. I went to the village with Matti and Odelia. I helped Emmon in the garden...played with the children."

"Ahhh, but what did you do this day?"

"Today?" Wide-eyed she looked to Matti at the far end of the table, but Matti was busy talking to Hugo. She worried her bottom lip as she glanced around the hall until her gaze fell back on Derek. "You're hurt," she said, gesturing at the sight of bandages beneath the open V of his shirt.

"Nay, I am well."

"You've been hurt. Let me take a look at it."

He held her back. "Since you were not here to greet me that lovely new wench, Sarah, saw to it. She did a fine job tending to me, I must say."

"She did, did she?"

His gaze fell to her hand as it rested on his thigh. The light stubble covering his chin brushed against her cheek as he whispered, "Fair damsel, do I dare hope that you are impatient for my bed?"

Shivers coursed up her spine. His words rang true, causing an inner heat to spread between her thighs and through her belly. Looking upon his handsome face, she noticed his magnificent dark brows curved so neatly above sparkling brown eyes. She gazed at his firm, sensuous mouth and then looked into his eyes and regarded him provocatively.

"It seems, my lord," Hugo interrupted from across the table, speaking loud so that he could be heard above the noise, "that the women here have been sewing and weaving all day, hoping to pass the time as they waited anxiously for our return. But I questioned my dear wife on that, for does she not wear an unusually healthy glow?"

Morgan rolled her eyes when at least six serving maids darted from the room, heading toward the kitchen.

"I dare say you are right my friend," Derek added, "for Matti's healthy glow turns healthier as we speak. I do believe my betrothed wears that same sun-kissed gleam." He turned to Morgan. "Do your fair cheeks hint of a bit more color, or could it be that my vision is blurred this eve?"

Morgan swallowed the lump in her throat. "It was awfully warm when we went to the village a few days ago. Blistering hot if I do recall correctly. Isn't that right, Emmon?"

Emmon glared at her as if she were the most farcical, senseless creature he'd ever laid eyes on.

Many of the knights and ladies within the hall stopped whatever they were doing and looked in her direction.

As she opened her mouth again, she noticed everyone looking past her instead of at her. She glanced over her shoulder and saw a Fabio look-alike holding her wet bikini, letting it dangle precariously from his thumb and forefinger. She'd accidentally left the bathing suit in the weaving room. Her face heated.

Fabio shot her an apologetic glance. Apparently he only wished to relieve her of bothering with another lie. Not knowing what else to do, she turned back to Derek and playfully kissed his cheek, laughing as if she'd been in on the joke all along. The room remained deathly quiet until Derek shook his head unable to stop the corners of his mouth from turning upward. The castle folk must have realized their lord wasn't going to throw anyone in the dungeons because they quickly resumed their chattering.

Morgan put a hand on Derek's chest. His half smile had already disappeared, his expression unreadable except for the flexing of lean muscle beneath a stern jaw.

"What harm could a little outing do?" she asked quietly.

"The people here at Braddock have a routine," he answered firmly, calmly. "It takes many servants to keep Braddock running smoothly, something that would not be possible if I were to let them run off and play at will."

She leaned forward and whispered so that only he could hear her, "I'm sorry. I only fibbed in hopes that you would punish me severely for my actions. In fact, I think justice could only be served if I accept the punishment intended for each and every maiden who had no choice but to follow in my indecent behavior."

Small lines appeared at the corner of Derek's eyes as the humor of the situation dawned on him. "Only you, my lady, could manage to turn a serious offense into a laughable matter. Keep smiling upon me in such a palatable manner and I may sentence you to far more than one night in my torture chamber." He stood up with her still cradled in his arms, pushed aside a chair with his leg, then carried her across the hall and up the stairs.

By the time they reached his room, their fingers tugged frantically at each other's fastenings. Eagerly, as if her very life depended on stripping him bare, Morgan helped him remove his shirt, sighing heavily as her palms slid over his brawny chest, careful to stay away from his injury. She nibbled his neck and raked her fingers though his hair as he removed his boots.

Before Derek could rip another dress from her body, she untied it and slipped it off. He tossed his breeches to the floor and they stood together, standing quietly for a moment, touching and exploring until their bodies became entwined in feverish abandon as though this moment together was their last.

There was no time to find a bed. With one swift movement of his arm, Derek shoved a chair out of their way and they took to the floor. She had no thoughts of anything other then the two of them at this moment. His lips felt like warm liquid heat as he caressed her body with his mouth. She felt out of control, feverish, hungering for more of him, impatient for him to quench her all-consuming desire as she moved splayed fingers through his hair, pulling his mouth impossibly closer, arching into him. He lifted his head. Kissed her hungrily. His eyes peered deeply into hers as he drove hard and deep.

Her body exploded with climatic pleasure, shuddering beneath him as they became a collaboration of two spirits, trembling and demanding, giving and taking, in one sweet whirlwind of passion.

# CHAPTER ELEVEN

The clouds gave way to the sun and the warm spring air fell around them as Morgan ran to catch a small redheaded boy. "Gotcha!" She mirthlessly tickled his tummy.

"Uncle, uncle," Timothy screamed, his small, skinny legs flailing about as he begged for leniency.

A clod of dirt hit Morgan's backside, causing Timothy to explode in laughter laced with intermittent hiccups.

Nine-year old Joseph had hit his mark, and he ran to escape Morgan's wrath after he saw her abandon Timothy and grab her slingshot. In one swift motion she made a ball out of soft mound of dirt, took aim, and hit Joseph's shoulder before he could get away.

Joseph grabbed his chest, fell to the soft grass, and let out an exaggerated wail. Morgan laughed at his foolishness.

"You have been practicing, my lady."

With a cool smile, she stood over the young boy, blowing on the slingshot as if it were a pistol. "Looks like I just beat you at your own game, Sir Joseph. I guess I am now officially the best sling shooter in town, wouldn't you say?"

Joseph whipped out his own slingshot before she had time to reload and shot her point blank. She fell down dead.

"There," Morgan said triumphantly, dropping the quill into the inkwell. "The books are in order and I'm ready to learn falconry."

Derek stopped writing in his journal and peered over at her with one brow raised in question. "How could that be? You have been at those ledgers for less than a sennight."

"Too bad your steward ran off," she said. "I would say he was worth his weight in gold. He kept a thorough account of your lands, listing in time-consuming detail the revenues, acreage and produce, etc., on each of your manors. There is only one thing that seems odd."

"And what is that?" Derek asked, coming to stand behind her. He could smell her familiar rosewater scent. He inhaled deeply, relishing in her nearness...and surprisingly her intelligence. Each day he grew more needy, searching for ways to keep her by his side. And each day he feared more than the one before, that he would wake up and she would be gone.

"Right here," she said, pointing to the ledger. "Every few days the number of pigs, chickens and rabbits used here at Braddock changes. That wouldn't seem odd if the numbers weren't so erratic. According to these notes...even when your men are gone the number of livestock used at Braddock increases. Everything else remains relatively the same from week to week. It's very strange."

"Are you saying someone is pilfering my food supply?"

"It looks that way. It also makes me wonder about this Steward of yours...you know, whether he ran off or not."

Derek raised a brow.

"What if he didn't really run away?" Her eyes narrowed suspiciously. "What if he just knew too much?"

Derek circled his fingers about her slender neck and kneaded her soft flesh. He swallowed dryly as the serenity of the moment brought images of a mother he hardly remembered and a father he knew too well. Had his father ever felt this way about his mother...had he felt the same suffocating fear? Would every day spent with Lady Amanda bring a new bit of trust, producing a need so great that he would soon be vulnerable and weak, dependent upon her lingering kisses, her calming smile, and possibly even her friendship and advice? He closed his eyes, taking in a deep breath until her voice brought him back to the moment at hand.

"Derek, are you all right?"

"It is nothing," he said, shaking all forlorn musings from his mind. About this missing livestock," he went on as if there had been no pause in conversation, "Are you suggesting mayhem at Braddock?"

She wriggled in her seat and regarded him with open fondness as she took his hand in hers, setting his very blood aflame. "I don't know what I'm suggesting other than keeping a closer eye on the livestock."

"You do have quite an imagination."

"And right now I'm imagining you keeping your promise and showing me your hawks."

"And I am imagining you wearing that bit of cloth you call a bikini. 'Tis absurd to think the French allow their women to waltz around in such…nothingness."

"Terrible, I know," she said with a devilish smile. "I need to change my clothes before we go. Meet me in my bedroom?"

"Better yet," he said, stroking her cheek with the back of his hand, "I will meet you in your bed."

As soon as the door closed behind her, Derek sat before his writing table and became quickly immersed in mounds of unfinished business. He wrote more than a few letters, including one to Simon DeGald, arranging for promotion of one of the servants at a nearby manor.

He addressed another missive to the steward in charge of the manor of Chelshire, inquiring as to the marling of the fields there. As he tried to think of the word he was looking for, he envisioned fields of wheat, the same color as…

"Bloody Hell!" He plunked down his pen and headed for the door. He'd forgotten that Amanda awaited him, naked and wanting. Although it might take more than a few moments of coddling to make amends at being delayed, he was pleased to know he had actually gotten some work done.

As he made his way through the keep, he nearly tripped over two small boys as they rolled across the stone floor in front of him. They were both red in the face and furious with one another. Derek grabbed the bigger boy by the collar and held him up so that his feet hardly touched the ground. "What is this about?"

One of the maids came quickly to the boy's aid. Her face red and pleading as if she feared for the boy's very life. "I assure you, my lord, it was only children's play."

"He tried to take my wood carving!" the smaller lad said from his place on the floor.

Derek set the older boy back on solid ground, keeping him close to his side as he bent down on one knee. "Let me see that."

Warily the smaller boy handed him a piece of oak that had been well carved into a knight.

"Fine piece of work," Derek said proudly. "Did you make this yourself?"

"Aye," the boy said, his eyes beaming with pride.

"And what about you?" Derek asked the bigger lad. "Perhaps you should make friends with the boy in hopes that he will teach you to carve."

"I hath not an adequate knife, my lord."

Derek pointed a finger. "Wait here," he said. And when he returned a moment later, he handed the older boy a carving knife, its handle carved from a rare blackish wood and inlaid with crushed pearls.

Both boys gasped at the sight and the maid said, "Nay, my lord. 'Tis too fine a piece to lend the boy."

"It is the lads to keep," Derek stated firmly. "I used the knife to carve when I was a small lad. It would serve me well to know that the lad will make good use of it."

As he sauntered off he heard the boys arguing anew. This time over who would use his lordship's knife first. Matti interrupted Derek's chuckle as she hurried to catch up to him. "My lord," she said, touching at his arm as she walked with him. "That was a kindly thing you did just then."

"My actions were only a means in which to keep peace, since it appears the dozens of maids I employ cannot handle such a small task."

"Oh, I see," Matti said with a knowing twinkle in her eye. "You did not think I was implying that you were getting soft, did you? Maybe I will return to those boys and remind them that you have a heart of steel."

"It would be good of you to do so." He walked off, leaving her smiling to herself as if she'd seen something inside of him that did not exist. "Women," he muttered. "Always making something out of naught."

Derek entered Lady Amanda's chamber expecting to find her awaiting him in bed. Instead he found her maid straightening the room. "Where is Lady Amanda?"

Odelia jerked around. "I b-believe her ladyship is playing with the children, my lord. Shall I go in search of her?"

"Aye," Derek said, feeling mischievous and abnormally light-hearted. Why, he wondered, did everyone seem to tremble when he was near? Was he not one of the most generous lords around? Did he not feed his people well?

He sighed as Odelia left in search of Lady Amanda, then he paced the room as he waited. Lady Amanda's wooden chest had been left open. A tightly rolled parchment caught his eye, and he thought it peculiar that Amanda had not mentioned receiving a missive. He picked it up and eyed it curiously before untying the ribbon.

His jaw tightened unmercifully as he read the unfamiliar scrawl. No signature, no date. All of the earlier fears from this morn quickly rolled into a ball of fury within. To think she did not even have the courtesy to hide the damn note.

Every muscle grew taut as he envisioned Amanda these past days, talking to him, listening with feigned interest as she continuously dug for scraps of him that had long been buried.

Lies. She was like his mother. He shut his eyes and squeezed his head between his palms as he watched his mother run off in his mind's eye. She had abandoned her family...her responsibilities. *Why could he not forget?* The biting hatred of such memories always contrasted with the warmth of her motherly arms about him. But he could still hear the words she'd spoken only days before she left. *Do not fret, my sweet, sweet boy. I will never leave you.* Chills washed over him as her words turned to intense screams within his mind. He watched himself as a boy reach out small arms. To help her or to stop her, he was not certain. He could never remember anything past the screams. And whose piercing cries woke him most nights he knew not. He only knew that his mother had left him. He could still see the faint blackness of her mantle, like the wings of a hawk, as she ran from Braddock. She lied to him. She left him. And she never came back for him.

And now this...

He dropped his hands to his side and opened his eyes. The blood in his veins thickened at the thought that he had dared to trust his betrothed these past days. Not once had he questioned her with regard to the bikini incident or the noise she brought to his castle as she chased children through the hall with her ridiculous slingshot. He had dared to think she might be growing content; he had dared to let his guard down.

He should have known something was amiss when she gave up her talk of being from another world. The fact that she had runaway twice should have convinced him she had other plans. He had failed to believe his intuition, shouting for him to be wary. He had no real inkling of what she was up to, but whatever it was no longer mattered. She should have run away whilst she had the chance.

He tucked the note in his belt as his eyes blazed anew with a raging bitterness that refused to stay buried. She was his betrothed, and he refused to spend another moment guessing at her games. Before sundown, she would be his wife.

Odelia could not find her ladyship anywhere. At the same moment panic set in, a clod of dirt hit her square in the chest. Odelia tapped her foot to the ground and glared at Morgan as she came out of hiding. "Sorry, Odelia. I thought you were Joseph."

"Amanda," Odelia said indignantly. "His lordship wishes to see you."

"Derek?"

Odelia put her hands to hips. "Who else? 'Tis not proper for you to call his lordship by his given name...his people may take offense."

Morgan hissed. "He was supposed to meet me hours ago. I figured he was too busy, so I came here. Where is he?"

"In your bedchamber and appearing quite mysterious," Odelia said. She took the slingshot from Morgan and handed it over to Joseph, giving the boy a harsh glare, unwilling to forgive him for teaching her ladyship how to use the thing.

Before Morgan and Odelia reached the main hall, Shayna rushed toward them, red in the face and out of breath. "Your ladyship," she said, "you'll not believe what has happened."

"What?" Morgan and Odelia asked in unison.

"Lord Vanguard has declared that the wedding is to take place today!"

"What wedding?" Morgan asked.

"Why yours, my lady, who else?"

Morgan's heart rate spiraled. "Why today...why now?"

"No one knows...but all within the castle are running about like dogs after their tails. Matti said we must hurry and prepare you for the ceremony."

"This is crazy," Morgan said, her voice strained. Why would he plan such a thing without talking to her first? "There's no way I'm rushing into this before I get a chance to talk to him. Where is he?"

Shayna glanced worriedly at Odelia.

Morgan swept past both women. Everything had been going so well. The last few days had been peaceful, bordering on wonderful. At times Derek truly seemed to have let his guard down. Lately he seemed relaxed as if ribbons of emotions inside of him were slowly untangling.

She opened the door to her room, hoping to find Derek. But the room was empty. Shayna and Odelia followed her in. Before she could head back out in search of Derek, five more maids scurried in circles about her. They carried baskets filled with combs, towels, and ointments. Morgan gasped as an elderly woman stripped her naked in record time. Two other maids prepared a bath for her. They came at her from all angles, ignoring her complaints. Odelia's brown eyes widened with the same worry and confusion she felt.

"I will see what this is about," Odelia said as she hurried out the door. By the time Odelia returned, Morgan had been bathed and slathered with assorted sweet smelling herbs. She sat stiffly on a stool, wearing only a prickly towel. For the last hour she'd been going over in her mind what she would say to Derek when she saw him. But her patience had all but left her. When she got her hands on Derek Vanguard, she was going to rip him to shreds for setting her emotions into such a wild spin.

A short plump maid held assorted headdresses up to her face. The procession of women gave approving nods or disapproving frowns.

Odelia came to her side. "Lord Vanguard is no where to be found. I know not what this is all about."

Morgan's head dipped from side to side as a maid yanked at her tangled hair with a wide-toothed comb. Another maid scrubbed at her fingernails. "Are you sure no one knows where he is?"

"Aye, I am certain. But Hugo promised to send his lordship above stairs as soon as he is located."

Morgan sighed, unwilling to get these women into trouble by refusing their services. When they finished with their primping and prodding, Shayna held up a mirror.

Morgan looked at her reflection. It had been weeks since she'd gazed into a mirror and it suddenly occurred to her that she'd sort of buried the fact that she was Morgan Hayes. Morgan Hayes from the future appeared to her now as a lost child in a woman's shell, like a caterpillar in a caccoon. Wanting to get out, but not sure how to go about it. Waiting for things to happen instead of making them happen. This new Morgan Hayes, the one staring back at her, had in a sense been set free. She was tired of worrying about why her biological parents left her. She was through worrying about things she had no control over, things she couldn't change. She was ready to experience life and all it had to offer.

As she looked at the people around her she felt that same keen sense of belonging that she'd felt the first day she'd come to Braddock. Her eyes watered. She was ready to let go of expectations and fears. More than anything in the world she wanted to call her mother, tell her not to worry. Tell her she was okay and most of all to tell her thank you.

The maids mistook her tears as a sign of her happiness to be marrying Lord Vanguard. And she hated to correct them in that regard, but she knew she must. Her hair looked elegant in an elaborately braided coif entwined with thin silky ribbons. She wore a silk, antique-white gown with gold embroidery. The dress clung to her hips, flowing to the ground in close folds. The sleeves were tight to just below the elbows where they abruptly expanded into small puffs of material until they reached her wrists.

"I don't know how to thank you all for everything you've done," she said, "but I hope you understand when I tell you I can't possibly marry Lord Vanguard."

Odelia's shoulders sagged.

"What ever do you mean?" Shayna asked.

Morgan wanted to tell them everything...who she was, where she came from, how she might disappear at any moment. Instead she said, "He doesn't love me."

Matti stepped forward. "Oh, but he does. 'Twill take some time, though, before he can say the words."

"Aye," the bloodletter said, "sometimes these hardened warriors need to have the words sucked right out of them!"

Shayna laughed and Morgan forced a half-smile.

"You don't understand."

They all looked at her…waiting, hoping she could indeed make them see the light.

"Nobody could possibly understand," Morgan said sadly as she turned and headed out the door.

Two guards resembling Doberman pinschers minus the iron-studded collars, awaited her in the hallway. They took a firm hold of her arms, one on each side of her, and led her through the narrow hallway so that she was sandwiched between the two giants as they pulled her along.

Horrified, the group of women followed close behind as she was ushered down the stairs, through the keep, and to the outer bailey where a crowd of people had gathered, including a priest.

Derek had truly planned a wedding. Morgan looked about, wondering where he was now. With a small jerk of her head, she motioned for Odelia to come closer.

"Aye, my lady?"

"Didn't you say that Derek was in a pleasant mood this morning when you saw him?"

Odelia nodded. "He appeared quite amiable when he entered your bedchamber."

"Is this pre-wedding stuff normal? You know…is it common practice to have a small trial wedding before the actual event?"

"Nay, my lady. Never have I heard of such a thing."

None of this made any sense. She looked up, as much relieved as she was angry to finally see Derek coming toward her. He wore tight fawn-colored breeches that were snug against his powerful legs. His white linen shirt hung loose near his collar, revealing curly dark hairs at the V. He wore elaborate boots and gloves, and a short leather mantle that hung like a small cape. She also noticed a slight instability in his walk.

"You look charming," he drawled in an icy, uneven tone.

"I thought we were getting along so well. I thought you could talk to me. What happened?"

He wore a sinister expression along with a silvery glint in his eyes that matched the polished sword at his side. Loose strands of crisp black hair hung about his brow. His eyes reflected off the blackness of his cape and if she wasn't angry with him, she might have felt proud to marry him. She might have gone as far as feeling sorry for Lady Amanda for giving him up.

Ignoring her question, he leaned close, giving her a good whiff of ale. "You're drunk," she said. "I won't marry you like this."

"How about like this?" His lips touched her cheek, sliding over her jaw as he staggered backwards.

She rolled her eyes. "If you needed to get drunk in order to marry me, why the big rush?"

It took him two attempts to get both of his hands firmly attached to his hips. "For some reason, my fairest bride," he explained, "I had a fleeting thought these past days that perhaps me," he pointed to his chest, nearly missing, "and you," his finger brushed and lingered, along with his gaze, upon her chest, "were meant to be."

"I waited in bed for you for over an hour today," she said in a heated whisper. "After you didn't show I went to the gardens. The next thing I know, a dozen maids are in my room, stripping hair from my legs and slathering me with oils."

"'Twould seem I missed out on the fun," he said with a childish pout.

She plunked her hands on her hips. "That's it? That's all you have to say?"

He let out a hearty laugh and swept his arms in a wide, exaggerated arc as he said in a boisterous voice, "Fate! The inevitable. That which is willed by God himself. Call it what you may, but since laying eyes upon thou…I find myself thinking only of you. You, my love, cause my heart to sing like any nightingale." He swayed, widening his stance in order to stay balanced. "Can you imagine that, my sweet?"

Of course she could imagine that since she'd memorized the note word for word. She, too, believed that destiny played a part in all of this. The pain in Derek's voice was clear, but none of this made any sense. She laid a gentle hand on his arm. "What is this all about?"

Ignoring her further, he continued his slurred speech. Morgan raised her eyes in frustration as he rambled on again in a loud, insulting voice. "I have been engaged in many wars, but never one such as this between my body and mind. A war between my keen sense and that which I see with my own two eyes. It was not until I found this note from your lover," he said, pulling the missive from his belt, "that I finally saw what I had refused to see before and felt suddenly impelled to swallow the spirits."

Morgan drew a hand to her mouth, straining her neck to look up at him, sure, that at this moment, he measured seven feet in height. "I thought the note was from you."

Derek leaned low. "Is that so, my sweet?" He nuzzled her neck, tickling her in the process.

"You're embarrassing me." She pushed him away. "The only lover I have is you. Why can't you get that through your thick skull?"

Derek wrapped a strong arm around her waist, turning her about so they faced the minister. The priest stood not much taller than herself and was of the same meager width as the trunk of the tree behind him.

Derek motioned for the priest to start the proceedings. The crowd continued to grow. Morgan recognized some familiar faces from the village. The minister began to talk about the sacred bonds of marriage, but mostly seemed to reiterate the endless duties of a new wife.

168

Morgan wrung her hands. Maybe she could pretend to faint...anything but stand here. She couldn't marry him like this. It was all wrong.

"If there is anyone present who has reason to believe this lady and this man should not be wed, speak now or forever hold your peace."

Morgan opened her mouth, ready to protest, emitting a loud shriek instead as a man swung from a thick, knotted rope, landing with a loud thud and a cloud of dust before her.

Gasps and shouts escaped the crowd. The priest's face was ashen. The big hulk of a man smiled pleasantly as if he were like any other messenger making a delivery. He held out a note for her to read.

Hesitantly, Morgan took it. She could feel Derek's shoulder leaning into her, his warm breath on her cheek as he read along with her.

*Amanda, my love,*
*I implore you not to go through with this farce.*
*Go with this messenger, for he will bring you to me.*
*Where I will be waiting with bated breath.*
*All my love, Robert*

The handwriting was different from the other note she'd received, but for some reason she felt certain that this note wasn't from Robert DeChaville. If Robert thought his beloved Amanda was about to marry Lord Vanguard he would have swung down from that tree himself. But if it wasn't Robert, who was it?

The big guy stood his ground, showing no sign of impatience or fear as he waited for her to make up her mind.

She looked at Derek, not for help, but because she didn't know what else to do.

"God's teeth and hell," Derek said through gritted teeth. And he stepped around her and brought a hard right fist into the man's jaw.

One swift sock was all it took. The giant fell to the ground like a cleanly sawed tree. Stunned, Morgan watched as the same two Dobermans who had brought her here, dragged the man off.

Calmly, Derek took his place beside her again and ordered the minister to proceed. Morgan swallowed. Everything was happening too fast. She thought of her mother then and of all the plans she had for her daughter's wedding day. Thank God her mother wasn't here now.

Derek ground out his marriage vows as if he had a gun to his back, ending his promise to love and cherish her with a grunt.

It was Morgan's turn and everybody looked her way. Watching and waiting. Her throat was parched, her voice strained. "I, Morgan Hayes—"

Odelia jabbed her in the side with a finger.

"I mean, Amanda Forrester, promise…or is it vow?"

"Promise, vow, it makes no difference as long as you do not break it," Derek muttered.

"Well then," she said, throwing up her hands in frustration, "I promise to put up with this man as long as humanly possible."

Either he didn't hear her or he didn't care what she'd said. He just grabbed hold of her hand and pulled her along, past the small orchard and through the inner bailey as the crowd shouted their approval from a distance.

They were through the castle in no time. Ignoring her complaints, he took the stairs two steps at a time until she was nearly out of breath. As soon as they reached his private chambers, he picked her up and tossed her on the bed.

Morgan jerked upright, then pushed strands of hair out of her face. Her mouth dropped open and she watched with some amusement as he hurriedly and awkwardly stripped himself of his clothes. When he was done, he moved toward her without a word spoken, covering her fully clothed body with his naked one.

She felt the hotness of his broad chest right through the thin muslin of her gown. He kissed any unspoken words from her lips before tracing a scorching path downward over her neck until he reached her shoulder.

"We need to talk," she said. "You can't just marry me and then drag me to your bed...it's not right and I'm mad at you."

He lifted his head, his lips grazing her temple. "What is done, is done." His mouth marked a warm trail across her neck. "You said 'I do' and now you must do."

"Do what?"

"Whatever I say."

She sighed. "We need to talk about all of this. There are things we should know about one another, especially now that we're married."

A long ponderous breath escaped him. He raised himself from the bed and went to the washstand where he splashed his face and chest with cool water. "Speak now, for these words will be your last tonight." He moved toward her again and his hard, naked thigh brushed against her knee at the edge of the bed. She tried not to stare as she collected her thoughts.

"Once again it is clear by the way you gawk at me," he said, "that you have intentions other than rambling on like a parrot."

The man's ego was the size of Mount Everest. There he stood, stark naked and immodest, wearing only an apathetic, slightly tipsy, self-possessed farce of a smile on his mouth. "How can I possibly not look when you flaunt yourself like a dog in heat every time we are alone?" she asked. "I would have to be blind not to notice."

Derek chuckled. "I, too, would need be blind not to look at you," he said truly grinning this time, letting his gaze drift slowly over her. "Have I not yet told you how beautiful you are?"

His compliment threw her for a loop. It was interminably quiet as she tried to remember what she had been about to say.

"You are my wife now," he added impatiently as if it suddenly occurred to him that he was sounding soft. "It is done. Whatever you had originally planned is no longer of any consequence, for you are legally bound to me. So what is it you wish to speak of? The note? I have no care as to whom the missive is from. You are mine now."

Morgan groaned. "You don't understand. This isn't about the note, although I really did think it was from you."

"Then pray tell, what is troubling you?"

"I'm not who you think I am."

He bent his head back slightly and closed his eyes. After a moment he opened them and peered into her eyes as if he hoped to stop her from saying more. "Who are you then?"

She was Morgan Hayes, raised by a wonderful compassionate woman, a woman who had lost her family and who had needed Morgan almost as much as Morgan needed her. But Morgan was also a woman thrown into another time and into the arms of a deeply tormented man who needed her, too, but who just didn't realize it yet. She loved him, that much was clear. And she hoped with all of her heart that he could someday love her back. Gazing into dark, beleaguered eyes, she prayed he would listen with his heart. "I know who I am not," she finally said.

She took hold of his arm and brushed her thumb against his warm skin. "You could help me find her. What harm could it do? Lady Amanda is out there somewhere," she said, gesturing toward the window, noting the familiar twitch beneath the hard muscle of his jaw. "I have no reason to lie to you. Open yourself to the possibility. If I'm truly your wife, then there shouldn't be any lies between us."

His brow creased and when he spoke an edge of impatience and resentment crept into his voice. "I have often wondered when you would continue this game of yours. So 'tis to be now, is it? Too bad you find yourself so discontent here at Braddock that you must resort to little games and dangerous pranks. Unfortunately, I like having you nearby. I quite enjoy your lustful play between the sheets. For the time being anyhow," he added mockingly.

He bent over her, slid his hands over her silk covered breasts as he brushed kisses across her cheeks, her neck, and her shoulders.

She fell back under his weight, refusing to respond to his sensuous kisses or the heat of his body as he glided gently over her like a boa constrictor. His words hit her like a thump to the head. He wanted her for one thing—a plaything for his bed. He never listened to a word she said. He'd done nothing but humiliate her since her arrival at Braddock. How she'd managed to attain feelings for a cocky, arrogant swine was beyond comprehension. But she had, and that was a horrifying problem, because even now her body begged for his attention.

A whisper to the ear, a look, a touch was all it took for him to excite her. He nibbled on her ear, but she refused to respond. Instead she lay like a corpse ready to be buried.

He lifted his head. "So, this is how it will be?" he questioned, his tone smooth yet biting. "You are my wife now and you will respond appropriately to your husband whenever he sees fit for you to do so."

Her eyes burned and she squirmed beneath his body, but it was useless. "I've tried to understand you. But you won't open up to me. You'll know the truth someday, Derek. I only hope it's not too late when you do."

He looked suddenly distant and sad. There was no reaching him. "You know what your problem is? I think you like me." She stared into his black eyes. "I think you like me a lot and it's killing you because you don't know what to do about it. You think women are callous, selfish people undeserving of respect, but you're wrong. You aren't the only one who was abandoned by his parents. I, too, was left behind…a sick baby left on a stranger's doorstep. But I was lucky enough to have been found by a lonely woman, a woman who found it in her heart to love me. Growing up, I never felt as if I belonged, but I always felt loved…because I allowed myself to be loved." She kept her gaze on his. "Matti and Hugo love you as if you were their very own. All of the people here at Braddock love you."

She saw him flinch and added, "All of that bitterness inside of you prevents you from seeing the truth."

"Touching," he said without passion.

She shook her head sadly. "Once I find the Earl of Kensington you'll see. Until then, go ahead and lock me in the dungeon for denying you, because I'd rather be stuck with the rats than be pinned beneath a heartless warrior such as you."

"Too bad," he said mockingly, "for tonight I hoped to plant you with seed so that you might give me a son. Have no fear, my sweet, for I will quickly teach you to be a respectable wife. It will not take long, I swear."

Morgan's heart wilted as she stared straight ahead, past his taunting face, focusing in on a cobweb that dangled and swayed from the beamed ceiling. He kissed her cheek and softly touched her soft skin. "Your body deceives you," he said huskily.

Her spine tingled and her fingers grasped quietly at the blankets beneath her. She spotted the maker of the web and felt only pity for the insect as it guarded the wrapped and wriggling prey beneath its spindly legs.

Derek felt her attempt to resist him. He had intended to have her whether she chose to participate or not, but now he thought otherwise. Without her warm arms around him, 'twas not enough. Shame and sorrow filled him. "So this is the game you intend to play although 'tis plain to see that you want me as much as I want you?"

She didn't move, hardly breathed.

"When you change your mind," he said as one finger grazed lightly over her collarbone. "When your body can no longer resist that which it craves, I will be waiting for you."

His fingers trailed upward along the column of her neck and to her lips before he pushed himself off of the bed and walked to the tub that had been readied near the hearth. He climbed into the cool water and began washing.

The hinges on the door creaked, alerting him to her attempt to depart. "Come here," he demanded.

"No," she said firmly. "Until you sober up and are ready to listen to what I have to say, I'll be in my room."

"One of the first duties a wife must learn," he went on, "is the washing of her husband." He held out a small linen cloth and a silver jar of soap.

Her eyes narrowed and her lip curled. She opened her mouth to speak, but for the first time since he'd met her, thought better of it. She left the room, not bothering to give him another glance.

Derek's stomach roiled. And his head felt foggy from all the ale he'd imbibed; so foggy it made it difficult to remember all he had said to make her so furious. But he did recall her ridiculous words of wisdom, words coming from one discarded child to another. His jaw twitched. Amanda Forrester, the most coddled daughter in all of England abandoned by her parents. Ha! The woman surely thought all men daft.

How, he wondered, did the wench keep all her lies in order?

# CHAPTER TWELVE

Outside Braddock's high walls, morning blossomed with an abundance of new life, suggesting spring was well underway. The trees were full and green and the sparrows that waited for their eggs to hatch swept down on intruders that came too close to their nests.

Inside the great hall, Matti watched his lordship walk her way. She pretended not to notice his impatient scowl. "Good morning, my lord. I was hoping to have a word with you. Just a quick chat."

"What is it now, Matti?"

"I was wondering if you could take Lady Amanda her tray."

Derek raised a brow. "I have no time for such nonsense. Acquire the help of one of the maids if you must. Where is her ladyship's chambermaid?"

"I know not, my lord. But if I am not too bold in asking, why did you bother wedding her ladyship yester eve if you cannot find time for her? And what, my lord, did you do to upset her?"

"What are you babbling on about, Matti?"

"When I took Lady Amanda some hot cider last night, she looked unusually pale and her eyes were swollen from crying."

"Bah," he muttered. "The woman does not cry. And as for why I wed her…'twas a bad case of too much ale and bitter wine. But it is done and I have no wish to talk of it further."

"But there is something else."

Derek exhaled heavily.

"That note you came across in Lady Amanda's trunk was found by one of the scullery maids the very morning you left with your men to aid the king."

Derek crossed his arms and drummed his fingers against his forearm.

"Lady Amanda thought the note was from you and was in high spirits for days because of it."

"What are you saying Matti?"

"I only thought you should know that Lady Amanda cares deeply for you. She was miserable when you were gone, and if you only gave her a chance." Matti's expression became perplexed. "That note bothers me, my lord, for if the missive was not from you, then who penned it and how did it come to be in the castle?"

"Of that I am not certain, but I plan to find out. Do not burden yourself with such matters."

"I promise not to...provided you take this tray to her ladyship for me." With that said, she plunked the tray into his arms and walked away.

Derek shook his head as he watched Matti disappear.

He would not apologize to Amanda, he thought as he made his way to his wife's bedchamber. He would hand her the tray and make a hasty exit. And then he would have a talk with Hugo about Matti, tell him that his wife's meddling was getting out of hand.

With a scowl on his face and a tray in his hand, he entered her room.

Morgan heard the door open. Thinking it was Odelia, she sat up, stretched her arms wide and said, "Good morning."

Derek grunted.

Her eyes opened fully then. It was him all right, the same arrogant sap who'd managed to keep her tossing and turning most of the night. She crossed her arms tightly against her chest. "What do you want?"

His cool expression changed to one of mock pain. "Surely you will not deny me the privilege of serving my wife a meal in bed?"

She eyed him suspiciously as he brought forward a serving tray filled with silver bowls of fresh fruit and a plate of warm apple tarts. There was a silver goblet of apple cider and a red rose.

"If you think this will make up for yesterday..."

"I only wish to make my wife more agreeable. Is that so terrible?" He set the tray beside her on the bed and popped a chunk of fresh green apple into his mouth.

"Ha, you think I'll fall for that?" Morgan admonished. "I know what you want. You made it all very clear last night. I'm sure there are many women who would be more than willing to help you out. Maybe you could order a porcupine or concubine...or whatever you call those women who assist men like you in bearing them strong healthy sons."

"I am sure you are right," he agreed. He raised one foot so that it rested on the wooden frame of the bed, then shook his head. "But I am afraid it would not do. Only you do I wish to be the mother of my children."

She opened her mouth to protest further, but he inserted a fresh strawberry into her mouth. She had no choice but to chew. "That was a dirty trick," she said after swallowing.

"The strawberry?"

"All of it," she said, talking with her hands. "Forcing me to marry you, coercing me into your bed...and the strawberry," she added.

"I did not mean to raise your ire so." His brows slanted as he added, "And I do not recall having to coerce you into bed."

She blushed.

The hard features of his face softened. Then he seemed to struggle with whatever it was that was on his mind. "I may have said some things last night that perhaps I did not mean to say."

He stood straight and then shifted his weight from one foot to the other.

"Are you apologizing?"

"Nay," he said matter-of-factly. "I do not find it necessary to apologize." His brow creased. "But you must cease this talk of being from another world and of being someone else altogether."

She opened her mouth to protest but he put up a hand to stop her. "And another thing. We will have daughters instead of sons. 'Twill please you to have daughters?"

Morgan grunted. His offer to have daughters instead of sons was his way of apologizing for last night. Silly, and yet also sweet because he looked so serious. And she had already decided she wouldn't bring up her being from another time again. Unless she found Amanda or the Earl of Kensington, it was useless trying to convince anyone of her situation.

As she peered up at him, she noticed something different about him this morning. Not just in his mood, but in his eyes. It was as if a layer of anger and bitterness had been peeled away.

"What?" he asked, looking at her with wide, somewhat innocent eyes.

"You can't do this," she said softly. "You can't say such cruel things to me one day, then come to me with breakfast and a flower the next..." She took the rose and breathed in the sweet aroma. "...expecting all to be wonderful between us."

"Hmmm," is all he had to say about that. "Get dressed."

She frowned.

"Please," he added before turning toward the door. "I will wait for you in the gardens."

"What about all the work you have piling up?"

"'Twould seem it has waited this long without dire consequence. Besides," he said, turning back once more, "it seems I have a new steward to keep my accounts. She is as clever as a fox."

"You mean me?" she asked, pointing to her chest.

His gaze shot toward the ceiling as he shook his head in playful annoyance. Then he left her alone to wonder what he was up to. The man was impossible to figure out. One minute he was kind and the next he was the devil himself.

"Lord Vanguard has been watching you," Ciara whispered to the new maid, Helena.

Helena put a hand to her chest. "I thought his lordship was newly married."

Ciara scoffed at that. "The ceremony was performed only to stop her ladyship from running away again. His lordship would not bother with Lady Amanda were it not for the king's alliance."

"If Lord Vanguard resembles the courtly image of the troubadours, then why does Lady Amanda run from him at all?"

"Because she is foolish and has many lovers. She has no sense and will do anything to cause Lord Vanguard hardship." Ciara frowned, disliking the trickery she had become involved in. Truthfully she had unexpectedly grown fond of Lady Amanda. But she had no choice but to do as she was told. Leonie had threatened her family. Ciara would do anything before she'd allow harm to come to her younger siblings. She was all they had left. She had already been stealing livestock to keep food in their stomachs. She was in too deep to turn back now.

"See how gentle his lordship is?" Ciara asked the new maid. "How many lords do you know of who play with children that are not even of their own blood?"

As Helena watched Lord Vanguard, Ciara noticed Helena's petite frame. The girl had darkened skin from so many hours spent in the fields. Her clothes were fairly worn. Verily she wondered why Leonie thought this woman could catch his lordship's eye at all. Lady Amanda was the only woman who had been capable of such a thing. And no matter what Leonie told her, Ciara felt certain that Lord Vanguard had already fallen in love with his wife. Everybody at Braddock thought so.

Ciara observed the new maid with curiosity. Her hair could use a bit of attention, she thought, but the woman did have a fair enough smile, making her eyes sparkle. Although 'twas difficult to tell since she wore a ragged tunic, Helena also had a shapely form which surely made men look twice. And how could any woman not take notice of such a handsome lord? A fine looking man such as Lord Vanguard with his thick black hair the shade of midnight and the charming indentation upon his chin.

Ciara sighed, drawing strength from the thought of her siblings to do what she must. "I realize you came to Braddock for Matti's training," Ciara said to Helena, "and 'tis certainly a privilege and an honor that you have been given the chance to do so. But to be Lord Vanguard's mistress could be compared to discovering a king's treasure."

"How do you know he is interested in me?" Helena asked.

Ciara twirled a lock of auburn hair about her finger. "I had the honor of taking his lordship's meal to him...'twas the day you arrived. I overheard his endless praise of you to his man-at-arms. I thought you would be pleased to know."

Helena's bountiful chest heaved with each breath against the woolen garment she had long outgrown. She gave Ciara a devilish smile before making her way toward the children and their lord.


"Lady Amanda...are you in there?"

"Come in," Morgan said, her voice lined with frustration as she tried to fasten another hard to reach lace. "Could you help me with this?"

Ciara readily obliged.

"Thanks. I don't think I'll ever get used to these strange clothes."

"Did you not wear these garments at Silverwood?"

Morgan winced. "I did. I've just never been good with tying laces is what I meant to say."

"I see," Ciara said as she finished with the last of the hard to reach ties.

"Thanks. Now what can I do for you?" Morgan asked as she shuffled through Amanda's trunk, looking for the slippers to match the royal blue gown she had on.

Ciara stepped closer. "I thought you should know that Lord Vanguard is in the gardens."

"I know," Morgan whispered back, wondering why they were talking in hushed voices, "he asked me to meet him there."

"He is with another woman, my lady."

"What?"

Ciara nodded.

Morgan stared at Ciara for a moment, dumbfounded, knowing there had to be a reasonable explanation. She slipped on the ivory slippers nearest her and left the room. Within minutes she was making a path through the many cooks in the kitchen. They waved and nodded, wondering what their ladyship was up to now as she rushed past without a word. Usually they burnt whole meals trying to cook and listen to her stories when she visited.

Morgan swept through the side door and up the winding path. She spotted Joseph immediately. He held his slingshot in one hand and his belly in the other as he laughed whole-heartedly, watching as his lordship brought the new maid, Helena, to the soft ground in one swoop.

"Joseph, what's going on?" she asked, unable to make sense of what she was seeing.

"N-nothing, my lady. A new maid-in-training only just joined in on our game of tag."

"Give me your slingshot, Joseph."

Joseph smiled mischievously and handed it over. He also handed her his ammunition of softly mounded dirt.

"This won't do," she said with a determined glint in her eye.

Joseph's eyes sparkled and his smile grew even wider. "Maybe these will do well?" he asked, showing her his prized projectiles, a large collection of acorns.

"Not good enough I'm afraid." She looked to the ground and grabbed a small, but perfectly round stone that lay on the edge of the path.

Joseph's eyes bulged as he watched her ladyship ready the slingshot with a stone. "Surely, you will be thrown in the dungeon for this, my lady."

Morgan realized he was right and replaced the stone with the biggest acorn in the pile.

Derek turned in her direction just as she let the acorn fly.

Joseph's mouth fell open when the acorn hit her target. Derek frowned as he touched the small lump forming above his brow. Then he took massive strides in their direction.

Without looking away from him, Morgan handed the slingshot back to Joseph. "Thank you, kind sir, for the use of your fine weapon."

"You're w-welcome," Joseph managed before running off as fast as his small legs could carry him.

"Saint John and horse flies woman! What do you think you are up to now?"

Morgan stood firm, plunking her hands to her hips. "How dare you question me when you're the one who invited me here just so I could see you flirt with another woman."

Derek threw his arms upward. "I have no idea what you are talking about." He turned to where she gestured and noticed for the first time since coming to the gardens that the child he had just tackled was indeed a full-grown woman; a woman with great mountains of breasts firmly pressed against her tunic he noticed as she came to her feet. She met his gaze and shot him a radiant grin.

Derek stood momentarily speechless. "Once again it seems you are correct." He chuckled to himself. "A man would have to be blind not to notice a wench such as that," he said, turning toward Amanda only to watch her disappear back the way she came.

What a saucy wench his wife could be.

His head cleared as he gazed about. For the second time he found himself in the gardens. Trying to please a damn woman, no less, an impossible task that should be saved for passing troubadours and romantic minstrels. He raked his hands through his hair. She already expected him to beg forgiveness for their wedding day, and now this! The idea of it was absurd. He would not allow himself to be led around by a chain, and certainly not by an acorn hurling, blathering she-devil.

"The man is unbearable," Morgan said an hour later as she packed a tin of soap, a comb and brush, and as many dresses as she could fit into the small trunk that Odelia had emptied.

Odelia kept her tongue as she helped sort her things.

"Do you know what he said last night on our wedding night?" Morgan asked. "He said he would teach me my wifely duties!" Her voice filled with indignation. "How do you like that? He said I would bear him sons, making it perfectly clear that I had only one use as his wife."

"Surely, it was only the ale talking," Odelia said in Derek's defense. "Did he not bring you a lovely meal to break your fast this very morn?"

Morgan shook her finger at Odelia. "Big deal. I've heard about men like him. They do one little thing like unload the dishwasher or put away their socks and we're supposed to be overwhelmed with joy, down on our knees and kissing their feet!"

"You speak nonsense," Odelia said with a chuckle before looking suddenly perplexed. "What is this dishwasher you speak of?"

"A dishwasher washes the dishes, of course," Morgan answered, exasperated.

Odelia sighed and began repacking her things to make them all fit.

Morgan gazed out the window. Down below, two young boys ran into the training field and mounted good-sized horses. They began to practice fighting with blunted swords and shiny lances. She winced as one boy rode toward a stuffed quintain, hitting his target at full speed. He fell off his horse, landing on his backside, coughing up dirt as it settled on top of him. Derek came into view, laughing heartily. Morgan stayed hidden behind the curtain. She watched him help the boy to his feet, brush the dirt off his small tunic, and then kneel so that he and the boy were at eye level as he talked to him. Man to boy. She smiled at the picture they made. Even though she couldn't hear what they were saying, she saw trust in the boy's eyes as Derek urged him to try again. According to Matti, Derek had not had a father to guide him when he was small. And yet instinct and his good heart allowed him to help others, to give freely of himself.

He'd spoken with such coldness on their wedding day and yet even then she could see clearly that he was fighting with his emotions. He was fighting demons she couldn't see, and that made it difficult to reason with the man at times.

"My lady, are things really so terrible that you must try so hard to displease his lordship? The man is merely trying to please you."

"Trying to please me? He forced me to marry him. And he had to drink a keg of beer to do it. Every time I turn around he is in another woman's arms. You call that trying to please me?"

"I think you embellish just a wee bit, but as I told you earlier, and as your little friend Joseph confirmed, his lordship thought the new maid was one of the children. Helena is quite small and she is new to Braddock. From behind she looks no bigger than Joseph."

Morgan gazed heavenward. "Don't tell me you believed Casanova's story?"

"Where do you come up with such names?" Odelia put a hand to the air. "Never mind—I do not want to know. But I dare hope you realize that Lord Vanguard went to the gardens for the sole purpose of pleasing you." She fastened the last strap on the trunk. "I need to get my own things together now so finish up and I will meet you below stairs."

After Odelia left, Morgan thought about what she'd done to Derek's head. She'd meant to hit his back and never would've used the largest acorn if she hadn't been so…so jealous. She shuddered at the thought. She wasn't a violent person. She'd never thrown anything in her life. Cringing, she realized she'd done exactly what Derek had done to her. She hadn't listened, hadn't given him the time to explain. She would make a point to apologize as soon as she saw him.

Her insides rumbled at the thought that before sundown she'd be at Windsor, socializing with royalty. Tonight she would meet the King of England. She'd read that King Henry VI was slightly insane. So what if he was a little off his rocker…she was going to meet him. How many people in the modern world could say that?

An hour later, she descended the stairs. Not an easy task considering she wore a long, silky black dress that she'd designed and Shayna had stitched. The dress was sleeveless with a backside that draped low. She lifted the hem to prevent herself from tripping.

Servants stopped their chattering to gawk at her. Emmon showed a rare tilt of the lips when he saw her. Hugo bowed and took hold of her elbow as she reached the landing, escorting her to where Derek leaned casually against the wall.

Her gaze landed on the knot on his forehead. Even with his eyes smoldering the way they were, she thought he looked breathtakingly handsome in his light-colored shirt stretched taut over powerful shoulders. Only a shadow of a beard covered his jaw and, dear God, she thought, this medieval man was her husband.

Derek straightened. "We are late." He seized her hand, pulling her along behind him as he made his way through the castle folk gathered around to wish them well.

She swallowed dryly and said to his back, "I'm sorry...I thought about what I did and I came to the conclusion that I was just a tiny bit jealous. It was stupid of me. But just so you know, I wasn't aiming for your head. You just happened to look over at the wrong time."

"So in a sense you are saying it was my fault—this knot on my head," he said without slowing.

"Well, when you put it that way, I guess maybe you could say we were both at fault."

Derek paused long enough to glance over his shoulder, stopping her with an aggravated gaze. No smile, no apology accepted.

"You don't have to be such a sorehead, you know." Realizing her unintended pun, she yanked her hand from his grasp and bent over in laughter.

Derek glared at her.

"*Sorehead*—get it?" Judging by the stern expression covering his face he didn't get it at all. She straightened, mumbled another apology of sorts, and followed behind as she tried to keep up with his lengthy strides.

# CHAPTER THIRTEEN

Derek rarely used the carriage, preferring to ride his horse alongside. But not tonight. He lifted himself up and sat beside his wife, taking in the fragrant smell of wildflowers and herbs. He stole a glance and feasted on her oval face and emerald green eyes rimmed with thick, sooty lashes. Golden streaks, newly bleached by the sun, swirled within her neatly pinned coif and her skin appeared flawless, softly hued with coral. God's teeth she was beautiful. He wondered if she was aware of how she tortured him with not only her beauty but her quick smile and laughing eyes. The back of her gown dipped low, revealing soft, alluring curves. Even the knot on his head failed to stop him from wanting her. He shook his head before leaning forward to give instructions to the driver.

Hugo helped Odelia and Matti to their seats on the bench behind them. Then he moved to the front to sit alongside the driver in order to help him avoid the larger ruts in the well-used roads.

The castle folk, with Emmon and Shayna in the foreground, waved and said their good-byes, bidding them a safe trip as the horses snorted and stamped their hooves in readiness. The driver jostled the reins and the carriage lurched forward.

Morgan waved goodbye. She waved to the cooks, the maids, the children, and to the two sentries at the gate.

Derek shook his head, staring straight ahead, but soon the corners of his mouth angled upward for her endless exuberance was contagious. She pointed and gasped at every windmill and manor, grabbing his hand or his arm at every turn, causing him to forget that he was angry with her.

Even a team of oxen pulling a man and his wagon caught her attention. Her excitement seemed sincere and he began to wonder if her parents ever let her out of Silverwood in her four and twenty years. He nodded when she pointed out yet another amazement in her eyes—a flock of sheep and endless rolling hills that to everyone else in the carriage was here nor there.

'Twas hours later when they approached the outskirts of Windsor, twenty miles west of London. The tillage lands appeared prosperous and the traffic increased tenfold. Although the sun was setting, there were people traveling the roads, selling their wares and working within the fields.

The horses possessed a gentle gait as they brought the carriage over smoother and wider roads until they reached the long path that led to the castle. The outer gates to Windsor were fitted with double swinging-doors of heavy oak, reinforced with iron.

Amanda held tight to his arm when she caught a glimpse of the huge towers. "What is it?" Derek asked.

"I shouldn't be here. I don't belong. And, I never should have worn this dress," she said firmly, gazing downward.

"You belong to me and thus have naught to worry about tonight. As for the dress, 'twill be the latest in fashion after the king's court gets an eyeful."

"I really am sorry about your head."

"'Tis what I get for trying to please a woman," he interrupted before leaning forward to speak to Hugo as they entered the gates. Out of the corner of his eye, he saw her wrinkle her nose at him, and he turned full around and pointed at her. "Do you think I do not see that?"

"See what?"

"Those ludicrous faces you make every time I turn around."

She sighed. "Only a child would do such a thing."

"Exactly the point I was getting to."

He stared at her a moment longer, waiting for her nose to wrinkle or her brow to crease. Then he gave up, returning his attentions back to Hugo and the driver.

After the carriage came to a halt, Odelia and the driver stayed behind to take care of their belongings.

Derek detested being late, so he hurried them along, leading them through throngs of well-dressed people and past impeccable gardens and great stone statues.

He knew Amanda was nervous and thus gave her hand a knowing squeeze. Briskly, they made their way past elaborately costumed guards who stood as straight as iron poles with jutting swords at their sides. As they stepped into the main entrance, her eyes widened at the sight of the red carpet sweeping before them in a long, narrow line. At the end of it sat the King of England on his throne.

Morgan tugged frantically at the hem of Derek's cloak. "Are we supposed to meet the king right now, this very moment?"

"It appears so. Take heed, for he is a kind and gentle man. He will not bite."

She gave him a lighthearted smile. "I just thought I'd have a chance to look around, warm up to the place. You know, get to know a few dukes and lords first. Maybe fix my hair," she added.

Derek continued to bring her forward, not bothering to glance back at her. "Your hair needs no adjusting, 'tis fine as it is."

All around them, heads turned and conversations dropped off as Derek Vanguard, Lord of Braddock Hall, passed by. Like the parting of the Red Sea, people divided, providing Lord Vanguard and his betrothed a path to the king. These people had no idea that they were already married.

As they came to the end of the crimson path, Morgan gave a semi-practiced curtsy and Derek went into a deep bow.

The king nodded Derek's way before letting his gaze fall upon her. "You are as beautiful as your father declared," King

Henry said, his voice soft and sweet like that of a young boy's. He waved a fragile white hand toward Derek. "Did I not tell you she would be a beauty? A treasure fit for a gallant knight such as yourself?" A mischievous grin crossed the king's face as he extended a pale hand Morgan's way.

"Aye, that you did," Derek said, nodding his agreement.

"So, my brave warrior, you hath no reason then to be disagreeable with me in the future, for your eyes fairly betray your fondness for the lady. I do believe she is not the shrew I believe you half expected." The king squeezed her hand in a playful manner before releasing her fingers altogether.

"My Lord and King," Derek said, "you have done well by me in this matter as you have in all matters concerning my welfare."

The king's lips curved upward before a frown suddenly creased his brow. He leaned forward to inspect Derek's injury. "I fair say that is a good size knot on your head."

Morgan directed her gaze to her feet when Derek glanced her way. "It seems my castle has been overrun with children and their slingshots of late," Derek said.

Thankfully, the king left the matter alone. While the two men chatted, Morgan couldn't help but stare at King Henry. He had the face of an adolescent and he looked much younger than his twenty-four years. His hair was cut short and his face appeared long and egg shaped. He had eyebrows as pale as his skin and lips that were small and pursed. Granted, he did look like a teenager, but he certainly didn't seem to be as crazy as the history books stated.

"Let us eat and make merry," the king said at last. "Our feast is spread before us. "We will speak privately of other matters before the morrow," he said to Derek.

Derek nodded in the affirmative and Morgan curtsied again before they headed back across the velvet-lined floor. "I just met the King of England," she murmured in disbelief as she walked briskly at Derek's side.

He glanced down at her with a lazy grin. Then in full view of hundreds of onlookers he leaned low so that his lips could fully meld with hers.

The kiss was fleeting, but long enough to garner a faint chorus of oohs and aahs. Contentment filled her as he straightened and led her through the hall, replete with barons, dukes, lords and ladies. Ardent torches spread a beacon of light throughout the castle and to the outdoors.

The sky was already black, the air warm, and a full moon shone with a marvelous luster. A pleasant scent of pine and lavender drifted from the nearby forest. Scores of bright waxen tapers stood upon the tables, illuminating the savory meats and excellent wines spread out for sampling. They ate, drank and danced beneath the moonlight.

Morgan's head reeled giddily from the effects of the wine. An orchestra of lutes together with the sweet smell of flowers and savory foods filled the air, adding to the excitement. She easily followed Derek's steps in a slow medieval waltz as she looked lovingly into his eyes, glimmering dark eyes that burned amber. Her heart pounded wildly, intoxicated by his nearness as she danced with him. Here, in the midst of royalty, she was alone with Lord Vanguard, her husband, and nothing else mattered.

After the dance was over, Derek filled their goblets with a sweet wine. Between sips, Morgan wondered again about the maid he'd rolled with in the gardens. She couldn't let it go without asking, "Is it true that you had no idea the child you tackled this morning was a grown woman?"

Derek's mood had softened. "I plead innocence with regard to the incident. She looked like a small child from behind, surely you could see that for yourself. Only when she turned around did I notice she had breasts the size of large melons."

Morgan poked him in the shoulder at his bluntness.

"Did you not see them for yourself?" he asked incredulously, unaware that he was digging himself deeper into a grave.

She raised a brow. The man was clueless after all. "According to Shayna, that child is almost seventeen, the perfect marrying age," Morgan informed him.

Derek brushed his fingers across her cheek. "Let us not speak of this now. Besides, it was only because of you that I ended up in the gardens and played with the unruly children to begin with."

"You make playing with the children sound like some sort of punishment."

He cocked his head. "'Tis not?"

She chuckled at his obvious teasing.

"King Henry seemed smitten by you," Derek said, changing the subject. "I would not be surprised if the king himself will be asking for your hand in marriage ere this night is over."

"Nice of you to say, but the king has someone else in mind altogether."

"And who might that be?" he asked. "Although I only ask out of morbid curiosity," he added, "for I know personally that King Henry has no interest in marriage."

"Well, if I remember correctly," she said, "King Henry will try to provide England with an ally against France by marrying one of two daughters of an important Count. After that deal falls through he will form an alliance by marrying Margaret of Anjou instead." She stroked her chin. "At least I think that's how it goes."

"You weave incredible stories, my lady. Will Henry and Margaret have heirs?"

"Well," she said, glad to have his attention. "They have trouble at first, but finally they do manage to produce a son who they name Edward." Morgan knew that Derek was fond of King Henry so she wasn't going to tell him the part about King Henry losing his wits at about the same time his son is born.

"Interesting," Derek acceded, "but I do believe it would be in your best interest to keep this information to yourself."

"Oh, don't worry, I will. I just want to get through this night without much ado."

Derek set down their cups and guided her back to the makeshift dance floor. He swung her around and let out a short husky laugh as he looked into her eyes.

"What's so amusing, my lord?"

"It seems, my sweet, that since meeting you, you have made all the jesters in England appear to be dull and tedious in comparison. Thus I was wondering what made you think this night would be any different?"

"Go ahead, laugh at me. See who will be begging for forgiveness later tonight."

"Unfortunately, it will not be me. The king is unaware of our marriage and I am afraid he would be put off if he knew. During our stay at Windsor we will be forced to endure separate quarters."

Morgan felt deflated by the news, since they'd already wasted the last few nights arguing about nothing. "Who will I sleep with then?" she teased.

"Not a bloody soul. In fact, you will most likely be busily employed with the interrogations of the king's ladies, who will be desirous of any news on the distinguished and gallant champion who is your betrothed. You could enlighten the ladies, describe to them how your eyes stick out from thy head whenever your lord is about. Or tell them how thy very breath is seized when he makes love to you."

The dance came to an end and Morgan nudged him playfully with an elbow. "Enough already. Maybe I will tell them that my betrothed is just another arrogant swine who thinks too highly of himself and they're the lucky ones to have avoided being trapped with such an arrogant lord."

Derek shrugged. "Tell the ladies what you like for 'tis only the truth that matters. And the truth shines almost as brightly as does your smile this night." He chuckled at the way her brows slanted in mock anger. He plucked her under the chin with a gloved finger.

Morgan sighed and leaned into him. He was right. The arrogant, pompous man was right. To think she even enjoyed his vainglorious, self-worshipping talk. He covered her with part of his mantle to shield her from a sudden breeze. Her insides swirled as he fastened his arm about her shoulder, filling her with a tingly warmth that she wished would last forever.

Some things never change, Morgan realized as she stood in a long line for a turn in the garderobe. She and Derek had danced for most of the night before he left her with a duke's wife and her daughter so that he could go in search of King Henry. It was late and her eyelids were growing heavy. Despite her exhausted state, she cocked her head when she overheard a group of ladies gossiping behind her.

"'Tis too much to fathom that poor man having to feign happiness when everyone knows he has no wish to marry."

"Aye," another lady agreed. "If you look into the depths of Lord Vanguard's eyes you will see naught but darkness, like endless black caves."

"'Tis his own mother's fault he has no soul," added another feminine voice. "Abandoning her child and leaving the poor lad in the hands of such an evil man as Simon Vanguard. Horribly unfair."

"Surely Lady Vanguard would have returned for the boy, though, had she not perished soon after leaving Braddock," another said.

"'Twas infection to the lungs that caused her death, was it not?"

Morgan stood still, tried to make sense of it all.

"The disease was Lady Vanguard's punishment," an elderly woman added spitefully.

"I disagree," the other woman said, "for I, too, would have run away if I had been beaten and abused so severely at every turn. Besides, I heard she came back for the boy, but Simon refused her even a glimpse of her own son."

Morgan heard murmurs of agreement at that last statement. Her breath caught in her throat. Wishing to hear more about Derek's mother she was disappointed when her turn came to use the facilities she'd been waiting for. If the women's words held any truth, then maybe Derek's mother didn't abandon him after all; maybe she'd had no choice in the matter like the woman had said.

Within the privacy of the garderobe, Morgan closed her eyes and took a deep breath. Not a good idea considering her proximity. She had to choose between cornhusks or stiff parchment to use as toilet paper, just one more household item she'd come to take for granted. Apparently she'd taken too long since the wooden door nearly came unhinged from all the pushing outside of it.

She opened the door, squeezed past the gossiping ladies with head down, then hurried back to the main hall. She spotted Derek immediately, involved in a group discussion between various men and ladies. One particular lady at his side caught her full attention. Even through the maze of tall hats and lacy attire, she recognized Leonie. Her shimmering ebony hair beneath an elaborate headpiece and her voluptuous curves gave her away. What was she doing here?

The light from the many candles adorning the wall reflected off Leonie's face, hinting at a porcelain complexion. The woman was perfection. Morgan's stomach gurgled as though she'd swallowed a pint of oil. Then a firm hand slid about her bare shoulder and a gentle kiss was placed on her cheek.

"Amanda, my sweet angel," a masculine voice crooned. "I have missed you so."

Morgan recognized Robert's voice at once. She turned swiftly about. "Robin Hood! What are you doing here?"

He grinned from ear to ear. "You look enchanting this evening. Certainly none-the-worse for having been lodged with that swarthy Vanguard."

"You shouldn't be here." Concerned for Robert's safety, she glanced about, remembering suddenly the question she'd meant to ask him the last time they'd met. "I do have one question though. Where were you supposed to meet Amanda after she ran from Vanguard's men in the forest?"

His brows furrowed in consideration as he brought her fingers to his lips. "Wilmead Farm is where we were to meet. I remember it was your idea to go there, in fact."

Morgan gently pulled her hand from his grasp. "Go to Wilmead Farm, then. If I'm wrong, you can continue to harass me."

His expression showed puzzlement.

"If you go to Wilmead Farm," she said, "and find that Amanda isn't there, you can keep trying to convince me that I am her. I might even believe you. But not until you go there and see for yourself that I've been telling you the truth all along."

She glanced across the crowded room. With his broad shoulders and ebony hair, Derek easily stood out among the multitude of guests. Having him nearby made her feel safe...and happy. Her initial surprise at seeing Leonie dimmed, for she refused to make the same mistake twice. She would talk to Derek and see what was going on.

Robert followed her gaze, then turned back to her, trying to see her face clearly in the softly lighted room. "Since when have your beautiful ocean-blue eyes turned to emeralds?"

"What?" she asked.

"Your eyes. The scoundrel has dared to change the color of your beautiful blue eyes!"

Morgan shook her head at the absurdity of his statement. "If you would just do as I ask," she said, "you'll see that Amanda's eyes are still as blue as they ever were." That gave her an idea and she asked excitedly, "Does Amanda have any moles or beauty marks to distinguish her?"

"Nay, I remember seeing naught. Maybe we should flee to the nearest inn so that I may examine you thoroughly and see if that prompts a remembrance of any unusual birthmarks."

"Your humor befits that of a jester," she added smugly, using Derek's own words before she glanced Derek's way once more. The intimate group appeared deep in conversation. Leonie stayed close to Derek's side, but he seemed too preoccupied to take notice.

"I have been wondering," Robert said, "the way you look upon him. Admiration clearly forms upon your countenance." He tilted his head. "I asked before and received no answer and fear I must know. Do you love him?"

Morgan drew in a breath. The question caught her off guard, but then also brought to mind Derek's stubbornness, his constant scowls and arrogant talk. She smiled to herself, for those traits endeared her to him as much as his more formidable qualities did. She did love him. She loved the way he caressed her with his eyes. She loved his dry humor and his subtle, yet obvious attempts to be more sensitive to others. The way he made her feel like the only person in the room warmed her insides, and the gentle guidance he provided the castle's children...

"'Tis written all over your face. You do love him, do you not?"

Morgan felt terrible for Robin Hood. He really did believe she was his beloved Amanda, blue eyes or not, and she didn't want to hurt him...she liked him.

Before she could answer him she was whirled about from her left side and Robert from his right as they were both enlisted in a giant circle, some sort of middle-age chain dance. The lute players had joined together in a fast tempo tune. The dance might have been enjoyable if she hadn't glanced across the room in time to see Leonie look her way, giving her a satisfied wink.

Following every pivot the dance called for, Morgan did her best to mimic those around her. When the dance finally ended the crowd became en masse, but she managed to dip into a hasty curtsey. "I have to go, Robert." She glanced about. "Derek said he'd kill you if he ever saw us together. Do us both a favor and find Amanda."

Robert gave her a sincere but fleeting grin. "You have been saved for the moment, fair damsel, but I assure you," he said, kissing her hand, "I am not ready to give up. I will be back."

The trumpeters announced the end of the dancing and the king it seemed was getting ready to make an announcement. She moved through the ever-increasing crowds of people, mad at herself for trying to spare Robert's feelings. Judging by the look in his eyes before he'd left, her hesitancy had probably added fuel to his determination to convince her to leave with him.

A silk veil lightly touched her face as she squeezed through the crowd. Many women wore high, pointed hats and headdresses horned with yards of fabric twirled about. The majority of ladies wore long, fur trimmed velvet and brocade gowns, heavy and cumbersome.

It was like being amidst a wonderful fashion show she decided as she made a determined path toward Derek. She'd almost made it too, until Leonie appeared, blocking her way. Morgan cringed at the thought of having to speak to her. Not now, she thought, not when she was eager to talk to Derek about what she'd overheard.

"I see you finally decided to join us," Leonie drawled, a husky twinge lining her voice.

"I would love to talk, but I've got to find Derek before he begins to worry."

"You mean your husband, don't you?"

Morgan tried to hide her surprise.

Leonie laughed, touching lightly at Morgan's arm. "Husband, betrothed, no matter really. Either way it is my warm bed he seeks out whenever he can."

Morgan pulled her arm free.

"Tsk, tsk, not very ladylike for such a high-born lass such as yourself. But then again, there are not many women who would not be just as furious under the circumstances."

"Derek has done nothing wrong." Morgan looked around, thankful to see him gesture for her to join him. "Ah, there he is now. I've got to go, my husband awaits me."

She could feel the animosity left in her wake as she made her way to Derek's side.

"There you are," Derek said, turning away from the other guests. She saw a glimpse of uncertainty in his eyes that disappeared the moment she took his hand.

"I'd like you to meet Lady Margaret Paston and her husband, John," he said as he eased her into the group.

Morgan listened attentively as introductions were made. Before long the conversation turned toward John Paston's travels to London where he spent the majority of his time studying law. Apparently his wife took care of the estates while he was gone.

As they all chatted, Morgan felt Derek's arm brush her side. At one point Derek laughed at a lighthearted comment made by John Paston's wife, and Derek's fingers touched at her shoulder as if to acknowledge his awareness of her. She'd never imagined that such simple things—a touch, a glimpse, the sound of his voice, could make her feel such an intensely feverish want. Hot and bothered was a term that suddenly made sense. She was hot all right, and she was definitely bothered.

As the pad of his thumb slid back and forth over her shoulder, she found it difficult to pay attention to what anyone was saying. She observed the slight crinkling of Derek's eyes when he smiled. Such a delicious thing to know that he was hers and she was his. To know they would soon, although not nearly soon enough, be entangled within each other's arms again.

The king's voice blared suddenly across the room as he readied to make a speech.

"'Tis something bothering you?" Derek asked with genuine concern as he leaned low, his breath caressing her ear. "You appear suddenly flushed."

"I'm fine." She squeezed his warm hand, wishing they were at Braddock...at home...where she belonged.

*Where she belonged.* The thought caused a flood of emotions to course through her.

After King Henry made an enthusiastic speech about a jousting event to be held the next day, he then made it known that he was retiring for the night. Morgan was thankful when he suggested his guests do the same. After saying goodnight to the Paston's, Derek led her through the castle decorated with detailed tapestries and artwork that belonged in a museum.

Stopping before one of the many royal rooms lining the hall, Derek opened the door and led her inside, leaving the door ajar. It was dark inside, shadowed only by a thin strip of light from the hallway and faint moonlight that filtered through the curtains. She could see shadows of the tapestries that hung from the ceiling, dividing the room in two. Derek took it upon himself to check behind the cloth divider, then turned back to her and whispered into her ear. "Your maid is asleep. Maybe I should wake her so she can help you undress."

Peering up at his face, her eyes not yet accustomed to the darkness, she boldly laid her hand on his solid flat stomach and slid her splayed fingers upward, slow and steady, reveling in the contrast between the soft fabric and his hard chest. Her voice came out husky and low. "Can't you stay?"

"Nay, I have unfinished business to attend."

She saw the hint of regret in his eyes and his whispered voice against her ear was enough to undo her. She hungered for him like never before. When he turned away and headed for the door without leaving her with so much as a kiss, she felt deflated and physically frustrated. She sighed, knowing his leaving was for the best. Odelia was only a curtain away and they both had a long day ahead of them.

She followed him to the door, gently putting a hand to his back. Before she could say goodnight, he turned back to her, took her swiftly into his arms and greedily claimed her mouth with his in a heated, desperate passion that matched her own. Their tongues mated eagerly as her hands slid around her waist.

After the kiss ended, he held her tight against him, then pressed a fleeting kiss to her forehead, leaving her standing in the dark…wanting him more than ever, missing him already.

# CHAPTER FOURTEEN

The intense heat from the sun beat down upon the crowds. The fields were a festival of color with everyone attired in bright colors. Sprinklings of silk and flashes of shining baubles glinted in the sun as people waved fans, handkerchiefs and caps to fend off the high temperatures.

The herald blew his trumpet and before Morgan or Odelia had time to take their seats, two armored parties rushed upon the other. The sharp clanging of iron against iron reverberated above the cacophony of noise coming from the onlookers.

Over a smaller man's head Morgan saw the air fill with dust, splinters, and scraps of silk. Out of the thickest cloud of dust, arose the neighing of horses and the continuing crash of blows. Morgan stood on her tiptoes and caught sight of two men charging one another with twelve-foot lances pointed straight and forward. "I can't watch this," she said to Odelia as they progressed through the cramped masses to find their seats.

"Close your eyes if you must, but I can assure you 'tis only for entertainment. That wounded knight yonder there," she said, flicking her hand to where two knights carried a wounded man off, "will derive the most pleasure of all. Every unwed maiden will tend to the knight with their fair kisses, then coddle him for his brave and courageous deeds this day."

This was worse than the stupid fights of modern days. What joy could be derived from wounding another? Morgan shook her head. She could hardly hear herself think through a herald's cry and the crowd's unwavering shouts. Perspiration dripped down her neck as she took the empty seat next to Odelia. Not too far away, the king sat perched within his throne on a high platform. She had no intention of watching any more jousting, but Odelia's nudge to her arm caused her to look back to the fields. Her mouth fell open as she watched two more knights mount their steeds.

Two very familiar looking knights.

She shot to her feet and rubbed her eyes. She had to be hallucinating. It was definitely Robert DeChaville on the left. His horse, in purple satin trappings trimmed with gold, stamped at the ground and snorted in anticipation. Over his suit of mailed armor, Robert's tunic blazed with his bright colored coat of arms. And with his basinet opened, she could clearly see his face.

She didn't need to see the other man's face to see that the Earl of Kensington had finally arrived. Her very own knight in shining armor was here at last. She shook Odelia's arm. "Odelia, it's the Earl of Kensington! I know that armor. He'll kill Robert, I'm sure of it."

"The weapons are blunted for their protection, my lady. Don't fret, for Lord—"

Morgan paid little attention to Odelia's words. The fact that the earl was actually here and…oh…Robert! He would be killed. She and her mother had read that the Earl of Kensington's knightly abilities would go unchallenged until his death. She couldn't just stand here and watch Robert die because of her.

Jumping off the pavilion, she ran through the railing of shiny ribbon, running as fast as she could toward the armored men.

Robert smiled, a great flash of straight teeth, apparently deeply moved that she was coming to his side.

"Robert, get off that horse this minute. You'll be killed. You don't know that man who sits before you the way I do. The Earl of Kensington will strike you down with the swiftest of blows. You won't know what hit you I tell you! Get off now before they carry you away helpless and most likely dead."

Robert bent over and kissed Morgan's cheek. "Ah, my sweet Amanda, you've seen the light. Surely you know that by coming to my side you have given me the strength of four knights. The strength needed to win the infamous Lord Vanguard," he added, raising both arms.

Beads of sweat appeared. The thick dress she wore clung to her skin like a wet towel. "What are you talking about? That isn't Vanguard. It's another knight entirely; a knight more fierce and dangerous. Look for yourself."

Morgan turned to face the man to which she now pointed. He was closer than she thought and he'd obviously heard every word. She couldn't take her eyes off of him. Here he was, the Earl of Kensington, just as she'd last seen him at her mother's antique store when her T-shirt had become stuck within the same glimmering plates of armor. There he sat, she thought, the proud knight, looking as chivalrous and fearless as the tales boasted. Through his basinet he stared at her as he'd often done while she was growing up.

But this was different.

The man to whom the armor belonged was actually beneath the metal suit. The plated armor, cunningly wrought and inlaid with gold and silver, was exactly the same. Unable to resist the impulse to touch, she took a step forward, her heart hammering against her chest.

At that very moment he pushed his visor up to finally reveal the face she'd longed to see since she was a child.

Her legs trembled at the sight of him! Her knight, her very own knight, holding his magnificent sword with golden hilt...was also Derek Vanguard, Lord of Braddock Hall. *One and the same.*

It couldn't be. She felt dizzy.

He must have sensed her imbalance for he dismounted and his arms came around her and she could feel the hard steel of his armor against her chest.

The crowd, the polished and civilized lords and ladies, could barely contain their excitement as they watched the ongoing commotion. Even the king watched in a merry frenzy, as if he knew he couldn't have summoned more titillating entertainment had he tried.

"Return to your seat," Derek said as she regained her footing.

"Derek," she said. "You are the Earl of Kensington, you're the reason I've been sent here...to this century. All this time it was because of you, don't you see?"

"Take your seat," he said firmly, "or I will bring you to it myself." He turned his back to her and went to his steed.

She followed him, still trembling from the shock of discovering that Derek was also the Earl of Kensington.

With help from a squire, Derek mounted his charger, then turned back to her. "'Twould seem I may be forced to have you confined to your room if you continue to disobey me."

"You wouldn't dare!"

"Go," he said calmly.

"My dearest Amanda," Robert called to her. "Do not fear, for there will be no later date for this man who dares to call himself a knight."

Morgan was about to let Robert have a piece of her mind, but stopped herself when she saw Leonie run up and tie her dainty, lacy handkerchief around Derek's arm. That did it!

Morgan went to stand by Robert's gigantic horse and glanced about for something to tie on Robert's arm. She didn't have a handkerchief, damn it! She tried ripping part of her velvet sleeve but Shayna's needlework was too good. She tried ripping at the hem. Damn. Still no luck. Finally she yanked the ribbon weaved within her braid, causing her hair to fall in a thick veil around her shoulders.

As she gifted Robert with a dazzling smile she tied the ribbon around his wrist.

Saucily, she glanced at Derek and instantly regretted her actions when she saw that he appeared officially ready to kill them both.

There would be no mercy when he jousted this day and the crowd knew it. Even from where they stood, the increasing hordes could feel the undaunted and intrepid vibrations of the two men. The anticipation alone made the unbearable heat suddenly very tolerable for the bloodthirsty crowd.

Derek looked straight at DeChaville, piercing the other's blue eyes with his threatening gaze of dark rage and said without compassion, "I bid thee make a final prayer, for I shall presently cast you down from your seat so swiftly that you shall never rise again."

"That shall be according to the will of Heaven, Sir Knight, and not according to thy own mortal will," Robert said without diffidence.

Morgan pleaded with them both to forget the ridiculous joust, but neither would pay her any attention, and she had no choice but to return to her seat when one of the squires led her to it.

She sat tense and pale, worried sick at the thought that Robert would soon be dead. An overwhelming numbness seeped inside of her as each knight saluted the other before riding to his station. Without waiting for the herald's cries or the high-pitched blows of the trumpeters, the two knights shouted out and launched forth.

They met with a thunderclap of hooves hitting dirt and the dust rose high and a giant sigh escaped the crowd as the dust cleared and they saw that both men still sat firm upon their mounts.

The trumpets sounded, a mere whisper to Morgan's ears. The horses whirled about to start at their allotted places. Morgan thought of Amanda, wondering how she would ever find Wilmead Farm so that she could tell her how sorry she was that Robin Hood had been killed.

The knights passed a second time, and she put her head to Odelia's shoulder, squeezing her arm when Robert's helmet was knocked clean off. Blood ran from his mouth and cheek, but he held his seat and wasn't overthrown.

The two men returned to their stations and requested new lances. Even from here Morgan could see that the new tips were sharper, deadlier. She grabbed hold of Odelia's hand. "Why are they doing that? Why are they taking a new weapon when nothing was wrong with the other?"

Worriedly, Odelia shook her head in wonder.

Both men saluted the king and when the brass horns fell silent they charged once more. The hooves of their mounts were again like thunder and when the sunlight hit both knights their armor flamed like lightning, and the people shouted their approval as the two men came together, lashing at each other with fearful strength. Morgan blinked to rid her eyes of the blinding tears, praying that neither man would die.

For a split second no one could see how the battle went. The crowds shouted in deafening roars, and she strained every muscle to see beyond the dust. Splinters of wood were cast into the air. Whole pieces of armor flew off from their bodies, and yet neither man yielded as they came from the cloud of dust, turned, and charged once again, this time without bothering to return to their starting places.

Derek's horse appeared to fall back slightly. Robert noticed the slip and charged toward him, hitting her husband a great blow with his sword.

Morgan cried out in agony. The sword stuck fast, and neither man could pull it out.

Morgan's heart sank as Derek slumped over and fell from his horse. Her body felt powerless and numb. Derek got to his knees, tried to stand before stumbling like a blind man before he finally hit the earth.

Morgan made it to his side before Robert made a full circle back to where Derek lay. She could barely see through her tears as she bent over him. The beautiful armor was dented now and blood seeped through his leather tunic where the armor had been punctured and where part of the awful lance still protruded.

She looked up at Robert, glad that he was alive but hating him for what he'd done. She was furious with both of them for bringing it to this, and yet, the only thing that mattered was whether Derek lived. For she felt certain she, too, would die if Derek, her beloved Earl of Kensington, were to expire.

Absorbed in her own pain that Derek's very life slipped away with every drop of blood, she didn't look up right away when Hugo came forward to carry him off the field. Robert, too, came close, gently taking her elbow. She looked at him with unbridled fury ready to strike if he continued to try and take her away. He let go of her arm, sadly defeated, and instead helped Hugo remove the lance from Derek's limp frame.

Morgan removed Derek's helmet and threw it aside. "Derek, talk to me, please." Tears clouded her vision. "I never meant for you to get hurt," she said, placing his head tenderly upon her lap as she stroked his cheek and cradled him in her arms. Her voice was raw with agony. "What have I done?"

"Don't let him die," Morgan prayed.

The castle's surgeon wiped his scissors and scalpel with a solution resembling egg whites. Derek lay on a hard cot covered with clean linen. His handsome face appeared bloodless. Other than a few shuffled footsteps and the gentle clinking of instruments being cleaned, the room was eerily quiet. Odelia and Hugo assisted the surgeon in stripping Derek of the rest of his armor and then his tunic. The physician took Derek's pulse while Odelia washed the blood from his chest and shoulder.

Morgan winced when she caught a glimpse of the gaping wound. Odelia finished her task and came to her.

"This is all my fault," Morgan said.

"'Twill do no good to blame yourself, my lady."

"I shouldn't have gone out to the fields. Robert was right. He said that by coming to his side I'd given him the strength of four knights. I would do anything to take it back."

Odelia patted Morgan's hand before she returned to the doctor's side to see if she could be of further service.

Morgan stepped closer, saw the fine lines etched on Derek's face, her husband's face, the Earl of Kensington's face.

To think the man she'd been looking for had been right before her eyes all along. He couldn't die. She was sent here to save him not send him to an early grave. How could this be happening?

The physician was way too old, she thought, as she watched him lean closer to get a look at the wound. He appeared half blind. As the man used a knife to probe the wound for pieces of metal, Derek twisted in agony, semi-unconscious, but not immune to pain. Hugo held him down while Odelia liberally applied a gooey balm. Then the doctor hastily stitched the wound and bandaged the shoulder with wide strips of cloth.

"'Tis the best I can do," the physician said, his voice weary from the effort. "The bluish color that already spreads, tells me the wound might be infected." He looked to Odelia. "Keep it clean, for if the rot should set in he will surely perish."

Hugo took the old man by his bony shoulders and hastily led him out the door before the man could say anything more.

Matti entered hours later and they were all relieved to see her. It was already nightfall and Matti was red in the face and out of breath. "I came as quickly as I could," she said.

Matti looked at Derek's pale face, made the sign of the cross, praying quietly before speaking again. "Poor man," Matti whispered. "He has been ever so hungry for love," she added after a long pause. She took hold of his limp hand and kept her eyes on Derek as she spoke. "A bit of kindness here, a smile there, that is what he craves and needs most of all. 'Twould make your insides weep to have witnessed the icy coldness his father lent upon him."

"Those scars," Morgan said, noticing for the first time how each thin faint line resembled the other, "what happened?"

Matti closed her eyes.

Morgan's stomach turned. "Did his father do that to him?"

The silence was maddening as it dawned on Morgan that there might have been some truth to the gossip she'd overheard last night. "Is this the reason Derek's mother left...was she beaten too?"

A tear fell across Matti's cheek as she nodded. "Lord Vanguard has sworn Hugo and I too secrecy on the matter. Though I had thought he would have told you by now. A horrible day it was the day his mother left. She hardly escaped with her life."

"But why would she leave Derek with a man like that?" No wonder Derek's soul was so badly bruised.

"She came back for her son, she did. With a small band of friends for protection, but Simon refused to let her see him. She died before she managed to gain help from either the king or the church."

"Does Derek know the truth?"

"I tried to tell him on many occasions, but he refuses to talk of his mother. As far as he's concerned she never existed."

"I overheard others talking about his mother. I never got the chance to tell him," Morgan said, stepping closer to Derek and touching lightly at one of his scars on his arm. "How could his own father do such a thing?"

"Worse than the beatings was the fact that Derek did all he could to win his father's love," Matti answered sadly.

"What did he do?" Odelia asked.

"He would make things. Surely you know of what I speak. Little things that make a child proud: a mud sculpture...an awkward sketch. Sometimes he'd spend all day with a chore he thought might please his father. But he did these things continuously, in a desperate, child-like frenzy, hoping to catch his father's attention. A fruitless endeavor, I'm afraid. Never a glimpse or a nod, or acknowledgment of any kind did he get from his father. We all tried to make up for Simon's neglect," Matti said, smoothing Derek's forehead with a wet cloth. "Hugo tried hardest of all, but the lad never gave up, not for a long, long time."

Odelia appeared hypnotized by the story.

"More than ten years ago," Matti went on, "when Lord Vanguard turned twenty. Aye, that was when something inside of Lord Vanguard died. It seemed he no longer cared if his father existed at all. Although Lord Vanguard and Hugo had become close, and the young lord had the loyalty of his father's people, he no longer smiled or took any joy in life. He began to concentrate on his training instead, becoming fearless with his sword. Strangely," Matti said as if she could even now picture Derek in her mind all those years ago, "after Lord Vanguard stopped seeking his father's attentions, Simon suddenly took notice of him. Only after Derek no longer cared, did Simon Vanguard dare to speak to the boy, who, of course by then, was a grown man. I believe Simon went to his grave a deeply remorseful man."

Matti looked Morgan square in the eye. "Until you came, my dear, only then did Braddock see a change in their lord. So abrupt was the change in him 'twould make a chameleon green with envy the way his colors changed so quickly. God's mercy child, you have made the man's heart smile again. A sight we have not seen for many years. So be glad for what you have given him…no matter what happens now. 'Tis a miracle you were sent to him."

"Let us not give up yet," Odelia said as she pushed her way to Derek's side. "The king's physician said there was still a chance."

A miracle, Morgan thought. A true miracle.

Morgan watched Odelia clean the flesh around the wound, trying to make Derek more comfortable. Watching Odelia and Matti huddle over him renewed her hope.

*Hope*. The impalpable thing she had thrived on as a child. Hope…that wonderful feeling of wishing for something with unwavering and confident expectation. It was an unrelenting desire she'd given up on when all the hoping in the world had failed to produce that which she desired most. Had hope made her parents come for her? Had hope made her any friends? She shook her head and pushed her thoughts to the back of her mind, for if ever there was a reason to begin hoping again, now was the time.

"I want you both to get some rest. I'm taking over now," Morgan said.

Odelia was reluctant to leave until Morgan added, "We will all take care of him in shifts. If we're going to help him get through this, we'll need to take turns."

Morgan stood by the window, staring out at the huge pale moon that hovered over Windsor. Four nights had past since Derek had been wounded. *When was he going to wake up?* Her stomach knotted as she glanced over her shoulder at him. He looked deathly pale. Her husband was the Earl of Kensington. But he was also Derek Vanguard, kind, yet courageous, strong yet tender, stubborn, bullheaded. She smiled fondly as she remembered dancing with him beneath the stars.

Rubbing an aching temple, she turned away from the window and moved to his side. The cool air felt good against her skin. She stroked her fingers through his hair as she'd done so many times over the last few days. Was it Derek's lost soul that had summoned her through time, or had the armor itself brought her here? Hadn't she always felt a bond, a unique closeness to the armor? And hadn't she felt compelled that night at her mother's store, driven by an invisible force to see his face beneath the visor?

She thought suddenly of the witch who spoke of her return from the dead, of Amanda who was without her own true love, and then of her mother, whom she missed so very much. She held her head between her palms. She needed answers but always came up with more questions instead.

Her gaze fell back to Derek. She'd never liked arrogant, obstinate, cold-hearted men, and yet, she'd fallen in love with one of the cockiest, most stubborn men she'd ever met.

She crawled beneath the blankets and drew close to his good side. His body felt warm and strong. "You cannot die Derek Vanguard," she said firmly. "I won't let you."

It was just after dawn when Odelia came into the room. "Amanda, 'tis morning. Time to wake up."

Morgan yawned, forgetting for a few fleeting seconds where she was. But seeing the concern on Odelia's face brought all the horror of the last days flooding back. She jerked upright, looked at Derek and felt his forehead with her palm. "He's burning up."

Morgan slid out of bed and quickly dunked fresh linens into a bucket of clean water. She began to clean his wound. Odelia used one of the cloths on Derek's forehead to bring his fever down. "I had a terrible dream, my lady. You were in a small cottage, drenched with sunlight, and you floated upward like the cottony seeds of a Dandelion. And then you disappeared. Gone in an instant."

"Not now, Odelia," Morgan said as she checked his fever. "He doesn't look any better, does he?"

"I am afraid not, my lady."

"Something is terribly wrong. He should be better by now."

Matti entered the room as Morgan unwrapped bandages from Derek's wound.

"You need to eat," Matti said.

Odelia gasped when she saw Derek's wound. The deep gash was red and raw, oozing with thick, yellowish fluid.

Ignoring them both, Morgan grabbed the doctor's utensils from the high table and sorted through them until she found the sharpest blade.

"What are you going to do?" Odelia asked.

"The wound isn't healing. There's got to be a piece of the sword's tip still left inside. I'm going to find out."

"My lady," Matti said, "mayhap we should seek the physician's help."

"The doctor is a quack. Yesterday he refused to look at the wound, saying once again that he'd done all he could. The only reason he came at all was because the king ordered him to." Morgan sighed. "I won't sit here another minute and watch him die...not when there might be something I can do."

Odelia padded across the room, bringing back with her a large goblet filled with a strong red wine. "I heard Lord Vanguard's plaints the first time the physician cut into him. Bloody hell if I will listen to him whine again." She propped Derek's head up in a hefty arm and poured the liquid down his throat. Wine drizzled over his chin and onto Odelia's tunic.

Morgan sterilized the knife in the fire before she came back to stand over Derek. She poured alcohol over the wound and blade. She licked at dry lips.

Matti wiped at Derek's feverish brow. Her hands trembled as she placed a leather strip between Derek's teeth before she took hold of Derek's left arm. Odelia held the other, and then they both looked at Morgan and waited.

Morgan removed hard to find stitches with the tip of the blade. Using wet towels to soften the damaged skin she managed to open the wound slightly. The process took interminably long, but all three of them were patient. She hardly needed the knife, using her finger instead as a feeler to search the wound, pushing her finger deeper as the wound opened.

Derek moaned. Odelia and Matti held him tight, every muscle tense. He was as weak as a wounded dog and Morgan winced as she added another finger, pushing farther downward. Her eyes widened, surprising even herself when she felt a piece of jagged iron embedded within the wound.

Derek groaned with a great passion of pain as she withdrew the metal. With the piece of iron came a new surge of crimson blood. Odelia used all her strength to hold him down until his head fell back into the pillows like a corpse.

Working quickly, Odelia cleaned the wound with alcohol as Morgan instructed, then Matti stanched the flow of blood with a pile of clean linens. Morgan found the doctor's needle and set about sewing Derek up. Biting her lip, intent on stopping the flow of blood as quickly as possible, Morgan made her first stitch, then her second with a steady hand. When she was done, she examined the stitches and frowned. Shayna would definitely scold her for such sloppy work, she thought.

Bright rays of morning light came through the window, hitting Derek smack in the eyes and making him grimace. He tried to sit up until the pain in his side tore through every muscle he possessed. He laid still, gritting his teeth in discomfort.

What day was this? he wondered. As he reached upward to wipe at his dry mouth he snarled in agony. His lips felt dry and parched. His insides burned. He looked to his bandaged shoulder and recalled with amazing clarity the reason for his suffering.

*DeChaville*. The name caused fury to override any pain he felt, and he clenched his teeth and pushed his legs over the side of the bed, swallowing the excruciating torture that followed. A terrific hunger gnawed at his belly.

He stood, his legs weak beneath him. The bed beckoned him to lie back down, but stubbornness prevailed. A fleeting vision of an angel passed within his mind, and he recalled memories of his wife calling his name and soothing his brow, confessing her undying love for him. But he knew well enough she would never have come to him. He had seen the way she gazed at her lover afraid for DeChaville's life. He had sorely wished 'twas himself she had gazed upon in such a manner. His gut ached to think she would always love another.

An under-the-weather smile crossed his lips as his next vexing thought turned to getting DeChaville's impertinent neck between his hands so that he could squeeze the very life from him. This deliberation made the wrenching pain a bit more tolerable as he took a few feeble steps toward the door. His muscles relaxed a bit after the first steps and the pain was not nearly so bad, he told himself. He took two more steps, grimacing as he tried to catch his breath.

Hugo entered the room in time to see a wicked snarl on Derek's face and one arm outstretched in hopes of finding some invisible support. Derek stumbled into the big man's arms.

"'Tis good to see you up, my lord, shall we dance?"

Derek grunted, pushing away from Hugo with his good arm. Somehow he managed to get back to the bed where he collapsed.

Hugo smiled brightly. "All will be glad to know that you have finally awakened. I will see that the maids have hot water brought up for your bath and—"

"Wait," Derek said weakly. "Food, I need food. And water first to quench this eternal thirst. And what day is this?"

"The twelfth of July, my lord."

Derek looked doubtful. "You mean to say I have been ill-functioning for five days now? Absurd. I will have DeChaville's head for this. I was to be back home ere two days ago." He finished his rambling and swept a hand through the air. "Send for the maids to see to my bath and food. And water, Hell's teeth get me some water!"

Hugo tried to take his leave, but he was not quick enough.

"And Hugo, have the men get the carriage ready for a quick departure. I expect to see the towers of Braddock before sundown." He laid his head back on the pillows and closed his eyes.

Hugo bowed low, glad to see that his lordship was back to his old, unpleasant self.


Morgan sort of liked the wacky, eccentric character that King Henry was and she added him to the list of people she would miss when she returned to her own time. The King did seem to be overly nervous at times, especially when she asked him what he thought about a woman ruler. His eyes doubled in size and he looked as if he might have a stroke. The seeds of insanity had definitely been planted, she decided sadly. Hastily, she changed the subject, deciding to forgo the tale of Queen Elizabeth and what little she knew about her reign.

The king wheezed with unrestrained laughter at her tales of Robin Hood and her much revised tales of Sir Lancelot. She was laughing, too, after he told her that next to Queen Guinevere she was the fairest lass in all the world.

Yep…she would miss him all right.

After the king's cortege escorted him off, she rushed back to Derek's room and noticed right away that his position on the bed was lopsided. He had moved!

She walked briskly to his bedside, excited by the possibility that he might awake soon. She went to the table to fetch some broth, hoping she could get him to eat.

Derek watched her out of the corner of his eye, surprised to see her here. As she turned back toward him, he closed his eyes and feigned sleep.

Morgan set the cup and spoon at the table by the bed and began adjusting the pillows behind his head, positioning him so that she could feed him. Derek groaned, a long, pitiful sound.

Morgan found a damp cloth and began dabbing at his forehead. "There, there, it'll be okay."

He smiled inwardly and yet he did not open his eyes. Instead, he gave an exaggerated moan and twisted his head into her soft breasts that were laid before him as she leaned close.

"Derek," she said, placing her soft hands on both sides of his whiskered face. "It's time for you to wake up. Please wake up."

He groaned louder.

Gently, she laid her head in the crook of his good arm. Derek managed another peek as she whispered soothing words, wincing when a searing pain shot up his side.

She jerked back. "Derek, you're awake!"

He gave her a pitiful look through one squinted eye and said, "Aye, but I feel as if I am dying." He shut his eyes.

"Tell me where it hurts." The desperation in her voice surprised him.

He pointed to his neck. She bent lower to take a look and he opened his eyes and smiled.

"You—you faker." Her smile broadened. And then she sank closer and kissed him firmly on the lips.

His fingers brushed the soft curls about her neck. He slid his hand upward and unclasped the pin that held her hair, letting the glistening locks fall past her shoulders and graze at his chest. She kissed his forehead, his nose, and his chin. Her hands trembled. "I love you," she said into his ear.

Weakly, he maneuvered himself so that he could look into her eyes. "Say it again," he demanded.

"I love you."

"What about..."

She put a finger to his lips. "Don't say it. Don't even think it. I love you."

He groaned with a combination of passion and pain as she brushed her lips against his again and again.

"Oh dear," Matti said when she shot through the door and caught them together. "Hugo, I thought you said Lord Vanguard was thirsty. Why did you not tell me his lordship was busy?"

"I was not aware," Hugo said in his defense grinning at the sight.

Derek tried to wave them away with a feeble gesture of his big toe.

"Verily he does not look so bad," Matti said as she followed Hugo back out the door, their hands fully occupied with trays.

The door closed then opened again and both Derek and Morgan looked over at Hugo as he entered and placed the platter of food and the pitcher of water just inside the door before making a hasty exit.

They chuckled in unison as Hugo hurried off.

"You do need to eat," Morgan said. She left his bedside and retrieved the tray of food, then filled a cup with cold water and brought it to him, bringing it to his lips.

He swallowed, then drank some more and said softly, "So what have you been doing while I have been out of commission?"

"I've been attending great feasts," she said with exaggerated glee. "Meeting dukes and lords and so many earls that I can't recall all of their names." She laughed at his scowl, adding sincerely, "I've been worrying about you, that's what I've been doing."

He looked thoughtful. "So you love me, you say? 'Tis because you think I am this Earl of Kensington you speak so fondly of?"

Morgan laughed. "You are the Earl of Kensington. Maybe not officially yet, but you are him—positively, absolutely. If it would make you feel better though, I loved you even when I thought you were just a lowly lord." She smiled at his continued frowning and her voice softened considerably. "Almost losing you made me see the extent of my love for you." Her eyes glazed. "When I thought you might not live to hear the words, I couldn't stand the thought of not being able to tell you. I have learned that anything can happen. Anything at all…at any moment, at any time…I wanted you to know how I feel. No matter what happens you must know that I love you."

Derek felt something strange happening within. Could it be that his wife, his sorceress, had chipped away at the stone walls so strongly built around his heart? Could his desire for her be something else entirely? Could it be love? The pain in his chest was deep, a persistent ache so unlike the wrenching agony of his shoulder. Aye, he thought, the affection he felt for her was based on benevolence and admiration, not just lust and desire. And yet his throat closed seemingly of its own accord for he could not bring himself to say the words in return. Her talk of being someone else, and now of his being the Earl of Kensington, prevented him from trusting her fully.

Morgan lifted her head from his good shoulder and placed a grape in his mouth. He kissed her fingertips. She slid her fingers over his whiskered jaw and made a feathery path over his temple and to his forehead. This was the face she'd longed to see as a child. The invisible face behind the iron mask. These were the hard planes of his jaw and cheeks. She slid her fingertips across his thick brow.

He closed his eyes.

Derek Vanguard was the reason she was here in this century. How odd that he could call her through time. How odd that she had immediately felt as if she belonged in this strange unfamiliar time. Bending forward, she kissed his forehead, and then the bridge of his sturdy nose. She traced a downward path with her mouth until she buried her head within his neck again and savored the moment.

Derek tilted his chin and listened to her sniffles. "Why do you cry?"

"Happiness, lack of sleep, mostly relief that you're alive," she said. She lifted her head so she could peer into his eyes. "It's taken me so long to find you." She wiped her eyes. "And now that I have...I never want to leave you."

He placed his good arm half way about her and said reassuringly, "Then you have naught to cry about, do you?"

# CHAPTER FIFTEEN

"You are doing extremely well, my dear. Don't bend forward overly much. You must keep a stiff upper back…aye, much better."

Morgan did as King Henry said, straightening her spine until she thought her backbone would snap from the strain. King Henry was teaching her to ride a horse of all things and she didn't like it one bit. This was her third day of riding instructions and the insides of her thighs felt like bruised peaches.

But how do you deny the King of England? More than anything she wanted to leave Windsor with her head still firmly attached to her shoulders. If Henry VI was anything like Henry VIII, she was doomed.

After Derek regained consciousness, the king had insisted they stay until he was fully recovered. His Majesty had been just as persistent in his request that she join him and his retinue in a ride about the countryside. Morgan had courteously declined and that seemed well and fine until Henry learned of her fear of horses. After that, His Majesty decided it was his duty to take her under his wing, firmly instructing, thoroughly explaining, and artfully drilling her on the joys of riding horseback.

Morgan disagreed. There wasn't an ounce of euphoria to be grasped as the king had promised, especially when he clicked his tongue and the beast reared up on his hind legs.

But how do you argue with a king?

So here she sat for the third day in a row, her spine as stiff as a steel rod while she sat upon a fine white palfrey, feeling no cheer, only cowardly angst instead.

The king's attentiveness seemed a bit much at first. After a few days though, she grew accustomed to the monarch's mothering. He was a kind and gentle man, much too nice to be king, she thought. She'd tried to hint about nice guys finishing last, but he'd launched into a squeal of merriment as if she'd told a great one-liner.

"Loosen up on the reins," Derek overheard the king say as he came toward them, his gait stiff and slow and his arm in a sling. He stood beside King Henry and watched as his wife did exactly as the king bid her.

"Good to see that you are well," King Henry said merrily to Derek as he watched his student with a stern eye. "How is it that she does not know how to ride? I have never heard of such a thing."

"So you see it, too?" Derek asked.

"See what?" the king asked, thoroughly baffled by the question.

"Emmon McBray," Derek said, pausing to watch with strained muscles as his wife made an unsteady circle around the field. Derek let out a relieved breath when the horse slowed its gait with Amanda still atop its back. "Emmon McBray, a young knight who escorted Lady Amanda back from Silverwood swore she could ride a horse as well as any man. But after seeing her ride my horse I had to question him on it."

The king laughed heartily. "Tell this Emmon McBray he is surely blind for before I took the matter into my own hands, the woman would not touch a horse unless the devil himself were after her."

Derek frowned at that.

The king's countenance grew serious. "I have been meaning to speak to you of my recently made plans."

Derek nodded, letting His Majesty know that he was listening.

"I am to marry."

Derek hid his surprise in a cough. He glanced at his wife to see if she was in on the jest. "Not Margaret of Anjou, I suppose?" Derek asked with a bit of humor.

The king paled and his brows slanted with concern. "How did you become enlightened of such news?"

Derek scratched at the back of his neck. "I overheard some people talking. Before I had a chance to see who it was, music filled the hall and the dancing had begun. Only speculation I am certain." He nearly growled as he looked again toward his wife, wishing he had said naught, never imagining that she spoke the truth about whom King Henry would marry.

The king eyed him closely for a minute. "Good, then I will not fret over it. The news will be made public soon enough. Mayhap after you are wed, we can go over the details and I could receive your advice on the matter."

Derek nodded, then gazed back at Amanda with a peculiar fascination. *How had she known?*

His wife noticed him watching her, and she flashed a bright smile, straining to remain upright as she veered the horse to the right. Before he could yell out for her to slacken the reins it was too late. She was on the ground, kissing the dirt.

The king's small goosesteps were no faster than Derek's sore measured gait as they went to her.

She pushed her face from the ground, felt whiskers on her cheek and screamed when she saw it was the horse who breathed down her neck.

The king nearly jumped out of his fur-lined slippers. The beast whinnied and trotted off. Derek plunked a hand on his hip as the king looked at her with disappointment.

"What?" she asked.

The moment she came to her feet, Derek took her by the elbow and excused them both before leading her a few feet away. Upon seeing Hugo he said, "Keep the king in good company until I return."

Hugo nodded and continued toward the king.

"It's good to see you up," she said sweetly to Derek.

"Why must you unceasingly make an oafish fool of yourself?" He raised her skirts a few inches and looked to her toes. "Could it be that you have two left feet or is it your cumbersome attire that makes you appear a bit graceless?"

"I realize you're on your way to a full recovery, but this is ridiculous," she told him. "How dare you call me oafish when you, a hobbling, inconsiderate, mollycoddled overlord just stood there, smirking at me while my face was buried in the dirt. I rode that horse for you and the king! For three days I listened to the big honcho's orders to sit straight, keep the knees in tight...go to the right, go to the left, check the bit, tighten the reins, adjust the blinders until I thought I'd go mad!" She plunked hands to hips. "And then I see you, looking pale, but handsome all the same, and I do my best to show you what I've learned. Nevermind that I'm sitting on one of the largest beasts known to mankind. Nevermind that I'm scared out of my wits. The point is that I trot, lope and canter my heart out to please you in front of the king. And this is what I get in return?"

A raspy chuckle erupted as he shook his head. "You are right. I have been nonfunctioning for too long and have turned into a roguish knave to treat you so."

Morgan looked back at him skeptically, unsure as to his sincerity.

"Quickly," he blurted, gently lifting her chin higher so that he could well see her emerald eyes. "Tell me again, while your ire is well heightened, that you love me. 'Twould be the validation my insecure sensibilities require to settle this once and for all."

Morgan rolled her eyes and dropped her arms to her sides. "I love you. There," she said with lingering stubbornness in her tone. "Now apologize for insulting me so that my sensibilities, too, will be mended."

It took him a while, but he did finally bend low and take her hand in his. "I, Derek Vanguard, wish to express my extreme regret for offending one so graceful and nimble as yourself."

She playfully tapped him on the head. "I accept your apology, Sir Knight, but I think you should know that you were a roguish knave before you were ever wounded in the jousting fields. And, the fact that you are a roguish knave has not been altered by your apology."

"Your things are packed, my lord," Hugo said as he came toward them.

"We're leaving?" Morgan asked excitedly.

"Aye. Odelia and Matti have collected your belongings and even now they await within the carriage," Hugo answered. "May I add that you look lovely, my lady."

"Must every man upon this earth verily foam at the mouth at the sight of her?" Derek asked. "It appears all men have been held in captivity and deprived the sight of a wench for too long."

Morgan blushed.

"Nay, you are wrong my most noble of champions," King Henry said as he came up from behind. "The death wound you received fair voided your memory, for it is not just any fair maiden that stands before us but one worthy of her very own songs and ballads."

Morgan smiled, leaving Derek to shrug in defeat as he followed her. Although he wasn't ready to confess his love for her, he wished only to trust her fully. Perhaps then he would gain the courage to tell her what she meant to him. Some day he wished to tell her that whatever he and Leonie had between them was over the moment he laid eyes on her. There was no other and never would be. Verily it made his flesh and body quake to think what Amanda Forrester had done to him. He could not eat, drink, or sleep without visions of her emerald eyes hounding him, as if her very soul seeped slowly through his veins. Damn it, he thought. She had corrupted every fool she had met with her charm. And now he, too, joined the ranks of foolish sops waiting in line for a mere glimpse, mayhap a touch of her soft hand, to make his breathing calm again. He was not angry with her, only with himself for losing all control when it came to his wife.

Derek stopped her on the path and when she looked up at him and smiled, he leaned low and kissed her, gently, ever so softly, knowing that he had lost the war, totally and completely, and now stood before her defeated, a mere shell of the man he once was.

By the time the carriage neared Braddock, the sun had set and a full round moon had taken its place, making a white haze of light above the treetops.

Morgan gazed at their surroundings. The night seemed embalmed in twilight and enshrouded in mystery. Between the intermittent creaking of the carriage wheels she could hear the eerie howls of coyotes and the croaking mating sounds of numerous frogs.

Derek held her within the crook of his good arm, and she felt a serene sense of peace like never before. His hair appeared as black as the midnight sky around them, and having grown overly long, his thick locks swept down his neck and over his collar.

When he glanced down at her, she noticed that his eyes, too, appeared extraordinarily black tonight. Their fingers entwined and the feel of his strong hand wrapped around hers made her feel content and whole.

"The king is well fond of you," Derek said, breaking the silence.

She smiled. "He had more than a few kind words to say about you, too."

Derek expressed mild curiosity, but didn't ask her to elaborate. "I'll tell you what King Henry said if you would like to know."

"Something tells me you will tell me either way."

She laughed. "You think you know me so well, don't you?"

He smiled, staring ahead into the night as she took a good look at his well-chiseled profile.

"The king told me," she began, "how he'd been assured from the first day you lay unconscious that you would live to see another day. He believes you are immortal. You don't believe that do you?"

Derek looked at her with exaggerated astonishment. "You dare confess to me that you are from another world, and yet, show skepticism to hear that perhaps I will enjoy eternal life?"

He had a point, she realized.

"Nay, 'tis not true what King Henry says," Derek finally let out. "I believe I am wholly mortal as are all men."

Again he gazed ahead. Then he pointed to the turrets of Braddock edging above the hills, understandable joy crossing his face to be so close to home.

"Did you know that King Henry takes full credit for raising you into manhood?" she asked next.

Derek shook his head, smiling thoughtfully.

"Well, he does. And he's quite proud of the fact that he knighted you himself. Although you've proved your worthiness many times over," she said with a sigh, "he is upset that you never stop to smell the roses."

"He said that?" Derek asked with a worried chuckle.

"Well, not the part about stopping to smell the roses. Those were my words." She gave him a sheepish grin. "But he did say that you seldom take respite as reward for your constant toil. Pretty much the same thing."

"Hmmm, verily, I will have the perfect reason now to do just that."

"To take a respite?"

"Aye, and to smell the roses." He kissed her forehead as the carriage swept through the main gates of Braddock. She could hardly contain her excitement at being back at the castle. She missed her friends and the children. For the first time since she'd come to this new world, she began to think about the possibility that she might never return to her own time. The thought did not bother her. She belonged here...with Derek. Of that she had no doubt.

A deafening rumble suddenly obliterated the tranquility, cutting through the air like a radio turned full blast.

Jerking her head around to look back to the gates, Morgan realized there were no guards there. Her heart jumped to her throat.

Derek's jaw hardened.

"What is it?" Her voice cracked with tension. She clutched onto his leg just before he pushed her to the floor. Without a word and barely any movement on his part, he unhinged a trap door on the floor of the carriage and shoved her through it. She let out a scream in surprised confusion as she fell to the ground. Rolling in a twisted heap with her arms crossed tightly over her face as the wheels rolled past both sides of her.

The rattle of the carriage and the shouts of men in the distance muffled her shrieks. For a moment, she remained perfectly still as the carriage continued on without her. She didn't need to come from this century to know that a battle was taking place. The smell of burnt tar raided her nostrils. Cinders and sparks carried by a breeze were deposited all around her, and the air became thick with soot and clouds of smoke. Jumping to her feet she remained hunched over as she ran a few feet in the direction of Braddock and then hid behind a tall shrub.

Her eyes widened at the sight before her. Braddock Castle was under siege. A massive catapult hurled a barrage of rocks and hand-crafted missiles toward the main entrance. Through the fog of smoke she could see the enemy scaling Braddock's walls only to be assaulted by arrows from the high towers. What in heaven's name was Derek doing riding into the midst of all that danger?

She tasted blood on her lip as she ducked low. Someone was coming toward her. As the shadowy figure came under the moon's light, she saw that it was Odelia.

She headed toward her. Terror filled her as she saw another dark figure grab Odelia and drag her back toward the castle. From here, with the moonlight on his face, she saw the man all too clearly. Otgar!

Frantically, Morgan searched for something to hurl at the hideous man. "Odelia, fight him," she whispered to herself, but Odelia's struggles appeared useless.

The dagger! Lifting her skirts, Morgan unhooked the knife she carried with her and ran forward until Otgar was in her line of vision. Two of Otgar's men stood close by. Kneeling down, she held the knife straight out, calculating the distance.

Odelia kicked and screamed while Otgar dragged her closer toward the castle.

Acrid smoke stung Morgan's eyes, blurring her vision. She swiped a dirty sleeve across beads of perspiration, squinting until she could see her target again. If she missed, it could be Odelia she hit. She took aim, the jagged point of the sharp blade aimed at Otgar's back. She couldn't do it, couldn't risk hurting Odelia.

She had to find a way to save Odelia and the others. Again, staying low, she ran until she came to a large oak further away from the commotion. She looked from her left to her right. She needed help.

The stables appeared quiet as she jogged that way, stopping at every tree and shrub to stay hidden. Within minutes she had made it to the first stall. The only noise she heard was her own heavy breathing and the nervous whinnies of the horses. And something else...the soft whimpers of a child. She tiptoed through the stables. The sound appeared to be coming from beneath the mound of hay. One of the horses neighed as she passed by. Taking hold of a pitchfork, she used it to toss back a pile of straw, then she jumped back, keeping the blunted tips of the pitch fork pointed outward. A small head popped up.

"Joseph! What are you doing here?" Morgan dropped the pitchfork and Joseph leapt into her arms. He clutched at her waist with one hand and his slingshot with the other.

"'Tis terrible, my lady. There is a spy within Braddock who helped those awful men through the gates."

"Who?"

"I am not certain, my lady. After the midday meal I found Thomas sleeping over his plate. Thomas never sleeps, and he had promised to help me train with a real sword." Joseph looked suddenly guilt-ridden. "'You will not tell his lordship, will you?"

"Of course not." That was the last of their worries.

"I ran outside to find my friend, Matthew," he continued. "I climbed a tree to get a better look and that is when I saw the enemy surrounding Braddock. After that, I hid." Joseph looked down at his feet as if he had failed somehow.

"Joseph," she said, smoothing his mop of tangled red hair. "You did the right thing and everything will be okay. But right now the people inside Braddock need our help." She hugged Joseph tight, wondering if Derek had been taken prisoner. And Odelia…poor Odelia.

"Joseph," she said with renewed urgency. "Can you ride a horse?"

His round eyes rolled upward as if that were the most lame-brained question in the world. He followed her as she haltered the smallest horse, oblivious to the animal as it nudged her with its nose. "If I can get you outside the gates, do you think you could get to the village?"

He nodded, his eyes wide and hopeful.

"Oh, Joseph, you're so brave." She tossed a pad over the horse's back and tightened the cinch, buckling it tightly in place just as King Henry had shown her. "When you get to the village I want you to knock at the first door you come to. Tell everyone you see that Braddock is under siege. Tell them Lord Vanguard needs their help. Tell them everything, Joseph, and you stay in the village until it's over. Do you understand?"

"Yes, my lady," he said bravely.

Morgan sighed, then linked her fingers together and gestured for him to use her hands as a stirrup to get on the horse's back.

"Good," she said as she handed him the leather straps. "Joseph, can I have your slingshot?"

He smiled, pulled the toy from his back pocket and handed it over. He reached into a leather pouch attached to his breeches and pulled out a large, deadly looking stone that had been sharpened to a fine point.

"Joseph! What wonderful ammunition you've made."

He grinned.

Quickly, she led the animal around the back of the stables and to the outer gates, thankful for the lessons the king had given her. She then watched Joseph ride off.

Morgan crept closer to the castle, close enough that she could see Otgar's men were gathering wood and throwing it to a fire built against Braddock's outer walls. Where was Odelia now? Running into Otgar's men in search of Odelia wouldn't do either of them any good. Of that much she was certain. She needed to think, but there was no time for that as she watched the enemy pick up a newly downed tree and use it as a battering ram on a postern gate.

This siege stuff was tedious work, she realized, and although she hated the terrible powers of modern world weaponry—what she would do right now for a grenade or a small automatic rifle to put these awful men in their place. Where were all of Derek's men? Certainly it would take more than two or three dozen men to take over an entire army. Derek's men-at-arms should have easily defended the castle. It didn't make any sense.

She ran toward the eastern side of the keep. A pitch-covered arrow doused in flames went hurling past her head.

She squealed and bent down. When no additional arrows came her way she took off again. Her thin slipper-like shoes were useless as she dashed over rocks and pine needles. Hopefully the black cloak she wore would keep her hidden.

No such luck.

A hand clamped around her mouth and she bit down.

"Damn," Robert swore, shaking his wounded digits.

"Robert, is it really you?"

"Who else?" he asked irritably.

"Thank God you're here!" She felt a rush of relief at seeing a familiar face. "We've got to stop these men from taking over Braddock!"

He grasped her wrist. "Let us be off whilst we still have our lives."

"I'm not leaving these people here to die."

"And what exactly do you have in mind? I beseech you to tell me how one man and one very small lass is going to save the day. There is naught we can do to help. I spied on Otgar's men. They are holding Vanguard's men within the castle's dungeons. Mayhap most are certainly dead."

Morgan shuddered. "They can't be!"

"It seems a scullery maid laced the castle's ale and wine with potent brew, causing Vanguard's men to sleep. That same traitor probably allowed Otgar's men into the castle."

"Why then," she asked, "are Otgar's men trying to get in the castle if they've already been inside Braddock?"

"I only speculate, but 'tis obvious Otgar's army lacks intelligence. My guess is that more than a few castle folk hid while Otgar's men carted the knights to the dungeon. When the enemy went back outside for supplies, I must assume the gates were shut upon them once again. 'Tis not an ingenious group of warriors that fight here," he said, scratching his chin. "Unfortunately, trained knights or not, I am afraid it shan't be long before Otgar's band has access to the castle once again. Invariably, whoever shut the gate on Otgar must be unable to free Vanguard's men, otherwise 'twould surely all be over by now."

Robert sighed as he looked deep into her eyes. "Amanda, my love, if we take leave now perhaps we can appeal to the villagers for help."

"I've already seen to that."

He gave her an incredulous look.

"I ran into Joseph."

"So many men at your beckon call," he said mockingly.

"He's ten years old and he's probably half way to the village already."

"Clever girl."

"It could take hours for him to gather enough people to make a difference though. I need to free Derek's men. It's the only way to save Braddock."

Robert's mouth angled upward. "Do the wheels in your pretty head ever stop their spinning?"

Morgan grabbed his arm as an idea came to her. "Robert, there's a way but I'll need your help."

His cumbersome sigh cut through the air between them.

"My friend, Matti, showed me a hidden passage. We could—"

"I've already tried the eastern door, 'tis guarded by two men," Robert told her.

"There's another way. An underground tunnel." She glanced around in all directions. "If you could catch those guards' attention over there, create a diversion of some sort, I could make my way to the tunnel."

He shook his head, clearly unconvinced.

"Please. If it doesn't work I'll go with you to the surrounding villages and we'll gather what help we can there." She looked up at him with pleading eyes. "I beg of you. Will you do it?"

"How could I do anything but?"

Morgan threw her arms around him and gave him a fierce hug. When she tried to push away though, Robert took full advantage of her close proximity and put his lips to hers.

"How touching," a deep voice drawled from behind them.

Startled, Morgan jerked around to see Derek standing in the shadows. The expression on his face sent a chill of dread down her spine. She shook her head at him as she stepped fully out of Robert's arms, denying whatever it was he was thinking, which was obvious to everyone involved.

Robert met Vanguard's glare, neither man having any reason to trust one another, but plenty enough reasons to despise each other. "I suppose you intend to challenge me to a duel?" Robert questioned flatly.

Morgan cringed at Robert's words.

An abortive laugh escaped Derek's lips as he watched the two of them with a hawkish glare. "I fear I have been misunderstood," Derek said in a caustic tone. "I do not bother with duels concerning objects I have no desire to possess." He turned and walked away.

"Stop," Morgan said as she ran to him. "It's not what you think. He's going to help us."

There wasn't even the briefest of pauses in Derek's step as he walked off. There was nothing she could do to stop him. If she ran after him she'd only serve to get them both killed. She swiped a shaking forearm across her forehead. Her head pounded and her heart filled with grief. Turning toward the castle, she saw parts of the western side of the tower in flames. Time was running out.

"I can't worry about all of this right now. There could be people dying inside the castle. My friends are in there." She ran to the darkest shadows, no longer caring whether Robert followed her or not. She stopped as before, huddled behind each tree and bush as she headed toward the opening to the tunnel, intent on getting there, diversions or not. She didn't bother glancing back to see if Robert was going to help, but before long he was at her side.

# CHAPTER SIXTEEN

"Where is she?" Otgar growled, spittle hitting Odelia's face with every word. "Where is that lady of yours?"

"She's not here. King Henry requested that she stay at Windsor."

"She lies," Otgar's man disagreed.

Otgar clutched tightly at Odelia's shoulder. His dirty overgrown fingernails became embedded within her skin as he shook her. "Tell me where your lady hides or else I will be forced to put hot timbers to your skin until you beg to tell me different."

The walls had been doused with tar and set to fire. Flames flickered violently behind Odelia, making it all too easy for her to see the details of Otgar's ugly face. Shivers coursed through her at the sight of his red-rimmed eyes that darted wildly about.

Suddenly Ciara stepped from the darker shadows of the outer bailey and cried, "Let her go! Leonie promised no one would be hurt. I demand that you release her now."

Otgar peered into Ciara's youthful face and spit at her.

Ciara stepped back, wiping spittle from her chin. His crackled snorts of laughter blended in with the flickering sounds of the blaze.

Odelia could hardly believe that Ciara was the traitor in all of this. But Ciara could not make eye contact with her, which spoke volumes.

"This is my fault," Ciara said to Odelia. "I thought Leonie was my friend. I trusted and confided in her; eagerly kept her informed of Lord Vanguard's whereabouts. But I did it all out of loyalty to a friend. A friend, that is, until Lady Amanda came to Braddock. That is when everything changed. Leonie began to ask me to do terrible things. She wanted me to steal and lie and when I refused, Leonie threatened to tell Lord Vanguard that I was the one stealing his livestock."

Ciara's head dipped low and Odelia's heart went out to the young girl.

"I gave in to Leonie's latest demand by slipping a potion of herbs into Braddock's ale and cider. When Lord Vanguard's men finally slept, I opened the inner gates and let the enemy in."

Otgar spit. "Shut up, bitch. I care naught about your sad tale."

"I like Lady Amanda and respect Lord Vanguard," Ciara told Odelia, ignoring Otgar.

"Did you have anything to do with the missive sent to Lady Amanda?" Odelia asked.

"Aye, 'twas I who left the love letter with the messenger as Leonie instructed. I also forged the missive inviting Leonie to Braddock, sealing it with his lordship's personal seal. She promised me nobody would be hurt."

Otgar's pig-like grunt stopped Ciara cold. And then Otgar raised his hand and his palm fell hard against Odelia's cheek.

Ciara cried out as she flung herself at Otgar, clawing into his face like a bear provoked one too many times.

Otgar fell to the ground. Odelia kicked at him, but it was a useless attempt since one of his men came quickly to his aid and pulled her away. A third man sauntered over and reluctantly pulled Ciara off of Otgar, too, but not before she managed to gouge into one of Otgar's eyes. Otgar let out a shriek as he came to his feet, and after one swift blow of his arm, Ciara fell silently to the ground.

Morgan crouched behind a low woody plant as Robert crept toward the open field with a handful of rocks. Her adrenaline soared and her heart pounded against her chest.

Only one of Otgar's men stood nearby, pacing slowly before Braddock's eastern entrance. The hissing, crackling sounds of the fire and the cries of war were loud and yet Morgan worried the man could hear her breathing. The few seconds it took Robert to sneak into the field felt like hours.

Robert stooped low and pitched one of the rocks into the air, then another to the right of that. Twenty feet away a bird flew up from the tall grass.

Morgan stayed low as the man turned to peer toward the fields. He whistled, drawing forth another man, and together the two of them walked past her.

She held her breath as they passed.

Seconds later, Morgan huddled over the tunnel with Robert at her side and pushed the wood planks to the side. She thought of Matti, Shayna, Ciara, and all of the other people she'd come to care about. She prayed they were alive and well. She thought of Joseph, too, hoping he'd made it safely to the village.

She slid through the opening, her heart racing as she disappeared underground, knowing this could well be Braddock's last hope. Robert slid in behind her, and she waited as he moved the planks back into place, muffling the sounds above.

The dark passageway felt more constricting than the last time she'd been here. Blindly, she crept through the burrows, using her fingers against the clay walls to guide her. Her body shook in repulsed shivers as little feet scampered away. They hurried forward and moments passed before the tunnel divided. She went to the left, fairly confident that this was the passageway Matti said would lead to the dungeon. Unlike the wooden hatch leading to the weaving room, this tunnel ended with a clay wall. Pinholes of light escaped. After removing bits of clay, she was relieved to see that the clay was their only barrier. Through the hole she saw the side view of a guard. He sat on a stool, whistling a merry tune as he whittled away at a stick.

Robert leaned over her shoulder to have a look for himself, but there was not enough room for both of them. He motioned for her to get behind him. They stepped back into the darker hollow of the tunnel and quietly struggled to change places.

Before she knew of Robert's plan, he rammed his shoulder through the hard mud and landed with a thud on the dirt floor. In one fluid motion, he rolled from the ground and pounced on the guard. Robert easily wrestled the knife from the man and used it to silence the guard completely.

Morgan gasped. "Did you have to kill him?"

He shrugged. "'Twas either him or me. Are you ready to give this mad game up and get away from here? 'Tis not too late."

Although the notion of getting away appealed to her more than ever, she shook her head. She couldn't leave her friends. She grabbed a well-lit torch from an iron wall bracket and held the light over Robert as he rummaged through the dead man's tunic. The corners of Robert's lips curved upward as he held up a heavy brass ring from which hung a single key.

Together they went to the dungeon's entrance where heard only a few coughs and muffled whispers.

Robert turned the key and pushed open thick timbered doors. With a loud creak of rusty hinges, the doors came open.

Derek's men were being held captive within an iron cell. They waved their hands furiously and shouted a cacophony of words as she and Robert came through the doors.

Both, she and Robert, took a few seconds too long to figure out that the men were warning them to stay where they were. Robert plucked the knife from his sheath but it was too late. One of Otgar's guards came up from behind and with a powerful blow to the back of his head, knocked Robert to the ground.

Morgan stood momentarily frozen.

Countless faces were pushed up against the cell, arms reaching wildly through the iron bars as they all called out to her, everyone shouting at once. She stared back at them with wide, frantic eyes. Her gaze darted to the floor where they pointed. The key! Robert must have dropped it as he went down.

Her gaze darted from the torch in her hand to the man a few feet away. He, too, looked down at the key. With thoughts of living to see another day, she threw the torch at him before he could lunge for her or for the key. The man's thick head of wiry hair went up in a fiery blaze. His screams of agony pierced her ears as he threw himself to the ground in a wild frenzy, rolling about, trying to smother the flames.

Morgan made a mad dash for the brass ring. Her hands trembled as she held onto the key and ran toward the cell. Out of the corner of her eye she saw a shadow of yet another man as he came through the doors. Knowing she'd never make it in time, she threw the key toward the outstretched hands of Derek's men and watched in horror as the brass ring fell to the beaten earth, just out of their reach.

She grabbed blindly for the slingshot hidden beneath her skirt when something solid hit her ankle. Without seeing what it was, she reached for the object and held it outward as the second man lunged for her. His eyes bulged and his lips curled in a deathly grimace as he fell, bringing them both hard to the ground. She fought for breath as she watched the man's eyes roll to the back of his head. He was dead. And he was heavy. It took muscles she didn't know she possessed to push the man off her.

Cheers and shouts filled the dungeon as she came to her feet. Dizzy and weak, she gazed down at the dead man before her. The wooden handle of a kitchen knife stuck out from his gut. She turned away, half expecting the man whose head she'd lit on fire to attack again. But he never came and she saw the reason why...one of Derek's men had managed to reach the key and now three burly men-at-arms held Otgar's man at bay.

Someone called her name and she turned back to the cell. "Emmon, thank God you're alive!" Morgan ran to him and hugged his lanky body when he approached her, laughing with relief when he held up the brass key in triumph. Emmon followed her to Robert's side. Robert's chest fell in even breaths. He was alive.

"How did you get in here?" Emmon asked.

"Matti showed me a hidden passage the day we went swimming at the lake. The tunnels lead to the eastern side of Braddock and to the weaving room. You and the other men can enter the castle that way and take Otgar's men by surprise."

"Matti never talked of a passage before."

"She told me there was no reason to tell anyone about the tunnel."

Emmon gazed curiously at Robert. "Why would this man risk his life to save Braddock?"

"Because like everyone else around here," Morgan said, "he thinks I'm Lady Amanda. And he's in love with her."

Robert's moans broke through their exchange.

Emmon left her side and quickly organized the men into groups, telling them that they needed to act quickly.

Morgan pushed back the hair from Robert's forehead, then squeezed his hand, smiling at him when he opened his eyes.

"You truly did it," he said hoarsely.

"We did it, Robert. We did it together."

He tried to smile, but grimaced instead.

"Robert, I have to leave you for now but I'll be back, okay?"

"'Twould make a difference if I told you nay?" he asked weakly.

She shook her head.

"Go then, before I find the strength to stop you as I should have done from the start."

Morgan squeezed his hand again, grateful for his help. She was relieved to see Emmon take charge with newfound leadership. In a bold, confident voice he instructed a dozen men to go back through the underground tunnel and veer to the right. Another twelve men were to take the stairway back and wait until he signaled for them to enter the castle. The rest of the knights would follow him and Lady Amanda to the weaving room, thus giving them three areas from which to surprise the enemy.

"DeChaville will be safer left here in the dungeons," Emmon called to her as they headed out.

Morgan nodded, knowing they had no choice.

"I will leave a man to guard him until the battle is over," he said.

"Thank you, Emmon."

After saying good-bye to Robert, she hurried to catch up with Emmon.

Minutes felt like hours by the time Morgan pushed through the trapdoor leading to the weaving room. She then pulled herself out of the tunnel.

"Matti! Shayna!" Morgan scrambled across the room where the two women were tied with thick ropes. She untied Matti while Emmon hurried over to untie Shayna. He pulled the gag from her mouth and she threw herself into his arms.

"Lady Amanda…Emmon," Matti said in a panicked whisper as his head popped through the trap door. "They only just managed to take over the top towers. They have Lord Vanguard…and Hugo!" Matti rubbed at her sore wrists when the ropes were removed. "Most of the women and children are locked in the upper towers. I had no idea the men were locked within the dungeon until 'twas too late. Otherwise I would have gone there first."

Morgan cringed at the thought of it. Matti would have been alone and most likely killed if she had gone to the dungeons.

"We must hurry," Matti went on. "The men who tied us will soon be back for they had eager eyes on Shayna."

Emmon's hands clenched into fists at his sides.

Chills raced up Morgan's spine as she realized Emmon, overnight, had become a man and a true knight. And he'd already chosen his lady.

After the last man came through the tunnel, Emmon turned to Matti. "Where did they take Lord Vanguard and Hugo?"

"We are not certain."

"Have you seen Odelia?" Morgan asked.

Matti and Shayna shook their heads.

Shayna placed an urgent, passionate kiss on Emmon's mouth. Renewed by the kiss, Emmon raised his sword to signal his small army to follow him. "You three stay here and bolt the door."

After the men were gone, Morgan turned to Matti and Shayna. "You know I'm not going to sit here and twiddle my thumbs." She bent forward to retrieve her slingshot and the sharp rock from beneath her skirts. Matti and Shayna stayed close behind as she crept out the door and into the hallway. Emmon and his men were already gone.

As Morgan came to the stairs she heard the clanking of swords and the shouts of Derek's men as they fought to regain control of Braddock. She had a clear view of the main hall. Derek's men came upon the enemy from all sides. She let out a resounding "yes" when she saw little Joseph lead dozens of villagers through the castle's entrance. The people were armed with hoes, rakes, and every sharp item they had made time to grab.

Failing to see Derek, Hugo, or Odelia, Morgan hurried back to where Shayna and Matti stood. All three then made their way slowly down the hallway, listening as they went. Matti gestured toward a half-opened door where they saw Derek sitting awkwardly within a high-back chair.

Morgan, Matti and Shayna crept quietly forward. A loud crack sounded and a man dropped to the ground before Lord Vanguard's feet.

"Hugo!" Matti said in a whispered cry.

Morgan grabbed her, stopping Matti from running to Hugo's side. Footsteps thumped across the wood floor and a huge tree of a man kicked Hugo in the gut with the tip of his boot.

The giant apparently had no idea that Otgar's men were losing the battle below. He yanked Derek's head upward by his hair.

Derek muttered a threat, causing the man to laugh before he put a punishing fist to Derek's face. Derek's chin hit his chest. The three women held their breath as they stepped back out of sight, hoping the man hadn't noticed them.

Morgan readied the slingshot, positioning the rock so that the sharp edge pointed forward. Pulling back on the leather strip, she stepped into the doorway and took aim, then watched the rock take flight. The big man raised a sword above Derek's head just as the stone hit his temple.

The giant fell forward like a newly cut tree, barely missing Derek with the sharp tip of his blade as he hit the floor with an earth shattering thud.


The clashing of swords within Braddock caught Otgar's attention. His face flushed with indignation as he stopped unfastening his breeches and sneered at the young girl. "Such a pretty name, Ciara. Too bad I have not the time to teach you a lesson."

"What do we do with these two?" his man called out to him.

"Whatever you want. Just get rid of them," Otgar answered before he ran to the high wall, climbed a thick twine rope and disappeared into the night.

The back door flew open and the thick planks hit the stone wall with a thundering crash. Emmon's eyes darted wildly about before he spotted Ciara as she lay in a bloody heap on the ground. He looked up in time to see Odelia being dragged off. "Unhand the lady now!"

A thick-bearded brute with tiny slits for eyes didn't waste any time grabbing his broadsword. The second man looked around nervously, dropped Odelia and ran off.

Odelia groaned when she fell to the ground. Otgar's man stalked toward Emmon without fear, ducking and shuffling his feet with practiced ease as Emmon came at him with his sword. Odelia gasped when the man thrust his sword into Emmon's leg, removing his blade just as swiftly. Crawling on her knees, Odelia tried to get to Emmon before blackness overcame her. The last thing she saw before her eyes closed unwillingly, was the man lunging for Emmon's heart.

Morgan glanced at the fallen giant with disbelief. Had she really put that huge freak of nature down with one sharp rock? She felt like David striking down Goliath. She shoved the slingshot beneath her belt, then quickly knelt before Derek. After untying the ropes binding his legs, she gently smothered his wounded face with kisses, thankful to find him alive.

Shayna finished with the rough knots that bound Derek's hands to the back of the chair. "There," she said, satisfied, "Now I must go see how Emmon is faring."

"Be careful," Morgan warned, but Shayna was already out the door. Morgan ripped the hem of her tunic and hastily wrapped the fabric around Derek's shoulder.

Groggy and weak, he moaned at her efforts. He had lost new blood from his old wound. She coaxed him into standing, hoping to get him to the bed nearby.

Derek blinked, tried to focus. Seeing that his wife was the one at his side caused his lip to curl. The teeth-clamping pain in his shoulder caused him to sway, but the searing sting was naught compared to the pain in his heart. He could not bear to look at her. She had betrayed him. And what ate at his gut most was the simple fact that he had known this day would come.

*Women cannot be trusted. Women are like scavengers, leaving naught but destruction in their wake.* How many times had his father said the words? A cruel and heartless man his father was, but at least he had stood up to his responsibilities. He had stayed and provided Derek with shelter and food. He had not abandoned him as his mother had or left him to die in the woods as his father's mother had done to him. *Bruised and battered...left to die. Scavengers, the lot of them.*

As he staggered to where Matti knelt beside Hugo, he recalled how every part of his being had alerted him to Amanda's intended deceit, but he had failed to listen to his instincts. And now he would pay the price.

Matti whispered soothing words in her husband's ear and brushed her fingers through Hugo's hair.

"How is he?" Derek asked.

"He's breathing steadily."

He shrugged Amanda away when she tried once again to tend to his wounds.

A loud groan emanated from the brute on the floor and Derek used his good arm to pick up the man's sword and raise it high above the giant.

"Nay, my lord," Matti pleaded. "There has been too much bloodshed already."

After a heavy sigh, Derek shoved the sword in his scabbard, then summoned the strength to drag the giant of a man to the bed. He tied him securely to a bedpost using his belt and strips of bedcloth. Noticing the gash on the man's head, Derek's gaze darted about until he saw the slingshot protruding from his wife's belt. Once again her weapon had proven dangerous, he thought sourly. After Matti turned her attentions back to Hugo, Derek took the opportunity to knee the man in the head and then the gut, making certain Otgar's man would no longer be a threat.

"You're not trying to punish me for what you think you saw, are you?" Amanda asked as she followed him out the door and into the hallway.

He gazed down at her and she touched his arm, begging for his attention. He flinched as her visage became that of his mother, promising him she'd always be there for him, her soothing voice drawing him in like sweet music draws out a snake.

"We need to talk," she said.

"Nay, I have heard and seen enough."

"I only hugged Robert because he agreed to help me get to the dungeons. The kiss was unexpected and he never would have done such a thing if he didn't believe I was Amanda Forrester."

Derek closed his eyes. Hot pain shot through his head as memories of his mother and father arguing filled his mind. Usually it was visions of his mother he saw as she made false promises or of his father as he lectured Derek on the evils of women. Not once before had he brought forth images of the two of them together. But clearly they were together now in his mind's eye. Plainly, he saw his mother as she swore to Simon that she had not been unfaithful. Her eyes were filled with remorse...or mayhap fear? He could not tell, for suddenly she raised her arms before her face, covering her eyes as the same high-pitched screams that so often filled his dreams came to him now. He covered his ears.

*I will not leave you, my son, not for all the riches in the world.*

"Lies," he said aloud, dropping his hands. "I am tired of the lies."

His wife blinked, but remained silent for once. He wondered if she understood as well as he that they had reached the beginning of the end. Aye, he thought...she knew.

"I must see to my people now," he said before he left her standing alone in the empty hallway.

Instead of grief or sadness, he was glad for the familiar hollowness that quickly took its place. He and Amanda would talk again as they would be forced to endure a lifetime together, but things would never be as they were at Windsor.

Never. He would not allow himself to be eaten up by jealousies, but neither would he listen to her endless falsehoods…or be taken in by her insincere declarations of love. Hogwash, all of it.

Emmon's very life flashed before him. For the first time since being ceremonially inducted into knighthood, Emmon realized he might not live to see another day. The man before him surely deviated from the norm, Emmon thought, for Otgar's man appeared to be an unnatural force as he came upon him with great swiftness. Emmon attempted to lunge to his right but his bloodied leg betrayed him. Had he perished then and there, his last thoughts would have been of Shayna's soft mouth and pale skin. But as it was, a huge iron cauldron came from the sky and fell upon his adversary, killing him in an instant.

Emmon lifted his gaze to the high window.

Shayna smiled down upon him from a high open window. He gave her a wide grin, and she put her fingers to her lips and blew him a sweet kiss.

Just past midnight there were no particular sounds to herald the end of the siege. But for the most part it was over and Braddock had withstood the attack.

Morgan made her way to the dungeons to check on Robert. Chaos and a foul odor reminding her of dead rodents filling the passageway. Otgar's men, injured and bloodied, were being dragged and carried to the same cell where Derek's men had been held captive earlier. A dead man was being carted away and Morgan maneuvered around the wheelbarrow when it passed. Anxiously, she gazed about the castle as she went. Robert was gone. Recognizing the man who'd been ordered to guard him, she hurried over to him and asked of Robert's whereabouts. The man stuttered and was difficult to understand, but if she understood correctly, Robert had been well enough to leave Braddock on his own accord.

As she headed back through the main hall, she saw that the western side of the keep had taken the worst of the assault. Cries of children were muffled in their mother's arms. The knights and men-at-arms already gathered supplies to cover the great gaps in the thick limestone walls. Maids, farmers, and all cuts of medieval life joined together in securing Braddock.

Odelia was nowhere to be seen. Outside, buckets of water were handed from one person to the next as the flames were slowly doused. Barrels of tainted ale, wine, and cider were being carried outside and dumped beneath the bushes.

The last of the dead were brought to the outer bailey and the bodies were counted. Nineteen dead: all Otgar's men. Another eighteen had been locked in the dungeon. Only a few had escaped, along with Otgar.

Morgan quickened her pace. Where was Odelia? Please, please let her be alive and safe. She entered the kitchen where a sick bay of sorts had been set up. At least two-dozen people were being tended to. Deep cuts were cleaned and bandaged. Broken bones were set and bound as she weaved her way through the wounded. She was losing all hope when she spotted a bruised and battered woman across the way.

"Odelia!" she shouted as she ran to her side.

Odelia peeked through a swollen, purplish eye and gave a smile of sorts. Between swollen cheekbones and a string of bruises, Morgan hardly recognized her. Her stomach churned as she knelt beside Odelia and whispered close to her ear. "I couldn't throw my knife. I was afaid I would hit you instead. My one chance at helping you...and I screwed it all up."

"Rumor has it that you saved us all," Odelia said, her voice barely audible.

"I didn't save anybody. Robert was the one who risked his life for all of us. And if it weren't for Derek pushing me out of the carriage—"

"Shush," Odelia whispered hoarsely.

"Boy, you're even bossy when you're sick," Morgan teased in hopes of easing the horridness of it all.

A corner of Odelia's mouth curved upward.

Morgan smiled down at her and pressed a light kiss to the top of her head. After awhile Odelia fell asleep and Morgan helped tend to the rest of the wounded before returning to the main hall where she found Matti, Shayna, and many other relieved castle folk. They hugged and talked, comforted by the fact that none of Braddock's people had been killed. Morgan learned that Emmon's leg had been badly cut, but miraculously main arteries had been missed.

She spotted Derek leaning stiffly against the wall near the hearth, staring into the flames. As if he sensed her watching him, he turned her way and their eyes met. A relentless twitch set within his jaw and his swollen eye, bloodied lip, and bandaged shoulder added to the savage look he emitted.

Morgan boldly gazed back at him, daring him to come to her and say what he felt, which was fairly obvious. Why couldn't he love her enough to trust her fully, to see that she would never betray him? Every bone in her body ached to hold him close, to bask in his familiar earthy scent, to have him look upon her with open fondness. She'd never loved a man before and the love she felt for Derek Vanguard was potent, passionate…and oh, so painful.

He gulped down the rest of his drink, cast the horn to the fire, and stalked from the room.

Morgan watched him leave. Not one of his men had been killed in the raid and that was a miracle she would have gladly celebrated with him if he'd only given her the chance. She stared at his unyielding face as he stalked by. Although he didn't look her way, she flinched, for there was no mistaking the cynicism there.

"What is bothering Lord Vanguard?" Matti asked. "Verily, he should be rejoicing his arriving in time to save Braddock."

"He thinks I have my heart set on Robert DeChaville," Morgan answered bluntly. "He's too stubborn to see the truth."

Morgan set her cup on the table. "I think I'll get some rest now."

Matti nodded as she watched her ladyship walk away. She leaned toward Shayna and said quietly, "'Twould seem Hugo and I have our work cut out for us, would you not agree?"

Shayna sighed. "Love, such a complicated sentiment. Someday I hope to be worshipped and adored like the return of the rose."

Matti raised a questioning brow.

"Emmon says naught is more beautiful than his roses," Shayna explained. "And he delights in the fact that each year they return; new blooms, each more striking, more colorful, more fragrant than the year before."

# CHAPTER SEVENTEEN

Early the next morning, Derek rose from his bed and washed himself. Every muscle ached. After the more imminent dangers had been put to rest yester eve, the women had hugged and fawned over one another, giving thanks to all, especially to his wife.

It had repulsed him to watch her last night, acting as if nothing had changed between them. It angered him further to find he had not the strength to look away, his gaze resting on the angelic face that had only hours before looked unto his own with feigned love and tenderness. How she must have laughed at his falling for her ploy of love. When was the final performance to be executed? he wondered. How confident and sure of herself she appeared, invariably quite certain she'd have him believing new fabrications on the morrow. He shook his head at the fool he'd been, recalling in detail her relentless falsehoods of another life and how she'd relayed her stories with convincing sincerity.

Damn the wench to Hell. He might have come to believe anything she uttered, including her tale of being from another world, had he not finally been forced to see the light.

He drummed a finger against the side of the tub. His wife had indeed held him within her slender palm just as Leonie declared she would. No longer though. Women were not to be trusted and not again would he forget his father's words. As far as he was concerned, Amanda was dead. Not buried though, he mused without feeling, for even last night her betrayal failed to stop his body from responding to her shapely hips and firm breasts. As his gaze had roamed over her curves, his arousal had fueled his anger all the more. Verily 'twas two necks he wished enwrapped within his hands just now.

Derek finished his bath with thoughts mainly of Braddock and his men. He donned his stockings and leather boots, then threw on a cotton shirt and leather breeches. Braddock would require many hours of repair before its walls were back to normal.

He rubbed the tenseness he felt at the back of his neck. He'd sent a dozen men-at-arms in search of Otgar. Ignoring Matti and Hugo's protests, he held DeChaville prisoner in the upper towers. Robert DeChaville refused to speak of Lady Amanda's plans and it was clear DeChaville would not stay far from Braddock until Amanda was in his clutches. Until Derek decided what to do with the man, he would stay locked up.

Without bothering to tie the laces on his shirt, he swept through his bedchamber door and into the hallway, intent on seeing that the repairs to Braddock were finished before sundown.

A feminine gasp stopped him in his tracks as he realized he had nearly run down his wife. She raised her hands to stop him and her splayed fingers rested against his chest as she gazed up at him. "Good morning," she said, appearing flustered, yet confident in her actions. "I was hoping we could talk."

At first he remained unyielding, then thought better of it upon feeling the tightening of his groin. Turning back toward his bedchamber, he motioned for her to enter. He followed her in and shut the door behind them.

Circling her, he tried to read her mind, surprised once again by her silence. Usually she twittered on like one of the birds that awoke him each morn. When he finally spoke, his voice rang deep and clear. "From here on out, you will address me as my lord as all others within Braddock see fit to do."

"You can't be serious?"

"Perfectly," he said flatly.

Her chin came up a notch. "Why are you doing this?"

He put his hands behind his back and arched a thick brow. "'Tis amusing to hear you ask one of the many questions I should ask of you. For instance, why do you find it necessary to wrap incredible stories around every lie? Why did you run away from my men all those weeks ago, and why, my dear wife, are you still here at Braddock?"

"Don't let your father's hatred of women stop you from opening your heart to others. I can't bear to see you suffer."

"What do you know of my father?"

"Only that he was a deeply bitter man ruled by possessiveness and a suspicious nature."

A sardonic smile curved his lips. "My mother ran off to share another man's bed. Mayhap my father had reason to be mistrustful."

"How can you be sure? Did your father tell you this or did you actually see your mother with another man?"

Derek stiffened. He did, in fact, see his mother leave Braddock for good. He would never forget it as long as he lived. Neither would he ever forget the sweet fresh scent of her or the softness of her skin when she used to tuck him into bed each night. "Do you know where your lover is right now?" he asked suddenly, ignoring her question, intent on changing the subject.

"He's not my lover."

"He is locked in the upper towers," he said with much satisfaction.


Morgan didn't believe what Derek said about locking Robert in the towers. But maybe that was why Derek's man had been so nervous when she'd questioned him as to Robert's whereabouts. No, she told herself, it couldn't be true. This was probably a test of Derek's. She would show him that Robert meant nothing to her. She stared into his dark eyes, unblinking, her heart filled with love.

"Let your hair down," he said curtly.

Startled by his request and surly tone of voice, she held his gaze and decided to do as he requested, now more sure than ever that he was testing her. She pulled the pins from the coil atop her head.

Derek stepped closer, his eyes resolute and vacant as though all emotions had been erased. She was conscious of a great fury burning inside of him, and yet, she could not resist the temptation to feel his arms around her, to feel the power of his touch. Her palms grew moist and her heart beat rapidly as he came close. Her skin tingled from the feel of his body pressed against her.

He felt warm and strong. It felt like years since they had made love. If only he could see that she truly loved him. A love like no other. Maybe if she could show him, he would give himself a chance to love her back.

She felt his hands slide up over her silk covered buttocks, over her hips and across her belly.

Morgan's lids grew heavy. She was hopelessly addicted to his touch. "Derek, I love you——"

He stopped her words with his mouth, driving his tongue deep and pressing his body hard against her until she was backed against the wall. His hands and mouth devoured her.

Morgan was taken aback by the primitive, turbulent feel of his kiss and the urgency of his touch, but she was losing all sense as she arched into him, craving the feel of him. Thinking he would carry her to his bed and make mad passionate love to her, she was surprised when he quickly suffocated any lingering appeal by stepping back, pulling away from her. He took hold of her arms and returned them to her sides. Then he straightened, smoothed his hair back from his face, and headed for the door.

"What are you doing?" she asked, a flicker of pain crossing her face when it became clear he was done with her.

His eyes roamed over her and he said in a bored drawl, "That was very nice. Is that what you wish to hear?"

Morgan met his gaze squarely and straightened her shoulders. "I don't understand. I mean nothing to you?" She felt only astonishment that after all they had been through he could so easily disregard her with such casual indifference.

He was a tall dark shadow as he turned and left the room without another word. Morgan stared at his broad back and shoulders as he walked out the door, her eyes stinging from the emotional blow he'd just tossed her way.


Three days had passed since the siege. It was late at night and the moon was hidden behind a band of fog. Morgan tossed and turned in bed. She had stayed by Odelia's side for most of the day. The bruises on Odelia's face were now deep shades of red and purple. After eating all of her broth, Odelia had fallen fast asleep downstairs.

The castle was deathly silent and even the birds seemed to be waiting for the sun to rise and brush the sky with streaks of orange and red. This world seemed yet unspoiled, and Morgan decided that whatever happened she would remember only the beauty of everything she had seen and done while she was here.

Her thoughts turned to Derek. She had not seen him since their last encounter in his bedroom. She'd hoped time would bring him to his senses but now she was beginning to see that his heart truly was impenetrable. Matti had been wrong to think that she could break through his hardened soul when he'd worked so diligently to keep the stone walls surrounding his heart.

Unable to sleep, she wondered suddenly if Derek spoke the truth and Robert really was held within the upper towers. Why she thought of it now, she didn't know, but she would not be able to sleep until she checked the towers upstairs. Sliding from bed, she put on a light shift and went to the stairs. She'd been up to the towers before and they were usually devoid of people, but she'd seen a maid descend the stairs only hours before she went to bed. She crept up the stairway and when she reached the top she tiptoed across the floor, peering into each room and alcove as she went. A noise caught her attention and she rushed to the next room. A guard slept on a cot before a cell, the guard's loud snoring a constant, irritating wheeze. Her mouth dropped open when she saw Robert curled up on the floor in the corner of the cell.

Derek had indeed locked Robert up. It was simply incomprehensible that Braddock's people would allow such a thing. Robert DeChaville had helped save the damn castle. And they all knew it. Her hands shook as she searched the room for the keys, her heart sinking as she spotted the metal ring attached to the guard's breeches.

She took quiet steps to the man's side and knelt slowly to the ground. The guard's snore was stentorian and she nearly fell back from his dragon's breath. Her brows drew deep in concentration as her fingers nimbly worked at the man's belt. His hand jerked up to scratch his nose. She held deathly still, dared not breathe. The guard rolled to his side until she was forced to look him square in the face. She took in a slow breath through her nose. When his snoring resumed, she clutched the keys tightly in her palm to prevent them from clanking together as she slid the ring off of his belt.

For a moment she thought Robert might be dead as she slipped the key in the lock. The snoring behind her grew louder.

"Robert, wake up," she whispered into his ear.

His eyes shot open. He stared at her in disbelief. "Has my dream become reality?" he asked in a whispered voice.

Morgan motioned toward the guard, gesturing for Robert to stay quiet. He sat up, taking quick notice of the key within the cell door. His grin revealed his joy at seeing her. He pressed his mouth to her ear. "You, my sweet one, never fail to

surprise me." He kissed her cheek. "'Tis good to see you faring
well."

Morgan whispered back, "Go. Before someone comes."

"You are not coming with me?"

She shook her head.

Robert tilted her face upward so that he could peer into her
eyes. "Do you not remember the vows we spoke to one another
before I set out to seek my fortune...our fortune? Can you
recall thy very own words before you so casually let me fly
away as if I were an old hawk of no use?"

He eyed her necklace, stared at it for a long moment before
reaching for the pendant. His somber expression changed
abruptly to wide eyes and a slack jaw.

The sudden change in his expression gave her chills.

His thumb rubbed over the rose-shaped pendant. Abruptly,
he gazed back at her with narrowed eyes, confusion clearly
lining his brow. "Look at me again," he whispered, tilting her
head upward toward the faint light coming through the high
window.

Seconds rolled by.

"Why did I refuse to see it before? Amanda's pendant is
nearly identical to this one, only hers is of a bird in flight
instead of a rose." He pulled the leather strap from around his
neck and showed it to her. "Amanda gave this to me for luck
until we met again."

Morgan could hardly believe what she was seeing.
Amanda's pendant was made from the same stone, carved with
so much detail and sanded smooth.

Gently, Robert grasped her shoulders, perusing her
thoroughly as though they had only just met. "'Tis the truth
you spoke all along," he said.

She felt his hands tremble on her shoulders as he spoke
again. "My Amanda is out there searching for the one who has
unknowingly abandoned her for another. Is that not so?"

She nodded. Relief flooded her insides like a tidal wave
within until the guard's loud snoring snapped her attention

back to the matter at hand. She grabbed Robert's arm and gestured for him to follow her. Quietly, she led Robert halfway down the stairs to the weaving room.

"Good luck," she called before closing the wooden hatch. Robert would be safe, she thought, which meant it was now time for her to leave Braddock for good.

Derek watched DeChaville leave. He sent word to the guards at the tower to let him be. And he did not have to question his wife to know she was the culprit.

He slammed into her bedchamber unannounced, moving toward her with lightning speed. "Sit down!" he ordered.

Her face paled, but once again she refused to obey him. "I'm busy, what do you want?"

"I came to see what my lovely wife was up to. Does she sleep, I wondered. Or does she dream of the husband she loves so dearly?"

"If you didn't come here to my room to talk rationally, I would prefer it if you left me alone."

She looked at him with sad, melancholy eyes. "You're making a big mistake, Derek. But I've come to realize that it's not me you're mad at." She stepped closer to him and peered into his eyes as if she could see into his very soul. "Who are you mad at really? Is it your mother?"

"You speak in riddles," he said uncomfortably.

"No," she said softly, "I only speak the truth. I love you, Derek. I've never loved anyone the way I love you. I only wish I had met you at a time in your life when you were ready to love me back." She shook her head and turned back to her things on the bed. "You're too busy holding on to the past. Condemning all women because your mother left you—it makes no sense to me, especially since you know she tried to come back for you."

"I know of no such thing. And I do not appreciate your speaking of things you know nothing about."

She seemed taken aback by his words. "You didn't know?" she asked as she moved toward him again. "Your mother came back for you but your father would not allow her to see you. She brought her case to the church but as she waited for their guidance she was forced to watch you from a distance. She died before she ever received word from the clergy."

He gave a small shake of his head. "My mother left for another man."

"Your mother left because she couldn't take your father's abuse any longer. She was running for her life."

"'Tis rubbish. My fathers only failing was loving her too much."

"You call that love? He nearly killed her with his bare hands."

Derek gave her a slow, appraising glance. "Your stories never cease to amaze me. You, Amanda Forrester, have caused only trouble since arriving at Braddock. I gave you time to settle in. I listened to your endless falsehoods of being from another time, another place," he waved his hands through the air and added scornfully, "And I allowed you to seduce me with your deceit. I must add though, how much I enjoyed your little game. I saw a side of you, or should I say, much more of you than I bargained for."

Her eyes burned fire and yet her voice cracked. "You're the one who doesn't care to know what happened that night we arrived back at Braddock or how that one-sided kiss took me by as much surprise as it did you." She touched his chest with a finger. "You shouldn't be here accusing me of this and that when it's you who is too wrapped up in your rotten past to ever let anybody through that scarred soul of yours. Many people in the world have been abandoned and abused as children, and yet many of them have dared to love and be loved."

His eyes bore into hers.

"I feel sorry for you. You are loved by everyone around you, but you are too stubborn to see it. I had hoped that someday you might love me, but it seems you lack the capacity to love anyone in return."

Husky laughter rumbled from his chest. "Once again you amaze me with your incredible acting abilities. Please, go on."

Her cheeks turned fairly red and she appeared to fight back tears.

He felt the damning want of her, not just with his body, but with his whole being. But he knew he would never again give credence to a word she uttered. His pride would not allow it. He had seen her dancing with Robert at Windsor, even before Leonie had come to him with the news. He had told Leonie he well knew whom his wife danced with that night, and then he had waited patiently for his wife to explain. But Amanda never did. He had every intention of talking to her about the incident, too. But then he'd left his burning castle to go in search of her and found her in Robert's arms. Seeing her in another man's arms had been too much. He would not play the fool again. His father had been right all along. Women were shrewd, devious creatures and were not to be trusted.

He looked at Amanda through narrowed eyes, surprised by her unfamiliar silence. "If you are quite finished with your—I must say—most powerful scene yet," he said derisively, "I have something to add to all of this. Sort of an ending shall we say to this incredible long...played out scene." His voice went from mocking to business-like as he added curtly, "In one week's time we will be married formally before the king as he so wishes. Before and after this ceremony takes place, you will cooperate fully with my people to see to it that things run smoothly here at Braddock. As for the two of us, we will live our lives as we see fit. I almost forgot," he said as if an afterthought, "as of tonight, you will share my bed. Give your room to your maid. I care not. You are my wife, and as long as I see fit to have you in my bed, you will sleep beside me." He smiled as if they were good friends.

She stared up at him. All anger had left her face and her voice softened considerably as she went to her trunk and pulled out an old blanket. "My other life has become a distant, faded memory, but I'll never forget how lonely I used to be," she told him. "I never felt as if I belonged. But you know what? I never had any regrets, not one. Not until this very moment." She released a shaky laugh. "You've made it easier for me to tell you that there won't be any formal marriage between the two of us. Please tell the king and Amanda's father whatever you want. Since I haven't disappeared into thin air as everyone here knows I thought I would, I guess I'll have to get home by foot." She sighed heavily and looked back at him. "I can't stay here at Braddock knowing how you feel about me, knowing you could never trust me."

He saw her tremble. His heart hammered against his chest, every word dripping with uncontrollable spite as he said coldly, "Get you from my sight ere I take exception to your leaving Braddock and keep you locked within the dungeon instead." He stalked savagely from the room, slamming the door behind him.

Morgan held a shaky hand to the bedpost. A dull ache throbbed within her chest as she tried hard to breathe. After a moment she changed into her jeans, a woolen tunic, and replaced her slippers with the tennis shoes she'd been wearing when she first came. Then she grabbed a leather bag and hastily filled it with one of Amanda's heavy cloaks, a pair of worn slippers, and bread from a tray. She pulled the drawstring tight and tucked her blanket safely beneath her arm.

As she went to the door, she gave the room one last glance. She hated to leave her friends without saying goodbye but it couldn't be helped. It would be light soon. The guard upstairs would wake and see that Robert was gone. She headed down the hallway.

"Lady Amanda, is that you?"

Morgan peeked inside the next room, surprised to see Emmon. She eyed him skeptically as she made her way to the side of his bed. His injured leg was carefully wrapped and elevated. She placed her belongings on the floor.

"And where is Braddock's savior off to?" he asked much too cheerfully, eyeing her belongings.

Wary of his sudden friendliness, she arched a brow at him. He'd never liked her, so why the sudden pretense? He looked a sorrowful sight, though, with his hurt limb and pale face. "I'm far from a hero," she said, stepping closer. "How's that leg of yours doing?"

She began adjusting his pillows before she realized she was doing the motherly thing again. She stopped and kept her hands busy by twiddling her thumbs instead.

Emmon peered into her eyes. "'Twould seem you are in somewhat of a hurry," he said.

"And 'twould seem you are a busybody."

"Tell me where the lady of the castle is headed?"

Her shoulders sagged. "You wouldn't understand."

"Has his lordship not yet forgiven you then?"

"How would you know about any of that?" she asked.

"Unfortunately, I know everything," he said with a hearty sigh. "I am like a snared and trapped ear for the maids' endless gossip. I know who is awash with tears and who is not. When there is loathing in the air or when there is love. I know it all…whether I wish to or not."

Morgan chuckled at his unfamiliar show of humor. "No," she said in answer to his original question, "your stubborn lord hasn't forgiven me. But I don't ask for his forgiveness, Emmon, because I did nothing wrong. Derek is not only stubborn, he is determined to stay exactly as he is. You were right when you said he doesn't need me. He doesn't need anyone. He has his whole life ahead of him carved out in stone."

Emmon shook his head. "Nay. I was wrong and you were right. His lordship does not know as much about women as he thinks. Even I, Emmon McBray, can now see that he needs you more than I first thought. It just took opening my eyes a bit to see the way of it all more clearly."

263

Morgan smiled and there was a moment's silence before Emmon asked, "So, where are you off to? And what is that you have yonder there?" He pointed to her bundle on the floor.

Morgan retrieved her blanket from her small pile of belongings. "This old thing. Just an old rag I've grown attached to. As for going anywhere, I'm taking this dirty laundry to the kitchen to be washed."

Emmon raised a disbelieving brow. "A bit late for washing. Or should I say early since it is nearly morn?"

"Never too early for washing," she said as she gathered her things. "I hope you're up and tending to your roses in no time." She went to the door and glanced back at him. "Take care of yourself, Emmon. You hear me?"

"Aye," he said quietly as she left. "I hear you."

# CHAPTER EIGHTEEN

"I should have you beheaded for your bungling incompetence!" Leonie hissed, throwing her goblet so that it soared past Otgar and hit the wall instead.

"Your worthless spy, Ciara, came upon me like a wounded bear and ruined our plans," Otgar told Leonie. She was the one who released Vanguard's men from their cell, for all entrances were well guarded by my men."

"If your men were so well trained as you assured me they were, how is it that all of Lord Vanguard's people are faring well? Why is Lady Amanda without a scratch and so dubbed Braddock's savior? Answer me that you oafish, dim-witted man."

Otgar licked his crooked lips, gazing upon her with lust.

Leonie waved her hand through the air. "Do not bother answering you doltish fool." She sauntered over to the table in the middle of the room and poured wine into a goblet. She paid little heed to Otgar's pensive mood as she went on. "It seems the Witch of Devonshire knows something after all. The man who spied Lady Amanda with the witch only just returned from Devonshire. He informed me that four and twenty years ago, there were two babes born to the Earl of Silverwood. Twin girls. Apparently one of the babes was ill and brought to the witch. No one in the surrounding villages has ever seen such a twin. But the witch calls Amanda's twin by the name of Morgeanna and swears she sent the babe through time itself. I have come to believe the witch hid the lass away all these years, waiting for the right time to bring her forth. But why, I wonder, would the old hag do such a thing?"

Otgar shrugged. "Mayhap she was going to seek a ransom from the Earl of Silverwood."

Leonie peered thoughtfully at her cup. "Aye. Or mayhap the witch became frightened by the idea, deciding not to risk it after all. I wager she set the girl free to relieve herself of such a burden. That would explain Lady Amanda's strange dialect and odd customs." Deep in thought, Leonie set her goblet down. "'Twould mean Lord Vanguard has wedded the wrong woman and the church would see the marriage as null and void. Before I confront Lord Vanguard on this," she added, strutting to Otgar's side and raking a long nail across his dirt-encrusted tunic, "I need you to do one more thing for me. It seems Ciara has confessed to her sins and Braddock's idiots all but fawn over the silly twit. But I have eyes everywhere," she said, twirling a finger around his ear, "and I learned before you arrived that Lady Amanda has left Braddock for good."

Otgar snorted and pulled Leonie against him, his eagerness making her laugh. Such an insignificant ghastly man, she thought.

"My good sense tells me Lord Vanguard will follow her. I want you and your men to hide near Swan Lake. When Lord Vanguard rides by I want you to surprise him. Make him suffer as I have suffered. Then bring him to me on bended knees."

"What about the Forrester wench?"

"'Tis Lord Vanguard I want." She glanced down in disgust as Otgar began suckling at her breast, caring not that he ruined her gown. "Get your disgusting tongue off of me you pig's ass!" She pushed him away, repulsed by his lack of control. Then she caught a glimpse of his abandoned wrath, realizing too late that she had pushed him too far.

Otgar slammed her to the ground, sending the table and wine crashing to the ground. Leonie's blood roared in her ears. She was sure that she was doomed until he began rubbing on her like the mongrel that he was. She trailed her fingers across his rounded shoulders, hoping a little coaxing would calm him, get him back under control. In the future, she would have to remember to be more careful with this horrid man. Perhaps after tomorrow she would rid herself of his groveling hands altogether.

Leonie sighed as he pressed his face between her bosom and rode her like a dog in heat. Closing her eyes, she waited for the storm to pass.

"Only a bloody blackguard would let her ladyship wander into the wilderness unaccompanied," Hugo said, his lips curling in disgust as he limped across Emmon's bedroom floor.

Shayna and Emmon exchanged fleeting glances.

Matti had called them all together, including Odelia, and the five of them stood, or laid in Emmon's case, about the room, discussing Lady Amanda's disappearance.

"Calm yourself," Matti said, concerned for her husband's health. He had lived a vigorous life and although he was as tough as a new hide of leather, he was well into his fifties and his injuries had yet to heal. "I have asked two men-at-arms to go in search of her. Mayhap they will find her before another night falls upon us."

"Could well be too late," Odelia said with a shake of her head.

Hugo grimaced. "Vanguard knew she was going to leave and yet he did nothing about it. She is his wife for God's sake!"

"It will do you no good to get your ire up," Matti said, "Besides, his lordship is punishing himself without any help from the likes of us."

"In what way?" Emmon asked.

"He has been locked within his study, drowning himself in his work since Lady Amanda left nearly two days ago. He refuses to speak to any of us."

"So he thinks to rid himself of Lady Amanda just like that?" Emmon asked with distaste. "And how I wonder is he planning to explain all of this to her ladyship's father, the Earl of Silverwood?"

Matti shrugged, having no answer to that.

"Lord Vanguard has the compassion of twenty devils," Emmon added. "You both knew that before you started your damned matchmaking."

Matti glared at Emmon.

Shayna and Odelia exchanged puzzled glances, for they had no idea of Matti's long-time desire to see Derek wed. Matti's attempts at matchmaking had doubled after Derek took up with Leonie. Unbeknownst to her husband or Emmon, it was her own letter sent to King Henry that spurred His Majesty's decision to see his favored knight properly wed.

Emmon glanced at his bandaged limb. "Was it not for this damnable leg I would go after Lady Amanda myself instead of lying here like a useless sack of bran."

Hugo, too, had wanted to go in search of Lady Amanda, but Matti would not allow it. Hugo's head still throbbed and his bruised ribs pained him when he walked. Yesterday he could hardly breathe without grimacing.

"Perhaps that DeChaville fellow will fall upon her before another night passes us by," Emmon said hopefully.

Shayna's eyes grew round. "You have not heard?"

Judging by Emmon's puzzled look, Matti could see that Emmon had not.

"Lord Vanguard," Shayna explained, "had Robert DeChaville locked within the upper towers after you gained control of Braddock. His lordship would not listen to Hugo or Odelia when they questioned him on it. We would have eventually released DeChaville ourselves if Lady Amanda had not taken the task on herself before she left."

"He locked the man up?" A shudder of irritation crossed Emmon's face. "My God man, if it were not for DeChaville, we would all be dead. Was Lord Vanguard aware of this fact?"

Odelia sighed. "Aye, but he cares not, for he also knows that Robert is in love with his wife."

Emmon threw up his hands in disgusted resignation. "Saint Anthony's Fire! Methinks Lord Vanguard has verily lost his head this time. Is it not clear to everyone but him that it is he, Lord Vanguard, who she gives her heart so freely? I should have listened to my instincts the other morn telling me she might go." Emmon adjusted his hurt leg upon the mounds of pillows, wincing at the pain it caused.

"What are you saying?" Hugo asked. "Did you talk to her ladyship before she set out?"

"Aye," Emmon said. "At the time it was not quite morn when I caught her walking by in a bit of a hurry. I questioned her as to where she was headed but she insisted she had only a few chores to tend to. Verily, I had hoped Lord Vanguard would come around. But I must say I saw it in her eyes...the pain he had already caused her. I should have known she would not wait."

"For a lass such as she," Odelia added, "possessing such courage and pride, 'twould have been impossible for her to stay."

"Aye," Shayna added, "especially loving his lordship the way she does. She never could have remained at Braddock under his scornful gaze."

Emmon reached out and took Shayna's hand in his. "Call me a bloody simpleton," he said, drawing everyone's attention once more, "but I must say, after all I have seen and heard, I have grave doubts as to her being Lady Amanda Forrester at all."

Matti gasped and all eyes fell on Emmon. Stunned that he, the most level-headed of them all, could dare to believe such a thing.


Thanks to the rising sun, Morgan's bones began to thaw. Spending more than one night in the forest had not been part of her plan. Unfortunately she'd taken a path off of the main road, hoping to find a village or a cottage at the very least.

She was lost. Only vast fields of tall grass lay before her. Her small blanket wasn't enough to keep her warm. Her teeth chattered and her stomach grumbled. The bread was long gone and her head ached with the taunting beat of a migraine. She'd never had a migraine before, but that didn't surprise her. She'd never climbed a tree before last night either, but here she sat, high above the solid ground, amid the bickering squirrels and angry ants.

She had roamed the countryside for days, forgoing the solid path and making her own trail through high grass and streams, rocks and mud. Her shoes had been sucked up within the hungry mouth of a mud hole when she'd crossed a small stream. And she hadn't had time to put on the slippers that were still snug within her leather bag...a bag she had sacrificed to a wild animal in exchange for her life. It seemed like a pretty fair deal at the time. She didn't even know what kind of animal it had been, but she'd seen its red eyes and heard its scavenger snarl all too clearly. Without hesitation, she'd thrown the bag its way and climbed the nearest tree.

Every part of her body felt bruised and stiff. Here she sat high aloft a spindly needleleaf tree, fighting a never-ending battle with an organized community of determined ants. She listened in vain for a crowing of a cock, the barking of a dog, any sound that would indicate human habitation. But besides a small breeze and the consistent upbraiding of an irate squirrel, it was eerily silent.

She sighed, knowing it was time to move on. One more glance about told her Derek wasn't coming after her. More than once last night she'd come awake with a start, sure that she'd heard the neigh of his horse and the pounding of its hooves. But then the crickets would lull her back to sleep where she would imagine he had come to his senses, and she was back in his arms, safe and sound.

Derek paced the floor of his study like an enraged beast. He felt the growth of a beard, more than just a shadow upon his jaw. He drew in a hefty swallow of amber brew, a gift from the king...a gift he had not planned to sample so soon. But there was no time like the present, he figured, as he finished off the last of the rum before continuing his pacing.

He deserved to be punished, he told himself, for allowing his brain to be controlled by the tightness of his breeches. Again he stopped before the table, this time filling his cup with a dark hearty wine, swallowing the contents in one long gulp. He stared into the cold empty hearth and even there he saw his wife's face. Looking exactly as she had at their first meeting. Oddly dressed, yet strangely familiar. Could it be possible that they met before? Nay, he thought with a shake of his head, he would have remembered her. Unless they had met in another time, another world...a drunken fit of laughter escaped him at the thought, echoing off the dense walls. His laughter quickly faded, and he stumbled drunkenly across the room. "Well, that would explain everything," he said aloud, teetering slightly before he fell awkwardly into the chair behind his writing table. Mounds of paperwork sat before him and he patted the pile as if it were a pet. He slid his daily ledger closer for a better look. The numbers blurred into nothingness.

Derek paid scant heed to the heavy footfalls in the corridor. He hardly glanced up at all when the door swung open and Emmon stormed in with a crutch, a bad limp, and a furious scowl upon his young face. Emmon took a seat before him, wrinkling his nose with disgust. "Have you not changed your clothes?" the boy asked.

Derek examined his wrinkled tunic, noticing how the ties of his shirt hung loose. His gaze then fell to the unchanged bandages on his arm. He tried to shrug but his shoulder pained him, so he returned his gaze to his ledgers and tried to remember where he left off.

"It smells like a brewery in here," Emmon complained.

"Then leave, boy."

"Not until you tell me what you intend to do about your wife's disappearance?"

Derek raised his head just enough until he peered into the eyes of the impudent man-boy who dared to bother him so persistently. He tried hard to remember when exactly the boy had become such a nuisance. "What I intend to do, is finish my work. For as you can see..." Derek paused as he realized he completely forgot the point he was about to make.

Emmon drummed his fingers against his crutch and waited.

"Ahhh," Derek said, gesturing towards the mounds of parchments. "As you can see, all of the chaos of late has caused me to neglect the work that keeps this castle running smoothly. 'Twould seem you have much to learn, my boy."

"With all due respect," Emmon ground out, "I believe it is you who has much to learn. And I thought we agreed you would no longer call me 'boy'."

"Aye, my apologies, boy." He chuckled.

Emmon's eyes narrowed considerably. "Did you ever ask the king, or mayhap Hugo, or even your own wife who it was who tended your serpent's hide while you lay dying and bleeding within the king's court? Were you aware that Lady Amanda is the one who stayed by your side, calming your fever and keeping you from joining the dead? You would be talking to the devil now if she had believed the doctor's words when he said there was naught anyone could do. But she would not listen."

Derek raked his hand through his hair, turning a frigid gaze on Emmon. "You are beginning to sound like Lady Amanda herself. Make your point and then get out before you set my hackles to rising."

"My point is," Emmon bravely continued, "if Lady Amanda had a plan as you assured us she did, then why did she not let you die? She is no doctor. And yet with only Matti and Odelia to aid her, she reopened your wound and removed this from deep within your battered soul." Emmon dropped a piece of iron on the parchment in front of Derek.

Derek raised both arms in a questioning gesture. "Methinks we both agree she is a talented wench. So what now? I did not force her to leave Braddock, nor did I punish her for releasing my prisoner."

"DeChaville should never have been locked up. He helped save the damn castle."

"He also tried to kill me."

"In self defense," Emmon argued.

"He will stop at nothing until he has my wife."

Emmon raised a brow. "A wife you do not want or love."

Derek's stomach roiled at the bluntness of Emmon's words.

Emmon refused to give up. "I spied upon her ladyship when DeChaville first found her outside these castle walls; 'twas only a few days after she arrived. Lady Amanda told him the same story she told you...that she was from another time, another place. She told him she was not Lady Amanda and she refused to leave with him."

"And yet you failed to tell me this before?"

"I was befuddled by her stories."

Derek pressed his palms against his aching temples. "And now you are not?"

Emmon leaned forward, his eyes brightening. "I believe she is not Amanda Forrester at all. It does seem odd that the people who know her best think she is someone she is not, but I trust she does not lie."

Stunned, Derek gaped at the boy. It was as if Lady Amanda were inside of Emmon's body this very moment, telling him what to say.

"My God man," Emmon went on, "listen to what I say. I believe—"

Derek's obtrusive laughter broke into Emmon's words. "You, my boy, have been bit by the spidery fangs of a woman!"

Emmon's eyes blazed as he jerked upright, sending his chair toppling behind him.

When Derek's laughter subsided, he, too, stood up to see the boy out, surprised when Emmon lunged at him with all the voraciousness of a bloodthirsty wolf.

# CHAPTER NINETEEN

A loud thump and a crash sent Matti running toward Lord Vanguard's study. She threw open the door and stood flabbergasted as she watched Derek and Emmon roll across the room.

"You two stop it right now! Derek, I mean it, you are going to hurt him!" Still shrieking, she hopped out of the way as they scuffled past her, colliding into the door with a crash. Wood chips flew about as the door splintered. They fought a winding path across the passageway and into the main hall, knocking over chairs and tables as they went. An old dog got in the way and yelped before it ran off with its tail between his legs.

A dozen castle folk gathered around to see what the commotion was about. Although both men were wounded and Lord Vanguard was half sowed, they managed quite well to snake across the floor, exchanging heated blows at consistent intervals.

Lord Vanguard finally pushed Emmon far enough away so that he could stagger to his feet.

Emmon looked like a crazed and injured animal as he scrambled to one foot, hopping on one leg before he thrust himself at Lord Vanguard once again.

His lordship stumbled backwards into the long table newly set for the morning's meal. The table split in two. Plates and utensils flew to the air. Matti ran to Odelia's side and they took cover behind a wooden beam.

Again Derek came to his feet, a carrot dangling from his shirt and mutton dripping from his pants. He kicked his way through the rubble to get to Emmon who was now slipping in a heap of porridge a few feet away.

Derek's jaw hardened as he grabbed Emmon by the collar and picked him up until the boy's feet no longer touched the ground.

Shayna screamed for his lordship to stop.

She had seen enough. Matti ran into the middle of the brawl shaking her finger wildly only to be mistakenly walloped by Lord Vanguard when he sent Emmon soaring backwards.

Hugo arrived in time to see his wife stumbling and staggering backward across the room. His face heated as he stalked toward Lord Vanguard with the strength of ten warriors coursing through his blood.

Seeing his wife take wing, gave him a rush of adrenaline as he picked his lordship up with one Herculean hand, pinning him helplessly against the wall. Eager to strike a hefty fist into his lord's insolent face, he stopped as the high-pitched shouts of a scullery maid cut through the room, piercing his ears.

"She's come back! Amanda and Robert DeChaville are here!"

Hugo held his position as if waiting for his picture to be painted as he and all else in the room looked towards Braddock's entrance.

Every face was open-mouthed and saucer-eyed as the mirror image of Lady Amanda entered the keep. She wore a loose shirt-like dress of dark bombazine with jagged hem and torn seams.

Derek's heart pounded in his throat as he watched the woman take a few timid steps forward. He could hardly trust his own sight. This woman's eyes were round instead of oval and so blue in color there could be no mistaking she was not the same woman that had verily turned this castle upside down. Her hair was the same shade of tawny gold as his wife, her height nearly exact. But her curves were not nearly as

276

voluptuous. How could this be? He rubbed at his eyes, certain that he'd been knocked in the head once too often. He gave Hugo a fierce scowl, but the man held him tight against the wall.

"Put him down," Matti pleaded. "He meant me no harm."

Hugo grunted, his veins throbbing at the temple, unwilling to let him go just yet.

Matti rolled her eyes at Hugo's stubbornness.

Amanda Forrester glanced about the room, her countenance resembling a wild hare that had suddenly run into the waiting jaws of more than one hungry dog. She clung tightly to Robert's hand.

Odelia walked slowly toward her, shaking her head, blinking with incredulity. "How can this be? How did I not see it before?"

"I am glad to see you," Amanda said as she crushed herself to Odelia's chest, hugging her tight. "And I am truly sorry for all the trouble I have caused."

"Where have you been?" Odelia asked, her voice a stunned whisper.

Amanda gazed at the maid with apologetic eyes. "After taking Emmon's horse I went to Wilmead Farm where Robert and I were to meet."

Emmon growled.

"Robert's friend was away so I made use of his cabin, eating berries and taking baths in the lake to keep clean." Her voice became soft. "I am dreadfully ashamed. I only knew that I could not marry a man I did not love."

Robert took her hand and tried to explain. "So many months had passed since Amanda and I had seen one another that I failed to see the truth. Not until Morgan released me from Braddock's towers did I see the grave error I had made. When I caught sight of the rose-shaped amethyst about her neck, thick clouds lifted from my head and I saw clearly for the first time that she was not my Amanda. I went to Wilmead Farm as she had pleaded for me to do all along." Robert smiled lovingly at Amanda. "And I found my love, just as Vanguard's wife said I would."

In light of what was happening or mayhap because his hand was tiring, Hugo loosened his grip and let Derek fall to the ground.

Derek scowled at the burly warrior, his supposed friend, as he came to his feet, finding great comfort in being upon solid ground again. He straightened his dirty collar and brushed straw and splinters from his torn linen shirt. He picked up Emmon's broken crutch and offered it to him as a token of apology.

Emmon humbly accepted.

After making his apologies to Matti, Derek appeared suddenly sober as he cleared the length of the hall with a few powerful strides. He towered over the woman they all referred to as Amanda. "Odelia," he bellowed, unable to accept what he was seeing and hearing. "I beseech you to tell me here and now why you call this lady before you by the name of Amanda?"

He waited. They all waited, hoping for some kind of reasonable explanation.

"My Lord, I have made a grave error. My eyesight is poor and I had only been at Silverwood a short time before I was instructed to accompany Lady Amanda to Braddock, which is why I failed to see the truth."

Derek squeezed the back of his neck as he tried hard to grasp what the maid was trying to say.

"Their resemblance is astounding," Odelia went on. "And I must say, because I was forewarned of Amanda's...umm, creative nature, and had heard many stories of her unruly antics, I thought little of her strange speech and odd tales. After a while though her consistent use of such odd dialect along with her mannerisms caused me to feel uneasy at times. I began to think something was amiss until I learned that Robert, too, believed her to be his Amanda. I knew not what to think after that."

This new Amanda peered up at Derek, studying him critically as she said, "The day your men came to Silverwood I had every intention of coming here to be your bride. 'Tis true," she added upon seeing his disbelieving scowl. "Although I was upset with my father for agreeing to the marriage, I packed my things, for I could not find the courage to tell him I loved another. And yet neither could I spend the rest of my life knowing that the man I loved was out there somewhere without me."

Derek rubbed his hands through his hair. He was losing patience and his mind reeled with thoughts of his wife. How could this happen? Morgan was the woman who possessed a creamy complexion and rosy cheeks. 'Twas Morgan who had fawn colored hair and a high, regular nose. So many times she had tried to tell him.

Her bright smile plagued his mind at the thought of her alone in the woods for so many days. Visions of her slain body upon the road made his gut ache. Emmon's angry words suddenly swirled within his mind, and he envisioned her now, back at Windsor, sitting by his side, night after night, going against the physician's orders and saving his very life. Why had she not told him? He recalled how she made him smile with her ludicrous stories and with her great gales of unfeminine laughter.

And now she was gone. She'd loved him, faults and all. Where was she now?

Amanda touched his forearm. "I beseech you, my lord, if you have any compassion at all, tell me of your wife's whereabouts, for I believe she may be my sister."

"Your sister?" he asked as if all the world had gone suddenly insane.

"When I was small I used to watch my father pick flowers from my mother's garden," Amanda said. "Taking great care in gathering a bouquet, he would hide the flowers beneath his cloak and leave the castle by foot. I knew of this, for I had spied his ritual many times. And on one occasion I dared to follow him. After a long walk he came to a mound of stones upon the ground. 'Twas there he laid the flowers, lowering his head in prayer. He said, "Return to us soon, my daughter."

Amanda looked at Odelia. "Is that not strange? Those words plagued me all that day, but I was young and forgot about it until Robert told me of this woman who is my mirror image and of the necklace so similar to mine."

With his fingertips, Derek felt the rose-shaped pendant within his pouch. After his wife had left, he'd found it in her chambers. He hadn't realized he carried it until now.

"Our pendants are of the same rare stone. A gift from my father…mayhap our father."

Odelia's eyes widened. "You think your mother gave birth to another daughter who died in infancy? It is your twin sister appearing as a ghost after all these years?"

"The Witch of Devonshire stated such," Emmon agreed, "except Morgan is no ghost. 'Twas more like she came through time itself."

"Emmon," Derek bellowed, turning to glare at the young knight. "What do you know of all this?"

"When you were gone," Emmon said. "When I escorted the women to the market to purchase cloth. Not too surprisingly, her ladyship disappeared. A while later, I found her running from the clutches of an old hag. Turned out to be the Witch of Devonshire who shrieked and pointed, declaring that the spell had worked and her ladyship had come back from the dead. Methinks the old woman was so excited I was sure she would expire from the high-strung shrieks she made as we took off."

Again, Derek threaded his fingers through his hair, wondering why Emmon had not bothered to say a word of this until now. And then it dawned on him that he was to blame. Did he not tell everyone in the castle that he wanted nothing to do with Lady Amanda? Look what happened to Emmon when he came forth.

Derek's face grew taut with grief and remorse.

A messenger arrived then and everyone in the room glanced toward the door where the newest arrival stood.

Shayna made her way through broken furniture, chipped goblets and broken plates to see what the missive was about. After a moment, Shayna turned to Lord Vanguard. "There is a message for the Earl of Kensington."

Derek's eyes narrowed as he came toward her. "I do not believe I heard you correctly." He took the scroll and read it for himself. He felt all color drain from his face as he turned back to the small crowd that had gathered. "The king it seems has bequeathed to me the Kensington lands as an early wedding gift. Thus honoring me with another title: The Earl of Kensington."

The room grew silent for they all knew something wondrous, a miracle of sorts, had taken place these past weeks.

"We need to find her," Emmon said, breaking the silence.

"But where would she go?" Matti asked.

"To see the Witch of Devonshire, of course," Odelia said excitedly. "Morgan mentioned the old woman on more than one occasion. She thought mayhap the witch could tell her why she was sent to this time. I am sure that is where she has gone."

Dread and misgivings had gnawed at Derek since seeing Amanda come through Braddock's doors. The thought of his wife disappearing into thin air tugged at his heart. Could it truly be that she spoke the truth all along?

After Odelia told him where he could find the witch's cottage, Derek took long strides through the hall and to his chambers where he donned a tight-fitting padded doublet. He snatched his broadsword from where it hung by the door and hurried back downstairs and through the lengthy keep, pausing long enough to let Matti place a belt about his waist from which hung a sheath and his dagger. Shayna swung his mantle about his neck and together the entire swarm of castle folk bid him good luck.

He made haste in getting to the stables where the stable master waited with a readied mount. The horse snorted and made a nervous sideways movement, sensing his urgency. Before Derek was full upon the animal's broad back, his destrier reared up and took off without waiting for the command.

In a blur of dust and rattling of hooves, he sped past the guards and past hard-working serfs as they plowed the fields. He leaned low to avoid the lower branches of alders that lined the path of beaten earth. His wounded shoulder burned and his mind buzzed with the absurdity of it all.

*His wife was not Amanda Forrester?* Every word she uttered had been the unvarnished truth? It made his head ache to think of it. How could any rational being have believed such a thing? And yet all that had happened pointed to her telling naught but the truth. She was thrown into a strange world and had tried to tell each and every one of them that something unbelievable occurred. But no one would listen.

He tightened his knees into the steed's side as he neared Swan Lake. He had to hurry and find her, tell her what he should have told her long ago. That he was in love with her and madly so. If everything she told him was true, then the Witch of Devonshire, in all actuality, could send Morgan back in time. He would not allow it.

Time was his enemy now, and he grasped the hilt of his sword, ready to do battle with his invisible nemesis.

His eyes watered, surely caused by the slaps of wind to his face. And yet strangely, he realized he no longer felt so hollow inside. Soothing warmth filled him and it seemed suddenly that he had no room for detestation. Pools of hatred for his father and the mother he hardly knew began to melt within. For the first time in years he felt a strange sense of forgiveness, exoneration for himself and what he had become. The acrid taste that had eluded him for most of his life was suddenly gone and in its stead was something sweet and mild.

He bent his heels into the horse's flanks. Should he find her, he would beg for her forgiveness and not stop until she relented. For was he not the infallible Earl of Kensington? Had Morgan Hayes not apprised him of just that? Even the ambush at Swan Lake was the truth he realized too late as four men with swords appeared from the denser brush without warning. His horse whinnied and reared high.

The men caught him ill equipped and unprepared as they blocked his path and came at him.

Had he not just gripped his sword, he would not have had sufficient time to retrieve it. But he had, and he did, thrusting the blade into the closest man's gut and just as quickly extracting the ancient sword so that he could swing forth once more, this time easily severing the arms that held his steed by the reins. That man screamed as he slumped to the ground in his own pool of blood.

Derek's steed took full advantage of its freedom and raised its front legs as if performing a capriole for its master, giving a snort as its hooves came smashing down upon a third victim. Derek let out a cry when a scorching pain shot through his side as another man lunged from behind and knocked him to the ground.

Derek jumped to his feet with sword firmly grasped. Heated fury bulged from every vein as he turned and spied his adversary. Otgar!

Having no thought other than killing the man, Derek prepared to lunge when five more men, bigger and more vicious than the others, came to stand behind Otgar.

A rickety bridge spanned across a wide creek. Morgan stopped to catch her breath and rub her throbbing feet before crossing. She was close. She knew she was nearing the old woman's cottage for she'd finally come across a small establishment called the Boars Head Inn. The innkeeper had taken pity on her and after filling her with stew and cider he'd pointed her in the right direction.

To think she'd been going in circles for two days now. She grimaced as she crossed the bridge, then climbed a small slope. If she'd stayed on the main road to begin with she would have reached the Witch of Devonshire's cottage long ago.

Now at last in the moonlight, Morgan caught a glimpse of a cottage set against a backdrop of enormous pines. Overgrown with tangled vines, the cottage had an eerie shadow of darkness veiling it. A shiver ran up her spine.

She stood silent for a moment. Her life held no purpose in this medieval world although her heart wilted at the thought of leaving Derek forever. She knew she could forgive him, for how could she expect anyone to believe the things she'd told him? But how, she wondered, would she ever forget him?

She listened for the pounding of hooves, still praying that Derek would appear, a knight-errant upon his horse, declaring his love for her. But she heard only the chirping of crickets and the wind as it brushed against the trees.

Her hopes withering, she moved on, feeling a sudden urge to get this over with. It was time to go back. The future was calling her like an invisible emissary whispering in her ear, pulling her closer. She made her way toward the witch's home.

A small breeze chilled her. Then a streak of lightning sliced through the night and a boom of thunder followed. Perplexed, she glanced upward. No clouds gathered, only myriad stars glittering against the dark sky.

Dread filled her insides and before she knocked, the door creaked open and a dark shadow filled the doorway.

*The Witch of Devonshire.*

Long white hair flowed down over frail shoulders. The old woman reached out and touched Morgan's arm. The woman's hand shook excitedly and Morgan forced herself to stay calm. "Do you know me?" Morgan asked.

The witch laughed gleefully as she nodded.

"Who am I then?"

"You are Morgeanna," the witch said elatedly, "twin sister to Amanda Forrester, daughter of the Earl of Silverwood. You were born a sickly child and only I could save you. 'Twas I, the Witch of Devonshire, who sent you to another world to be healed."

*Twin sister to Amanda Forrester? Daughter of the Earl of Silverwood?* The woman was insane, Morgan realized. Over the woman's shoulder, she saw that the inside of the cottage was bare except for a few crates and an old faded rug atop a dirt floor.

She needed to go home; now more than ever. "Can you send me back? To the future where I belong?"

The witch let out a string of mumble jumble as she threw up her arms. "'Twould not work!"

"Why not? If what you said about sending me to another world is true, then I don't see why you couldn't do it again."

"Too soon. There is no halo about the moon," the witch said sharply. "The time is not right and it is not your calling to do so. You belong here now."

"I don't care if it's my calling. I read once that destiny is an invention of the cowardly and the resigned. I believe it's true and I'm making my own destiny now. I want to go back and see my mother. Do you understand? Show me that you can do this. I don't care about the moon's nimbus or where you think I belong. I only know I would be a fool to think that a knight from another world could ever love me. If I can't have him, then I don't want to live in his world...your world." She waved her hand through the air. "Now send me home."

"The prophecy does not call for sending you back. You are not ailing. What you ask for is absurd." The old woman turned and went inside, shutting the door behind her.

Morgan stood dumbfounded for a moment, then pounded on the door as if her very life depended on getting inside. "I won't leave here until you do as I say," she shouted at the door. "If you don't send me back, I'll tell everyone I meet that you're no witch at all, just an old hag who grows herbs. I'll forever deny that you sent me through time unless you prove to me that you can do it again!"

The door opened again and this time the witch looked her up and down, scowling with obvious malice as she let her in. "I will rid myself of such an ungrateful wench. What do I care which world you wish to live in or if the time is not right. I have done it before and I shall do it again."

Ignoring her complaints, Morgan watched the old woman go from one cupboard to another, gathering a large bowl and many small wooden ones. The woman licked at her lips as she mixed and blended assorted herbs. A foul-smelling liquid was added before the witch began to chant and hiss as if she'd forgotten Morgan was in the room.

When the moon was at its brightest, the old woman was ready, and she gestured toward a couch of moss for Morgan to lie on. Morgan did as she said, laying on her back and holding tight to her blanket as if it were a lifeline.

She shut her eyes and listened to the woman's strange words. A fine dust fell across her face and neck. Within minutes her body felt weightless. And her only thoughts were of Derek and how much she would miss him when she was gone.

"At last, Vanguard, we meet face to face," Otgar said.

Derek's chest heaved beneath his torn doublet as he glared at the toad-faced man. "So, Otgar, you have naught better to do than hide in the thicket and wait for one lone man?"

Otgar's lips pursed with suppressed fury. "Aye, there is only one man whose neck I wish to snap like a twig. My brother will not rest in his grave until the deed is done. And neither, it seems, will Lady Leonie, for she proved right in telling me we would not have long to wait for you to come. Braddock will be mine before this day is out and Lady Amanda will celebrate my victory at my side."

It mattered not that they numbered six and he only one. The veins in Derek's jaw throbbed and every muscle was taut as he stalked forward. His eyes locked on Otgar's pitiful face, and he cared not that he was devoid of a horse and armor and only possessed one good arm. He had something mayhap they did not—the determination and will of a dozen warriors. He raised his broadsword skyward in warning, astounding all six men by his steadfast perseverance and by what some might consider to be the harebrained actions of an irrational fool.

Hugo nodded for Emmon to be silent as they came upon Derek's war-horse. They could hear the shouts of men in the distance and paid little attention to the dismembered bodies strewn about the ground as they urged their mounts onward. They easily discerned that a small war had already taken place, but to come forward and see their lord staggering toward six men with raised sword, gave both Hugo and Emmon cause to wince.

Emmon moved first. With a quick jerk of his wrist he sent a sharp javelin through the air, impaling a man's throat. A heroic gesture, Hugo thought, worthy of only the most adroit of knights and one that would surely launch Emmon to his glory.

Hugo's mount was fast and agile, and he urged the steed close enough so that when he flung his ax it hit its mark square on. His victim went mute as he stumbled and fell before Lord Vanguard's feet. By the time Hugo took out his target, Emmon was charging forward again, piercing another man with his lance, pinning the bulky frame to a seasoned alder.

Derek lunged, bringing his sword swiftly earthward, dealing a swift blow to another man's gut. Otgar had run off the moment he spotted Hugo. There was only one man left.

The last of the enemy peered about wild-eyed as if he were trying to decide which way to run. Instead, he stood rigid with terror, knowing it was too late as he watched Hugo retrieve an ax and Emmon pluck a small dagger from his sheath.

Derek raised his broadsword and the man jerked about, tripping on his own feet. Derek motioned for Emmon to let the man be and Hugo chuckled as the gutless coward scrambled to his feet and ran into the denser part of the woods.

"It seems you needed no help from us, my lord," Hugo mocked, bearing little sympathy for his lordship's weary state.

"Indeed," Derek said to his men, "for as you could surely see I had the situation well under control."

Derek walked toward Hugo as the big man came down from his horse. Derek squeezed his friend's broad shoulder, knowing full well he should even now be breathing his last breath.

"What made you think to come?" Derek asked as he bound his side with strips of cloth torn from his mantle.

"Your wife told her maid and most of the people at Braddock of an ambush near Swan Lake. An ambush that was to be the cause of the Earl of Kensington's death whilst he searched in desperation for his true love."

"Aye," Derek said, "it seems my wife related the story to me also, but I am afraid it was not the first time I failed to take heed of what she said. Verily, in all honesty, 'tis a good thing you came when you did, else I would not be around to listen to your insulting barbs." They shared an amiable look between long-time comrades before turning to Emmon.

"You have done well," Derek said, clapping Emmon's horse on the rump, wincing from the pain it caused him.

"You are badly hurt?"

"Naught to fret about," Derek said as he gathered his things and whistled for his horse.

Emmon tossed back his long hair. "Any more brave, chivalrous deeds and I am certain the king himself would seek to reward me."

"My young knight," Hugo supplied, "I am afraid the king would not take kindly to the fact that you nearly killed his best knight only this morn. Aye, 'tis the king's own dungeons that you almost found to be your just reward."

They all chuckled at that, recalling the damage they had caused within the keep, eager to find humor where they could, relieved to see all before them alive and well.

"It may not surprise you to know that one of the two men running off was Otgar," Emmon ground out.

"Leave him be for now," Derek said as he mounted his steed, ignoring the pain in his side. "I believe Leonie is also behind this bloody mayhem."

The corners of Emmon's lips curved upward. "Apparently, my lord, the ladies are not as enchanted with you as I originally envisioned."

Derek grunted and then urged his horse onward, leaving Hugo to scramble for his mount.


With her eyes clamped shut, Morgan concentrated on all the new friends she'd made, hoping they would all find happiness after she left. She wondered if Robert had found Amanda. She felt saddened to think she and Amanda would never meet. Inhaling deeply, she listened to the shattering claps of distant thunder together with the strange garbled chants of the old woman.

Her feet and hands tingled as she felt her body lifting, floating upward. A wispy beam of light filled her head with visions of the same man she'd seen so many times in her dreams. He was carrying wild flowers and praying for her return.

# CHAPTER TWENTY

The air appeared suddenly thick and Derek prayed he was not too late as he charged toward the witch's cottage.

Leaving Emmon and Hugo in a wave of dust, he heard chanting and saw an eerie light flicker through a small window. Before his horse slowed, he jumped, launching himself against the door. The ancient planks ruptured into a splintering rain as he rolled across the dirt floor inside the small hut.

A cacophony of jarring thunder and high-pitched chants rang in his ears. His eyes widened in horror as he glanced across the room. His wife, his angel from another world, floated upward out of arm's reach. Scrambling quickly to his feet, he leapt through the air, grabbing Morgan about the waist before falling to the ground. For a moment he lay still and held her tight against his chest as he watched the blanket she'd been holding hover above them as a hawk would hover above its prey. And then the coverlet disappeared before his eyes.

Just inside the door, Emmon and Hugo, having seen the blanket vanish into thin air, stood speechless. The witch failed to acknowledge the men at all as she paced the darkest corner of the cottage and mumbled to herself of moons and faraway places.

With Morgan draped in his arms, Derek came to his feet. She did not stir but she was alive. He could hardly believe his good fortune at finding her in time. "We will take her to

Silverwood," he said to Hugo. "Hopefully her father can shed some light on the matter of his second daughter."

Impatiently, Leonie waited for Otgar, knowing full well he had failed once again to do her bidding. When he finally did arrive, his repulsive countenance made her inwardly cringe. She did not like the bitter taste of defeat. More than anything she had wanted to see Lord Vanguard on bended knee, begging forgiveness. She had planned to take him in her arms and pardon him his fleeting lapse in judgment; assure him of her undying love. But it was not to be. She had no one. Her heart shriveled, and a dull, empty ache gnawed inside of her.

She glanced within the cup she held and watched the wine swirl about. After Otgar tasted the sweet brew, she would never again be forced to lie beneath such a disgusting denizen of the forest.

Otgar's tread fell noiselessly against the floor as he came to her. He did not question her unusual readiness for him, and she was glad for it. But his swiftness in discarding his garments, then and there, startled her. Within minutes he was standing over her.

He pushed aside the cup of wine she held out to him.

"Drink with me first," she pleaded.

Otgar took the cup and put it to the table by the bed. "'Tis not wine I yearn for."

"Surely there is no hurry when we could talk awhile first."

His chest heaved with ragged breaths of desire as his eyes roamed hungrily over her.

Before Leonie could reach for the cup, he forced himself full upon her, casting his body this way and that like a newly caught salmon. His callused palm cupped her breast as his rotted breath covered her mouth. Desperately, she reached to the bed table, grabbed a vase and slammed it atop his ugly head.

Otgar growled like the demon he was and in a new fit of rage he stumbled from the bed. Staggering to his heap of clothes, he grabbed for his dagger. When he swiveled back around, he came at her so quickly she had no time to flee. He plunged the knife deep.

He appeared to shudder in pleasure as he watched her fall back, struggling for breath. And then bored with watching her die, he rolled his shoulders to stretch the tenseness there before reaching for the goblet of wine. Sitting upon the edge of the bed, Otgar held the cup above her, giving cheers before downing the dark brew in its entirety, unaware of the smile that played upon her lips as he drank.

By the time Derek arrived at Silverwood it was morning and the air was brisk, stinging his face with its coldness. Derek grew haggard with worry as he climbed the wide stairs, carrying his wife in his arms. *Why had she not yet awoken?* Her breathing was steady and her color had returned. It made no sense.

The sentries recognized the woman in his arms as their lord's daughter and hastily opened the round-headed doorway of the castle. Servants scurried through the hall to inform the Earl of Silverwood of his daughter's arrival and to prepare a place for her. A pallet was provided near the hearth. Carefully, Derek placed her there and knelt beside her.

Hugo and Emmon followed him inside and stood close by.

Richard Forrester swept into the room and to his daughter's side. Pale sunlight streamed in through the mauve drapes and hit her face just so.

"It cannot be," the Earl said as he looked upon her pale face.

"Morgeanna, is it you?" The Earl of Silverwood looked to Lord Vanguard for answers. "Where did you ever find her? And where is her sister?"

"Amanda is well. I will explain later. Right now we need to warm her. She is chilled to the bone." Derek took an offered blanket from a maid and wrapped it snug about her.

The Earl of Forrester knelt down beside him and took his daughter's hand in his. "Surely I am dreaming," he said as the ball of his thumb rubbed against her soft skin. "Seems only like yesterday that I held the wee infant in my arms. My beautiful Morgeanna has come home at last."

"Mother...is that you?" Morgan's eyes fluttered half open before closing again.

Eleanor Forrester came into the room next. She had heard the calling and her eyes darted about the room as she moved closer, slowly at first. Her skirts rustled as she went to the side opposite of where her husband knelt. Her hand trembled as she swept back her daughter's hair from her brow.

"'Tis not Amanda I fear," Richard told his wife, "Her name is—"

"Do you think I know not when I see my own flesh and blood?"

"Of course you do, my dear, 'tis only that..." Richard paused, looking heavenward as if for guidance.

Eleanor's voice was soft and sure as she stroked her daughter's cheek. "Your mother is right here child, where she has been all along." She looked to her husband, then back to Morgan. "After all these years of longing to touch my baby, my beautiful baby."

The Earl's eyes glazed with bewilderment. "You have known all this time...all these years? Will you ever find it in your heart to forgive me?"

Eleanor stood, tears wetting her cheek. "There is naught to forgive, my dear. Our beloved child is home...my sweet daughter has come back."


Derek kept a steady gaze on Morgan as she slept in Amanda's bed. Her parents were in the other room, but every few minutes one of them would peek through the chamber door. "Wake up," he whispered hoarsely, "I demand that you do."

Heavy eyelids slid open and Morgan's eyes narrowed as she tried to focus. She lifted her hand as she gazed into his eyes, reaching upward to touch his cheek, his jaw, his hair. "You came for me?"

He took her hand and nodded. He was about to kiss her palm when suddenly her eyes became focused and she snatched her hand back and sat up as if she only just now realized who she was talking to. "Where am I? Where is the Witch of Devonshire? What have you done with her?"

Relief swept over Derek at seeing her awake and talking, and he smiled at her. "I finally came to my senses," he said. "I should never have let you leave Braddock. Everything you ever told me was naught but the truth and I was but a fool all along."

"Why?" she asked skeptically. "Why the sudden change of heart?"

"The king sent messenger to Braddock. You were right. I am the Earl of Kensington."

"And that's why you came? To tell me what I already knew?"

His eyes said it all. "I wish to apologize. I should have listened to you, I should have known."

She rubbed her forehead. She loved him so much it hurt, but she couldn't live with a man who could never love her back. "Nobody could have known," she said softly. "I hardly believed it myself. But you had no right to stop me from returning to my true home."

"Amanda Forrester came to Braddock looking for you," he explained further.

"You're not listening to me, Derek. I don't care about all of that anymore. I'm tired. I want to go home…I belong in the future."

He lifted her chin, forced her to look into his eyes. "Amanda came to Braddock to meet her twin sister."

"You can't stop me, Derek. And if you think you can—" She stopped mid-sentence. "Did you say twin sister?"

He nodded.

Edging off of the bed, Morgan came slowly to her feet and tested her legs as she gazed curiously about the room. She went to a high table and touched the small hand mirror and dainty combs and brushes. She picked up a silk glove and breathed in the sweet familiar smell of lavender. She was in Amanda's room.

The witch, too, she recalled, had said she was Amanda's sister, which would mean... Slowly, she turned about, sensing someone other than Derek in the room. Her heart nearly stopped.

Beneath the rounded doorframe stood an elderly man. The same man she'd seen so many times in her dreams. She moved toward him, wondering if all her dreams and prayers were being answered in this one glorious moment. The gray at his temples and his sparkling blue eyes were the same.

It was him. Chills coursed over her. It was her father.

He held out a hand to her and she was sure she'd never make it that far. Her knees wobbled and her hands shook. A tear fell, sliding across his softly bearded cheek.

She put a hand to her chest and breathed in.

"My sweet daughter," he said. "How I have waited and yearned for this day."

"Father," she whispered, "is it really you?"

He held out his arms and she fell into them before he could answer because in her heart she already knew. She stayed wrapped in her father's arms for a long time and when her mother entered the room and joined them in their embrace she wasn't sure if she could take the multitude of emotions coursing through her, making her feel as if she'd literally burst from happiness.

Her vision was blurred, but out of the corner of her eye she saw Derek leave the room. She didn't have the strength to stop him. He didn't need her. He wasn't ready to love.


Derek walked out of the castle and past the outer gates of Silverwood. He made his way through the low misty fog until he could no longer see any signs of daily life. He took a seat upon the ground beneath a large oak and looked about. Had the trees always been so tall? he wondered. He couldn't remember hearing the birds as he heard them now with their rhythmic singsong of notes and whistles. Beneath a layer of dirt he spotted a bit of color and easily pulled forth a tiny bloom. He put it to his nose, surprised that something so insignificant had any scent at all.

Had he truly lost her? he wondered, his heart twisting in a slow, tortuous anguish.

A loud screech caught his attention as a bird protected its nest. The high-pitched sounds drew forth his darkest moment, the present becoming intermingled with the past, until the noise was deafening. He covered his ears. When he squeezed his eyes shut he saw clearly his father's bloodshot eyes as his father came at him with a raised iron poker and the combined wrath of a dozen wolves. At the time, Derek was eight years old at best, and he opened his mouth and screamed, bracing himself for what was to come.

Usually he opened his eyes or woke up and the horrible vision disappeared, but this time he kept his eyes shut. He felt strangely disembodied as he watched himself as a boy, peek through swollen eyes to see his mother enter the room. She placed herself between him and his father and in so doing received the blows meant for him. She shouted for Derek to run, pointing a bloodied hand toward the door, but all he could do was stand there and scream.

Derek opened his eyes, tried to breathe.

It could not be. But even as he denied it, he knew that it was true...the shrieks he'd heard so often, the cries that had awoken him most nights...were his own. Matti had told him many times that his father had been a troubled man, but Derek had refused to listen. Although he despised the man for the coldness he had lent upon his only son, 'twas his mother he blamed all these years for leaving him. Nothing else had mattered after she left Braddock.

The crackling of brush caused Derek to drop his hands and look in that direction.

"Are you all right?" Morgan asked as she stepped into view.

"Aye." He inhaled deeply of pine and moss, rolled a twig between his fingers. "You were right about my mother," he said after a quiet moment. "When I was young I used to see a darkly cloaked woman watching me from afar. I never considered until now that the woman could have been my mother. It was her though, I am certain of it, for I saw her the day she left Braddock. She wore the same dark cape then as she did when I spotted her near the training fields, at the market, then again on the day I turned nine...that was the last time I ever saw her."

"Ohhh," she said. "I'm sorry about your mother, and your father."

"And I am sorry I stopped you from returning home."

"You shouldn't have interfered."

"I know." He came to his feet and brushed himself off. As she peered up at him he wondered how he ever let her leave Braddock. "You were right about many things," he went on, "including my following in my father's footsteps. I have been smothered by bitterness, ever so close to becoming the one man I never wanted to be." It all seemed clear to him now, he thought. Judging by her blank expression and somberness he worried he might indeed lose the one thing he needed most. His throat went tight. He could hardly swallow. "I lied," he said in a hoarse whisper.

"About what?" she asked, looking toward the bird's nest of all things instead of at him as she always had before.

"About my being sorry."

Her brows knitted.

He began to throw his arms into a wide arc, then thought better of it and lowered his hands back to his sides. Again he attempted to explain, his voice audibly strained. "I am not suited to this...this apologizing nonsense."

She gave him a pitying look.

He swallowed a lump in his throat. "I did not mean 'nonsense.'"

She sighed.

"What I meant to say is that I lied because I am not at all sorry I stopped you from leaving this world. Because you see I...I like you. I like you very much." He waited for her to throw her arms about his neck in gleeful bliss as she always did. But she hardly moved. Perhaps she was too overjoyed to speak.

When she finally turned back toward him, he fully expected to see her eyes glistening with tears of happiness. Instead he saw dry eyes and a meager half smile.

"That's nice," was all she said. "I should go now." She made a small gesture toward the castle.

*Tell her the truth. Tell her you love her.* Derek's pulse roared in his ears at the thought that he still could not summon the courage to say the words. Damnation he thought as he watched her walk away.

"Morgan Hayes!" he said as he went after her.

She stopped, but still failed to turn fully around. She was a stubborn wench, he mused, and if she thought he was going to drop to his knees and beg...

"I love you," he said, dropping to his knees the minute he saw her look at him with empty, non-expressive eyes. "Do not look at me like that."

Her hands went to her hips. "Why?"

"Because as you told the maids so many times at Braddock, those frowns will cause lines about your eyes."

She rolled her eyes. "I meant, why do you love me?"

"Ahhh," he said, wondering why women made everything so complicated. "There must be a reason?"

She did not walk away or present him with a scowl, and thus he surmised his question to be a reasonable one. After pondering the question for less than a moment, she crossed her arms and simply said, "Yes."

He scratched his chin and did his best to ignore the pain in his knee. His head throbbed as did his shoulder, making it difficult to think. "I am not certain of the reason."

Her shoulders drooped, and she appeared ready to turn away again so he reached out a hand to stop her. "I do know," he quickly added, "that the birds are singing. Do you hear them?"

She listened for a moment and nodded, clearly puzzled.

"Do you not see?" he asked her. "Until I met you my world was quiet and dark. But your love has set me free. Because of you, Morgan Hayes, I can hear the soothing song of a single bird and take pleasure in the sweet smell of a single flower. I do love you," he said as if he only now just realized it, "from the very core of my heart. I love you for all you have given me."

A tear slid over her cheek and Derek mistook her crying as a sign of displeasure. "I told you I was no good at this. Only because I have not had enough experience courting the ladies. That is not to say I did not charm the ladies, but—"

"Derek," she said, gazing down at him, placing a finger over his lips. "Stop. You were doing just fine."

"Then you do love me again?"

"I never stopped loving you."

"So this was all for naught?" he asked.

"Be quiet…just be quiet."

"But I dare say I was not yet finished."

She got down on her knees so that they were face to face. "Just kiss me," she said. "That is an order not a prayer."

Derek quickly obeyed, relishing in the thought as their lips came together that his very life had only just begun.


Ten days later, Morgan was the epitome of elegance. She wore her newly found mother's silk dress, trimmed with lace and embroidered with gold thread. She smiled at her father and as he came to stand between her and Amanda, she took hold of the crook of his arm.

"I missed you all those many years we were apart, every day…every moment," her father whispered close to her ear, repeating the same words he had told her almost every day since she arrived at Silverwood.

"I missed you, too," she said. "And yet I saw you so often in my dreams. You brought me flowers and prayed for me. I always hoped we would meet some day."

His fatherly pride filled her with joy. She straightened, then turned to watch Derek move through the crowd until he came to stand before the king. Seeing him in all the layers of refinement, his eyes burning fire into hers when their gazes met, caused a warm ribbon of tingles within.

Derek wore a rich, emerald green cloak over a dark tunic with a leather belt that was gilded and jeweled. As he stood with both legs firm and steady, his dark stockings melded to his muscular thighs. She was going to marry the Earl of Kensington. If only her mother could be with her now. And then she wondered how she'd ever stop missing her.

Amanda leaned close and said, "I am so glad to have you as my sister. We will have a lifetime to catch up."

They embraced. Upon looking up again they saw Robert grinning at them both as he passed by, taking brisk jaunty steps toward the king.

Their father urged them forward, escorting both daughters toward the wedding platform where King Henry sat upon a temporary throne. The king dipped his head in acknowledgement.

As the trumpets blared Morgan gazed proudly at the people flocking about Braddock. Her eyes widened when she spotted an old woman half hidden behind a tree. The Witch of Devonshire had come after all. She'd paid the witch a visit a few days ago, to thank her for all she'd done and to invite her to the wedding. The old woman had obviously been a hermit for most of her life and thus had balked at the idea of coming. But here she was. Morgan smiled broadly and blew her a kiss that prompted the witch to hide behind the width of the tree.

At the front of the crowd Morgan saw Hugo and Matti. Emmon winked fondly at her as he held Shayna's hand tightly in his. Odelia stood between the Chippendales and wiped her nose with a hanky. Little Joseph saluted Morgan with his slingshot and Eleanor Forrester stood close by basking in her daughters' bliss.

For the first time in her life Morgan knew what it felt like to truly belong. She felt at peace. Something told her that her mother, Cathy Hayes, felt it, too. Destiny had proven stronger than all of them.

# EPILOGUE

*California, 1985*

"What happened? Where am I?" Cathy Hayes cried out. Her eyes were swollen and her head throbbed beneath the thick bandages. A nurse walked in and Cathy blinked, trying to remember how she came to be here. The walls were bleached white and unadorned. The smell of antiseptics overwhelmed her. Frowning, she hesitated in asking the nurse why she was here, fearing the worst.

The last thing she could remember was her five-year old daughter, Ashley, singing *Old McDonald* in the back seat of their car and her husband's hand flying across her chest as if he meant to shield her from...from something terrible.

Anguish filled her as she recalled being in a crash. The three of them had been in a terrible accident. Something flew in front of the car and landed on the windshield, blocking her husband's view of the road. He slammed on the brakes and there was an explosion. Her husband, her daughter...they were dead. She was sure of it. It was written all over the nurse's face.

"Are they—"

The door to her room came flying open, interrupting her question.

"Daddy! Come quick! Mommy's awake," Ashley yelled, running to the bed and into Cathy's arms. "I knew you would be okay, I just knew it."

Cathy looked to the door where a shadow appeared. She squinted her eyes, hoping for a clearer image, sure that the man standing there was an apparition. Her husband, Eric, looked just as she'd remembered him all those years ago.

*All those years ago?*

She frowned, tried to brush the strange thoughts from her head as she touched Ashley's hair and face, kissing the tip of her daughter's pug nose. She could hardly breathe. She held both chubby cheeks between her palms and looked deep into her daughter's eyes. "You're real, aren't you?"

Ashley gave her father a perplexed look as he came forward. Then Ashley looked back at her mother and giggled. "Of course I'm real. And daddy's real, too...see?" Ashley placed her father's hand within Cathy's hand.

His hand felt strong, his fingers vibrating with life.

"Your husband's a hero," the nurse said. "The hospital is filled with reporters. They all want to interview the man who risked his life to save the driver of a burning truck. And only minutes before it exploded."

Cathy felt her heart hammering against her chest. *What was wrong with her?* "What stopped us from going up in flames?" she asked, remembering too vividly a completely different scenario.

Her husband spoke next, the soothing richness of his voice causing Cathy to inhale.

"It was the strangest thing," he said as he went to a closet and withdrew an old blanket.

Chills crawled up Cathy's spine at the sight of the coverlet. Even from here she knew she'd seen it before.

"This very blanket fell from the sky like an angel with wings. It landed on my windshield, blocking my view completely. Since I couldn't see, I slammed on the brakes." He gave Cathy a sorrowful look, obviously blaming himself for the injury to her head. "At that same moment, a truck came barreling out of nowhere, barely missing us as it flew across our path and slammed into a tree. I didn't try to be the hero...I only knew I had to get that man out before it was too late. Minutes after I dragged his body from the truck it exploded."

Eric returned to her side and slid his warm hand over hers. "If this blanket hadn't appeared when it did—" He shook his head. "I hate to think what would have happened."

Cathy took the blanket from him, her hand trembling as she felt its velvety texture between her fingers. A tear made a path down her cheek.

And the tick of the clock was set right once more.

# ABOUT THE AUTHOR

Theresa Ragan didn't know she wanted to be a writer until she read her first romance novel in 1992. She spent the next five years researching medieval times and writing *Return of the Rose*. She was also working full time and raising four children, but she knew she was a writer when nothing could stop her from getting the words to the page.

Theresa has garnered six Golden Heart nominations in Romance Writers of America's prestigious Golden Heart Competition for her work. She lives with her husband, Joe, and the youngest of her four children in Sacramento, California.

*Return of the Rose* was written for busy women around the world, women who work full-time at home or out of the house…women whose job never ends because they are cooking, cleaning, taking care of kids, and they are in serious need of a few hours of escapism. Enjoy!

Made in the USA
Lexington, KY
20 December 2011